Once A Princess

Johanna Lindsey

CORGI BOOKS

For Vinny and Martha

ONCE A PRINCESS
A CORGI BOOK 0 552 13909 2

First publication in Great Britain

PRINTING HISTORY
Corgi edition published 1992

Corgi Books are published by Transworld Publishers Ltd, 61–63 Uxbridge Road, Ealing, London W5 5SA, in Australia by Transworld Publishers (Australia) Pty Ltd, 15–23 Helles Avenue, Moorebank, NSW 2170, and in New Zealand by Transworld Publishers (NZ) Ltd, 3 William Pickering Drive, Albany, Auckland.

Printed and bound in Great Britain by
Cox & Wyman Ltd, Reading, Berks.

Chapter 1

Cardinia, 1835

The Crown Prince of Cardinia drew to a halt upon entering the anteroom outside the royal bedchamber. Maximilian Daneff awaited him there alone, a portentous reminder of the prince's youth and the punishments he'd received, deservedly and sometimes not. Whenever he had been called to account for his misdeeds, it had been in these chambers, with no attendants to bear witness—other than Count Daneff, who had always served as a buffer between two hot tempers. Daneff was Prime Minister now, but even before he had risen to that exalted position, he had been a friend and advisor to the king.

He spoke now in the soothing accents bequeathed him by a Romanian mother. "Your expediency is appreciated, your Majesty. I feared we would have to scour the countryside in search of gypsy camps to find you."

The censure was there, unrestrained as usual. Max disapproved, even more than the king did, of the way the prince sometimes took his leisure. But the words

1

didn't affect him in the usual way, neither heightening his color nor producing anger. It was the address, *Majesty* rather than *Highness*, that arrested the prince's attention, draining color from his features.

"My God, he's dead?"

"No—*no!*" Maximilian shouted, horrified that he had given that impression. "But—" He paused, aware that the Crown Prince had had no forewarning of what he was about to impart. "Sandor has abdicated, formally, with the Turkish Grand Vezir as witness."

Color furiously returned to the prince's cheeks. "And why was I not invited to this momentous occasion?"

"It was thought that you might be moved to protest—"

"As well I would! Why, Max? His physicians claim he has improved. Were they lying for my benefit?"

"He *has* improved, but . . . it will not last if he returns to his duties, and even so, you knew—were told—that the time he has left is limited. Your father has reached his sixty-fifth year. This condition that has affected his heart has taken his strength from him. A few more months is the most we can hope for."

No expression crossed the prince's features to tell of the pain those words caused, other than the closing of his eyes. He *had* been told what Max had just reminded him of, but as any child might do when faced with losing his only remaining parent, he had ignored the warnings and clung to hope. And the physicians had given him that hope, a false hope, he now realized.

"Is this why I was summoned," he asked bitterly, "to be told I am to be crowned before the old king is even in his grave?"

"I know you feel it is wrong, but it cannot be helped. It is what your father wants."

"You could assume the reins, as you do whenever he leaves the country. He need not have relinquished the honor before death took it from him."

Maximilian smiled sadly. "Do you truly believe he would not involve himself in the rigors of office when he is here and kept well informed? The only way he will have the peace necessary to survive a while longer is to remove his right to rule. He knew this, and this is what he has done. And it is only one of the reasons you were summoned, not the most important."

"What can be more so?"

"Sandor will tell you. He awaits you now, so go in to him. But a word of caution, if you will. Do not remonstrate with him for what has already been done and cannot now be changed. He abdicated willingly and even with happiness, because you are and have always been the pride of his life. As for the rest, restrain your temper and arguments, and bring them to me when you leave him. I am prepared to deal with both, your Majesty."

The address was said deliberately this time, and meant to tell him that even though he was now king, Max would treat him no differently than he ever had, with love and calm reasoning in the face of his royal rage. Speculation over what was going to cause that rage filled him with dread as he entered the royal bedchamber. Max knew that he rarely lost his temper anymore. Certainly he would argue with anyone regardless of rank, but since he had become a man, he prided himself on having developed more control of his temper.

The abdicated King of Cardinia lay propped up in his bed, a huge monstrosity that required steps to reach the dais it sat upon, then more to reach the top mattress, which was draped in fine velvet and silks and was attached to a solid gold headboard displaying the royal crest at its head. The rest of the room was just as opulent. Marble floors reflected the candlelight; walls draped in the finest silk were adorned with artwork from the masters of Europe, some paintings spreading from floor to ceiling, all in solid gold frames. But the king's bedchamber was no different from the rest of the palace, where gold and silver abounded and assured any visitor that Cardinia, although relatively small in comparison to her neighbors, contained within her borders innumerable gold mines that made her one of the richest countries in Eastern Europe.

"Already he scowls," Sandor grumbled as his son drew near. "My last mistress confessed you frightened her to death when you looked just so."

"With a countenance to send children screaming for their mothers, I am not surprised."

Sandor grew uncomfortable with a subject that, by unspoken agreement, was never to be broached. He quickly changed it with the promise, "If Max has overstepped his bounds, I will have his tongue cut out.''

"He told me only that I am king.''

"Ah.'' Sandor ignored the sharp tone and relaxed back into his pillows, patting the mattress beside him. "Come, join me as you used to do.''

The prince didn't hesitate, but bounded up the dais and stretched out his long frame on the foot of the mattress. He rested on one elbow, staring at his father with the patience he was becoming renowned for. Sandor knew in that moment that his abdication wouldn't be questioned, no matter how much his son might abhor his decision. He sighed in relief. That had been the only contention as he saw it. The rest was a matter of record that merely needed to be recalled.

"Yes, you are king, to be crowned within the week, before the Grand Vezir ends his visit.''

"What, no gold-engraved invitations to the crowned heads of Europe?''

Sandor grinned despite his son's sarcasm. "At present we have guests representing eight of those monarchs, three princes, an archduchess, several counts, our esteemed friend from Turkey, and even an English earl who has tracked Abdul Mustafa across our borders. We will make use of them all to witness the occasion. No one will doubt that you are my heir not only by right but also by choice and favor, well loved by your people—only lacking a queen at your side.''

The prince stiffened. Deep inside he had known what it was he dreaded hearing, and he had been right.

''You survived without a queen these past fifteen years since my mother died.''

Those words told Sandor how upset the prince really was. Instead of shouting and raving, he had made an absurd statement like that that didn't warrant an answer, much less acknowledgment. Yet because his son was managing to restrain his rage, Sandor did answer.

''I had my Crown Prince, so what need had I of another wife—other than for a political reason, which never arose. You cannot say the same.''

''Then let me choose.''

The words were whispered, as close to pleading as the prince would ever come. Sandor had heard them before, the last time this subject had been brought up, when his son returned from his European tour claiming he had found the woman he wished to make his own. Of course, that time he had not been so quiet in his protests when he was denied. This time, Sandor didn't think he could withstand such protests.

To avoid them, he said, ''It is my last wish, my death wish if you will, that you will honor the betrothal made the day Tatiana Janacek was born. Her father was our king, and it was his wish and decree that you rule as her consort. He could have chosen from any of the royal houses of Europe, but he chose my son. The honor was overwhelming—''

''The honor would have been negated with the birth of another Janacek son.''

''When the Stamboloffs swore to wipe out his

whole line? And within months they did so, everyone except for the girl child, whom I secreted out of the country. All that amazes me is that no one has ever whispered that I had more to gain than the Stamboloffs. With the Janaceks' deaths, I gained the throne."

"Their feud was legendary. You had no part in it."

"Be that as it may, the last Stamboloff has finally been found and eliminated. At long last it is safe for the princess to return to her homeland and sit on the throne that is her right by birth."

"She lost that right, Father. No one wanted an infant queen, especially one whose chances of surviving an assassin's bullet were next to nothing. Though she still lived, you were declared king. Even if she returns now, she no longer has a claim to the crown."

"Except through you," Sandor reminded him softly. "Circumstances have made you king instead of consort. You no longer must rule through her. But hers is the true royal line, and your children can only benefit from it."

"Ours is as royal—"

"Certainly, but indirectly descended. My God, eleven Janaceks had to die before I became next in line to the throne. Eleven! The crown should never have been mine, nor did I covet it, cursed as it was. But it came to me, and now to you, and you, my boy, are the end of the royal line—you and this one surviving Janacek. So whatever maggoty reason you have in your head for not wanting her, you will ignore it and honor my last wish. You will go to the Americas, where Baroness Tomilova has raised her. You will bring her home and wed her with all the pomp and circumstance a royal wedding decrees. And, God willing, I will live long enough to see it done.''

Without those last words, the prince might have continued his quiet arguments, might even have given his reasons for not wanting the Janacek princess, though that was doubtful because his reasons were locked away in the darkest part of his soul. But with those words, the hopeful words of a dying man . . .

''So be it.''

Maximilian Daneff was not treated to the same acquiescence, however, not by any means. But despite the fact that he was nearly half a head shorter than the Crown Prince soon to be crowned king, and frail of body next to the younger man's military-honed frame, he was not the least bit intimidated by the blast of fury that met him outside Sandor's chamber.

''Who even remembers that this royal bitch is alive?'' the prince snarled the moment he closed the door.

Maximilian nudged him out of the anteroom and away from Sandor's hearing before he answered. ''Everyone present at your betrothal, I don't doubt, which, by the way, is binding not only by our laws but by your honor.''

''You bastard!''

''I hope you had more restraint with your father.''

''Shut up, Max. Just shut the hell up!''

The words were shouted without the least heed to

the guards and attendants they passed, who had been temporarily banished from the royal chambers. If Maximilian weren't thick-skinned, he might take umbrage at being spoken to that way before those of lesser rank, who were now wide-eyed as they watched the prince stalk away. But being associated with autocrats almost demanded the suspension of one's pride, certainly of one's temper.

"I don't believe you've ever mentioned what it is you object to," Max called out as he tried to keep up with the prince's long strides. "Perhaps if you told me—"

"What difference now? He's made it a last request. Not an order, but a death wish. Do you know what that means?"

"Certainly. You might have ignored the order, but now you will put your heart and soul into fulfilling the wish."

The prince swung around, eyes blazing. "Did you know he meant to employ such vile manipulation?"

He was too volatile to remain still long enough to hear the reply. Maximilian had to hurry again just to stay within shouting distance.

"No," he said. "But it was ingenious of Sandor to think of it, since he hasn't the strength now to coerce you in the usual way."

"Go away, Max, before I forget that you have been like a second father to me."

Max stopped abruptly, not because of that supposedly dire warning, but because he was out of breath—and because the new king in his rage had missed the turn that led to the east wing of the palace where his apartments were located. The corridor he had taken led to a dead end, but it was still several minutes before he discovered that for himself and returned, allowing Max enough time to consider what information he possessed that might make the younger man accept the inevitable with a little more princely grace than he was showing thus far.

Before the prince reached him with his black glower, Max said, "Perhaps you worry that, being reared in a country so dissimilar from ours, the princess will have beliefs opposed to ours. But such could not have happened, not with a guardian like Baroness Tomilova, who was her mother's closest friend. The child will have been prepared for her destiny with great care, taught to love the country of her birth as well as her betrothed. A fortune was also supplied for her keep, so she will have been raised in splendor—"

"And spoiled right down to her toenails, no doubt."

"Possibly." Max grinned. "But her appearance is likely to more than compensate for that. You may not remember her parents, since you were living outside the palace at the time, but they were a magnificently handsome couple. The queen was a renowned Austrian beauty who could have had her choice of husbands from any of the royal houses across the land, but she chose our Janacek king. Their daughter can be nothing less than exquisite in her beauty."

This did not seem to relieve the prince as Maximilian had hoped. Instead the prince appeared even more enraged, if that were possible, snarling as he passed Max, "I spit on her beauty, for I will come to hate it, and her, each time she turns from me in revulsion."

Pain filled Maximilian's eyes, for he finally understood. Dear God, he had not thought of that.

Alicia slumped down in her bath with a start of surprise when the prince slammed into his apartment. It took only a glance to grasp the reason for such a loud entrance. She sighed inwardly and dismissed her two attendants, who were only too happy to get out of there. She couldn't blame them. The first time she had seen this man angry, she had been terrified too. It was those eyes, hotly glowing, that could make a God-fearing soul want to cross herself. Devil's eyes, she'd heard them called more than once. But it was the power of his rank that was the true cause for fear, for if he killed someone in a rage, whether by accident or not, nothing much would be done about it. And who didn't know that, including him.

That first time, he had been furious with his friend Lazar Dimitrieff, for some silly reason she couldn't remember now. But she hadn't known that at the time and had thought she herself had done something wrong to make him look at her like that. This had been over a year ago, not long after she had become his mistress, and she hadn't known him so well then as she did now.

She had thought he was going to kill her, with the way he had come after her as soon as he noticed her, dragging her to the bed in the next room, throwing her down on it. But all he had been interested in was expending his passion by the means their relationship allowed him.

It had not been a pleasant experience, certainly, with her fear making her stiff and unresponsive, but she was too experienced for it to be traumatic either. In fact, the only reason she had cried when it was over was because she was so relieved that that was all he meant to do to her. But he didn't know that. He thought he had actually hurt her, and she let him think so, for his guilt could be measured in gold, and was, by the magnificent gifts he had showered on her to make amends.

She no longer feared him, even when he looked like this, as if he would strangle the first person he could get his hands on. In fact she stood up from her bath in full sight of him, deliberately prodding the passion he was in the grips of, to the one she was more familiar with. And it worked. He came toward her, and without a word, yanked her into his arms and carried her naked and dripping into the other room.

Alicia laughed, but only to herself. She wasn't stupid. There was a magnificent sapphire necklace that she had been after him for the last month to buy her and now he would, if she could just manage to squeeze out a few tears when he was done with her. An easy task for one as accomplished as she.

Chapter 2

Natchez, Mississippi

"Tanya, you lazy slut, where's my breakfast!"

In the narrow hall, the girl with the heavy tray of food stopped short, cringing at that bellow. Wilbert Dobbs had the kind of voice that carried, and his did with regularity, right out his open window to their neighbors up and down the street. It was embarrassing, or used to be, to go out and hear the snickers, and worse, the mimics, but then her neighbors weren't the kind who might feel sympathy or pity over the verbal abuse that came her way each day. And after so many years of the same, one became less embarrassed, almost immune.

But it wasn't as bad as it used to be, not since Dobbs' illness had made him dependent on her. That thought made Tanya smile suddenly, which lit up her face and brought a rare sparkle to her pale green eyes. She still wasn't used to her change in circumstances. Verbal abuse was all Dobbs could give her, now that he was bedridden and could no longer beat her. She'd seen to that the very day he took to his bed, when she'd burned the stick that had been his constant companion for more years than she could remember.

She cringed again, recalling that stick. Her circumstances might have improved beyond her wildest dreams, but some twenty years of misery was not easy to forget.

She took the tray in to him now, dropping it on the table next to his bed, unmindful of the noise it made.

"What the hell took you so long, missy?"

"The beer delivery arrived early."

He grunted, which meant he accepted that excuse, when the truth was she'd decided to eat her own breakfast first for a change, before she brought up his.

"And what was the take last night?" he wanted to know.

"I haven't tallied it yet."

"I'll want an accounting—"

"After I'm done cleaning up last night's mess."

He flushed red at her answer. She flushed some herself at her audacity. She would never have spoken to him like that six months ago, and they both knew it. She would have rushed to do his bidding, forsaking any other chore, and she certainly wouldn't have interrupted him.

"I'm sorry," she offered out of habit. "But I'm doing two jobs now, both yours and mine, and there never seems to be enough time in the day to do it all. We really need to hire—"

"Now, now, you're doing just fine on your own.

We already have three others to pay. Any more will cut into the profits.''

She wanted to argue, she really did, but knew it wouldn't do her a bit of good. He made a good profit, he always had, but he never let her spend any of it, not on the tavern that was their livelihood, nor on herself. What the devil did he think he was saving it for? He was sixty years old if he was a day, and he was dying, a fact that elicited not the least bit of sadness from her or anyone else who knew him.

For the first ten years of her life, Tanya had thought this man and his wife were her parents. Finding out differently had brought her joy, not pain. But who her real parents were she didn't know. Iris Dobbs had been able to tell her only that the woman who had given her to them when she was a baby had claimed to be her mother one minute, then no relation to her the next. But the fever had made the woman say all kinds of crazy things.

Iris had died eight years ago. She had been Tanya's only buffer, taking many of the beatings meant for her. In fact, it was one of those beatings that had killed Iris, though Dobbs had got away with calling it an accident simply because she was his wife.

The things a husband was allowed to do didn't bear thinking of. And not for the first time Tanya swore that a husband would never make a chattel out of her, because she'd never have one. If she'd learned anything living with Dobbs all her life, she'd learned how precious her few rights were, and she wasn't about to give them up for anything. She just wished she'd known she had some sooner, wished she'd known that she could leave if she wanted, without being hunted down like a runaway slave. It had taken one of the barmaids to point this out, when she had witnessed Dobbs taking the stick to her, by asking why Tanya stayed.

In fact, Tanya had threatened to leave then. She'd been all of eighteen, or thereabouts, and could easily get a job in another tavern, since she knew everything there was to know about running such a place. That was when Dobbs had first tempted her with ownership of The Seraglio. But the promise of his leaving the tavern to her was all she'd had, until his illness. Then she'd insisted on having it written down on paper, that precious paper hidden under a floorboard in her room.

The Seraglio was all but hers now to do with as she would. It might exhaust her and cause one headache after another, but it represented independence, peace, and total control, or soon would—things she'd never had before, and which she craved now with a passion. To have them, she only had to take care of Dobbs for his remaining days, no more than she'd done all her life anyway.

Tanya left him as soon as she could, for she hadn't exaggerated. There was never enough time in each day to do all that was required of her. The three helpers were no help where cleanup was concerned. Dobbs had never wanted to pay them extra when he had Tanya at no cost, and so they left at the close of business even if the common room looked like a storm had come through it.

It usually was a filthy mess, with mugs left on

tables, ale spilled, chairs toppled, some broken, cigar butts mixed with spittle on the hardwood floor. Tanya usually attended to it all before she retired for the night, but last night there had been a fight over the current barmaid, Aggie, between one of the local planters' sons and a sailor from *The Lorilie,* just docked that morning. Dobbs used to handle all the fights, with a cudgel in one hand and a pistol in the other. Now Tanya had to depend on Jeremiah, who tended the bar; and while Jeremiah might have the bulk necessary to intimidate two drunken customers, he did not have the gumption.

It wasn't the first time Tanya had had to step in between two brawlers since she'd taken over the running of The Seraglio. Getting a couple of bruises before the fighters realized she was interfering was pretty common, too, but last night had been an exception, since she had been tired and out of sorts, and in no mood to reason first.

Normally she drew no notice, for she'd learned at an early age how to mask delicacy and fine features with severity, drabness, and a gauntness that could be achieved by using theatrical makeup, if not by actual exhaustion. She was a fixture of the place, sometimes serving customers when Aggie was harried because April was performing, sometimes working behind the bar when Jeremiah didn't show up for work. She was always there, ready to attend to whatever was necessary—even breaking up fights, she, not even five and a half feet tall, with her hair severely pulled back and bundled at her nape, wearing a serviceable black skirt, unadorned and unbustled, and

one of Dobbs' old gray shirts that reached her knees.
The shirts were belted to accommodate the wicked-
looking knife she'd been wearing at her hip ever since
Dobbs had taken ill, a longer-bladed weapon than
the knife she'd carried in her right boot for as long
as she could remember.

She'd brought both into play last night, slashing
in a wide circle that effectively separated the two
antagonists. She hadn't had to say a single word after
that. The planter's son, who was a regular and well
aware that she didn't palm her weapons unless she
was prepared to use them, apologized for the disturbance and resumed his seat. The sailor, there for the
first time, was too surprised to offer any more trouble,
and Jeremiah, late into the fray but handy just the
same, escorted him to the door.

But despite the ease with which she'd ended the
fracas, Tanya's nerves had still been on edge for the
remainder of the night, and such extreme tension was
debilitating. That was why she'd gone straight to bed
as soon as she'd locked up. She could accept violence
against herself more easily than she could accept
having to dole it out, because receiving it had been
a matter of course her whole life. Inflicting some of
her own went against her grain. Yet she didn't hesitate to do so when it was necessary, and it had been
necessary a number of times over the years, and more
often in just the past six months.

In spite of everything she did to appear unappealing
to The Seraglio's customers, a drunk sometimes
didn't see too well, and all it took was the sight of
a skirt to make one think he'd found an available

female. She'd had her share of pinches and pawing, for the most part ended with a sharp word or a well-placed cuff to the side of the head. If a man was drunk enough to have blurred vision, he was drunk enough for her to handle. It was those times when she was caught alone outside the common room by men not so drunk, in either the storeroom or the kitchen, or on her way to the stable out back, or even followed into her room once, that she'd had to get serious about protecting herself. But those attempts were made by men who'd known her for a long time, weren't fooled by her normal appearance, and now thought to take advantage of Dobbs' incapacity.

The only good thing she could say about Dobbs was that when he'd been hale and hearty, he'd been a potent discouragement to anyone who wanted to lay his hands on her. Once, he'd nearly beaten to death one of his own friends who had tried to kiss her, and that kind of news spread fast. Not that he had been protecting her virtue then or in other instances. He simply hated fornication with a passion and wouldn't stand for it under his roof. If Aggie and April wanted to accommodate customers in that way, and both of them often did, they made private arrangements. More recently they sneaked off to the stables whenever things slowed down. Dobbs' reaction wasn't normal, certainly, but it was amusing, since Iris had once confessed that it was because he couldn't do it anymore himself. Typical of Dobbs, then, not to want anyone else to do what he couldn't.

Tanya spared only one sigh as she looked over the common room before she got busy. There was also the beer shipment to see to, lunch and dinner to prepare, new candles to order, which required a three-block walk past gambling dens, brothels, and seedier taverns that were open day and night, since The Seraglio was located in one of the worst sections of Natchez. And then, just before it was time to open the doors, April's little brother stopped by to tell Tanya that The Seraglio's main attraction had sprained her ankle and wouldn't be able to perform tonight or any time soon. Just what she needed to hear minutes before opening. A headache began immediately.

Chapter 3

"What in hell are we doing here, Stefan?" Lazar complained as he watched a red-bearded man in fringed buckskins banging on his table with an empty beer mug, crudely demanding that the show begin. "We could have awaited Serge at the hotel, which at least offers a modicum of comfort."

"You have gone slumming before—"

"Not where every mother's son is armed to his teeth," Lazar hissed.

Stefan chuckled. "You exaggerate, my friend, but even so, like Vasili, I'm feeling restless enough to welcome a diversion, no matter its form."

"Oh, God," Lazar groaned, slumping down in his chair. "With both of you seeking trouble, we're bound to find it."

Stefan cocked a black brow. "Who said anything about trouble?"

"A diversion to you is nothing less than a rousing good fight. And I know you are exasperated—we all are after what we learned today. But you, if you will forgive my saying so, are an unpredictable bastard in such a mood.''

Stefan snorted without taking offense. Long-standing friends were occasionally allowed to insult him with impunity.

''I assure you I will start nothing that I can't finish.''

''Assurances like that I don't need.''

''Stop worrying, Lazar. We are here only to keep Vasili company, and to keep from going at each other's throats while we play this waiting game again.''

''And what is Vasili's excuse?'' Lazar queried, watching the man in question move casually about the room, speaking to the patrons as if he were a regular.

''He was intrigued by the name of this place when he heard it mentioned on *The Lorilie,* along with a description of its main attraction. But then he is so homesick he will settle for even the most laughable performance if he can see one single belly undulate.''

''That damned concubine Abdul gave him, she does dance like an angel, doesn't she?'' A chuckle broke through Lazar's concern. ''She undulates even better in bed.''

''So you've tried her?''

''Vasili is ever generous . . . you mean you haven't?''

''Slaves, even freed slaves, are too submissive for my tastes.''

Lazar grinned at that opinion. Submissiveness was nice on occasion, as far as he was concerned, especially when you had a termagant for a mistress, which he did. That one he had been glad to leave behind for this journey, but he hadn't expected to be away so long.

None of them had expected it, since their task had been so simple. They had merely to contact a Madame Rousseau in New Orleans. Hers was the one name that had come to Sandor all those years ago, as prearranged, and she was to have led them directly to Baroness Tomilova and her royal charge. A week at the most to pack up the princess, and they would have been on their way home. So simple . . . except Madame Rousseau had passed away three years ago, and her husband had moved to Charleston.

A week was wasted making inquiries in New Orleans about the baroness, but it was as if she had never been there, for no one remembered her. So they sailed to Charleston to speak with the lady's husband. More time wasted, for the gentleman had become a drunkard since Madame Rousseau's death. He could barely remember his wife, much less some woman he might or might not have met twenty years ago. His only suggestion, petulantly given after a great deal of browbeating, was that they speak with his wife's sister, who he thought, to the best of his recollection, though he wasn't positive, had been living with them at the time in question. The only problem, however, was that she had married ten years ago and moved to Natchez, Mississippi.

So to sail back to New Orleans on the oft chance that Rousscau's doubtful memory might be correct, and journey up the Mississippi River to the old town of Natchez? But what else could they do? Tatiana Janacek had waited all these years to be summoned home to assume her rightful place in Cardinia. She had to be found, no matter how long it took.

However, frustration was keen by this point. They all felt it. But until the new King of Cardinia lost his patience and said to hell with it, no one else would. But that was before their visit to Madame Rousseau's sister this morning at her plantation just south of town, which proved the worst frustration of all because of the incredible tale she had to relate to them.

Now Lazar was for quitting the country and simply reporting the tragedy that had befallen the Janacek infant. Serge was for finding another to take her place, someone more to the king's liking, but the trouble with that was the princess had an identifying mark on her left cheek, her sitting cheek, that Sandor had put there himself. But the cousins, Stefan and Vasili, were adamant still for following every lead, no matter how cold, until there was no place left to look. No telling how many more months could be wasted on that kind of doggedness. And what did they have to go on now but the name of the last person who supposedly had seen the baroness alive?

Learning that Tomilova had died soon after her arrival in this country was a shock to them all. She was to have contacted Sandor only under the direst emergency; otherwise there was to be no communication that could be intercepted and lead the Stamboloffs to the last Janacek. Was her imminent death not considered an emergency? But who would have thought she might die, and worse, done so before the child was old enough to care for herself, or even old enough to know whom to contact?

According to Rousseau's sister-in-law, the baroness and the infant, assumed to be hers, had spent no more than two days with them after making Madame Rousseau's acquaintance. But she had not been well, having barely recovered from a fever she had contracted on the journey to America. She was suffering delusions of grandeur one moment, persecution the next. She claimed to have been robbed of a fortune in jewels her very first night in the city. But when she learned of the yellow fever that could run rife through New Orleans, killing indiscriminately, she became nearly hysterical, insisting she could not stay there another day.

"My sister could make no assurances that she would listen to," the bearer of these bad tidings told them. "The lady made arrangements on her own to leave the city, but when she told us who with and to where, we tried even more to dissuade her. The woman she meant to travel with was steeped in scandal for marrying white trash. But would your baroness take heed, or care that the area she intended to travel through was the most lawless in the land? We suspected her fever had returned, she was behaving so erratically. We even offered to keep the child, for its own protection, but the lady was simply not open to reason. I, for one, wasn't the least surprised when her body was brought to us for proper burial less than a week later, because my sister's calling card was the only thing found in her purse. She'd been left on the side of the road, only partially covered by rocks, as if that Dobbs woman had at least tried to bury her.''

Another name to track down, and the only piece of good luck yet, if it could be considered such, was that this Dobbs woman's destination had been right here to the town of Natchez. But would she still be here after twenty years had come and gone? The Rousseau sister had never heard of her again, and she'd been living here ten years herself. And if she was here, would she know what had happened to the child?

Serge had been sent to speak with the town officials as soon as they returned to town, hopefully to find an answer or two to those very questions. If not, then they would all begin tomorrow to canvas the town, a tedious task, as they had learned in New Orleans. The possibilities were endless, but uppermost in all of their minds right now was the simple fact that the princess might never be found, might even be dead, and as much as the king had hated coming here to fetch her, he did not want to go home empty-handed.

''I have decided that table over there has the best view of the stage,'' Vasili remarked as soon as he rejoined them. ''Shall we bribe the occupants into a trade . . . or simply confiscate it? After all, royalty has its privilege. Even these peasants can understand that.''

''When we have been traveling incognito?'' Stefan countered dryly.

''So we have.'' Vasili sighed. ''Then I suppose we must just take it. Might also has its privile~.''

''The devil you will,'' Lazar hissed, coming instantly to his feet. "My chair has an unobstructed view of the damn stage. Here, take it!"

"If you insist, my friend."

Stefan grinned to himself at how subtly Vasili had maneuvered that, with Lazar merely gritting his teeth, relieved that he wouldn't have to draw his sword in their defense—yet. They all had a degree of arrogance, Stefan would be the first to admit, but Vasili used his like a weapon sometimes, with precision and skill, and a good deal of amusement. Lazar knew that. How could he not, when they had been together since childhood, suffering the same court tutors, the same training, the same enemies. They thought alike, they were alike, they were the best of friends. Lazar just had trouble concentrating on more than one thing at a time, and presently, he had made up his mind that both Vasili and Stefan were eager for trouble as a way to relieve their latest frustration, and he was determined to worry about it.

Lazar also hadn't realized that Vasili had already found an outlet for his tension—this show. His desire for Lazar's better seat had been very real. He was caught up in the anticipation of the crowd that was growing impatient at the delay in the entertainment.

The performance was supposed to have started by now. More patrons were noisily banging on their tables in complaint. But perhaps the wait would be worth it. Perhaps this harem dancer was as good as she was touted to be. And whom was he kidding? She had to be a rank amateur, merely giving her interpretation of what she supposed the famed harem dance would be like. These Americans wouldn't know the difference, however, and Vasili was easily pleased, which was fortunate, for Stefan was afraid there'd be the devil to pay if Vasili's present eagerness turned to disappointment.

He leaned toward Stefan now to whisper, "It was confided to me that the dancer can be had for a few coins. If she is even one tenth as good as my Fatima, I will request a private performance."

Lazar heard that and scowled. "You take too many risks with these whores, Vasili. Three in New Orleans, one on the steamship, now this belly dancer. You'll take home a souvenir from this country that will have you scratching your—"

"Lazar has been bitching since we walked in the door," Stefan interrupted before Vasili's changeable temper took a turn for the worse. Those two had been known to go at each other with murderous intent before they realized what they were doing and fell over laughing about it. "He cannot believe that we are here merely to swill this horse piss they call beer and watch an ignorant foreigner make a ridiculous fool of herself up on that stage."

"Put that way, I would have doubts myself," Vasili said, his light brown eyes laughing as he turned to Lazar. "You see what your bitching has brought us? You know how vicious Stefan can be when he is annoyed with us."

"Jesus, Vasili," Lazar groaned exaggeratedly as he slumped down in his new chair. "Why don't you just ask him to cut us to ribbons?"

Vasili turned back to Stefan, wide-eyed with innocence. "Was I prodding you, my friend?"

"You were trying," Stefan replied inscrutably. "But then the braying of an ass has never bothered me."

"I see what you mean, Lazar." Vasili winced. "Cut to the bone."

"If you both don't shut up, you will miss the show entirely."

Vasili glanced at the stage and sat forward, the teasing forgotten. The crowd erupted into applause at the same time, which brought Lazar up, alert and then dumbfounded as he too stared at the stage. Stefan, however, scowled as the dance progressed. Whatever else he had expected, he had not thought he would want the wench for himself.

Chapter 4

She was exquisitely delicate and fine-boned, this angel of Babylon. Stefan, along with every other man in the room, was entranced, unable to take his eyes from her. Here was a dance meant to inflame the senses, yet the girl's movements were so sensually graceful, she lent it a kind of innocence. Perhaps that was for her own protection, performing before so many men as she was. It was too late to work on Stefan, however. She might be the kind of female who could drive a man crazy with warring instincts of lust and protectiveness, but right now he felt only lust.

He had wondered what kind of costume she would use—certainly not the revealing transparency of the true harem dancer, who was after all a concubine or a slave, and danced to entice a master into noticing her among so many other slaves. This was America, where women thoroughly covered all limbs; at least good women did. But this one was a whore, dancing for an all-male audience, so she would be allowed to bare her arms at least, and a portion of her legs, and, because of the dance, a good portion of her belly. Such was not the case.

The material of her harem trousers started just below the navel, was snug across the hips and abdomen, but baggy down the legs, where they gathered tight at her ankles. The lavender material was not at all transparent, but was so thin that with certain movements it molded itself to her legs. Her top, of the same thin material, was short, though not as short as the audience would have liked, hanging down to the waistband of the trousers. The sleeves were long and full, gathered at the wrists. The top fit snugly across her firm breasts but thereafter fell loosely, so that it swayed with her body. Dotted about this costume were small silver sequins that flashed as they caught the candlelight, as well as a wide band of bangles about her hips, wrists, and ankles that clinked rhythmically with her movements, proving she was no amateur to this dance. But then that had been very obvious from the moment she glided onto the stage.

The same lavender material was used for the long veil that covered her hair to her waist, but her hair was a bit longer than the veil, and unbound, so long locks of it, as black as ebony, fell over her narrow shoulders or were flipped back as she dipped and turned. A shorter veil concealed her features, all but her eyes, which at first seemed slanted. Watching her so intently, Stefan soon realized it was the heavy kohl she'd used that gave them that effect, that and the fact that she kept her eyes lowered to avoid looking directly at the audience. Her feet were bare, but that was the only part of her that was, other than the inch or two of navel that appeared infrequently when her chest rose during her slow undulations.

Hopefully, Vasili would be satisfied with that teasing glimpse of exposed belly, for he wouldn't see any more if Stefan could help it, not tonight anyway. But how to manage that, when Vasili had already announced his intentions? Directness seemed the easiest route, which was what he tried the moment the girl ended her dance and disappeared through a back door.

"You have gorged yourself recently, Vasili. This one you will leave to me."

"I will?" The golden-haired man swung around in surprise. "Did you hear that, Lazar? He wants to steal the wench right out from under me."

"Ah, but she's not under you yet, and he's right," Lazar said in complete agreement. "You *have* gorged yourself lately. Besides, for you, any female will do, but our Stefan is much more particular in his tastes."

"I'm willing to share."

"I am not," Stefan said, stressing his words with the very softness of his tone.

"So it's like that, is it?" Vasili demanded, half indignant, half amused. "Well, why didn't you say so? You're welcome to her—if she'll have you."

It was said lightly, yet hearing Lazar suck in a horrified breath, Vasili realized the cruelty of his taunt, unintentional but there nonetheless, and he went white as a shroud. He was the most handsome among them. Women adored him because of it, and it was a typical joke in their youth that he would lord this over the rest of them. But that was before Stefan had been disfigured trying to save his only brother from a pack of hungry wolves.

"I didn't—"

Vasili was so appalled at himself, he couldn't finish. His chair scraped back and long strides carried him out the door without a backward glance.

"He meant it only in jest," Lazar offered hesitantly into the silence that surrounded only their table. "He would have said the same ten years ago."

"Am I so ignorant I don't know that?"

"Jesus, Stefan," Lazar complained. "If you weren't so touchy about it—"

"Go after him before he cuts his throat, thinking he has wounded me. Assure him my hide is much thicker than you both seem to think."

But it wasn't. Vasili's reminder that women, beautiful women at any rate, would avoid Stefan if possible cut deep. Like most men who could afford to, Stefan enjoyed them when the mood took him, but only whores, women who had little choice in the matter once they saw the color of his gold. Yet he still sensed their reluctance, and so he did not often indulge himself in that way.

He wondered why he had forgotten that when the little houri had begun her dance. Was it just the dance, then, that had made him want to possess her so badly? Or was it only that it had been long since he'd had a woman beneath him? This one had certainly stirred something deep within him, and yet ironically, he hadn't thought the dance all that erotic.

Not that any of it mattered now, for the urge was gone.

But he had no wish to return to the hotel yet, where Vasili and Lazar would be waiting, and would realize that he had changed his mind about the girl.

He was still sitting there, broodingly watching the occupants of the room as he finished his beer, when the new barmaid came in. He wasn't sure why he noticed her. She was certainly nothing to look at, with her haggard face that was downright gaunt, with her severely drawn-back hair and mannish attire. But his eyes followed her as she picked up a tray and cleared a table that had just been vacated. Her step was jaunty, her movements brisk—too brisk for such a tired-looking woman.

Tanya noticed him right off, and had to fight the urge not to cross herself. If the devil ever came to life, he'd have eyes like that man's, aglow with yellow hellfire.

Fanciful. She must be more tired than she thought, yet she'd felt exhilarated only moments before. It had been so long since she'd had to dance, six years to be exact. She'd been afraid she would have forgotten how, but she hadn't, and why should she? For almost half a year she'd danced every night at Dobbs' insistence, after Lelia had run off with a riverboat gambler.

Lelia had been the first dancer, the one who taught Tanya. She'd come through town with a troupe of actors, had had a fight with one of them, and had decided to stay. That had been Dobbs' lucky day, for Lelia and her foreign dance had turned the tavern around, from a business that barely paid for itself to one that made a decent profit. He finally had an attraction that could compete with the brothels and gambling dens that surrounded him. He even changed the name of the place to suit the dance. And did he ever have a fit when Lelia ran off.

But Tanya knew the dance by then, or her own special version of it, which was good enough for Dobbs, since she was all he had to keep the customers coming in. She was young, but her body was pretty much grown to what it was now, and Lelia had taught her how to use the powders and creams of the acting profession to dramatically change her looks. That was important, because Dobbs didn't want anyone knowing it was she up there on that stage, and neither did Tanya. When a few of the regulars finally figured it out, Dobbs found a girl for her to teach the dance to.

She'd been glad to quit. As much as she loved dancing, she'd hated the way the men in the audience looked at her, and their crude comments while she was performing were even worse. But until April's foot healed, she'd be dancing again, or lose the business to her next-door neighbors, which she refused to do. She had to protect what would soon be hers. And she made a vow right then that when The Seraglio was hers, she'd have extra dancers trained so she wouldn't have to expose herself to discovery again.

She shivered, knowing damn well those glowing yellow eyes were still watching her. And despite every instinct that screamed, *Don't look at him again,* she did—and got summoned to his table with a beckoning hand.

Don't be a twithead, missy. He's not the devil, he's not. But she'd never walked so slowly in her life as she did to that swarthy-faced, richly dressed gentleman. And then she almost erupted with giggles at her own foolishness, because two steps away from him, she saw that it had only been the candlelight reflecting in his eyes that had made them seem to glow from within. They weren't yellow at all, but a very light brown, like golden sherry wine, and beautiful, really, in such a darkly bronze face.

When she reached him, she was smiling, her relief was so great. But that was something she never did in the common room, because good humor just didn't match the haggard appearance she strived for. She was old Tanya, supposedly Dobbs' spinster daughter. However, this was a stranger, most likely from the riverboat that would be leaving in the morning, so she wasn't going to worry about one little slip.

"What can I do for you, sir?"

The smile confused Stefan, not because it was incongruous in that work-worn face, but because women rarely smiled at him, not at first anyway. They were usually overcome with embarrassment for getting caught staring in fascinated horror at his scars, which were what everyone, men included, noticed first about him now. But this barmaid had yet to even notice, or if she had . . . perhaps she didn't find him quite so objectionable for the simple reason that she was beyond plain-looking herself.

He was inordinately pleased by her reaction to him,

however, particularly after his previous dark thoughts, but that didn't blind him to the fact that something wasn't quite right about her, something that nagged at the back of his mind.

She had the eyes of a laughing child, bubbling with humor. Certainly they didn't suit her, nor did the fine white teeth she'd revealed, but he had unusual eyes himself and all his teeth, so he could discount that as what bothered him about her. Her gray shirt and waistcoat were manly, bulky, ugly on her, the black skirt unadorned peasant's clothing, the knife on her hip—what the devil could *she* need that for? Her hands were small, red and callused on one side, peach- and cream-tinted on the other side, a sharp contrast to the sallow complexion of her face, engraved with dark smudges of exhaustion—another sharp contrast considering the bouncy step he had first noticed.

Intuition finally stirred and he took a wild guess. "Such black eye paint is the very devil to come off, isn't it?"

At her gasp, he burst into laughter, which only increased when she swiftly tried to correct the oversight he'd hinted at by wiping vigorously at her eyes. She made sense now, in all her strangeness. On the stage, she camouflaged her face, and no wonder, for she was singularly unattractive, except for those pale green eyes and perfect white teeth. Here in the common room, however, she camouflaged her body, again no wonder, for the costume she'd worn, though for the most part loose, had still revealed an emi-

nently desirable form. The girl obviously played at
two roles—the dancer who whored on the side, and
the barmaid who didn't want to be bothered.

"It's not funny, mister," she said in a curt, irritated tone, glaring down at him now that she assumed
she'd taken care of the smudges.

Still chuckling, Stefan asked, "Would you like me
to help?"

"You mean it's still . . . ? No, thank you," she
gritted out ungraciously.

She grabbed the bottom of her shirt this time to
try again, unaware that she left him staring at a patch
of smooth stomach when her belt was pulled upward
with the raised shirttail. Stefan's humor fled as lust
instantly returned, full-blown and prodding.

When her clothes were smoothed back into place,
there were indeed faint smears of black on the material, though Stefan hadn't really seen any remaining
kohl on her eyes. They were slightly puffy now,
however. Even the dark shadows beneath them were
lightened in color from all the rubbing she'd just
done, which gave him a twinge of conscience that
just upped the price he would offer for her.

"If you're finished picking out my flaws, maybe
you'd like to tell me what you want now. I have other
customers—"

"You."

"What was that?"

"I want you."

So she'd heard him right the first time! But he had
to be making sport of her. She knew what she looked
like. She'd spent seven years perfecting the disguise

that now only took a few minutes to effect. Her appearance was meant to put off, not attract. Yet he was darkly good-looking in a rough sort of way, like an uncut gem. He was also well-to-do, if the cut of his navy coat was any indication, fitting so snug across broad shoulders. But that combination, money and looks, made him the exact type of man she was always invisible to.

She'd thought him Spanish or Mexican at first glance because he was so dark and definitely foreign-looking, but she would recognize a Spanish accent, and that wasn't the accent she heard in his very correct English. Maybe he was a Northerner. They didn't get too many of them coming here, being too fastidious for the rough crowd The Seraglio drew. This one had lean, hawklike features, with flaring black brows, thin, straight lips, a very strong jaw that was smooth-skinned—except for the scars. They dotted his upper left cheek in half-inch, downward slashes. The same kind of marks appeared on his lower jaw, as if some animal had sunk its teeth into the man's face and started to bite the whole side of it off, but had been stopped in time.

The scars made her feel a kind of empathy with him. He'd suffered pain because of them, and she understood pain very well. But that empathy wasn't going to let her accept a joke at her own expense.

The man's bald statement that he wanted her didn't even deserve an answer, so all she said was, "I think Aggie should be handling this order. I'll send her to you."

She turned and walked away, only to feel something catch her belt and yank her back—his hand. She came up against his legs, which precipitated a fall, right into his lap. For a moment she was too incredulous to move, much less speak.

She finally glanced up and said with clear warning, "You're really pushing your luck, mister."

"Shush," he told her, grinning. "You have nothing to be angry about." And he dropped five twenty-dollar gold pieces into her lap.

Tanya just stared at the money, never having seen so much at one time before. She knew for a fact April and Aggie earned only a dollar or two for their favors, which was still a lot more than Dobbs paid them for a night's work. When she thought of what she could do with that money, such as hire more help, buy new clothes, which she'd never had . . . then he wasn't joking?

Lord help her, she'd never been tempted like this. The urge was so strong to palm those coins . . . he really was a devil to make her even consider it. But all she'd have to do was let him have her virginity, which she wasn't saving for anyone anyway, since she was never going to marry, and how bad could that be? This close, he smelled heavenly. She'd already noted he was clean, impeccably groomed, and she didn't find him the least bit unpleasant to look at. She might just enjoy . . . oh, Lord, what was she thinking?

"You *must* be a devil," she said wondrously, more to herself than for his benefit.

He didn't know what had brought that on, but he replied, "A belief shared by many."

Her green eyes narrowed on him. "You should at least deny it!"

He laughed. "Why should I?"

"Because—because . . . oh, never mind."

She tried to get up, but his arms, which were wrapped around her waist, weren't letting her. Her eyes narrowed even more. He was still grinning.

"Look, mister, you've picked the wrong—"

She was cut off by an impassioned new voice. "Stefan, I refuse to feel guilty about a stupid slip of the—"

"Not *now*, Vasili," Stefan growled impatiently. "Use your eyes and notice that I am busy."

Tanya turned her head and found herself staring bemusedly up at what could only be described as a golden Adonis, blond hair in soft curls, golden skin, and brown eyes as light in color as those of the man who held her. But this newcomer, Vasili, held her just as firmly—spellbound, for he had to be the most handsome of God's creatures, certainly the most handsome she'd ever seen.

Likewise he was looking at Tanya as if he couldn't believe his eyes, but then he groaned, demanding of his friend, "You gave up without even trying, didn't you? But you don't have to settle for *that,* for God's sake," he said in disgust, jerking his head toward Tanya. "I will procure the dancer for you myself."

It took Tanya a moment to comprehend that she had been insulted in the worst way. She wasn't supposed to be pretty, but common decency kept a man's mouth shut about it. But to be made to feel that she wasn't good enough to be the rug they would walk on—that hurt, more than she would have thought possible. That she *could* be hurt by a few insensitive words, and from a stranger no less, also infuriated her. Two emotions that didn't sit well together raged within her.

Who did they think they were, these strangers, the one sure she could be bought, the other sure no one in his right mind would want to buy her? She wanted to disappear. She wanted to retaliate. First she had to get off the lap of the dark one.

She settled on two out of three, since the arms that had held her were now loosened. She rose with as much dignity as she could muster, carefully placed the gold coins on the table, and mindful that The Seraglio had witnessed a scene just last night and didn't need another, she turned to leave. A wise decision she could have been proud of, but her anger suddenly got the better of her and she swung around and slapped the golden Adonis with all her might.

What happened then was swift, no one's reflexes lagging. Vasili raised his arm with the clear intent of slapping her back, Stefan leaped up and caught his arm, while Tanya unsheathed her knife. But for once she didn't care to make good on her threat, didn't even demand that they leave. While they both stood unmoving, staring at her knife, Tanya backed away, turned, and ran out the back door.

As soon as the wench was gone from sight, Stefan turned on his friend with a snarl. "Vasili, you are about as sensitive as a pig!" At the same instant, Vasili burst out incredulously, "That bitch pulled a knife on me!"

"Not surprising, since you were about to hit her," Stefan noted with disgust.

"Deservedly, after she slapped me."

"Which you deserved."

Vasili shrugged and then grinned. "What does it matter, as long as you have forgiven me my loose tongue. Now, would you like me to find the dancer for you?"

"Idiot, *that* was the dancer."

Only the merest widening of Vasili's eyes showed his surprise, before he said imperiously, "Then I returned to save you just in time. You may thank me later."

Chapter 5

After hearing Serge's discouraging news that the Dobbs woman was another lead who had been dead many years, Vasili had been in favor of returning to The Seraglio last night, but Stefan had talked him into waiting until the morning. It was ironic that they had been so close to their quarry without even knowing it. But the woman's husband, the owner of the tavern and their only remaining hope for some solid information about Tatiana, had lived in this town for over twenty years. He wasn't going anywhere.

The truth of the matter was that Stefan was embarrassed to face the little dancer again, after he'd sat there and let her be wounded by Vasili's arrogance. Granted, he'd been amazed into momentary speechlessness by Vasili's insensitivity, but that was no excuse. He'd chosen the wench for the evening, so he should have protected or at least spoken up for her sooner than he did.

Of course, it had not taken him long to understand why his friend had been upset enough not to care whom he insulted. Vasili had seen the entire situation as being *his* fault because of his earlier remark, and so had tried to correct it as swiftly as possible, and contempt was a specialty of his, developed to perfection.

At any rate, Stefan didn't want to return to the tavern until he could be assured the wench wouldn't be there, which was this morning, while the place wasn't open for business. Yet who should open the door to Serge's pounding but the very one Stefan had hoped to avoid. And what did she do upon seeing them standing there but immediately shut the door, and none too gently.

It was a new experience for all four of them, having a door closed in their face, and they each reacted differently.

Serge became aggressive, asking, "Shall I break it down?"

Before anyone answered, Vasili voiced his indignation. "More audacious behavior by the wench. Do you still maintain she doesn't deserve to be put in her place, Stefan?"

Stefan was purely disgusted with himself, for his first reaction to that closed door was relief, which smacked of cowardice, something no one in his right mind could ever accuse him of. Accordingly, his tone was a bit clipped when he shot back, "And what is her place, my friend? She's not a Cardinian peasant, you know."

"She's an American peasant. What, pray, is the difference?"

Lazar was laughing by this time, he was so

amused, and answered, "Damned if I know, but I'm sure she can tell you. Why don't we ask her?"

"We'll have to break the door down to do that," Serge reminded them.

"I didn't hear a lock turn," Vasili said. "Just open—"

The lock clicked even as he spoke, so Serge asked again, "Shall I break it down?"

With a sound of annoyance, Stefan stepped forward and rapped sharply on the door, calling out, "Mistress, our business is with Wilbert Dobbs, not with you. Kindly—"

"Dobbs is sick," the female voice shouted. "I run the place now, so you'd have to deal with me, and *that* means you might as well leave."

She'd answered so quickly, it was obvious she'd been listening at the door, knowledge that would have increased Stefan's embarrassment if her stubbornness hadn't just pricked his temper. "Unless you wish to do without a door until this one can be repaired, I would suggest you open it very quickly, mistress!"

Magic words, apparently. The door opened, but the wench stood there blocking the way, hands on hips, one on the hilt of her knife. The knife was still sheathed, but Vasili and Stefan knew how quickly that could be amended, and the light of battle in her eyes said it was likely to be. Her clothes were similar to those she'd worn last night, with merely a different colored shirt, one that cast a gray pallor to her complexion. The bright light of day was definitely not kind to her.

"You speak English real good for a foreigner,"

she told Stefan directly, not bothering to look at the others. "But you sure don't understand its meaning very well. I told you Dobbs is sick. That means he can't be disturbed by the likes of you."

Stefan took an intimidating step toward her, but she held her ground. Her courage was commendable, but foolish under the circumstances. He was, after all, nearly a head taller than she and in prime physical condition, and she had no idea what he was capable of. His eyes had begun to glow with his annoyance, though he was unaware of that fact, or that it was the reason her hands had started to sweat.

"If you understand English yourself," he said with soft menace, "then understand that we will speak with Wilbert Dobbs because it is imperative that we do so, and nothing you can say or do will alter that. If my own understanding is correct, I believe that means you would be wise to step out of the way."

She hesitated for a long moment, glaring at him, before she said, "Go on, then, disturb a dying man. It's on your conscience, not mine." And she whipped around, leaving the doorway and their presence as quickly as possible.

"You could have at least asked her where the fellow is," Vasili grumbled as he and the others followed Stefan inside.

Lazar chuckled, still finding the situation highly amusing. "It will be easier to find him ourselves, Vasili, than to get any more information out of that one. We have not a palace to search, after all, but a few measly rooms."

"Then let us proceed, by all means. This place is

hard to stomach in the light of day."

Actually, it smelled of lye soap, rather than stale beer. Tables were moved aside, chairs upended on them, and the floor was still damp in spots from being scrubbed. The tavern was as clean as it was ever likely to be. Vasili's finding it distasteful was merely a reflection of his mood, primed for ridicule after their unexpected reception.

Up a narrow flight of stairs and down an even narrower hallway, Wilbert Dobbs' voice, raised in complaint about the tardiness of his breakfast, drew them directly to him. He did not sound like a sick man. He sounded like an irate, hungry man.

Lazar was still finding this part of their quest very entertaining, likely because Vasili was not. Close to laughter again, he wondered aloud, "Do you suppose that green-eyed dragon below is the lazy slut he's calling for?"

"Slut maybe, but lazy?" Serge replied. "She's working herself into the grave, if you ask me. She looks about two steps from it."

Serge could be even more blunt than Vasili in speaking the obvious, and having the obvious pointed out so blaringly stirred Stefan's guilt for his sharpness with the girl just now. She did look overworked, cruelly so, and that could be the cause of her bad temper, rather than what had happened last night. At any rate, he shouldn't have let her prod his own temper.

"What is this?" Vasili demanded impatiently. "That impudent bitch isn't worth our curiosity, particularly when the whereabouts of the princess could be revealed in a matter of moments.''

"Or not," Serge pointed out, though he reached for the door handle. "And I would just as soon have delayed another 'not.' ''

"Damn you, Tanya!" they were greeted before the door finished its inward swing. "What excuse . . .''

The words died off as the four men filed into the small room, crowding it with their size. Wilbert Dobbs jerked up in his bed, no easy feat with his bloated body.

"Here, now, how'd you get in here?" he blustered, though there was a marked improvement in his tone of voice, a deference for his betters, which they personified in the richness of their dress as well as their bearing. "Tanya knows I don't want no visitors.''

"If you refer to the wench below, then you may absolve her, for she did her best to turn us away," Lazar volunteered.

"Not good enough," Dobbs snorted. "All right, then, let's hear it. What do the likes of you fine gentlemen want with me?''

"We are here on a matter concerning your deceased wife," Lazar answered.

"Iris? What, has she been bequeathed something by that fine family that disowned her for marrying me?''

Dobbs laughed at the thought that something might finally have come out of that mistake. Iris had married him in desperation because her rich lover wouldn't have her after she got with child. Dobbs had thought she'd add a little class to the tavern he'd just opened in Natchez, so he'd jumped at the chance to offer his name. But she'd lost the brat and got slovenly after that, so they'd both lost out on the bargain.

His hope of a belated inheritance was quickly dashed, however. "We know nothing of your wife's family, Mr. Dobbs," he was told by the same man. "Our interest is in the woman with whom she departed New Orleans nearly twenty years ago."

"The crazy foreigner?"

"Your wife mentioned her to you, then?" Lazar asked.

"I met her myself when I caught up with Iris."

He didn't like being reminded of that time his wife had run away from him, going home to New Orleans to beg her folks to take her back, futilely as it turned out. He'd had every intention of beating her senseless, despite the fact that she was returning to him. But she'd had that foreign woman with her who'd died of the fever within hours of his finding them, and the woman's baby. It had galled him to forgo beating her, but Iris had needed her faculties intact to care for the baby. And the baby had been more important at the time, for he'd already decided to keep it. In a few years she'd be as good as any slave, and she'd cost him nothing.

As he recalled how he'd come by Tanya, his expression turned wary and his tone became belligerent. "There's not much to tell about that woman. She didn't have a penny to her name, but she managed to talk Iris into taking her along with her, even though the going wouldn't be easy traveling by wagon. But Iris always was softhearted.''

"With a direct river route between New Orleans and Natchez, why was your wife traveling by land and without escort?'' Lazar asked.

"She didn't have the fare for no riverboat either, not that it's any of your business. But she'd gone down there with the wagon, *my* wagon. She's damn lucky she didn't sell it—'' Dobbs fell silent with a scowl, aware that he was saying more than they needed to know, but having already blurted out so much, he confessed, "The wife thought to run off from me, but realized she had nowhere to go. She was coming back when I found her camped along the river road, trying to nurse the woman. But she was burned up with fever, and shouting all kinds of nonsense about assassins and kings, mostly in languages we'd never heard before, and mostly about failing her duty, whatever that was. She died in her sleep that night, and that's all there is to tell.''

"I think not, Mr. Dobbs,'' said the clipped voice of the dark man with the devil's eyes. "You forget to mention the child.''

More than the others, who were all too serious-looking by half, this man unnerved Dobbs with his strange, piercing eyes. He seemed to be in the grip of some powerful emotion, tightly controlled, but frightening just the same. The same intense emotion was apparent in all of them, really, just more obvious in this one, but it made Dobbs wonder what was so important about the information they sought and why, after all these years, they were even seeking it.

His expression still wary, but his tone more affable, he said, ''I didn't forget. It's just a sad thing to remember, is all. There was a baby, yes, but it caught the fever from its mother. There just weren't nothing me or Iris could do to save it, much as we tried.''

Chapter 6

"Dead!?"

The incredulous exclamations came at Dobbs from two different directions at once. He didn't know whether to elaborate on what he'd said or demand some answers of his own. But his hands had begun to sweat, his brow, too, not because he was lying, but because those devil's eyes were trying to see right inside his head. He was sure of it.

He cleared his throat, surreptitiously wiping his palms on his blanket. "What's your interest in that baby? You're all kind of young to be the father, ain't you?" No answer came, which unnerved him even more.

And then the blond one, whom he'd barely noticed because his handsomeness made him seem less dangerous than the others, flung a retort at him. "There was only one grave found, the woman's. A mere pile of stones, guaranteed to crumble."

The contempt in that voice, making it sound as if

Dobbs had been deliberately inept, got his dander up.

"What was I supposed to do, dump her in the river?" Dobbs demanded. "When you don't have no shovel, you make do in these parts."

"There was still only the one grave, Mr. Dobbs," observed the one with blue eyes.

"The baby didn't die the same day. We'd already moved on."

The questions came at him from all of them then, and he had barely enough time to answer one before the next was shot at him.

"How many days later?"

"A few."

"Exactly?"

"Two, dammit!"

"What time of day?"

"How the hell should I remember?"

"What time did he die, Mr. Dobbs?"

"He? What he? She's a girl."

"She is? Or was?"

"Was! Was! What the hell is this? It don't make a peck of difference what she was, or what time she died. She's dead—that's all you need to know!"

"I'm afraid not, Mr. Dobbs. We require proof."

"Proof that you will have to supply, Mr. Dobbs, since you claim to have buried her."

"In other words, Mr. Dobbs, you will have to lead us to her grave."

Dobbs stared at the three who had just spoken as if they were crazy. But they were serious, dead serious. The dark one with the unholy eyes hadn't said a word during the interrogation, nor did he now. He just watched, and listened, and made Dobbs even more uneasy with his silence.

"I can't lead anyone anywhere," Dobbs told them, for once glad it was true. "I haven't left this room in six months, not since—"

"The nature of your illness has little bearing," he was informed with a distinct lack of sympathy. "We will supply you a comfortable conveyance, and pay you for your time."

"It wouldn't do no good," Dobbs insisted nervously. "I put that baby in the ground, since she didn't need but a tiny grave, easy enough to scrap out with a sharp rock. But there weren't nothing to leave as a marker, and with twenty years come and gone, even with that other grave to judge the distance by, I'd never find—"

"You needn't explain further," the dark one cut in. "Thank you for your time."

As soon as it was said, they all turned and left the room. Dobbs fell back on his pillow, finally wiping his brow. He couldn't imagine what that had been all about, but he hoped never to go through it again.

At the top of the stairs, Stefan paused to state the obvious. "He was lying."

"Yes," Lazar agreed. "But why?"

"There can be only one reason," Serge said.

Their minds traveled the same path and came to the same appalling conclusion. It was Vasili who burst out, "Don't even think it! She's a tavern whore, for God's sake, and ugly—"

"She has the right color eyes," Lazar pointed out.

He was no longer the least bit amused.

"There are probably a hundred women with green eyes in this town alone," Vasili insisted. "And besides, that horrid female downstairs cannot possibly be only twenty years of age. She's thirty if she's a day."

"Hard work can age anyone," Serge said. "And even her name, Tanya, is—"

"Enough!" Stefan hissed. "We each of us know how proof is to be established. I would suggest we establish it one way or the other, rather than argue the possibility."

Vasili still protested. "But even to consider her is insane."

"There is nothing *to* consider if she is the one we seek, Vasili. You know that as well as I."

"Then I would just as soon not find out," Vasili replied. "But then I can't believe for a minute that she's the one. Mere circumstance doesn't make it so."

"But the crescent moon on her left cheek will."

"Damn you, Stefan! All right, if you insist on looking for it, you will do so without my help. I refuse to go near that foul-tempered wench again."

"I doubt your assistance will be necessary," Stefan said tightly. "I believe I can spare a few coins, which is all it should take to get a whore to raise her skirts."

Vasili flushed crimson at those words. He'd said it himself, called her a whore more than once, but that wasn't the same as hearing it from Stefan. How could his cousin even consider the possibility that a whore could be the future Queen of Cardinia?

Before the two cousins got physical in their disagreement, Lazar stepped between them. "Why don't I find the girl and just ask her if she has any unusual marks on her person?" he suggested. "If she can describe the damned moon, it won't be necessary to embarrass her or ourselves."

"She's not going to answer a personal question like that without knowing why she's being asked," Serge said. "And if she's told why, she'd carve the crescent on her backside herself to have a chance at the life we're offering."

"We're not going to tell her what we're looking for, Serge," Lazar said patiently. "She'd have to tell us—"

"You're still here?" the female in question demanded from the bottom of the stairs, a tray of food in her hands. "Well, there's the door, and hurry up, will you? Dobbs is waiting for his breakfast."

"So we heard," Stefan said, coming down the stairs. "Take it to him, by all means."

"But, Stefan—"

A hand waved Lazar to silence.

Tanya had to wait until they'd all come down, the stairs were so narrow. She did so nervously, because her hands were encumbered with the tray, leaving her defenseless for the moment. That devil's eyes weren't glowing now, but she'd been mistaken last night in her relief. They really did glow, or seemed to, they brightened so much, and it had nothing to do with candlelight, for there'd been none this morning.

The handsome one's eyes were glowing, though
. . . Lord help her, they burned as brightly as the other
one's, they just didn't seem as satanic or frightening
in an angel's face. But they were burning at her. That
man despised her for some reason. She'd been
slapped with his contempt last night. This morning
he looked as if he'd like to erase her from the face
of the earth. Well, the feeling was entirely mutual.
She'd spent the night choking with the hurt he'd
caused her to feel, the kind that went so deep it cut
and bled tears. She'd rather feel Dobbs' stick across
her back any day than suffer that kind of contempt
again. At least physical pain went away, but she
didn't think she'd ever forget last night's shame.

The other two men weren't nearly as intimidating
as the two she'd already met. One was tall and slim
of build, with dark brown hair and blue eyes that
raked her from head to toe, as if he knew she hid
something and was determined to find it. She wasn't
accustomed to such curiosity. The other man was an
inch or so shorter and stocky, with black hair and
eyes, but a fair complexion. Tanya could have sworn
there was sympathy in his dark eyes, and that more
than anything kept her back straight and her lips
tightly compressed, despite her nervousness.

But as soon as the last one reached the bottom of
the stairs, she rushed up them, praying that was the
last she'd see of any of them. She didn't know that
four pairs of eyes turned to watch her ascent, or that
one of the men was signaled to follow her. She simply
rushed into Dobbs' room and kicked the door shut
behind her with a great deal of relief.

Chapter 7

"When she asked, he told her our business was none of hers," Lazar said when he came back downstairs from eavesdropping outside Wilbert Dobbs' room. "But he warned her to stay away from us if we return here."

"What else?"

"Nothing that pertains to us. He spent most of the time complaining, in particular that his breakfast was late, but about a goodly number of other things, too. Apparently she really does run this place as she claimed, and without help."

"A good reason why he wouldn't want to part with her," Serge commented.

"Perhaps, though he had no way of knowing what we wanted with her," Stefan said, then asked Lazar, "Will she be long, do you think?"

"I doubt it. With the way he talks to her, berating her for every little thing, if I were her I wouldn't stay in that room any longer than I had to."

Even as he said it, they heard the sound of a door

closing. And then the girl was running down the stairs, once again belying the exhaustion in her face. She tripped to a stop at the bottom upon seeing them, and without caring that the gesture gave away her apprehension, she put her hand on the hilt of her knife.

Stefan stifled a laugh that would have told her plainly what little deterrent that weapon was to men trained to war with other men. He didn't want to take away whatever security it provided her, but it really was amusing, seeing a woman trying to give the impression she was prepared to do battle.

"Couldn't you find the door?" she asked, looking pointedly at Stefan.

He ignored her attempt to goad him. "We need to talk to you, mistress."

"You claimed your business was only with Dobbs and you've concluded that."

"Not to our satisfaction."

One flaring feminine brow arched. "I hope you don't think I care whether you're satisfied."

Lazar hooted with laughter. Vasili made a sound of disgust, but fortunately kept his mouth shut otherwise. Stefan cringed inwardly, seeing a double meaning there whether it was intended or not. Outwardly, he frowned.

"We have a few questions—"

"I don't have time—"

"—for you to answer."

"I said—" she started to reiterate, only to be drowned out by sheer volume.

"Enough, mistress! We apologize for last night.

We also apologize for our sharpness with you earlier. But now we must insist that you cooperate.''

A shouted apology wasn't worth a lick of salt as far as she was concerned. And while this apology was being forced on her by the one called Stefan, the other men were moving restlessly about the room, clearly not the least bit interested in what was supposedly a joint offering. But in that she was mistaken. What she'd taken as restlessness was a deliberate maneuver to block every exit from the room. Even the stocky one now stood close enough to her and the stairs to prevent a retreat in that direction.

Obviously, Tanya wasn't going anywhere until she "cooperated." That she was being denied any choice in the matter infuriated her. Of course, she could just sit down and stubbornly wait them out. They couldn't force words out of her mouth, could they? But she'd rather get rid of them, the sooner the better, and that meant answering their damn questions. Only she wasn't going to pretend she liked it. And if she could exact a little retribution, she would. To her delight, an opportunity came her way immediately.

She'd hesitated in replying just long enough for Stefan to offer, "If all you are worried about is your time, then consider it paid for," and he tossed a coin at her.

Tanya caught it by reflex, but just as swiftly tossed it back. "Keep your money. You want information from me, it'll cost an apology from *him*.''

The "him" she dared to try bringing down a peg was the golden-haired Adonis. The others looked at him and waited, as if it were a foregone conclusion that he would comply. But he'd turned several shades of red, and was staring back at Tanya with murder in his eyes.

Well, it had been worth a try, to see that one humbled, but she hadn't really expected it to work, not when the other one had more or less spit out his apology as if she should be honored to receive it. And now she'd backed herself into a corner by putting a price on her cooperation. She'd have to attempt to leave. Her pride demanded it. She just hoped they weren't too rough in stopping her.

She waited another long moment before turning toward the door that led out back. The brown-haired man moved to block her way, as she had expected he would, but she didn't stop. She drew her knife instead, surprising him and herself, for she hadn't intended to go that far to protect her pride. Damned self-defeating emotion it was, too, having earned her a lot of extra beatings over the years. Today it just might get her killed, for the man wasn't backing down either. The very reason she hadn't insisted those other two leave last night, after she'd drawn her knife, was because she'd sensed they wouldn't. And this man was cut from the same cloth.

"Vasili!"

Tanya didn't know who had prodded him, the voice was so angry, but she heard Vasili grumble in response, "Oh, all right," then louder, imperiously, he added. "Attend me, mistress, and consider yourself apologized to for whatever it is I am supposed to have done or said that you found offensive to your so-called tender sensibilities."

He even apologized with contempt, and managed to insult her again by implying he didn't know what he'd done wrong to begin with. But Tanya knew she wouldn't get any better from the likes of him. He'd at least given her the out she needed to sheath her knife, which she did. The blue eyes in front of her were clearly relieved. She hoped her own relief was more concealed.

To that end, she swung about and gave Vasili a brilliant smile. "Thank you, kind sir. It does my heart good to know I wasn't mistaken about you."

Vasili frowned, aware that she was no more sincere in her thanks than he'd been in his apology. But he was unable to figure out if she'd just returned the insult, so he said no more.

Stefan cleared his throat, drawing her eyes to him. "Are you satisfied, mistress?"

Her smile didn't waver. "Oh, certainly. I'm just a tavern wench, after all, so ignorant I couldn't possibly know what he just wrapped up in that crock of eloquence. So why shouldn't I be satisfied? No, don't bother to answer that." The smile was gone, along with the sarcastic tone. Her voice and her expression were now quite frigid. "Just ask me your questions and leave."

Vasili was flushing red again, but warning looks from the other three men kept him silent for the moment.

"You put that rather eloquently yourself, mistress," Stefan remarked as he moved to the nearest table and took down the chairs from it. "Who taught you to mimic your betters?"

"My betters?" she repeated, her eyes narrowing. "I don't have any—"

He cut in quickly, "Let me rephrase that. Your speech improves when you choose. Did your father have you educated?"

"My father? If you mean Dobbs, he doesn't believe in schooling or anything else that takes away from good work time. But Iris Dobbs was an educated woman. What I know I learned from her."

He held out a chair for her. "Will you sit, mistress?"

"No, thank you."

"Do you mind if I do?"

Her lips quirked slightly. "By all means. I'm used to looking down on men."

He almost didn't take the other chair after that, particularly with Lazar chuckling in the background. Stefan assumed she referred to serving men who were usually sitting down, but that other meaning . . . He sat down, only to get right back up and pace in front of her instead.

"Is Wilbert Dobbs not your father, then?"

"No, thank God."

He was curious enough about her to want to know why she was thankful, but that wasn't what they'd just gone through that unpleasant scene to discover. "Then you only work here?"

"I've lived here for as long as I can remember."

"Ah, then Mr. Dobbs' wife must have been your mother."

Tanya frowned. "What is your interest in the Dobbses? Iris is dead, and Dobbs almost is."

"Just bear with me, mistress, and we will be fin-ished the sooner. Now, *was* Iris Dobbs your mother?"

"No, she wasn't. Iris said my mother died when I was just a baby."

"How did she die?"

"The yellow fever."

"Do you know her name?"

"My mother's name?" Her frown was back, not just because he was getting personal, but because she sensed an urgency in him now that hadn't been there before. "What has that got to do with anything? Either stick to the questions about Dobbs that you so *politely* asked me to answer, or I'm not answering any more."

"Everything that I ask you is related, mistress," he said sternly. "If my questions become personal, that is because you have lived with Wilbert Dobbs all your life. Now, your mother's name?"

"I don't know," she answered stiffly, dissatisfied with his explanation and not caring that he was frown-ing at her now.

"What of your own name? Tanya, isn't it? Was that the name you were born with, or was it given to you by Iris Dobbs when she took you in?"

"Both, I guess you could say. Iris was told my name, but she said it was too unusual-sounding for her to remember all of it, so I ended up with just a portion of it, or what sounded like it, which is better than nothing, I suppose."

He stopped in front of her then, staring at her for a long nerve-racking moment before he asked,

"Would you like to know all of it?"

"Stefan." The warning came from behind Tanya. "It is still only circumstance."

He looked over her head to the man behind her. "It is much more than circumstance, Lazar. What more do you need to hear?" Silence was his answer. Stefan's eyes dropped back to Tanya. "Were both Dobbses with your mother when she died?"

"Yes," she replied, still confused over the last question he'd asked her.

"Why is that?"

"They were traveling together at the time."

"From where?"

"New Orleans."

"By riverboat?"

"No, wagon." He was looking at Lazar again, triumphantly. Tanya couldn't hold back the incredulous thought any longer. "Do—do you know who my parents are?"

"It is possible—if you carry a certain—birthmark that is—hereditary."

She didn't even notice his hesitation over those pertinent words. She was trying to tamp down her excitement, because what he was suggesting was just too unlikely to be true. And yet—ever since she'd found out that she was unrelated to Dobbs and Iris, she'd wondered about her real parents, where they came from, what they were like, *who* they were.

It had been frustrating beyond belief that Iris couldn't tell her more than she had, couldn't recall her mother's name though she'd been told it, couldn't recall her name either, not all of it. But then Iris had been upset at the time with her own problems as well as those of the dying woman she'd agreed to help. So Tanya couldn't blame her for not retaining those memories. But that left Tanya with a burning curiosity, unsatisfied.

Other girls had backgrounds, rich in detail and color. Her life was a blank page begun in a tavern. Now here were four strangers hinting at knowledge she craved as much as, if not more than, her independence. To finally have a real identity, a family history, possibly even relatives still living—a birth date! It was just too wonderful to be true, and if she allowed her hopes to be raised, she'd be doomed to disappointment. And to have it all hinge on a birthmark?

Tanya had been staring blankly at the wide chest in front of her while her thoughts whirled. But years of self-preservation enabled her to catch sight of the hand raising to lift her chin to reclaim her attention, and she jerked back instinctively, before the carefully applied makeup on her face could be disturbed. Stefan took her movement personally, however.

As accustomed as he was to rejection, he still felt bitterly disappointed that this girl couldn't bear his touch, even impersonally, for unlike the others, he found that he was fiercely glad that she could be the one they sought. Of course, he kept forgetting that she was a whore and utterly unsuitable to be a queen. He wouldn't forget again.

He turned away from her and changed places with Lazar, giving him a curt order. "You ask her."

Lazar was convinced by now that it was unnecessary to go any further in their questioning. The others obviously felt the same, for Vasili was leaning back against the wall, his eyes closed, slowly pounding his head against the wood. Serge was sitting at the bottom of the stairs, his head lowered in his hands, his shoulders slumped. Stefan was merely furious. But no wonder. If the girl could scorn him now, as they'd all just seen her do, imagine her degree of disdain when she knew who she was.

Lazar certainly was no happier about it than the others. It was unfortunate that she wasn't the beauty they'd been led to expect, but that was nothing compared to *what* she was, a common performer, a barmaid—a whore. Jesus, the knowledge would probably kill Sandor, that this was what had become of the child he himself had sent away and would now force his son to marry.

No, Lazar needed no further answers or visual proof for himself, but just for the record. Accordingly, he afforded Tanya the first respect she'd had from any of them. Standing before her, he bowed formally and introduced himself, though he left off his title. He would have taken her hand and brought it to his lips, but she crossed her arms over her chest and gave him a narrow-eyed look which warned him off. It took him only a moment to realize that she thought he was making sport of her. Vasili's derisive laughter in the background did nothing to disabuse her of it. Lazar decided not to try.

"Can you tell us, mistress, if you possess any unique birthmarks?"

"One, but I wouldn't call it unique."

"Will you describe it, please?"

"It's a pink patch on my skin, the size of a large mole, but smooth."

"And located where?" When she blushed, Lazar decided she just wasn't describing it right and assured her, "The location is important, mistress."

"It's on my—in the area of my—"

"You may simply point to the area," he offered as she got even pinker.

Scowling now in her embarrassment, she snapped, "My arms are covering it just now."

"Covering?" He frowned, staring at her chest. "But—no, you have another mark."

"No, I don't."

"But you must have," he insisted.

"Well, I don't!"

Tanya was definitely angry now. As she'd known would happen, her hopes had been dashed. What they were looking for, she obviously didn't have.

"I don't understand—"

"For God's sake, Lazar," Vasili cut in. "You have your answer, twice repeated. Let us be grateful and go before it changes."

"A splendid idea," Tanya agreed, though no one was listening to her.

"It makes no sense at all. Everything points—"

"Coincidence, just as I said before."

"With two women dying in the same way, around the same time, and that old man upstairs burying them both?"

"Bizarre, certainly, but not impossible," Vasili said.

"Hasn't it occurred to either of you," Stefan remarked, "that, considering the location of the mark, she may never have seen it?"

"Of course!" Lazar chuckled.

Vasili wasn't so amused. "Dammit, Stefan, why couldn't you leave well enough alone?"

"Because we are here to discover the truth, no matter how distasteful we may find it."

Tanya stiffened, recognizing another insult when she heard it. By the time Stefan stood in front of her again, her green eyes were glittering with ire. But his eyes were softly glowing as well, for he was still reacting to her earlier rebuff. So her anger didn't bother him. In fact, he was delighted that he'd caused it.

"We are certain of your identity, mistress. The mark that will prove it should be found on the underside of your seat, on the left cheek. It will no doubt require a mirror for you to examine it, but go and do so now, and do so carefully, so you may return and describe the mark to us."

"And if I won't?"

"Then you may possibly be offended when we locate the mark ourselves, to end all doubt, you understand."

She was quickly learning that he could be as cruel as Vasili in his remarks. Her cheeks flaming, she hissed, "You bastard," but he merely crooked a brow at her, showing her how little it mattered to him that he'd insulted her—again. "What happens if the mark *is* there?"

"Then you will return with us to Cardinia."

"Where is that?"

"It's a small country in Eastern Europe. It's where you were born, Tatiana Janacek."

A name. Her name? God, this was becoming real again, her hopes soaring again. "Is that why you're here? To take me back?"

"Yes."

"Then I have family there? They sent you to find me?"

"No." His tone softened for the moment. "Regrettably, you are the last of your line."

Up and down, these hopes. Why did she let herself be lured in by possibilities? All right, no family. But a name, a history—if they were telling the truth, and if she had the mark.

"If I don't have any family left, then why did you bother to find me?"

"These questions are pointless, mistress, until you prove to us all, yourself included, that you possess the mark that names you a Janacek."

"I don't care how pointless you find my questions, I'm not moving an inch until I know the real reason you came here."

Stefan took a menacing step closer, but she didn't budge. He growled down at her, "For no other reason than to collect you and return you—"

"*Why?*"

"For your wedding!"

"My *what?*"

"You are to marry the new King of Cardinia."

Chapter 8

Tanya took a wide step back, to look at them as a whole. Finely dressed gentlemen, probably educated at West Point or some other officer training school, which would account for the military precision of their movements and bearing. Young bloods, though these were a bit old for that label, all of them more in the area of thirty years. But she knew their type. Rich, privileged, and no doubt bored—which made them great practical jokers.

She should have known none of this was real. They obviously thought it would be hilariously funny to dupe a poor, ignorant town girl into believing in fairy tales. Cruel was what it was, because most girls wouldn't see that it was only an elaborate joke, not until they were hurt by it. Now that Tanya did, she could explain it all away so easily.

Dobbs, of course, had given them the information they needed about her mother, probably for a few coins. Even the birthmark on her backside, if there really was one, could have been glimpsed through her window, for just last night she'd been in such a hurry to change out of her costume, she hadn't closed her curtains. But it mortified her to think of one of these men up in that old tree outside her window, watching her in the altogether and noticing something on her body that even she didn't know was there.

Hopefully, they hadn't gone to that much trouble and there really was nothing there. In fact, there being no such mark was probably the end of the joke. But until she actually looked, they were having a high time, weren't they? Anticipating that they were making her deliriously happy by what they were revealing, and how disappointed she was going to be when it finally dawned on her that she wouldn't get her fairy-tale king.

But they'd picked the one girl who wouldn't get down and kiss the feet of the so-called king who'd deign to marry her, because she was never getting married, not to any man, not even to a king if a real one ever asked. If they hadn't tried to carry it so far—a *king*, for God's sake—it would have worked. But that was probably the whole idea, to get her to believe something that was so fantastically unbelievable.

In fact, the joke had worked up to this point. She'd believed they actually knew who she was, that she would learn about her real family, her history, everything she'd always wanted to know. *That* was what was important to her, not some happy-ever-after marriage. But they didn't know that. She'd been ridiculously gullible. But they weren't going to know that either, not if she could help it.

"A king?" she said now, forcing her eyes wide with amazement. "My oh my, will wonders never cease." That tepid bit of excitement was the best she could do, so she changed her tone to skeptical, laced with scorn, wanting to see just how far they'd go to convince her. "Who?" she asked Stefan. "You? No, you're not arrogant enough. It must be him."

She was looking at Vasili. The others were looking at Stefan for his reaction to what could be considered another rebuff.

"Indeed," Stefan said stiffly. "King Vasili of Cardinia. That should delight you, mistress."

"Should it?" she replied, but her eyes were still on Vasili, whom she asked, "So you're a real live king?"

Vasili came away from his slump against the wall with a look of utter disgust which he bestowed first on Stefan, then on Tanya. "So it would seem, mistress."

"And why would you want to marry the likes of me?"

"I assure you I don't."

"You were betrothed at birth," Stefan quickly told her. "Whether the king wishes to marry you or not, his duty demands that he do so—if you bear the mark. It is time to establish—"

"I don't think so," Tanya cut in. "What it's time for is the end of this joke, and for you to leave. You've wasted enough of my—"

"You don't believe you stand before royalty?" This interruption came from Vasili, who showed some amusement at last in the slight tilting of his lips.

Tanya snorted. "I don't know what gave you the idea I was stupid, but I assure you I'm not."

"That is most definitely debatable, mistress," Vasili shot back. To Stefan he added, "Why don't you just lift her damn skirts and be done with it?"

Tanya's fingers curled immediately around the hilt of her knife. "The hand that touches me gets cut off," she promised. "Now I want you out of here!"

Stefan sighed, wondering how a simple matter had become so difficult. "We cannot leave here in doubt, mistress. If you would but *try* to understand our position—"

"But I do understand, perfectly. I'm just not believing it."

"For what reason would we fabricate what has been revealed here?"

"I can think of several reasons, none of them very nice. You could even be actors for all I know, rehearsing some stupid play that deals with royalty. In that case, you definitely need more practice—on everything but the arrogance and condescension. You've got those attitudes mastered very well indeed."

"The mark—"

"I don't care about the damned mark!"

"We do!"

Now Tanya sighed. "Then let me put it another way, since you insist on keeping up the pretense. I wouldn't marry your king if you paid me. So whether I have the mark or not no longer matters."

"If you have it, mistress, you *will* marry the King of Cardinia. Your wishes in the matter do not count, since it was your father who betrothed you."

"A father you say is dead, so it makes no difference to me what he did or didn't do. And you better believe my wishes count. I can't be forced to marry anyone."

"You *can* be ordered to, mistress."

"Like hell!" she snapped. "I don't take orders from anyone anymore, not even from Dobbs."

"You are a Cardinian—"

"I'm an American!"

"Where you were raised doesn't matter in the least," Stefan told her. "You were *born* in Cardinia, and that makes you subject to your king's will."

If what he was saying was really true, Tanya would be just about petrified by now. Subject to that despicable Adonis? Forced to marry him, when he couldn't stand her and didn't care if she knew it? No, she didn't believe it, couldn't believe it. But then why weren't they ending this joke, now that she'd told them she didn't want their pretty-faced king? It made no sense to go on with it.

She wasn't going to. "I've had enough of this nonsense," she said, and turned toward the back door.

"The mark, mistress!" she was reminded once more, this time furiously. "At the risk of repeating myself, we must know if you possess it, and again, either you describe it to us or you will force us to look for ourselves."

She stared hard at Lazar, who was blocking her

way just as he'd done earlier. God, did they all have to look and sound so serious? They must have played this joke countless times to make it seem so convincing.

"All right," she gritted out, swinging around and heading for the stairs instead. "We'll play this out your way. But when I return and tell you there isn't any mark to be found, you'd damn well better leave the premises and . . . not . . . come . . . back!"

Serge barely got out of her way in time, before she marched past him and up the stairs. Stefan watched the sway of her skirt as she went, and imagined her lifting it in a moment to examine an area he would have become familiar with last night if things had worked out differently. He wished to hell they had.

The scars on his jaw turned white, he clenched it so tightly before turning away—and catching Vasili's look. "Don't say it," Stefan warned. "I assumed her attitude would change if she thought . . . Hell, she's not normal, that girl."

"I'll agree to that," Vasili sneered.

Lazar chuckled. "You're just annoyed that she didn't swoon with happiness at the prospect of winning your esteemed self. And maybe she would have if she had believed what she was told. But in case you didn't notice, my friends, she didn't believe any of it."

"Then she'll change her tune once she sees the mark," Serge predicted.

"We don't know what she'll do," Lazar said. "Who would have thought she'd scorn a king? And you heard her. She doesn't want him either way.''

"As Stefan said, she's not normal," Vasili remarked.

"Yes, but even if she finds the mark, I'll wager she will return and say it isn't there. Are we to believe that?"

"You know as well as I that she *is* Tatiana Janacek," Stefan said.

"But she's so set against us, Stefan, I wouldn't be surprised if she cuts the mark out just to thwart us. Then we could never be entirely sure."

"And consider this, Stefan," Vasili added. "That could work either way. Her attitude could be pretense."

"How so?"

"If she is *not* Tatiana Janacek, and knows she doesn't possess the mark, how better to make us think she is than by adopting her present attitude? She could gouge out an area on her backside and insist the mark wasn't there. She'd be telling the truth knowing we would doubt it, and get everything we offer when it isn't hers by right."

Stefan didn't want to believe there was any likelihood in what they were saying, but in fact, it wasn't at all inconceivable that in order to become a queen, a woman would mutilate herself in an obscure place on her body that no one would ever see but a husband. A woman of little prospects might do so even in a highly visible spot for such a reward. And in the same respect, a woman dead set against marriage, even to a king, and a woman as stubborn and hot-tempered as this one apparently was, would think nothing of scraping a mark off her lovely backside to keep herself unwed. And they had sent her upstairs with a knife on her person.

With a foul expletive, Stefan pinned Lazar with his fiery gold gaze, snapping out, "I will need one other witness." And he headed for the stairs.

Chapter 9

Tanya was going to wait only five short minutes before returning below. The men would probably be gone by then, knowing as well as she did that she didn't have an unusual birthmark on her backside. End of joke—she hoped. If not, if there was a mark, it only meant they'd spied on her through her window, not that they were telling the truth. But to what end?

She could think of one motive, and she paled at the mere thought of it. She'd heard of girls being stolen from one town and sold into brothels in another, always far from home, so there would be plenty of time to find them and bring them back if they managed to escape. But escape usually wasn't one of the options of those places, they were so heavily guarded. And there were unscrupulous men who actually made their living by supplying the girls. Were the men downstairs such unscrupulous characters?

You're really getting fanciful now, missy, just like

*thinking that Stefan was a devil. Who'd want you
anyway, looking as you do?*

The devil did, and if he did, maybe he thought
other men would too. No, the other three didn't think
she was desirable—but they didn't realize that she
was the dancer they'd seen last night. That damned
dance! Stefan knew she was the dancer, and a girl
who could dance like that would be an asset in any
brothel. And how better to get her to one with no
trouble at all than a ruse that would make her *want*
to go with them? Lord help her . . .

The door to her tiny room flew open, making
Tanya leap off the bed where she'd been sitting,
working herself into a panic. Seeing Stefan fill the
doorway, scowling at her, made the panic very real.
She tamped it down only with a concerted effort.
Getting hysterical at this point wouldn't help, and
she could be wrong. After all, how many times had
she already been wrong about them? But her latest
suspicion was a far cry from a cruel, though harmless,
practical joke.

"You were not even curious enough to see if it is
there, wench?"

What? The mark. They were still sticking to the
pretense of a birthmark. Then it really must be there,
she realized dismally. And they assumed it would
get her to pack up and happily leave with them.

"How long do you think it takes to examine such
a small area?" she demanded. "I looked. It's not
there. I was merely sitting here, giving you enough
time to get tired of waiting and leave. But I see that
was too much to hope for."

"Indeed," he said in a quiet voice that belied the anger in his sherry-gold eyes. "It was also rather stupid of you, since we have stressed the importance of your identity to us and the only way it can be established."

"Well, I have established that I'm *not* the one you're looking for."

"I am afraid I must doubt that, mistress."

"That's too bad—"

"Yes . . . for you. It now becomes necessary to attend to the matter ourselves."

"Attend—? Oh, no, you won't!"

Her knife was in her hand before the last word was out. Stefan sighed, but he had anticipated no less.

"Mistress, the only one who might be hurt by that weapon of yours is yourself. Put it down and submit to the inevitable, and I will try not to embarrass you any more than I have to."

"Just like that? God, you've got your nerve. Well, come ahead, then, and we'll see who gets hurt."

His lips turned up the slightest bit. "I applaud your courage, little one, but might I suggest an alternative first?"

Her eyes narrowed suspiciously. "I thought you said there wasn't any."

"Just one. We could make love."

God, was it the way he said it, or the way he was looking at her just then, that made those words sink inside her with a slow swirl of delicious sensation? She stiffened, trying to shake it off, but the feeling persisted. And she knew what it was. Lord help her, the man had done what no other ever had. He had just given her her first taste of desire. Him? *Now?* Oh, God, he really was a devil. He really, really was.

"Ah," he said, watching her closely. "I see that is not an option at this time."

"Or at any time," she assured him stiffly.

The angry glow was back in his sherry eyes, which indicated she'd definitely struck a nerve. "On the contrary, mistress. Before our journey ends, I will have you, no matter how high the cost."

Had he forgotten the grand pretense already? She decided to remind him with a sneer. "Even though I'm supposed to marry your friend?"

"Oh, Vasili won't mind. You aren't wed to him yet, after all, and you are no virgin, so one more man before the nuptials won't matter, will it, when you have already spread your favors among so many."

If that last insult was supposed to incite her to careless fury, it succeeded better than Stefan had intended. She leaped for him, knife raised, her target his heart. But since she was blinded by outrage, it wasn't surprising that she didn't notice the hand that whipped up to catch her arm. Fingers tight about her wrist now, he held her like that for a long moment, showing her just how futile her efforts were against him, before he slowly squeezed. When her other hand came up to beat at his face, that too was caught. And despite her struggles, it was only seconds more before the knife clattered harmlessly to the floor.

"Now we lift your skirts, mistress. A shame this couldn't have been done in a more amicable way."

"Devil's spawn!" she spat in answer. "You can't

do this!'' she screamed when he started dragging her to the bed.

"Certainly I can," he replied with calm assurance, and proceeded to prove it.

She was shoved back on the narrow bed, flipped over onto her belly, and before she had time to even screech into the bedding, he was sitting on her lower back. Only her right hand was still held. Her left couldn't reach him anyway, or manage to push herself up.

"I'll kill you for this," she vowed before her own hand, with his directing it, was placed behind her head to shove her face into the pillow, to discourage any more comments like that, she supposed.

She felt the air rush over her legs next, as her skirt was yanked up. Then she heard a barely audible gasp, and just as quickly the material covered her again.

"Lazar?" he called with some difficulty.

That was the first Tanya knew that Stefan wasn't alone. She twisted her head toward the door and flamed scarlet, seeing Lazar filling that open space now. God, were the others behind him, all eager to witness her humiliation?

"You found it?" Lazar asked, his eyes only on Stefan.

"Not yet. Leave us."

"I thought you wanted a witness."

Stefan had thought so too, but he had assumed he would be able to uncover just a small area for Lazar to take note of, a mere patch of skin amidst ruffles and lace. But the girl wore no underclothes of any sort, not even a single petticoat.

"A witness would be nice, except the wench is appallingly naked beneath her skirt. So I trust you will accept my word on the matter?"

"That goes without question," Lazar replied, but he was chuckling as he closed the door.

Nerve-racking silence followed while Tanya struggled to hold back tears, her humiliation was so great. She was also having a hard time breathing beneath his heavy weight. But not once did it occur to her that she was now alone, in her room, on her bed, with a man who had only minutes before suggested they make love.

Stefan was very much aware of that fact, however, and to put it from his mind, he said derisively, "You really *don't* believe in wasting time, do you, mistress? Your paying customers must be delighted by your lack of under—apparel."

"Go to hell," Tanya snapped, intending to say no more. But the excuse came out anyway. "If there was money to buy some, I'd wear some. But it's certainly no business of yours."

"I believe we will discover in a moment that everything about you henceforth will be very much our business."

He shifted, telling her he was reaching for her skirt again. And there wasn't a single thing she could do to prevent him, unless . . . "Please"—she choked on the word—"don't."

He did hesitate. She'd give him that. But the skirt came up anyway, slowly this time.

Tanya gritted her teeth, glad that her face was already hidden. It was beyond embarrassing, what he was putting her through. And for what? For a stupid pretense that was supposed to make her abduction easy for them, when she'd already assured them it wouldn't work. That left her with only one conclusion. The man on top of her was deriving some kind of diabolical pleasure out of shaming her this way.

Stefan was feeling no reluctance at this point, in fact just the opposite. And shaming her was the farthest thing from his mind. So was the mark he was supposed to be looking for, as inch by inch he revealed what he had seen no more than a glimpse of before. It was a view a man was rarely accorded unless he was in the process of making love to a woman, so it wasn't surprising that such a sight could stir a man's blood. Just a gracefully turned calf could do it, but he was already seeing much more than that, as the skirt rose up slender thighs and finally was tucked above her hips.

She made a groaning sound of distress that drew him back to his purpose, but still he didn't hurry. And there was nothing in that moment, certainly not conscience or scruple, that could have prevented him from running his hand over the firm mounds of both adorable cheeks.

Her sounds of distress got much louder, approaching outraged fury. Stefan sighed regrettably and got on with the matter at hand, smoothing the left cheek toward him so he could see the underside of the mound. The crescent moon was there, just as he had thought it would be. But Stefan hadn't expected his reaction upon finally seeing it.

He changed position, not even bothering to lower her skirt. He caught her left hand and pressed it down upon the mattress, leaning over her to murmur by her ear, "It's there—all the proof necessary to put you under our rule and will."

Tanya jerked her head up to rail at him, but got no further than "You bas—!" before she was turned over and her mouth covered by lips that tried to claim her soul, they were so fiercely possessive. She wasn't prepared for such an onslaught. She'd had kisses stolen from her before—that was the only kind she was familiar with—but none like this. This kiss was so compelling, she wanted to give in to it, an insane notion that took her several long moments to shake. But then she bit down hard, tasted blood, heard a curse, and found her face suddenly gripped between two strong hands.

It wasn't those glowing devil eyes that struck fear into her then, staring down at her with such rancor. It was the sure knowledge that when he let go of her face, her masterpiece of creative camouflage would be utterly ruined. To delay that, she didn't even try to push him away, though she wasn't sure she could get her arms out from under his forearms anyway.

"Whores are not usually so particular," he growled low. "Why are you?"

She was getting damned tired of being called a whore, but there wasn't much point in denying it. As insistent as he was at proving things, he'd likely demand proof of that, too, and she could just imagine how he'd want to establish it.

With bravado she wasn't really feeling, she said

caustically, "I don't accept men I intend to kill at the first opportunity."

He laughed then, and there was nothing derisive about it. He was genuinely amused. And the man became downright handsome when his face softened in humor, a fact Tanya wasn't pleased to note at this particular moment.

When he quieted down to mere chuckles, then finally a smile, he said, "A remark worthy of the future Queen of Cardinia. I am impressed, Tatiana."

Now he was making fun of her. "You can go sell your fancy tales elsewhere, mister. I told you I'm not a believer."

"But it has been proved beyond a doubt that you are Tatiana Janacek."

"All that has been proved is one of you knows how to climb trees and spy through windows."

His smile widened. "An interesting idea. Untrue, however. Now, where were we?"

She gasped to see his gaze drop to her lips. "Don't you dare kiss me again!"

"Ah, wench." He sounded so regretful. "You will learn, slowly I hope, not to issue me such intimate challenges."

This time she tried to bite him the moment his lips touched hers, but he avoided her teeth for nearly a full minute of sensual warfare. When he did quit, it was with another laugh. The devil really was enjoying himself.

"You will have to forgive me, Tatiana, though surely you will agree the fault cannot be entirely mine, since it was your lack of certain garments that aroused my amorous instincts. Mind you, I am not complaining in the least. In fact, when we supply you with a new wardrobe, I will remember to overlook such items as well.''

She had the ridiculous notion that he was merely teasing her, rather than trying to embarrass her again with the reminder of what he had gotten a good look at. She still felt the heat rushing into her cheeks.

''Why don't you just end this pretense now?'' she asked in a small, tight voice. ''I know I'm not this Tatiana you've made up, and you aren't going to buy me new clothes. And you *certainly* aren't going to marry me to a man too handsome for words. I won't accept clothes from you anyway, or anything else, and I'm not, repeat *not*, going anywhere with you. And don't call me by that damned name again—''

''Enough!''

Chapter 10

Tanya supposed she *was* pressing her luck a bit, listing so many of her doubts and insistences all at once for Stefan to acknowledge and heed. But that "Enough!" wasn't just a burst of impatience from him either. She was afraid she'd struck another nerve somehow, without intending to this time, and she knew that wasn't the smartest thing to do when she was still lying half under him on the bed.

But she needn't have worried—over that at least. Whatever had set him off, his mood had definitely changed. With one final long glare from those searing eyes of his, he left her side and headed straight for the door.

It took Tanya a moment to realize her good fortune—he'd moved away from her so quickly, he hadn't even seen her face when his hands let go of it. She turned immediately toward the wall, just in case he changed his mind about leaving, but all he did was issue an order. "Whatever you care to take with you, gather it now. You won't be returning to this place.'' Then he slammed the door shut behind him.

That's what he thought, the arrogant devil. But Tanya didn't waste any time fuming over that terse command, or even how to avoid it. First things first, and her immediate priority was to repair whatever damage his firm grip had done to her face. Thankfully, that would take her only a minute or two.

She scrambled off the bed and rushed to the dressing table she'd fashioned years ago from old crates, where she kept her box of colored powders and creams and her precious chunk of broken mirror, which she'd confiscated out of her next-door neighbor's trash. However, the sight of the mirror leaning upright against the wall at hip level was more than she, or her piqued curiosity, could bear, overriding even her sense of self-preservation. She turned around before it and hiked up the back of her skirt, then glanced over her shoulder—and felt the heat rush up and suffuse her face once more. God, he'd seen her like *that?* She felt shamed to the core—and something else, something she couldn't name in her naïveté.

Tanya might know all about fornication, having been reared in a tavern where men didn't curb their language or topics of conversation. She might even have seen it being practiced a time or two, having come upon some of the bolder barmaids they'd hired over the years entwined with men in the most unlikely places—anywhere Dobbs couldn't find them. She'd even had desire described to her by one helpful wench, which was why she'd been able to recognize that swirly jumble of sensations she'd felt earlier when Stefan had suggested they make love. But a "fluttering in the middle innards" was all she knew about, and that was quite different from the hot gush of achy pleasure she felt now in a spot much lower than her middle, as she pictured that dark devil seeing her like this, and touching . . .

Like Stefan, she forgot for a moment what she was looking for. Unlike him, when she finally spied the small crescent moon under the curve of her left buttock, she was hit with another wave of shame, knowing now without a doubt that one of those men had seen even more of her than her bare backside through her window. But which one? Stefan? Her shame lessened somewhat, and because she realized it did, it came flooding right back.

Daft-witted idiot, you can't like *the idea of him watching* . . .

"What in the hell is this?" he snarled at her even before the door slammed against the inner wall, too late a warning that the golden-eyed devil had returned.

Tanya dropped her skirt instantly, but she was much slower in turning to face Stefan. Lord help her, she was going to burn to a cinder with mortification this time, to have been caught ogling her own backside. It was just too much on top of everything else. But when she was finally looking at him, he wasn't looking at her. He was staring at his hands, which he held out in front of him as if he'd sprouted a few more fingers than he should have. And for a girl who was supposed to have been repairing her face, it didn't take much guessing to know what the "this" was he was asking about. Not her unseemly behavior, as she'd thought, but the gray powder now coating his long fingers.

She quickly decided that he'd be staring at her if he had figured it out yet, so she turned her back on him and tried as unobtrusively as possible to smooth out the damage he'd done to her camouflage. She didn't quite dare to bend over to see in her mirror if she'd managed to get rid of all his pale fingerprints. That would draw his attention to her face—and answer his question, which she was anxiously hoping he'd forget.

Attempting to distract him, she said, "If you don't know how to knock, I'd be pleased to teach you."

"I believe I asked you a question, wench."

So much for distracting him. "And I believe you've asked one too many questions for one day. I don't feel like—"

The grip on the tight bun at the nape of her neck put an end to her defiant evasions. She hadn't even heard him come up behind her. But she couldn't miss the large hand that appeared mere inches in front of her eyes.

"You will tell me, now, how it can be that when I touch you, my hands change color."

"Ash?" she offered as a possibility. "I was cleaning the hearth this morning."

"And rubbed your face in it?"

"No, but—"

"Of course, it could be ash," he said thoughtfully as he rubbed his fingers together. "It has that consistency.'' Just as she started to relax, her head was twisted sideways and back, until she was staring into his eyes. ''But somehow I doubt it. Tell me why I doubt it, wench,'' he commanded, while one finger traced a diagonal line down her cheek.

Tanya closed her eyes for a moment against the turbulent emotions she read in his. He knew, and was furious about it, though she couldn't imagine why. So her appearance was an illusion. She should be the one enraged to have it discovered, not he.

''Let go—''

That got her another tug on her bun that pulled on hair that had already been drawn back as far as possible. Tears popped into the corners of her eyes, accompanied by a gasping sound of pain and a reproachful glare that had no effect on him that she could see. In fact, for half a breath she thought he was going to tug even harder. He didn't. His grip slackened, and Tanya didn't spare a second to leap out of his reach, only to screech mightily because he hadn't actually let go of her bun. It was pulled loose from his fingers with her movement and now unraveled down her back. Her hair whipped over her shoulder as she spun about to glare murderously at him.

''I'll be lucky if I have any hair left, you bastard!'' she cried, her hands coming up to massage her scalp. ''Where do you get off treating me like that?''

Her question was ignored, totally. And she lost the space she'd gained as he took a step forward to grip her chin, forcing her head back.

''The truth, wench. Do you paint your face to enhance—or to conceal?''

Even as he asked this, his eyes were determining the answer for himself, probing so deeply. Tanya stiffened and knocked his hand away, but it only fell to her shoulder, keeping her from turning away from him.

She had nothing to lose at this point by demanding, "So you want the gory truth and the last of my pride with it? I don't have much *to* improve on, but then you've already guessed that, haven't you? You're a cruel devil to make me admit it."

Trying to sound as if her pride had been wounded when all she felt was anger just didn't come off, but she was sure the conscience she was trying to prick was nonexistent anyway.

He only grunted to acknowledge her effort before scoffing, "You are a lie from head to foot, mistress, but that ends here and now. I give you five minutes exactly to emerge from this room as your true self. Defy me and I will scrub you down myself, then heat your backside for putting me to the trouble."

Chapter 11

Tanya's eyes were still wide with disbelief after Stefan closed the door behind him, for the second time leaving her alone in her room. Heat her backside? Did that mean what she thought it did? She'd like to see him try it. On second thought, she'd rather not.

She glanced at the washbowl that he had shoved her toward before leaving. Since he'd already found her out, she had no reason not to wash her face clean—except one. She simply didn't want to, and that was an excellent reason as far as she was concerned. No one had the right to order her about anymore, and the freedom she'd tasted since Dobbs' illness was too precious to give up. Dobbs might still think he was in charge, but Tanya did whatever needed to be done because it needed to be done, and she did it in her own time, not when ordered to.

Now here was this devil acting as if he had some kind of right to assume control of her life, taking away her freedom and choices, even the choice of how she wanted to look, and threatening dire consequences if she didn't jump to obey him. A spanking, for crying out loud. God, that was rich. She'd suffered beatings that had laid her low for days, sometimes barely able to move, and she was supposed to be frightened now of a measly child's punishment? Not even a little, but she still didn't want that devil anywhere near her backside again, to spank her or to do anything else.

However, she didn't doubt for a moment that the man would do exactly as he said. And he'd already proved how easily his strength could force her to his will. So she'd just have to make sure he didn't have the opportunity again.

She set to motion, first retrieving her knife, then sticking her head out the window on the slim chance that something might be different out there. But the view was just as she knew it to be: the ground too far down for her to jump, and the tree just out of reach, even if she pushed off the windowsill and leaped toward it.

She turned to face the door, and sent up a little prayer as she approached it that Stefan wasn't waiting for her on the other side. There was only the one stairway that led downstairs, but there was another room across the hallway next to Dobbs' room. Both rooms faced the street and had windows only a few feet above the sloping porch roof, a roof she was well acquainted with, since she'd replaced several of its shingles. And from that roof it would be easy to swing down to the ground. Then she'd simply disappear until those four devils got tired of waiting and went off to dupe some other poor girl.

As a child, she'd often take off for days at a time, once for a whole week, when she knew Dobbs was looking for her with his stick. She came home each time to an even worse beating than she would have had, not because she couldn't survive in the wilds, but because she got too lonely being by herself. But she wouldn't have to be gone long this time, a few hours at most. And even if she had to stay away for a few days, now that she was older, she was sure loneliness wouldn't be a problem at all.

Briefly she thought of telling Dobbs about her dilemma, but she just as quickly dismissed the notion. Even if he would help her, what could he do in his present condition? He was, in fact, more likely to aid those devils than her if the price was right, and she'd already seen how quick Stefan was to toss money about.

With knife in hand, Tanya put her ear to the door, but could hear nothing. Best as she could figure, she had about two minutes left to make herself scarce. Would he have gone downstairs to wait?

She wanted to open that door stealthily so she could determine if her own window might be the better option after all. But the damned hinges on her door squeaked, giving her no alternative but to yank it open suddenly, using surprise to her advantage if Stefan was there.

He wasn't, but she wasn't lucky enough to find the hallway empty either. The one who had introduced himself as Lazar Dimitrieff was there instead, standing with his back to her door. It was the only bit of luck to come her way yet, and she made quick use of it, pressing her knife into his side before he could turn around.

"If you move even an inch, mister, we're going to spill blood on this floor, and I wouldn't like that, since I'm the one who will have to clean it up later."

"Then by all means," he said agreeably, "I am yours to command, Princess."

Tanya cringed. She'd whispered her threat. His answer sounded like a trumpet blast by comparison, guaranteed to bring on the cavalry—or one dark devil.

"I take it you consider yourself expendable?" she asked, and jabbed her knife forward a bit.

He got the point, both points actually. Still, he didn't sound too concerned, even though a small circle of red appeared around the hole her knife was making in his jacket.

"What exactly do you hope to accomplish?" was all he wanted to know.

"I'm leaving."

"Ah, then you mean to take me with you?"

"No farther than I have to," she assured him. "So just turn slowly when I turn, and keep your back to me."

"Our king won't like—"

"Your king can go polish his teeth for all I care," she bit out. "It's that dark devil Stefan I don't want to deal with again—ever."

That brought a burst of laughter from him that had Tanya grinding her teeth together. "I believe he feels exactly as you do right now."

"I'm absolutely delighted to hear it," she retorted. "Now move!"

The door she wanted was closer to the stairs, so she backed that way, pulling Lazar along with her, sparing a look once, twice, to make sure no surprises came up behind her. She knew her time was running out—unless Lazar hadn't been there just to guard her, but to escort her downstairs too. She didn't waste time asking him, especially since he was cooperating now. She had to concentrate on figuring out how she was going to get out the window and still keep him from stopping her. Damn, why had she never learned to use a pistol instead of a knife? This would have been so much simpler if she didn't have to keep Lazar close at hand.

She had almost reached the room she wanted when she decided she would have to leave him out in the hall for the few extra seconds that would gain her. A shove to his back, the door slammed behind her, and a running dive through the window ought to see her rolling down the porch roof before he even entered the room. And he was too big to follow her with any kind of speed. She'd be out of sight before he could do anything.

Another step brought her to the door, and up against a solid wall of immovable man. Even as she groaned in frustration—to be so close!—a large hand closed tightly over hers and moved it carefully away from the man in front of her.

"Just what do you think you are doing, Lazar?"

Tanya blinked, hearing that question put to her rescued captive rather than to herself, as if he had been assisting in her escape. But more importantly, it wasn't Stefan who asked, but that stocky fellow they called Serge.

"Humoring her," Lazar answered as he turned about and casually pried the knife loose from Tanya's fingers. "She is soon to be our queen, after all."

"So she is, and all the more reason she shouldn't be playing with knives where she might get hurt. Stefan should have unarmed her himself."

"He did, but I would guess she made him so furious, he forgot to take the weapon with him when he left her."

Tanya was gritting her teeth by now. She dearly loved being ignored most of the time, but this was ridiculous.

"If you wouldn't *mind,* I'd appreciate it if you realized I'm still here, much as I wish I weren't."

"Sorry, Princess." Lazar grinned down at her, then suddenly laughed as he got a good look at her face. "I don't believe she has done what Stefan ordered her to do," he said to Serge.

That one's hand came around to turn her face toward him, giving him a quick look at her before she knocked his hand aside. "So she hasn't."

Lazar's blue eyes were back on her, full of amusement. "I distinctly heard what our friend promised to do to you if you defied him, Tatiana. Perhaps you would like to return to your room now and wash before we take you below?"

That would be the wisest thing to do at this point, sandwiched between them as she was, with her chance to escape postponed for now. But Tanya had always had a rebellious, stubborn streak that had been responsible for more than a few of the beatings she'd received over the years. And she hadn't been promised a *real* beating after all, so she'd rather they knew right up front that she was going to be as difficult as she possibly could be, no matter what threats came her way. Just maybe, they might then decide she wasn't worth the trouble.

"I wash once a month—when I feel like it," she said brazenly, smiling so there'd be no doubt that that was a lie she intended to stick to. "And I've got at least three weeks to go before I get anywhere near water again."

"So you intend to defy Stefan?"

"Absolutely."

Serge groaned behind her. Lazar chuckled. Tanya tried slipping out from between them while they were both distracted, but was chagrined to have an arm slip around her waist from behind in what she would swear was no more than reflex.

"It's not funny, Lazar," Serge grumbled over her head, totally ignoring the small hands prying at his arm. "She's going to make Stefan even angrier than he is now, and right now he's too angry to be around."

"He knows it. That's why he left." Lazar tipped her chin up to study her face now that at least half of her haggardness had been rubbed off. "But I have a feeling his mood won't improve either way," he added thoughtfully. "We expected to find a beauty, and it looks like that is what we may have here after all."

"Yet he seemed to like her better when he thought she wasn't," Serge concluded with another groan.

"My thoughts exactly. But I wouldn't worry about it," Lazar said with blatant cheerfulness now. "For a change, he's not going to take his black mood out on us—he's going to take it out on her."

If that was said just to make Tanya rethink her stubborn position, it didn't work. But that didn't mean she liked hearing it. And she definitely didn't like the way they continued to talk around her.

She jabbed Lazar in the chest with a pointed finger, demanding, "If I'm to marry your king, why is Stefan the one giving me orders?"

That had Lazar grinning again for some reason, a joke shared with Serge obviously, since he glanced at him before answering. "Because until you are wed, you have been placed in Stefan's care—at our king's insistence. So it would be to your benefit, Princess, to pacify him rather than antagonize him, don't you think?"

Lord help her, they had an answer for every little discrepancy in their scheme that she tried to point out. "What I think hasn't mattered one bit so far, so why should it now? But answer me this. Does my being placed in Stefan's care mean that he can take liberties with me?"

If everything they had told her was true, that she really was to be married and all the rest, then that question should have angered Lazar, or at least disturbed him. But his grin didn't even falter.

"Stefan can do whatever he likes, Princess," he

said offhandedly. "He is answerable only to the king."

"And Vasili couldn't care less." She pointed out the obvious.

"Vasili frequently defers to Stefan. They are cousins, after all, and Stefan is older."

"But Vasili is king."

Lazar shrugged, as if to say it was all in the family, but he asked, "Would you rather Stefan were king?"

"I would rather Stefan dropped dead."

"Unfortunately for you, Princess"—Stefan's frigid tones drifted toward them from the top of the stairs—"I haven't yet."

Chapter 12

Tanya would have avoided facing Stefan—or, to be more exact, letting him see her face—for as long as possible, but she didn't have much choice in the matter. When Serge turned around at the sound of Stefan's voice, he took her with him, his arm still firmly around her waist. In fact, that put her in the forefront to receive the full blast of those devil eyes. And if her words hadn't made them glow, then her unwashed face definitely set fire to the coals.

But when he moved slowly forward, it was his friends he addressed. "You two were not, by any chance, trying to persuade her—gently—to do as she was told, were you?"

"Certainly not," Lazar assured him. "We were merely discussing responsibilities and the like."

"And keeping her from leaving on her own," Serge added.

"Ah, so we have that to watch for, do we?"

Tanya's bootheel came down hard on Serge's toe to thank him for his big mouth. He grunted, but not until Stefan stood before her did Serge release her. This he did with a little shove that sent her careening off balance into Stefan's chest. That one's arms came around her to catch her, and stayed there like a steel cage, tangling in the hair at her waist and keeping her pressed to his length. She imagined she could actually feel the vibration of his anger, surrounding her in waves.

"Let go of—" she began, only to be cut off with an emphatic "No." Ominously, for her ears alone, he added, "You will wish to God you had not defied me, Tatiana."

She turned white under the gray pallor of her makeup for about ten seconds. By then her conviction that to them she was a commodity worth a certain price reasserted itself. Accordingly, they wouldn't deliberately damage the goods, no matter how angry one of them was with her. Stefan had to be referring to the spanking he had promised, and as far as she was concerned, that was nothing to worry about.

In the meantime, she heard that there was a carriage now waiting below, that someone named Sasha had been instructed to meet them at the docks with their trunks, that they considered it fortuitous that their quarry had been found in time for them to leave on *The Lorilie*. But there was no time to waste. The riverboat was to depart within the hour.

And then they were silent, and Tanya felt they were all three looking down at her, though to be sure she'd have to crane her neck to see, pressed so close to Stefan as she still was. Were they waiting for her to react to what she'd just heard? She wasn't dense.

They intended to get her on that boat with them. But perhaps it had finally occurred to them to wonder just how they were going to accomplish that when they didn't have her cooperation.

Apparently she'd read the situation correctly, for Stefan's very next words were, "A crate, I think."

Tanya stiffened, and was about to protest heatedly, but surprisingly, Lazar beat her to it, reminding Stefan, "She is a royal princess."

The *royal princess* would have snorted in derision that the pretense was still being played out, except Stefan's casual rejoinder was the last straw.

"When she begins to look like one, she may be treated like one."

Tanya twisted around then, no easy feat in her steel cage, to demand of Lazar and Serge, "Are you going to let him get away with that just because he's angry at me?"

Serge wouldn't meet her eyes. Lazar looked chagrined at being put on the spot and said, "I believe it was explained who has authority over you, Tatiana. Whether you are transported or escorted is his decision, but perhaps if you ask him sweetly . . ."

The thought was allowed to trail off, for her to interpret as she would. Sweetly? No chance in hell would she be sweet to the devil at her back, who was even now turning her around again so she couldn't tempt his friends to her aid with eye contact or a pity-stirring expression. As if she would. . . . Of course she would! How else was she going to escape? Certainly not stuffed in a crate, and one probably from her own storeroom, none of which were big enough to offer her any degree of comfort.

She dropped her head back so she could finally look up at Stefan. He seemed to have been waiting for her to do just that, for she met his gaze directly for a heart-pounding moment. And then his eyes moved slowly over her face, so she couldn't doubt that the only thing he was thinking about right now was her gray-smudged complexion, and how it should have been roses and cream.

"You surprise me, Princess," he said in a voice that was merely conversational in tone. "I was fairly certain that you would have done everything possible to keep me from lifting your skirt again."

Lifting? Oh, God, she hadn't even considered that he might "heat her backside" without letting her skirt serve as padding. Suddenly a spanking from him became something to be concerned about and to be avoided at all costs.

"I'll wash now," she offered in a breathless whisper, hating to make that concession but seeing no alternative.

"Now there is no time."

He wasn't going to give her an out? "I'm not a child, to be—to be—!" She couldn't say it, and a shuffling foot behind her made her realize, horribly, that this conversation had an audience, that they'd heard . . .

As much as she was coming to despise the man who'd made her blush more today than she ever had in her life, right then all she could think to do was bury her face in his chest and be grateful it was wide enough to do so.

"What you are, Princess," she heard above her in what she hoped was a sigh, rather than a gust of exasperation, "is exceedingly stubborn."

"You expect me to go along with my own abduction?" she mumbled resentfully against his shirt.

"We expect you to honor the betrothal that was arranged and decreed by your own father, and to stop fighting what you cannot change."

She flung back her head furiously. "Stop fighting, when you can't even be truthful? You can't even make up a decent lie to get me to go along with you! You create one that's so implausible—"

"That it can be nothing but the truth."

"The *only* truth here," she said angrily, "is that I don't want to go with you."

His expression was skeptical. "So you would have us believe you prefer a life of drudgery and servitude, is that it? A life which includes salacious performances both on the stage and in the bedroom?"

Tanya sucked in a sharp breath, then drew back her foot to give his shin her reaction to this latest defaming innuendo. His arms tightened slightly around her, but in reflex rather than retaliation. In no other way did he acknowledge the pain she'd inflicted, so she answered his question in a calm voice that belied the fury behind that kick.

"What I prefer is no one telling me what to do. It took all my life to get to this point, where I have no one to answer to but myself. Now you show up here with your ridiculous tale, your threats, your *insults,* and your arrogant assumption that you can take over every aspect of my life. Well, you can't.

You don't have that right. No one does anymore, and no one ever will again.''

"It's too bad there is no time to discuss this unusual existence you desire for yourself, which so few of us ever achieve. As for our right to take you in hand, you are Cardinian by birth, and every Cardinian is subject to the supreme power of his ruling sovereign.''

"Like hell. *That's* what I don't accept, Stefan, so that excuse is not valid as far as I'm concerned. In this country you can't justify what you're attempting to do. It's unlawful no matter how you look at it.''

He looked up toward the ceiling to say, ''Why am I arguing with her?'' which made Tanya bristle until he added in sharp command, ''Lazar, Serge, wait for us below.'' Then she stiffened, filled with apprehension.

His gaze came back to her as the others squeezed past them, and the very fact that his eyes were only sherry-hued eased her tension somewhat. But he also brought one hand up to caress the back of her head in what was clearly an attempt to soothe her, and she simply wasn't sure how to interpret that.

"I have concluded, Tatiana, that I was, perhaps, a bit hasty in demanding the removal of your clever disguise. Of course, just now,'' he added with the softening of his expression which presaged a smile, ''it merely gives you the appearance of a grubby urchin. But if that is how you wish to look, so be it.''

She didn't trust this mellowness after the storm, not one little bit. ''What exactly are you saying?''

"That we will forget the consequence I promised for your defiance, and go on from here with a bargain."

She distrusted that even more, but said, "Go on, I'm listening."

"If you will agree not to cause a disturbance of any sort, then you may board *The Lorilie* without restraint."

Her eyes narrowed to green sparks. "Otherwise I get crated aboard?"

"Bound, gagged, and crated," he clarified.

"What about this one instead?" she said tightly. "I agree not to tell anyone what you tried to do here, if you simply take yourself off and never darken my door again?"

The arm still around her lower back squeezed just enough to remind her who was ultimately in control right now. "Make no mistake, Tatiana, you *are* coming with us. Your choice is merely how."

"But I don't want to!" she cried. "Doesn't that matter in the least?"

Slowly he shook his head. She hissed through her teeth in frustration. She was going to be abducted no matter what she said or did, but there was no choice to make in what was being offered, not if she intended to escape at the very first opportunity.

"All right," she said with ill grace. "I'll walk if that's my only option."

"Without causing a disturbance?"

"I won't speak to anyone, if that's what you mean."

"Excellent. Just remember, Tatiana, that this is a

bargain, and like any bargain, there will be a consequence to bear if it's broken. I believe you already know what that is.''

Don't you dare blush again, missy! He's just trying to put the fear of—him—into you, but his threats won't be worth sour beans once you escape.

To him she said, ''If you're in such an all-fired hurry to leave, don't you think it's time you let go of me?''

''What I think is that this bargain needs to be sealed with a kiss first.''

''N—!'' was all she got out before his lips covered hers.

Tanya would have struggled right away, except it occurred to her that this was a golden opportunity to lure Stefan down a path of confusion, at least where her feelings were concerned. If he was arrogant enough to think she liked his kisses and because of them might be resigned to her fate all the sooner, then he could let down his guard, making her escape that much easier. The trouble was, she did like his kisses. There wasn't the least bit of unpleasantness in the way his mouth moved sensually over hers. So there was no pretense in her yielding to that kiss.

But there was definite danger in her strategy, as she discovered when he finally set her away from him, and it took her a long dreamy moment to be drawn back to the present. Losing herself to the kiss hadn't been part of the plan. Nor had she counted on feeling a very strong desire to draw him back to her mouth for more of the same.

Tanya quickly tamped down that crazy urge, as

well as the mushy feeling in her innards. The damned
devil had powers she'd better not tempt again. But
looking at him, she didn't think he seemed any more
pleased with the results of that little experiment than
she was.

His next words proved it. "And to think I had
actually begun to wonder if a mistake might have
been made, that you might—miraculously—be
chaste after all. Foolish of me, wasn't it?"

Tanya fought this newest wave of heat surging up
her neck to her cheeks, hating for him to know he'd
scored another hit so easily if he should notice. But
it wasn't just embarrassment that she felt, it was anger
too, that he could say something like that just because
she had kissed him back. And the anger prompted
her reply.

"Well, *you* won't ever know for sure, will you?"
she taunted him.

Stefan merely smiled, a smile that smugly stated
as plain as any words, *That's what you think*. And
he *had* made a promise to her in that regard, hadn't
he? Something about her sharing his bed before their
journey ended. *Why* were they all so convinced she
was a whore? She almost asked him, but she didn't
think she could stand any more insults right now.
And there wasn't any time, if his sudden look of
impatience could be interpreted correctly.

It could, since he reached for her arm as he turned
toward the stairs. "Come along, Tati—"

"Wait a minute!" she cut in sharply. "What about
my things?"

He didn't even glance back as he continued to pull

her along. ''Perhaps next time you will do as you are told *when* you are told.''

In other words, she'd lost her chance to take along even a change of clothes. Tanya almost dug in her heels to protest, just for the hell of it, but she'd just as soon have all her possessions here awaiting her return than risk having to leave anything behind with these devils when the opportunity came to part company with them. She was aware, however, that Stefan thought he was getting some subtle revenge by denying her. So let him think it.

But there was one other matter she had to take care of. It wouldn't hurt to have a little help in getting away from these men, and only Dobbs could supply that by sending someone after her. He couldn't do that if he didn't even know she was gone. And he wouldn't have heard all of the commotion in the hallway to alert him that something was wrong, because it was his habit to sleep right after he finished his breakfast. This he did like a dead man until The Seraglio opened for business in the late afternoon. If he *had* heard anything, he'd be yelling to find out what was going on.

Tanya dug in her heels this time. ''You have to let me at least say good-bye to Dobbs.''

He didn't stop, and she was jerked along despite her efforts to hold him back. ''Why?'' he demanded. ''He lied about you, without even knowing why we sought you. That man is no friend of yours.''

''I know it, but he's still the closest thing I've ever had to a relative.''

''Not anymore.''

He said that so automatically, it had a ring of truth that disconcerted her. Lord help her, he was a convincing liar, but she wasn't fooled.

"Let me guess," she sneered. "I suppose you'll tell me now that *you* are a relative of mine?"

He had her halfway down the stairs, and still didn't even glance back to answer. "We share a common ancestor, five generations removed. We are, in fact, very, *very* distant cousins."

"And I believe that about as much as I do the rest of what you've told me. You're afraid to let me tell Dobbs I'm leaving."

"I believe he would try to prevent your going, yes. You are, after all, of great service to him, aren't you? A slave without the cost. Very convenient for the man."

She'd thought the same thing herself when she had become old enough to realize that Dobbs didn't have any right to demand so much from her. Now she was his housekeeper, maid, cook, laundress, nurse, and—for the tavern—manager, clerk, purchasing agent, waitress, sometimes bartender and dancer, and as Stefan and his friends would have it, a whore when she had the time. When, she'd like to know, did she ever have any spare time? But she was finally going to be paid for a whole life of servitude—with The Seraglio.

However, if these men had their way, she was going to lose that, and her freedom as well. They intended to make her a whore in truth. Well, there was no way she was going to let that happen.

They were halfway across the common room when

Stefan paused, perhaps realizing that, for the sake of the pretense, he'd been a bit harsh. "If you *do* have friends you would like to bid farewell to, and they live close by, I suppose we could spare a moment or two for good-byes."

Friends? The only friends she'd ever had were barmaids, and that was before she'd become their boss. But that wasn't the kind of friends she believed he was referring to, for she'd never felt close to any of them. Only Lelia could she call an actual friend, and that had been for a very short time a long time ago.

"There's no one," she said, her answer immediately saddening her since she'd never really thought about this lack in her life before.

"Not even a lover you are particularly fond of?" Stefan persisted.

Anger instantly replaced her sadness. "Oh, too many. Do we have all day?"

She got jerked along again for that piece of sarcasm, and could have kicked herself when she saw the carriage and the rest of the men, who were going to do all they could to prevent her escape, standing ready to surround her. Couldn't she have named *someone,* even one of Dobbs' old cronies, instead of trying to get in a dig to annoy Stefan? *Great going, missy. Why don't you just help with this abduction? You couldn't be making it any easier for them if you tried.*

Chapter 13

"For God's sake, Stefan, have her do something with her damn hair," Vasili said the moment they were all settled in the carriage. "She looks like a slattern."

"Neat and smudged, my friend? Is that the effect we're looking for?" Stefan asked, his tone so dry it wouldn't soak up water.

Tanya went one better. She was angry enough at the look of disgust Vasili had shot at her to sit forward and shake her head vigorously, sending her hair first into Lazar's lap, then into Stefan's, making it messier than it had been. Stefan sat on one side of her, and Lazar, who sat on the other, burst into laughter. Serge held his mouth tightly and stared up at the ceiling. Vasili flushed and looked out the window, ignoring her if he couldn't improve her, but oh, how nice it was, she thought, to see someone else turn pink for a change.

Stefan, however, gathered the entire cascade of her hair into his hands and began to salvage whatever pins still clung to it. When he had them all, he held them out to her.

"Would you mind, Tatiana?" Her mutinous expression told him she would. He shrugged. "Since I brought it down, I suppose I could put it back up."

Have him perform such an intimate task for her? She swiped the pins from his one hand, then her hair from the other. Lazar continued to laugh, so she sent him a furious glance, which didn't affect him in the least.

"Who would have thought there would be so much of it, rolled up in that little bun you sported," Lazar commented, still grinning. "Your mother had golden hair, I'm told. I never met her myself, but Stefan did. He was there at your betrothal, I believe. He could probably even describe her for you, if you asked him."

"I'm not interested in that fairy tale, so don't continue it for my sake."

"What's this?" Vasili turned to ask. "You mean she still doubts who she is?"

"There's no doubt about it, mister," Tanya answered before anyone else could, as she worked at putting her hair back in order. "You men have to be half-wits if you think I believe any of the nonsense I've heard today."

"Is that so, wench? Then how do you explain that mark upon your arse?" he sneered crudely.

"Ask Stefan," was all she said, despising even conversation with that disdainful peacock.

All eyes turned to Stefan. Even Lazar leaned

around Tanya to hear the explanation. Stefan actually smiled.

"She thinks one of us is adept at climbing trees to peek through second-story windows."

Vasili snorted. "Much too undignified."

"Speak for yourself, Vasili." Lazar grinned. "I for one see some definite merit in such an endeavor— if the view is interesting enough."

"*You* are more likely to be climbing out of windows, rather than up to them."

Tanya was surprised to hear Vasili sneering at someone other than herself. A glance to the side showed that Stefan was clearly amused at the turn the conversation had taken. Tanya wasn't. Everything seemed to be either amusing jokes or ridicule to them, with no middle ground. How was she supposed to deal with that? Hopefully not for long.

She gave a last pat to her bun, not caring if it was crooked, and looked out the window to determine how much time she still had. Not much. They were nearing the docks now. Another minute or two . . .

The one thing she couldn't risk was getting on that riverboat with them. With so many other people about, Stefan was sure to have her locked away in a cabin where she couldn't talk to anyone. It was amazing that he was taking the chance that she would remain quiet and docile. Did he really think she would stick to a bargain when her freedom was involved?

The carriage stopped. The door was opened by a swarthy little man who immediately started jabbering away in some foreign tongue. The men appeared to know him. The servant, Sasha? He sounded complaining, though Tanya couldn't comprehend a single word he was saying. He was also anxiously urging them to hurry, if his wild gesturing was any indication, and then he rushed ahead, probably to inform the captain that his last passengers had finally arrived.

Was the riverboat that close to departing, then? Tanya certainly hoped so, for that would definitely aid her in what she planned to do. The plan she had come up with in those past few moments before they arrived wasn't the most ingenious. Timing would be everything. But it could work, *if* she could be rid of Lazar and Stefan.

Vasili she didn't worry about. He out of all of them didn't want her along and made no bones about it. So he wouldn't expend himself to try and stop her when she set off down the docks. Serge would likely give chase, but he was too stocky to be able to catch her. And the docks this time of day were crowded, another point in her favor, particularly if Serge came after her. She'd be wending her way agilely through the crowd while he'd be knocking people down trying to keep up with her. There would be no contest.

The only difficulty in the plan was getting Lazar and Stefan out of the picture, because either one of them, she was sure, could catch her with little effort. Those damn long legs would do it, not to mention the fact that they were in superb physical condition. They both had to be eliminated from the chase before it began, and there was only one way to do it. But Lord help her if it didn't work.

To her immense relief, Vasili and Serge got out

of the carriage first. For the plan to work, she needed them in front of her, not behind her, when they all started up the ramp to the boat. If they went on ahead, so much the better, but she wasn't that lucky.

Serge took care of paying the driver of the carriage while Stefan lifted Tanya to the ground. Their baggage was apparently on board already, along with the servant, Sasha, another reason they wouldn't want to risk having the boat leave without them while they chased down a troublesome captive. They would give up because of that, and she could then go home and put the whole unpleasant encounter behind her— somehow—*and* start carrying a pistol.

The ramp was wide, but not quite wide enough for two to walk abreast with any degree of safety, since there were no railings. Thank God for that. And Serge and Vasili did go first, with Lazar behind them and Stefan behind Tanya, so he had to go over first. If she wasn't so nervous, she might enjoy this. But she hadn't counted on his being so close behind her that he could hold her elbow, which he did.

"Watch your step, Tatiana," Stefan said, which gave her the idea to trip.

But with strong resentment, what she replied was, "The name is Tanya, Tan-ya. If you call me by that foreign-sounding Ta-ti-a-na one more time, I will probably scream, and to hell with bargains. And furthermore, I can get up this ramp without your assistance, thank you."

She jerked her arm forward then, but he was expecting that movement, as she knew he would be, and held fast. Which gave her the excuse to turn around to take issue with him about it. This she did with her elbow jabbing backward. There was the chance, of course, that he'd take her over the side into the river with him, but instead he let go of her when she started to turn. He had probably been anticipating that *she* might try jumping over the side, not that she would dare to push him over, and that assumption allowed the plan to work.

It was executed beautifully, better than she could have hoped for. And even before Tanya heard him hit the water, she had turned and was tripping into Lazar with an added little shove to the right, which sent him over the opposite side of the ramp from Stefan.

She didn't wait around for Serge's and Vasili's reactions to what she'd done. Since they hadn't been watching, all they could know, until they were told otherwise, was that two of their party were in the river, not how they got there.

Tanya leaped for the dock and took off at a full run, which lasted all of five seconds. "Noooo!" she wailed as her feet literally left the ground and the last voice she expected to hear growled into her ear, "Shut up, wench, or I will cuff you to silence."

That son of a bitch would, too. His arm around her waist was already trying mightily to *squeeze* her to silence as he marched her back to the boat.

Hell and high water, Vasili wasn't supposed to have come after her. He was just as tall and long-legged as Stefan and Lazar. She'd known he could catch her if he tried. But he wasn't supposed to have tried!

"Why don't you just tell them you couldn't find—"

The suggestion was cut off as her stomach made hard contact with his shoulder bone. She started struggling then, and screaming for help as soon as she caught her breath, but he managed to keep her up on his shoulder, and another hard bounce stopped her protests for a few more seconds.

Long enough for her to hear him say to someone who was probably staring openmouthed at them, "My servant's wife. She hates boats, but he refuses to leave her behind."

"I would," the stranger replied.

"So would I, but the silly man loves her, so what can you do?"

"That's a lie!" Tanya screeched, only to get another bounce on Vasili's hard shoulder.

By the time she caught her breath, she was already on the boat. Her hair had come loose again in her struggle and was trailing on the deck. She had a difficult time pushing it out of the way when she reared up, then wished she hadn't when she saw the many passengers lining the rail all watching Vasili and his squirming bundle, rather than getting a last view of Natchez. The men looked amused, some actually laughing, while the women were stern-faced, likely feeling affronted. And farther away, Serge was talking to an officious-looking man—the captain?—and probably telling him some outrageous lie just like Vasili's, to explain why she had to be carried aboard. The passengers had no doubt been told something similar, which was why not a single one stepped forward to help her. Of Stefan and Lazar there was no sign. Maybe they'd drowned—hopefully.

Tanya still tried to get the truth out for whoever would listen, her last and only hope, but it came out a jumbled concoction of frantic words, interspersed with all her *oouffs* each time she was bounced into silence. Finally she just screamed in pure frustration, which was also interspersed with *oouffs*.

Too soon, she heard a door slam behind her and Vasili's irritated voice saying, ''Come and stuff something in her damn mouth, will you, Sasha?''

And then she was pulled off his shoulder and set down jarringly on her feet. But she wasn't so jarred that she didn't immediately take a close-fisted swing at her tormentor. Uselessly, however. He was as fast as Stefan was in avoiding what she could dish out. She ended up turning herself half around with the swing and was left staring at Sasha—and the cloth he had wadded in one hand.

The servant got blasted with everything Tanya was presently feeling. ''Don't even think about it, you sawed-off little toady!''

Unaffected by the insult, he merely turned his black eyes on Vasili. Tanya did too, *and* moved out of his reach.

''Never mind, Sasha,'' Vasili said, having suddenly found something to be amused about. He even chuckled. ''We'll leave her to deal with Stefan and his devil's temper. It's bound to be the worst we've seen in a long time.''

If that was said to frighten Tanya, it worked quite well. Until that moment, she hadn't remembered Stefan's promise of unpleasant consequences. And she hadn't just caused a commotion. She'd dunked two men in the river, one of whom supposedly had the authority to do with her anything he cared to do. Her fear didn't subdue her, however, not when she didn't have to face it yet.

Her lip curled with contempt for the golden Adonis and his vindictive amusement. "And I'm supposed to be betrothed to you? You see *why* I don't believe it."

His contempt was much more effective, all in the amber-brown eyes that raked over her. "I hardly believe it myself. But I can assure you, little wench, you'll never share *my* bed." With that he laughed derisively, before adding, "Royal marriages don't even require a degree of civility between the partners. No, after the nuptials, I will see much less of you than I am forced to endure now, thank the good Lord. And you, Princess, can take what lovers you care to."

"With your blessing?"

"Certainly," he said magnanimously. "I'll even make recommendations if you like."

"Wait, let me guess. Your dear cousin?"

Vasili shrugged. "For some reason I can't possibly fathom, he's not as adverse to you as he should be. Yes, you would do well to cultivate his interest, instead of his fury. He does, after all, carry a great deal of influence at court."

A choking sound was heard from Sasha, who had

been standing quietly through all this. Tanya couldn't believe she was even having this conversation.

"Enough!" she said in the same commanding tone she'd heard Stefan use. Vasili's brows went up, hearing it. "I don't know why you think you have to continue this farce, but we both know you don't want me along, no matter the destination. So why did you stop me from leaving?"

"Duty before preference, Princess," he replied simply. "You'll learn."

"Like hell I will!"

Again he shrugged, then motioned Sasha to precede him out the door. But he paused there and gave Tanya a smile that was full of wicked humor.

"Stefan's mistress is fond of telling one and all how he frequently takes his anger out on her whether she's to blame for it or not. The way she puts it, he pounds the hell out of her. You shouldn't have long to wait."

How diabolically cruel of him to leave her with that parting shot to think about. But then Vasili had to be the most hateful man she'd ever met in her life. He was, amazingly, even more detestable than Dobbs, and that was saying a lot. At least Dobbs only beat her, then went about his business, not giving the beating or her another thought. But Vasili was making a point of stinging her with his barbs at every single opportunity. And she was supposed to like the idea of marrying that jackassed peacock? They should have told her Lazar was king, or Stefan. Stefan . . .

So he had a mistress, did he? What sort of woman would want to make love with that moody, dark devil? she wondered. *You almost did, missy. You were so lost in that kiss you participated in, it could have been done and over with before you knew it even happened*.

She flamed crimson with the thought. Her only consolation was that at least this time no one was there to see her blush.

Chapter 14

The Lorilie was one of the larger riverboats that plied the Mississippi, double-decked, with a full-sized dining room, a separate gambling room, a small library, and well-appointed cabins. The one Tanya had been left in was medium-sized, certainly much bigger than the room she was used to sleeping in, and much, much nicer.

The bed was covered with a flower-sprigged quilt, the table beside it with white lace. On the table sat a lovely stained-glass lamp, already lit when she had been brought inside, since there were no portals in the cabin. There was a thick-piled rug of Oriental design on the floor, and in a corner an ornate washstand painted white with gold leaf, with a fine porcelain bowl. Fluffy white towels monogrammed with an L for Lorilie were stacked underneath.

There was a shelf built into one wall to set things on. And two trunks were stacked one on top of the other against another wall. To put things in? Or did they belong to one of the men? There was also a single well-padded armchair. Drawn up near the small table with the lamp, it would be an ideal place to sit and read. When had Tanya ever had time for such a luxury since Iris had taught her to read? All that she read now were the account books and the bills that came in.

The door was solid wood, and of course locked. That was the first thing she found out, before looking over the cabin. She thought about banging on it, but that just might bring Stefan that much sooner, so she didn't.

She sat in the chair now, feeling her apprehension mount as she waited. But she wasn't completely discouraged. So her second attempt to escape had failed just like her first. If she could walk—*pounds the hell out of her?*—when Stefan was done with her, then she would try again. Vasili's damned "duty before preference" had ruined the whole plan this time, but next time she wouldn't make any assumptions about any of them. She had probably even been wrong in thinking that the possibility of missing the boat would deter them from giving chase, since they had already put so much effort into her abduction.

She still couldn't understand why they had chosen her—unless some brothel owner had hired them specifically to find an exotic dancer. That would explain why they hadn't given up when she didn't believe their fairy-tale story, or when she started causing them difficulty. But still, all this trouble and expense just for one girl? Or were there more, already tucked away in other cabins, girls who had come willingly, believing the ridiculous tales they'd been told?

She'd find out when the boat docked, wouldn't she? No, she couldn't wait that long to escape. The farther away they moved from Natchez, the harder it would be for her to get back.

He *pounds* the hell out of her? she mused.

She had fair warning before the storm arrived. "Not *now, Sasha!*" she heard just before the door opened and closed quietly behind Stefan.

That soft entrance was deceiving, however. Tanya wished he'd slammed the door like before. The slamming of doors at least expended a little of one's anger. And looking at Stefan, she had no doubt at all about the state of his emotions. He was absolutely livid, eyes filled with that mesmerizing golden glow, jaw and fists clenched, scars whitened, more prominent, body taut with whatever restraint was being practiced—not much, she'd wager.

His boots, cravat, and jacket were gone. Someone had given him a towel, which he'd used on his face and hair, but it now hung around his neck, forgotten. His lawn shirt was clinging wetly, delineating every muscle across his chest and arms, pointing out that she had merely guessed at his strength before. Too tall, too lean and hard, too damn masculine, and much too angry.

Against her will, Tanya dropped her eyes to his hands again, which looked like large iron mallets right now. Pounds? *Pounds!!*

Panic rose suddenly and drained the color from her face. She shot to her feet and was behind the chair in seconds. But her movement set him in motion, too. Restraint gone, obviously too angry even for words, for he said not a one, he closed the distance between them before she could even think to scream. And then she was so terrified at having her only barrier violently knocked aside, all that came out of her was a gasp, followed by a mere whimper as she was lifted and tossed through the air. But she landed with a soft bounce that told her the bed had caught her fall.

No sooner did her relief register the fact that she hadn't been thrown through a wall than it felt as if one had dropped on top of her. Stefan—his body fully covering hers.

Unprepared for the sudden weight of him, she had her breath knocked out of her, then stolen further as he took her mouth with fierce demand. It wasn't a punishing kiss, but it was too impassioned for her, an innocent, to appreciate. She was stunned, and did not understand. Why wasn't he pounding her to dust with his huge fists?

And then she knew, instinctively, that it wasn't his fists he was going to pound her with, but his body. Relieved laughter bubbled up in her, but it never got past their joined lips. And the urge to laugh was gone as quickly as it had come. There was no playfulness to this kiss, no sensual exploring, no sense that she could end it if she tried. He was dead serious about what he was doing. He was actually going to make love to her—in anger.

She began to fight him with everything she had. Weighted down as she was, it wasn't much. But he didn't seem to feel anything, not her punches, not her yanking on his hair, certainly not the little bit of pushing she managed. He continued kissing her, taking full possession of her mouth, his breath becoming her breath, his taste her taste. It was draining, debilitating, but stirring, too. All the emotional energy she'd expended in her struggle left her wide open to his passionate onslaught.

But she was afraid. She had avoided this kind of contact with a man for so many years, and had done everything possible to make herself undesirable to men. Yet this one wanted her despite her looks and was going to take her despite her wishes. She wasn't even sure he knew exactly what he was doing. That was what frightened her the most. He was too passionate, too out of control in his fury. He didn't even seem to be aware of her resistance.

And he was so hot! Instead of a cold clamminess from his dunking, heat emanated from him in waves, soaking through her own clothes like wet steam. It made the barrier of their shirts seem like nothing between them . . . Lord help her, she was starting to feel things other than fear.

It was the first downward thrust of the huge paddle wheels, setting *The Lorilie* to motion, that was jarring enough to draw Stefan's attention away from her. Suddenly Tanya's mouth was hers again, free to let her scream and rail. But she didn't make a sound, for he was staring down at her, his eyes still aglow, his expression so intense she even feared to breathe, afraid it might disturb his tenuous control. But control of what? She couldn't tell which emotion he was still in the grip of, which passion he was restraining, the desire to take her or the urge to beat her.

And then he turned his head slightly to look at his hand, which held her hair in a tight fist, then his other hand, holding her wrist tightly. Instantly he released her hand as if it had suddenly become hot enough to burn him. He reared up on one arm at the same time.

"Go!" Stefan commanded. "Get away from me before . . ."

She needed no more urging and was grateful he didn't elaborate, for she simply didn't want to know what came after "before." However, he wasn't exactly making it easy for her to flee him, still half covering her body as he was, and making no effort to move. But she managed to pull herself out from under him, all but her now sodden skirt, which took some tugging. The moment it gave, she rolled to the side of the bed—about one second too late.

"No, by God!" she heard behind her as his hand caught her trailing skirt to jerk her to a halt. "You'll at least have what you deserve."

She took that to mean only one thing. She'd received a reprieve from his angry lovemaking, but not from the beating she'd been expecting. At the moment, she wished he hadn't come to his senses.

She wouldn't beg, however. Begging had never stopped Dobbs. But she wouldn't just accept this punishment either. She couldn't. She had to be hale and hearty to get off this boat, not broken and bedridden.

As he moved to the side of the bed, she had the leeway to get off it. Her feet were on the floor, but her skirt wasn't giving, and neither was his grip on it. She tried to twist loose, but turning around she saw how determined he was—and still so very angry. Lord help her, he was going to hurt her.

Instinctively she reached for the knife on her hip, but before she gave her intention away, she recalled that it was no longer there. But she had another one in her boot. Not as long-bladed and impressive, but it would still serve her purpose, which was just to hold Stefan off until he could be reasoned with. But as she bent for it, she saw his hand come up.

She reared back reflexively, raising her arms to block her face from the coming blow. It didn't come. He caught one of her arms instead to pull her over his lap into a position that was self-explanatory.

Tanya's eyes flared wide. Oh, for God's sake, he wasn't actually going to spank her, was he? Unbelievable. Was that all she'd had to worry about? But she was forgetting the raising of her skirt, which he did with swift efficiency. No, even that didn't matter now, not after what Vasili had led her to anticipate. She'd been fearing the worst, and this spanking was nothing in comparison.

She felt like laughing, her relief was so great, but all she did was smile, wince slightly when the first smack came, then smile again. Resisting the urge to tense her muscles, she relaxed to lessen the sting, and busied herself thinking about how she'd like to torture Vasili very slowly for the anxiety he had deliberately put her through. Her seat got hot, then quickly numb—Stefan took this business seriously and no doubt wouldn't finish until he'd got some of the anger out of his system. Better a spanking than his other means for expending it, though. Imagine anger making him want to make love. What kind of habit was that for a man to get into?

Chapter 15

Stefan's hand felt engulfed by flames. He couldn't begin to imagine what the girl's backside felt like. And yet not a single sound had he heard from her. Her tears had to be silent ones. He wished it were otherwise, for he couldn't bear the sound of a woman crying. He would have stopped sooner . . .

He resisted the urge to gather her in his arms and comfort her. He was not to blame. She had been warned. Her present behavior could not be allowed to continue. She had to be made to understand that it was her *duty* to return to Cardinia, that she mustn't try to avoid it again.

But the method he had chosen to instill this lesson had been too harsh. He could see that now. Her backside was cherry bright. But as usual, he was careless in his anger and sorry too late. That didn't relieve her pain. It merely made him ache with regret that he couldn't even reveal, or the lesson would lose its effect . . . To hell with that.

Stefan carefully turned her over and drew her up

against his chest, tucking her head beneath his chin and holding her tenderly. Still she made no sound. But she didn't reject his offer of comfort either. She just sat there with her head bowed, her hands in her lap, and let him soothe her.

Stefan held back a sigh. She confused him more than ever, this girl. From the moment he first saw her, she had stirred up powerful emotions in him. And each time thereafter it was the same. Lust, shame, fury, frustration—and possessiveness from the moment he was certain who she was. And right now confusion, remorse, and tenderness were tearing him up inside.

He had never intentionally hurt a woman before. What had made him think he could do so now with indifference? He knew from experience what kind of guilt the tiniest bruise would cost him, yet he had inflicted more than that on this delicate girl. How much worse could it have been if he had made love to her instead? That, at least, she was accustomed to. But it would have served no purpose other than to rid him of his anger. He still would have had her attempted defection to deal with.

Clearly, he didn't know *how* to deal with her. She was a royal princess, yet she wouldn't believe it. He would prefer to treat her as such, but she wouldn't let him. And when she finally cleaned herself up, he was afraid she was going to be as beautiful as her mother had been. Yet she didn't want to reveal her true self, even though they had already guessed the truth. And quite frankly, he was dreading the moment when she would reveal her beauty.

He had wanted her in all her unremarkable plainness. Beauty was for single instances of pleasure and no more. Beauty wouldn't return affection. But for some reason he had thought that this plain-looking girl could, possibly because she didn't seem to notice his scars when she looked at him. But she wasn't plain. He didn't know what she was, or why she hid it, but it wasn't going to be unremarkable, of that he was sure. And just because beautiful women no longer found him desirable didn't mean he wasn't attracted to them. He still wanted this girl—and was bound to suffer for it.

The situation was hopeless, no matter how he looked at it. Maybe he should just let her go as she wanted.

His arms tightened around her, his whole being rejecting that thought. This caused her to move finally, squirming in protest at the strength he was applying. He immediately loosened his hold, his hands soothing her again, caressing her back, her hair, her cheek—which was dry.

Stefan frowned and tilted her chin up. "Where are your tears?"

"What tears?"

"The ones that should have left gray streaks along your cheeks."

"Oh, *those* tears," she said with a shrug. "I wiped them off."

"Liar."

"Well, that makes two of us, doesn't it? No, don't start scowling at me again. You want tears, get a stick. On second thought, that probably won't do it either. My tears dried up years ago when I figured out that Dobbs liked the sound of them.''

"What has that to do with—"

Her laughter cut him off. "You seem to forget where you found me, Stefan. I'm not saying my life with Dobbs was all hardship and misery. It wasn't. But my defiant nature did bring frequent beatings. That tends to harden the soul, as well as the flesh.''

He paid less attention to what she was saying than he did to what it meant. She hadn't cried. It was doubtful that he had even hurt her a little bit.

He asked her as much. "Did that spanking even hurt you?''

"Certainly." His eyes narrowed, so she added, "Well, not much.''

He stood up so fast, she was dumped on the floor. "Of all the . . . what I went through . . . damned impudent wench! So your skin is as tough as hide, is it?''

"Are you going to get a stick now?''

"No!''

"Then what are you ranting about? I got your point. You don't think I want to go through that again, do you?''

"Why not?" he replied with dripping sarcasm. "You didn't *feel* it.''

"I felt it," she grumbled as she picked herself up off the floor, starting to rub her backside, then thinking better of it. "It just wasn't as disabling as what I'm accustomed to.''

Stefan stiffened, the rest of what she had said clarifying in his mind. "Jesus, he *beat* you?" She blinked at him as if she didn't understand the question, so he rephrased it. "Did Mr. Dobbs beat you, Tatiana?"

"I thought I already said as much. I also told you I don't like that name."

"Devil take the name!" he snapped irritably. "How did Dobbs beat you?"

"Now, what difference does that make? A stick, a hand, the intention is the same—to hurt me."

There was a wealth of bitterness in that statement that Stefan understood very well. Bitterness was his own constant companion.

"I'm sorry for adding more unpleasantness to your life, Tanya. It was not my intention to hurt you—"

"You could have fooled me," she snorted.

"—merely to impress upon you not to try to leave us again."

"So consider me impressed."

She wouldn't even allow him to assuage his conscience with an apology. Just as well. He didn't *want* to forget what his temper had wrought this time. If she had not learned a lesson, hopefully he had.

"It is intolerable what you have suffered through fate," he told her with feeling. "You were supposed to be reared gently. A fortune was sent with you and Baroness Tomilova to ensure it. She would have trained you, thoroughly, in the duties that await you as Queen of Cardinia, the etiquette of court—"

"If you don't want another fight on your hands," Tanya interrupted coldly, "then do us both a favor and end the pretense for now. I've heard all I can stomach of that fairy tale for one day."

"Very well—if you will tell me why you don't believe it."

"Because things like that don't happen. A lost princess, Stefan? Like hell. How can you misplace someone as important as a princess?"

"Through secrecy and neglectful assumptions. Communication was forbidden because it could have led to your death. It was assumed you were being cared for in the manner that your status demanded. And you would have been told how to obtain help if something had happened to the baroness. But how could anyone know that she would die before you were even old enough to know who you were?"

"You've got a ready answer for *everything,* don't you?" she retorted angrily.

He smiled at that burst of temper. "Such is usually the case when one is dealing with the truth."

"Enough!"

He laughed now. "Very good, Princess. You have a definite knack for command, at least. You will learn the rest soon enough."

She crossed her arms over her chest and glared at him, an affectation, he supposed, meant to silence him on the subject. And he was silenced, not by that, but by finally noticing that her shirt had been so dampened by his that it was now clinging quite provocatively to her breasts. Fortunately, they were just barely covered. The last thing either of them needed right now was for his damn lust to run amok again.

"I—ah—believe I need a bath to get the filth of your river off me," he remarked and turned toward the door to summon Sasha.

"My river? Are you admitting I'm American?"

He glanced back with a grin. "*You* think you are. I know differently. Now, would you by any chance like a bath also?"

"No," she staunchly maintained.

"Then a change of clothes?"

"Are you offering to swim back and fetch mine?" she asked with a falsely sweet smile.

"Oh, clever, Princess, but I think I must decline. You may, however, feel free to avail yourself of my wardrobe. Since your taste in attire seems to run toward the masculine, that should prove no hardship. Once we reach New Orleans, we will have you outfitted properly."

"In dancing costumes?" she sneered.

"I don't know where you get these intriguing notions, but that one definitely has merit. If I had known you wanted to dance for us again, I would have spared the time to bring your own costume along. You will, however, have a captive audience, no matter what you choose to dance in. Wearing nothing at all would be even better."

She looked so furious at being misunderstood, Stefan left the room quickly before he burst into laughter again.

Chapter 16

As soon as the door closed behind Stefan, Tanya rushed to it to see if Stefan would forget to lock it. At the sound of the click, she kicked the door in frustration—and heard his laughter on the other side.

Damned devil. His mercurial moods were going to drive her batty. Right now she didn't like his humor any better than his temper. Dance for them indeed. On his grave maybe.

She whipped around and began to pace, feeling caged and suddenly desperate. What if they didn't let her out of the cabin until they arrived in New Orleans? Then she wouldn't have a chance to escape, would she? It was that simple.

Like hell. She wasn't about to settle for no options when the stakes were so high—her freedom, her dream of independence. There had to be something she could do, anything, even . . . no, she wouldn't go that far. Sleeping with Stefan was no guarantee of his trust, or of her release. She would do better to lull them into thinking she was resigned—no, not them, just Stefan, since he obviously made the decisions where she was concerned. She had to convince him that she could be trusted to leave the cabin. The question was, how?

Her eyes lit on the trunks against the wall, which she supposed were his. Well, that was one place to start, by accepting his suggestion to use his clothes, a new shirt anyway. She could also stop fighting with him, and stop letting every mention of kings and betrothals rile her so. And it wouldn't hurt if he thought she couldn't swim. That at least would make him think he had nothing to worry about other than her causing another scene for the entertainment of crew and passengers.

She approached the trunks reluctantly. It seemed such an intimate thing, wearing something that belonged to Stefan, that had been on his body. She'd prefer not to, but she wasn't getting any of her wishes granted today. And her own shirt *was* uncomfortably wet, thanks to him.

The blush came on unexpectedly with the reminder of what had almost happened in this cabin. Tanya would like to say it had been the most horrible experience of her life, but that wasn't so. She had been frightened of his anger, true, but the fact was, he hadn't hurt her when he had lain atop her on the bed. He would have if he hadn't stopped, but he didn't know that. He thought her a whore, and whores supposedly did that kind of thing all the time.

What had happened instead, she would just as soon forget, but still, he hadn't hurt her with that child's punishment. She might be a little tender for a few days and not enjoy sitting down, yet it could have been so much worse. He could have used his belt and welted her, or his fists, for he'd felt justified after she had broken their bargain.

What she didn't understand was his attitude afterward. If she wasn't mistaken, she would have to say he really had been sorry for laying a violent hand on her. He had tried to apologize. He had certainly tried to comfort her—until he realized she didn't need comforting.

She made a face as she threw open the lid of the top trunk. Dumping her on the floor had not been nice of him. Of course, dumping him in the river had not been very nice of her. She giggled, wishing she could have seen his expression when he found the surface of the water. It must have been priceless.

She rummaged through the trunk, finding a number of things, boxes and such, that she would have liked to examine further, but just opening the trunk made her feel like a thief, so all she did was grab the first shirt she came across. It was white lawn, and too thin to appear bulky on her, as she discovered when she made quick work of exchanging it for her own and could see her nipples through the material. It simply wouldn't do, not by itself, since she wore no chemisette and never had, relying on the thickness of her shirts to adequately cover her breasts. And she doubted she would find a chemisette in Stefan's trunk.

She searched for and found a waistcoat instead, brocaded satin in black and silver, and about the richest piece of clothing she'd ever touched. She probably shouldn't use it. It was too fine for the likes of her. But she'd been given permission, so if Stefan objected, that was just too bad. Of course, considering that parting comment of his, he'd probably prefer her in just the shirt—or nothing at all.

Remembering that comment about her dancing and Stefan's humor brought back her annoyance with both, and she was still stewing when Stefan returned a few moments later. And the look he passed over her was salt to the wound, chock-full of amusement, sherry-gold eyes crinkled with it. It was fortunate that he wasn't alone, or what she'd decided to set in motion would have had to wait until after she had vented her spleen. But Sasha was with him, and a number of crewmen followed through the door, toting buckets of water.

When Tanya saw the tin tub being carried in, however, she ground her teeth together. All that plotting and planning, and here, already, was her ticket out. Stefan was going to bathe in here, which meant she would have to leave—with an escort, no doubt, but that was all right. All she had to do was get *near* a railing, and she'd find some way over it.

While the bath was being readied, Stefan came over to her and drew the waistcoat together to fasten it. She brushed his hands aside and did it herself, but recalled she had to start the lulling.

Nervous with him standing so close to her, she remarked, ''There were so many clothes in that top trunk, they can't all be yours. Do I have you to thank for what I've borrowed, or one of the others?''

''I believe I will feel bourgeois now if I admit that

both of those trunks are mine alone, so you have only me to thank.''

She glanced up in surprise. ''You can't have even *more* clothes in the bottom one.''

''Certainly I can, not that I will use them in this country. Much too conspicuous. That trunk should have remained on the ship that awaits us in New Orleans, but Sasha is of the absurd belief that everything brought along for this journey should be brought along for the *entire* journey.''

''Conspicuous?'' She dared not ask about that waiting ship if she was to keep her temper.

''They are clothes I would wear only in Europe, where the sight of nobility is nothing out of the ordinary.''

Lord help her, was he going to prove as condescending as Vasili? ''I see—no, I don't. Are you saying you're a titled aristocrat?''

''In Cardinia, it is customary for the king to draw his personal guard from his nobles. It is fortunate when those he has to choose from for this honor are the friends he happened to grow up with.''

''In other words, you all hold titles? What would yours be, then?''

''Would a *count* strain your belief?''

Everything he was saying strained her belief, but all she did was shrug and say, ''You have me curious now to see what's in that other trunk.''

''Ah, curiosity.'' He grinned. ''A reason to remain with us.''

She almost choked on that one. Give up freedom merely to appease curiosity? He had to be teasing her. But his mood was mellow and she wanted to keep it that way. And she hadn't once snapped at him for his talk of nobility. Her ploy was working, and now was an excellent time for the crowning touch.

"You haven't given me much choice about remaining with you, but it would have been easier to bear if you were traveling by land."

"I fail to see—"

"I hate boats," she cut in with a feigned shiver. "Most people do who can't swim."

"You needn't fear the water, Tanya. You are my responsibility on this journey, so be assured I will protect you with my own life."

In other words, if she jumped in the river, he'd jump in right after her to save her from drowning. How gallant of him, but she didn't appreciate his gallantry under the circumstances. She'd have to make sure he wasn't around when she did her jumping, like while he was taking his bath.

However, she said, "Thank you—I think . . . no, a little relief is better than none at all."

"You really are worried about it, aren't you?" he asked with concern.

"These steamboats *are* known to explode, particularly if the captain is in a hurry to reach his destination. Ours isn't, is he?"

"If he is, then I will have to disabuse him of the notion. Does that reassure you?" She gave him a doubting look, which brought on a smile. "I can see, then, that I will just have to get your mind off this worry. I wonder if you know how adorable you look in your sloppiness, with your hair in wild disarray, your clothes hanging as loose as a nightrail, and your dirty little face. Now what are you frowning for? Don't you want to look adorable?''

She didn't need *that* kind of distraction and told him so by picking up her belt and slapping it around her waist. Her hair was another matter. Running her fingers through it, she could only find two pins left.

''Sasha,'' Stefan called, chuckling, ''I believe our Tanya needs a brush.''

He moved off then and began pulling his shirt out of his trousers in preparation of removing it. The tub had been filled. Only the servant, Sasha, remained in the cabin.

When the shirt was lifted over Stefan's head, Tanya stood there mesmerized by that broad expanse of male back, darkly bronzed and well defined with muscle. Sasha, holding out the brush to her, had to clear his throat to gain her attention. Disconcerted, Tanya took the brush and turned her back on the scene.

Watching Stefan undress was . . .

She whipped around to see his belt come off and drop to the floor, where his shirt now lay. He was undressing, actually undressing! And he didn't appear the least bit concerned whether she watched him.

''Don't you think you ought to wait until I leave the room before you—''

''No.''

That was all? Just ''No''? She started for the door. She was halted before she even got close to it.

''Where are you going, Tanya?''

She wouldn't look back at him. "I'll just wait outside until you're finished," she offered.

It didn't work. "I don't think so."

"Look, I'm not going anywhere, Stefan. The boat is in the middle of the damned river, so I *can't* go anywhere. Summon one of the others to watch me if you must, but I can't stay in here with you . . . while you . . . This isn't proper by any standards, but particularly yours."

"Perhaps," he allowed. "However, we must by necessity make a few exceptions now. Besides, you aren't going to convince me that seeing a naked man is going to bother you, Tanya. So we will worry about what is proper and what isn't when we reach Europe, where it will matter."

This was an insult to her country as well as to her, and a flat refusal to let her leave the cabin. But the door was probably unlocked. She could just . . . who was she kidding? He would be after her instantly. And even if she managed to hit the water, he would be too close behind her for her plan to work. She'd be losing her only chance, because he wouldn't trust her again after that, no matter what she said or did. Unfortunately, he didn't trust her right now either, or he wouldn't be so adamant about her remaining with him.

She'd have to wait a little longer for her freedom, and wait until Stefan wasn't around. She would have a better chance of succeeding at night anyway, when they would have a hard time seeing her in the water. That might lead to their thinking she had drowned, and in that case, she wouldn't have anything else to worry about—except the long walk home.

In order to continue her pretense of accepting the situation, she had to ignore that insult about her familiarity with naked men and silently endure Stefan taking his bath in her presence. One was easier to do than the other.

She vigorously began to brush the snarls from her hair, pausing only when she heard distinct sounds of water splashing. Her face was heating up again, and that infuriated her. Why should she be the one embarrassed when *he* was the naked one?

"Your Highness?"

Sasha's hand appeared at her side, offering a strip of leather for her to use on her hair. She took it, keeping her mouth shut about correcting his form of address. That they even had the servants trained for the pretense was almost a guarantee that the royalty ploy was used frequently. She again wondered if they didn't have other girls stowed away on *The Lorilie* right now, all thinking they were betrothed to the handsome Vasili. So how did she get so lucky to end up with the devil in control of her? Probably because he was allotted the troublemakers, which they had found her to be from the start.

She was getting really angry again at the fate she had stumbled into through no fault of her own. She also felt like a fool standing there in the middle of the cabin with her back to Stefan. Well, no more of that. If he wanted to disconcert her with his nakedness, she'd see how he felt with the shoe on the other foot.

She crossed over to the chair, sat down, and proceeded to stare at Stefan while she continued to brush her hair. He really was in the tub—and naked. But she'd seen bare chests before, and more. There had been a fire scare one night at the brothel next door to the tavern, and all the girls and their customers had run out in the street in their various states of undress, providing some hilarious entertainment for everyone else along the street who came out to watch.

But there wasn't anything funny about Stefan in that tub . . . well, maybe a little bit funny. The tub was a small round one, and he had to scrunch up to fit in it, his knees bent to his chest. Presently, Sasha was pouring water from an extra bucket over Stefan's just-washed hair, so he didn't even know yet that she had decided to be entertained by him.

Even naked, he was a swarthy-skinned devil, though his knees weren't nearly as dark as his upper torso, proving that some of his coloring was helped by the sun. And the hair on his body was minimal, except for a Y-shaped thatch of black curling down the center of his chest. She looked at the scars on his face, barely noticeable from a distance, and tried to recall the empathy she'd felt when she first saw them. She couldn't. The man had proved too aggravating since then to arouse any kind of compassion in her now.

Sasha handed him a towel to wipe the water from his face and eyes. When the towel was lowered, Stefan was looking toward the spot where Tanya had been standing. It didn't take him but a second to turn his head and find her in the chair. He raised a black brow at seeing her watching him. She lifted one of her own. He laughed. She didn't. He stood up. She was positive she was going to faint. She wasn't that lucky.

Lord help her, he was raw masculinity, hard and splendidly formed, broad of shoulder, narrow of hip, thick of leg. And the root of his manhood . . . She closed her eyes. He laughed again, a wicked sound that mortified her. And she had thought she could play this out and embarrass *him?*

He must have had a similar thought, for he said, "When it is your turn, Princess, I assure you I won't be so shy."

She was never going to bathe again.

Chapter 17

Tanya didn't know how she got through that next half hour, watching Stefan being dressed and groomed by Sasha. Mostly she kept her eyes averted, or on the little servant, who turned out to be amazingly bossy for a man a good inch or two shorter than she was.

Stefan had warned him to speak only English, and once Sasha started, Tanya got to listen to a whole stream of grumblings and complaints that only a servant of long standing would dare to voice. Stefan merely shrugged, or ignored, or teased—which was interesting. Tanya wouldn't have thought someone as unapproachable and as volatile as Stefan seemed to be would be the sort who teased. Playful just wasn't synonymous with diabolical. But hadn't she suspected him of teasing her a few times today, only to dismiss the idea as being too unlikely?

She didn't like seeing this other side of him that even included affection for a servant. And she really hated it when he smiled, for her heart did a double beat each time, whether he was looking at her or not. He wasn't incredibly handsome like Vasili, but the more she looked at him, the more attractive he became, and that, for some reason, annoyed her the most. She preferred to keep their relationship black and white. Enemy—captive. No middle ground. Yet his kisses and the feelings they had evoked in her were never far from her mind. And the image of his naked body . . . She needed to get away from this man for more than just her freedom.

She breathed a sigh of relief now to see that he was finally completely dressed. The buff-colored trousers were too snug, if you asked her, and the forest-green coat was so well tailored it did nothing but accentuate his fine figure. The shirt he wore was identical to the one she now sported, with pleated cuffs, but the waistcoat wasn't as fancy, merely embroidered yellow silk. His offsetting red cravat was tied in the careless *primo tempo* style, and Sasha produced a tan top hat that took all of twenty seconds to be placed just so over his black hair.

He was definitely dressed to leave the cabin, and Tanya could only wish at this point that he would hurry up and do so. Except now that he was ready to, he turned his attention back to her, approaching her with a mirror in hand. She stiffened with an idea of what that meant. She wasn't far wrong.

"Wash the paint off or repair the damage," he said, dropping the round mirror into her lap. "But do one or the other before we go to supper."

She was actually being offered a choice? Yet it was an order, plain and simple, no matter how mild the tone. And she simply hated orders these days.

She was about to hand the mirror back and tell him what he could do with it when she caught a glimpse of her reflection that made her gasp and cringe. He'd said she looked like a grubby urchin, but that wasn't even the half of it. Tanya looked as if she had stuck her head in a fireplace and had cold ashes blown in her face, then had merely dabbed at the mess. Lighter splotches were everywhere, on her chin from having it gripped, on her cheeks and forehead where she'd rubbed against Stefan's chest. How could she repair this mess when she didn't have her powders and creams?

As best as she could, that was how. She still wasn't willing to give up her camouflage without a fight. Stefan had been provoked to lust with her looking as she did. How much more difficulty would she be facing if he saw her as she really was? But there was a devil's voice whispering at her to show him, a bit of vanity that had never troubled her before. She very swiftly squelched it.

"Will this do?" she asked after a few moments of smoothing, blending, and borrowing from the thicker color still beneath her eyes.

"The tired hag again? I think I liked the dirty urchin better."

Tanya gritted her teeth as she felt another urge to wash herself clean of her disguise. He suspected the truth anyway. But a suspicion was nothing compared to clear evidence. She resisted temptation again and changed the subject.

"Did you mention something about going to supper?"

"Unless you would prefer a tray brought to you here."

"I wouldn't," she quickly assured him, amazed that she was going to be allowed out of the cabin this soon. "But aren't you worried that I will enlist someone's aid, in particular the captain's?"

"You would only embarrass him and yourself if you did."

Her green eyes narrowed. "What absurd lies have you told him about me?"

"Nothing too taxing on the imagination. You are my runaway wife. You deserted not only me but two small babies as well. I'm afraid you won't engender the least bit of sympathy if you try to tell anyone otherwise."

He smiled, letting her know he knew how furious that would make her, so all she said was, "Did you have to make me sound so heartless? No one could blame me for deserting you, but babies?"

He didn't take the bait, possibly because her eyes were so hot with rancor. He chuckled, grabbed her hand and pulled her to her feet, and started her toward the door.

On the way to the dining room, he asked, somewhat on the same subject, "How do you feel about babies, Tanya? You will be expected to give the king at least one heir."

"Not according to him," she snorted. "He doesn't intend to ever touch me, for which I am immensely grateful."

"Most women adore Vasili. I assumed you would be pleased by the thought of marrying him."

"You assumed wrong."

"And if you had another choice?"

"That's the second time I've been asked that. *Do* I have another choice?"

He didn't answer. They had reached the dining room, small but comfortably furnished from what she could see through the open doorway. Serge and Vasili were already seated. Lazar was probably still cleaning up from his dunk in the river. No other girls were present at their table, but then if there were other girls like her, the men wouldn't allow them all to come together to compare fairy tales, would they?

Stefan paused before entering, holding Tanya back by her elbow. "We were discussing babies," he reminded her.

"You were, not me."

"You didn't say how you felt about them personally."

"I'm afraid it's a subject I never gave much thought to, since I had never planned to marry."

"And under these new circumstances?"

"I just told you Vasili said he wouldn't be sharing my bed, so I don't see how . . . wait a minute. Are you suggesting a bastard heir would be acceptable?"

"No! I mean yes—never mind."

He propelled her into the room without another word. Tanya glanced sideways at him and saw that he wasn't just flustered, but quite annoyed for some reason. Now, what was she to make of that? Not that it mattered. If she could go to supper, then it was likely that she could go to dinner that evening, too, and that was all she was interested in at the moment— another opportunity to escape.

So she behaved herself that afternoon, didn't argue, and refrained from any more caustic remarks, even toward Vasili, which was a major feat since he wasn't nearly as tactful. She also managed to ignore the disapproving looks that came her way, either because of the outlandish story circulating about her or due to her half-mannish attire, either reason sufficient to condemn her in the eyes of everyone there.

Instead she amused herself by watching every other female in the dining room trying to catch Vasili's eye, not just once, but continuously. Stefan was right in that respect. Most women seemed to adore him, and probably did—right up until they got to meet the insufferable peacock.

It was the same that evening, though even worse where Vasili was concerned, for several women managed to finagle introductions through the captain, who seemed so put upon, Tanya didn't even consider enlightening him with the truth about herself while she had the chance. It was perhaps because she did keep her mouth shut that when she confessed a need to use the convenience before their first course arrived, Stefan let her go without his escort, though she caught his nod toward Serge, which no doubt meant he was to follow at a reasonable distance. Of course, she would never have been allowed even that if Stefan thought she could swim.

Serge's unobtrusive presence on the deck was no hindrance to her plan, however, since he wasn't following close enough to stop her. Tanya even had time to pick her spot to jump, which was an added bonus, for she could barely make out a bend in the river coming up. If she could jump just before it, *The Lorilie* would be around the bend and out of sight long before she reached the riverbank, so no one would see her leave the water, if they *could* see her in the dark.

Being unable to swim was the smartest lie she'd ever told, definitely worth a mental pat on the back. Now, if she could only find the convenience.

Chapter 18

As soon as Tanya was out the door, Lazar leaned back in his chair and asked casually, "Do you think that was wise, Stefan, letting her go off on her own?"

Stefan's expression was devoid of concern. "Serge will keep an eye on her."

Vasili wasn't so casual in his grumbled opinion. "He ought to keep a hand on her—or better yet, a chain."

The suggestion wasn't taken seriously, but Lazar felt it necessary to point out, "It would take no more than a moment for her to jump ship."

"That is at least one worry we won't have," Stefan answered, adding, "She can't swim."

"Who told you that?"

The dubious question broke through Stefan's confidence, the implication waking his lagging instincts. With a particularly foul curse, he shot to his feet and left the room. Lazar and Vasili exchanged a glance before swiftly following him.

Serge was just lighting a cheroot when they joined

him on the dimly lit deck. "Where is she?" was all Stefan asked.

Serge nodded ahead of them to where a door was just opening. There was no time to experience any relief, however, at finding Tanya still aboard, for there was a flash of white legs—her skirt had been tucked up into her belt—as she ran straight to the railing, vaulted onto it, and dived cleanly into the river—right in front of the paddle wheels.

Stefan would swear his heart stopped beating in that moment of fear and dread as he leaned over the railing, searching frantically for a sign that the girl hadn't been pulled in and ripped to pieces by the huge side paddle that was churning the water on that side of the riverboat to foam. And then it dawned on him that because of the paddle wheels, which gave them added speed on top of the current already propelling them downriver, Tanya would now be behind the ship—floating broken and lifeless, or swimming to shore. Drowning wasn't a possibility, after he'd witnessed how skillfully that dive had been executed. His own dive over the side wasn't nearly as well done.

The three men left standing at the rail held their breath until they saw Stefan clear the path of the paddle wheel. It was Vasili who broke the silence. "I don't suppose we could go on to New Orleans and simply wait for Stefan to join us there?"

Serge shook his head slowly. Lazar chuckled. Vasili groaned. A moment later three more bodies hit the water.

* * *

Tanya was struggling for breath by the time she crawled out of the water. She was a good swimmer, but she'd never tried it before with boots on, and definitely wouldn't try it again. And swimming against the current? Her muscles were screaming with strain, her legs and arms trembling. She couldn't have got up and walked away right then to save her soul.

Fortunately, she didn't have to try. A glance over her shoulder showed that *The Lorilie* was gone from sight around the bend in the river, just as she had counted on. She couldn't make out anything else in the water, not even floating debris. Of course, it was extremely dark now, a solid sheet of clouds obscuring moon and stars. That had been to her benefit in case anyone tried to ''save'' her, that and waiting for the boat to pass so she could swim to the opposite side of the river from which she had jumped into.

But if her luck held, Serge might not even have noticed her swift departure. And she couldn't quite picture him jumping in to rescue her anyway. He would have gone to fetch Stefan, and she would have ''drowned'' by the time he had removed his coat and boots to make the valiant effort.

So they would assume. However, that was an assumption on her part as well, and she wasn't going to be that careless again. After a few minutes' rest she would head inland, away from the river. She had an advantage over any of her pursuers even if Serge had followed her into the water, simply because of the distance she would have gained between her jump and anyone else's occurring farther downriver. Besides, what she couldn't see she could hear, and the only noise, aside from her labored breathing, was the soothing river sounds of water rumbling past—until she heard a man's voice.

It was indistinct, but it could have been a shout for all she knew. Distance was deceiving. It could also have just been the wind, but Tanya wasn't taking any chances. She pulled herself out of the mud and scrambled up the riverbank, then had to stop herself from panicking and running pell-mell through the brush, thereby giving her own position away.

Although it was nerve-racking not to run when every instinct prompted her to, she managed to proceed quietly at a hurried walk. But uppermost in her mind was the blaring question: would they really come after her, strand themselves in the countryside without clothes or money, go through all that hardship, just to sell her to a brothel? The answer was no. They would find someone else to take her place. But if she were a genuine princess? Then yes—no! She couldn't let herself fall into the trap of believing their crazy tale. Besides, if she thought there was any truth in what they'd told her, especially that she would have to marry Vasili, she would run even harder to escape them.

Tanya made good headway considering the thickness of the wooded area she was presently passing through. But it wasn't long before she was wishing she had waited until after dinner to make her escape. As dark as it was, she couldn't even begin to look for food until morning. And unless she stumbled upon a plantation or other dwelling where she could beg a meal, she'd have to hunt for it herself.

But she did have her knife with her, so finding food wouldn't be too difficult, just time-consuming. She had tucked the weapon into the bottom of her boot so she wouldn't lose it in the river. But now she stopped long enough to empty her boots of water and put the knife back on the side where she usually wore it, using the time to listen carefully to the sounds around her.

If that was a voice she had heard earlier, it could have been on the other side of the river. That was why she had swum to the Louisiana shore, an added precaution she had decided on at the last minute, and just possibly a stroke of genius. With a river between her and any pursuers, she had very little to worry about. But that was another assumption, so she wasn't going to count on it.

On the negative side, she had stranded herself on the wrong bank of the river, with no money for the ferry to get back to Natchez. But before she considered swimming back across, which she wasn't at all sure she could manage, she would try bartering Stefan's fine waistcoat for the fare. She'd have to clean it first, for it along with the rest of her was coated with wet mud.

Being reminded of the condition of her clothes, Tanya headed back toward the river. She had walked a mile at least already, possibly two, so it should be safe enough to get near the water's edge for the few minutes it would take her to wash her clothes. Then she would have to find some place to get a few hours' sleep, for after the day she had been through, she was utterly exhausted in both body and mind, and she couldn't afford to make any mistakes simply because she couldn't think clearly.

She found the perfect spot on the riverbank, with a fallen tree on one side holding back the river's full current, and a drooping tree on the other side, both thickly branched enough to block her from view up and down the riverbank. She had planned to merely dunk herself again, then leave the water more carefully this time, without getting muddy. But with the added concealment from the two trees, she decided she could spare the extra few minutes to scrub her clothes properly and wash herself more thoroughly, especially since she felt so uncomfortable and itchy she could barely stand it.

Scanning the opposite riverbank first, which was no more than a barely discernible black outline, then the area behind her, thickly shadowed but quiet, Tanya proceeded to strip off everything but her boots. And from long habit she was nothing if not efficient, even when she was tired. It took five extra minutes at the most before she was dumping the water out of her boots again, shivering but clean, and wishing she could take the time to let her clothes dry before putting them back on. But time she didn't have, and even though it was dark as sin in her little spot on the riverbank, she was too self-conscious to remain naked any longer than she had to.

She was squeezing a few more drops of water out of her skirt when she heard the crunch of leaves directly behind her and froze, praying it was an animal, a dog, even a wild one. But if it had to be a man, considering her present naked state, she hoped

it was only Stefan and not some stranger who might
. . . Was she crazy? Stefan? Let it be Serge . . . no,
not even him. Vasili. Vasili wouldn't give two hoots
to see her naked, much less be tempted by it—oh,
God, she wasn't thinking clearly! But the voice behind her was clear and familiar, and as cold as the
river water still dripping from her hair.

"First the white shirt, now the beacon of your
white body. If I didn't know better, Princess, I would
think you wanted to be found."

Chapter 19

The very idea of wanting to be found by *him,* was so absurd it didn't bear comment. Not that Tanya could think of anything to say in that mortifying moment of knowing that Stefan's eyes were upon her, and probably so brightly glowing, she wouldn't be surprised if she now stood in two beams of yellow light. And that awful word—''found.'' He'd found her because he'd spotted that damn white shirt she was wearing, *his* white shirt. She hadn't even considered how noticeable it would be in the dark.

All her precautions for nothing. Caught—no, by God, not until he had his hands on her.

Tanya whipped around, swinging her wet skirt high as she did, hoping Stefan was close enough—and alone. He was both. The heavy skirt slapped across his face, blinding him for the seconds she needed to dash past him.

His sound of rage was terrifying, more like an animal's growl, and prompted her to run faster. If he hadn't been furious already, she'd just tipped the scales. But she couldn't think of that now. She simply ran, tearing through the brush, to hell with the noise she was making. She had to gain distance on him, enough to find a place to hide.

The first sharp sting of a branch against her side reminded her that she was wearing boots and nothing else. Lord help her, where did she think she was going naked? But she couldn't worry about that now either, not with that enraged devil so near. She couldn't hear him behind her, but she was making too much noise herself to hear anything, and that just frightened her all the more, not knowing. She had to know.

She sprinted to the side from the direction she had been running in and dropped to her knees behind a clump of ferns. She had to hold a hand to her mouth to silence her labored breaths, but no sooner did she hear Stefan's pounding footsteps than he dropped down to his knees right in front of her, scaring the life out of her.

She shrieked, then shrieked again as his weight bore her down to the spongy ground. A hand in the back of her hair brought her face up, and then his mouth was over hers and warning bells went off in her head. Not again! Didn't the man know how to deal with his anger any other way? She kicked and bucked under him, but that just moved his body into a more threatening position. Without her skirt to hamper him, his hips settled easily between her legs. If he weren't fully clothed himself . . .

It didn't seem to matter when the bulge of his manhood pressed against the core of her. What she felt had to be as devastating to her senses, for her innards came to life, spiraling downward to protest, or welcome, Lord help her, she wasn't sure which. But she'd never felt anything so strange and debilitating, frightening and thrilling at once. It temporarily took the fight out of her as she stilled to examine the sensation, but then she was snared by the passion in his kiss.

She'd never tried to deny how much she liked his kissing, much as she wished it were otherwise. Now was no different, and it took everything in her to resist the urge she now had, to put her arms around him and kiss him back. Was he still angry? She couldn't tell any longer, nor did she particularly care, if this was all he was going to do to her.

That thought and every other one froze, however, when Stefan's hand came between them to slowly discover the feel of her breasts. New sensations burst upon her senses, a tingling and tightening in her nipples that shook up her innards again. But his hand didn't stay there. It moved down over her stomach, down to where he was pressed so tightly to her core. Then his fingers were there, entering her, and she tried to tell him to stop, but his mouth wouldn't release her lips. And then she didn't want him to stop.

She bucked again, but it was an involuntary reaction this time, because what she felt could only be described as wildly pleasurable. All because he was angry? The man could get angry at her anytime he wanted . . .

They heard it at the same moment, his name being

called. It sounded a long way off, the voice unrecognizable to her, but probably not to Stefan. His head came up. She was being given another reprieve, only this time she didn't want it. And this time she couldn't see his expression as he looked down at her, to tell if he had worked off enough of his anger or if it was still there, just subdued—which was worse as far as she was concerned. He made love when he was furious, but he spanked when he was only half so. She didn't care to have another child's punishment, thank you, yet she had no idea what to expect now. Even his eyes were too shadowed for her to tell if they were glowing.

"If you ever risk your life again as you did by jumping off *The Lorilie,* I will find a stick, which is apparently all you are impressed by, and beat you with it," he promised, his voice low at first, but it picked up in volume as he continued, leaving his no doubts about the depth of her anger. "Do you have any idea what I went through, searching for you in that river? For ten minutes I combed the water, thinking you had been struck by that paddle wheel, going crazy with fear because it was too dark to see anything! And when I do finally see something, it is your white-sleeved arm, pulling you steadily toward shore without the least difficulty."

Tanya's eyes had rounded incredulously long before he finished. His anger stemmed from concern for her? If he hadn't said it so passionately, she might think this was another ploy. But she didn't doubt that she had really frightened him, and strangely enough, she now felt guilty about it, which was utterly ridiculous. He was a despicable purveyor of prostitutes, wasn't he? An abductor for nefarious reasons, at the very least. But a moment ago she hadn't thought so. A moment ago she hadn't thought about anything except the incredible new things he was making her feel, some of which she still felt, for he hadn't removed his fingers from inside her yet.

She doubted he was even aware of that fact, but she certainly was. It made it extremely awkward for her to answer him in kind, even to remind him that as the unwilling member of their little group, she had every right to try to escape, whatever the means.

"Why don't you say something?" he demanded.

She had the feeling he expected an apology. He wasn't getting it.

With great effort, she remarked in a casual tone, "You know, if I *was* traveling with you across a whole ocean to this Cardinia of your imagination, and I had to worry about this kind of thing happening every time someone got you angry, I'd go crazy. What do you do when there isn't a woman around for you to jump on?"

"I wait until I find one." There was a measure of amusement in his answer, but not in his voice when he added, "Did I hurt you, Tanya?"

"A fine time to wonder," she snorted. "Are you finished berating me?"

"Probably not."

"What about the kissing? Are we done with that?"

"Definitely not."

The mention of kissing must have recalled to him

the position of his fingers. Suddenly they moved slightly.

Tanya gasped and then snapped, "Well, you can't have both."

"Certainly I can."

She was positive he was only teasing her, for his humor was blatantly clear now. He was probably grinning from ear to ear, though she couldn't see it. She didn't care either. It was the languorous combination of feeling tired but sexually aroused that weakened her protest. She had to fight to resist him. She managed it.

"You aren't even angry with me anymore, Stefan, so let me up."

He didn't budge. "It would be a misconception on your part, little Tanya, if you are thinking I have to be angry to make love to you." His head bent, his lips grazing her cheek all the way to her ear. With his warm breath sending tingles all over her, he continued in a whisper, "I wanted you last night, today a dozen times, right now more than ever. Tell me to love you, Tanya. Demand it of me!"

Nothing in half measures for this devil. Demand it of him? She definitely liked the sound of that. But she didn't dare—did she?

Tanya was that close to giving in to what she was feeling when some loud throat clearing announced that they were no longer alone. Stefan sighed, kissed her cheek, and leaned away from her. His voice, however, was terse when he addressed his unwelcome friend.

"Though the loyalty that sent you into the river

after me warms my heart, right now I could wish you to Hades. The princess requires a moment of privacy, so turn around.''

Her cheeks flushed with embarrassment again. She was naked, but had temporarily forgotten that mortifying fact. He hadn't. He sat up and shrugged out of his coat, dropping it into her lap as she sat up also. She donned it quickly, savoring the heat inside from his body, even though the coat was still quite damp. For a covering, it was far from adequate, with only a few buttons that would have closed at Stefan's lower chest, but didn't even begin until Tanya's navel. But at least it was a frock coat, full-skirted, that reached below her knees, so it served its purpose as long as she held it tightly closed.

More sounds were heard in the brush now, as the other two drew near. Tanya found out who had discovered them first when Lazar called out, ''Over here.''

Coming back at him was the question, ''Did you find Stefan?''

''Yes, and he our little fish.''

The ''little fish'' made a face that no one could see in the dark. She wondered if she could *quietly* slip away while they were shouting back and forth. The hand she didn't see coming lifted her to her feet and stayed at her elbow to disabuse her of that notion. She wouldn't be getting away again tonight. Stefan was definitely going to make sure of that. But tomorrow . . .

Chapter 20

It had been a goodly number of years since Tanya had slept outdoors, but she wasn't startled when she awoke to humid river smells and grass tickling her nose. She was used to waking clearheaded and alert. Dobbs had taught her that, for he was his grouchiest in the mornings and quick to slap if an order wasn't understood and acted upon immediately.

She wondered about Dobbs now, and what had happened yesterday when he awoke in the late afternoon and she didn't come running at his first yell— or his third or fourth, which had been the case lately as her independence asserted itself more and more. Who had opened The Seraglio for him? Jeremiah? But he was only good at pouring drinks. He didn't even know how to replenish the supply.

The list grew in her mind, of the things that needed to be done at the tavern that neither Jeremiah or Aggie would know the first thing about. And they had no dancer until April's foot healed. For one or two nights they might be able to get away without entertainment, but then the word would spread and their business would drop drastically.

Panic crept up on her as she began to envision her future livelihood suffering a severe setback because she wasn't there to watch over it. The Seraglio might even be forced to close, or worse, Dobbs might make a deal with someone else. Her entire future could be ruined by this forced absence. Damn Stefan for finding her last night.

They had returned last night to where she had left her clothes, she and Stefan going on ahead, so she had time to dress before the others joined them. Stefan had decided to wait out the night there, and much to Tanya's disappointment, since she had hoped to slip away again while they were all sleeping, he had set up a watch, with each of them taking turns through the night. They had had no fire, no blankets to keep warm, and she had slept in her damp clothes, while the men had stripped down to almost nothing so they could spread their clothes out on the surrounding shrubbery to dry.

Tanya hoped they had had the decency to dress, now that it was light, but she hadn't looked yet. She had turned over onto her stomach during her sleep, so her own clothes were still damp where she had lain on them. But the men were awake. She could hear low-voiced conversations, though they had reverted to that foreign language they all knew, so she didn't bother to listen.

They were undoubtedly making plans, deciding which direction to take. She wondered if they knew the area, because she certainly didn't, not on this side of the river, nor on the other side for that matter, not this far from Natchez. But that was their problem. Hers was finding one more opportunity to part company with them, a virtual impossibility because none of them would trust her farther than they could reach.

She finally turned over and sat up, finding them gathered near the water's edge. Vasili and Serge sat on a log, Vasili trying to buff the mud from his boots with a handkerchief. Lazar squatted on the ground counting money, so one or more of them must have been carrying some when they decided to come after her. Stefan stood facing the water, possibly considering hailing some passing river craft. She could have told them that was a good way to get robbed and killed with so many unsavory types traveling the Mississippi these days, an option only for the really desperate. *She* was desperate, but they weren't, not yet anyway. But then they weren't exactly upstanding honest people themselves, were they? she thought disagreeably. So they would probably fit right in with thieves and murderers.

Her movement had drawn Serge's eyes to her, then Lazar's. When they didn't look away from her, she glanced down to make sure the waistcoat was still covering her breasts adequately. It was. Looking back, she saw Vasili staring at her now, too, and he seemed surprised, almost amazed. Well, what the hell?

"Have I grown two heads or something?" she demanded irritably.

Stefan turned at the sound of her voice, took one look at her, and uttered a curse that burned her ears.

Lazar started laughing at that point, Serge smiled, but they all still stared at her as if they were looking at something that totally defied belief.

Tanya wasn't usually so dense, but she was so used to being properly made up before she faced anyone, even Dobbs, that it didn't occur to her immediately that her camouflage was washed clean away. When she did finally recall scrubbing herself from top to bottom last night in the river, she repeated Stefan's curse, though silently. She wasn't supposed to have run into them again after she did that. And look at their damn reactions. She was rendering them speechless, for crying out loud. Well, not quite.

When Lazar had finished laughing, he said to no one in particular, "It stands to reason that she would look like this with her mother a renowned Austrian beauty and her father one of the handsomest men Cardinia has ever produced. *This* is what we expected, not the well-worn hag she painted herself. And Stefan warned us she was not as she appeared to be."

"I expected worse, not better," Vasili said.

"You merely call this better?" Serge asked, chuckling now. "They will come from all over Europe to have a look at her, once it is known she outshines even her mother. And to think I felt sorry for—"

Two throats cleared so loudly, Serge was effectively cut off. Stefan, silent so far, stepped forward stiffly to help Tanya to her feet.

"The question is," he said in a tone frigid enough to predict what was coming, "why would a whore hide a face worth her fortune?''

The fortune-producing face turned bright crimson, which infuriated Tanya even more than the insult did. She was getting sick and tired of blushing every time they dumped their contempt on her. Obviously, nothing was going to stop the insults from coming her way, so she had to stop letting them affect her. She didn't even know *why* she was reacting this way, when she had been called worse things in her life than a whore and had been too thick-skinned to even notice. She definitely needed to toughen up here if she had to pass another day with these four, or start fighting back in kind.

Right then fighting back appealed to her, so even though it had been a rhetorical question, at least not asked of her, she answered anyway, her smile deadly sweet. "I'm only one woman, Stefan. There was never enough time to handle all the customers this face attracted.''

Incredibly, color drained from his face, only to come back in such a rush she knew *he* was flushing in reaction. *Well, score one for you, missy. Fighting back is going to be easier than you thought.*

But she heard from behind him, "Jesus," and from another the warning "Think before you do anything, Stefan.''

And they couldn't even see that he had turned livid, since he was still facing her. They *expected* anger from what she'd said. Why? What difference did it make if she owned up to what they all thought anyway? If she told the truth instead, Stefan would probably get just as angry. Maybe she would try that next time.

Right now she braced herself, wondering if he would pounce on her as he usually did. Not with his friends present, apparently, for he merely tilted her chin up with one finger, his golden eyes roving over every inch of her face as if he would commit it to memory.

She knew what he was seeing, or she thought she did. Actually, she hadn't had a good look at her reflection in decent light for a number of years. But even if she had, she wouldn't have seen what he was seeing. Spiky lashes framed eyes that were captivatingly tilted, and weren't pale at all without the gray around them, just light in color and quite brilliant. Petal-soft skin was a roses-and-cream hue, and gently flaring brows were as black as her midnight hair. He saw the aristocrat in her high cheekbones, and passion in her lush mouth, with lips full and inviting. And he saw the strength, or stubbornness, in her jaw, as well as the slight curve at the tip of her small nose that kept her face from being haughty. He saw a face so lovely, even a poet couldn't do it justice with flowery description. And he disliked every inch of it.

Tanya saw that clearly in his expression, she just didn't understand it. The man had wanted her a dozen times yesterday, or so he claimed, when she had been at her most unappealing. Now he didn't? For crying out loud, she should have washed her face sooner.

When he finished his inspection, he said with deceptive nonchalance, "I see your point, Tanya. They would be lined up in droves, wouldn't they? Or do you service more than one at a time?''

Lord help her, he was going to get *really* nasty, now that he no longer wanted her for himself. Tanya didn't know whether to cry over that horrid insinuation or slap him. But she had forgotten how to cry . . .

The crack across his cheek was shatteringly loud in the stillness. Tanya had to bite her lip to keep from shaking her hand, it stung so badly. Stefan's cheek turned white, then filled with blood in the shape of her hand print, almost making his scars underneath it disappear.

Tanya felt such satisfaction on seeing that print, she didn't care if he turned around to look for a stick to beat her with, or slapped her back, as Vasili would have done the other night if Stefan hadn't stopped him.

But he did neither. He merely touched a finger to his cheek and raised a black brow, saying, ''I take that to be a no?'' She almost slapped him again. He must have sensed it, for he shook his head in warning. ''Ah, no, Tanya. Once was perhaps deserved, but twice I will not accept. Behave—''

''Then get the hell away from me, because I've had a bellyful of your vicious taunts!''

She turned her back on him, but he didn't reply. After another moment, she heard him walk away, and it was all she could do not to break into a run in the opposite direction. But there were four of them to give chase, so all she'd end up doing was wasting her strength.

Another moment passed and Lazar approached her, extreme wariness in his expression. "I hesitate to ask, Princess, but are these edible?"

She glanced down at the branch of foliage he held in his hand. Wild berries. If she weren't so hungry herself, she'd tell him no, then sit back quietly and watch them all try to throw up what they had probably already eaten. She took the branch from him instead and popped a few of the succulent berries in her mouth, a good enough answer as far as she was concerned, since she was done talking to the lot of them.

But the damn berries wouldn't go down. She had a lump in her throat that felt as big as her fist, something she hadn't experienced since she was a child. She guessed she could still cry after all.

She didn't make a single sound, but the tears started flowing copiously. Lazar blanched upon seeing them. Tanya didn't notice his reaction or that he left her side. And then an argument started behind her that got really heated for a moment, though she wasn't paying attention to that either. Maybe they'd kill each other. She could hope . . .

The arms that came around her were achingly tender, drawing her against a comforting chest. She assumed it was Lazar, but didn't look to be sure since she didn't care at that point. Sympathy broke the dam, it seemed, for she became loud then, great racking sobs echoing through the woods. Crying, for crying out loud, and when she'd been so furious just minutes before. How utterly embarrassing. And she couldn't even say why she was doing it—certainly not because that devil-eyed devil didn't like her anymore.

She was making so much noise, it was a while before she could even hear the soothing words coming her way. When she did hear them, she stiffened, pulling back. But the arms around her only tightened. She was going to be comforted whether she liked it or not, by *him*. What unmitigated gall. There wasn't anything he could say . . .

"I'm sorry, Tanya. At times I am the devil they call me. I did warn you of that, did I not? And sometimes when I am surprised—"

"You mean disappointed, don't you?" she interrupted bitterly.

"Surprised will do," he replied. "I have never dealt well with surprises."

"You have unusual reactions for a lot of things, don't you, Stefan?"

Pointing that out wasn't the wisest thing she could have done just then, when his arms were still around her. But she was in danger of being kissed only when he was angry, or sealing bargains, and that danger was undoubtedly gone now that he knew what she really looked like. She should be relieved. So why wasn't she?

He was quiet for so long, she was sure he wasn't going to reply to her remark, but he did. "You deal with my *unusual* reactions very well, do you not?"

Up came the color to her cheeks, and she had no gray pallor to hide any of it, only his wide chest for the moment. "That was a short truce," she said tiredly.

His hand ran over the back of her head, pressing her even closer to him. Comforting even while he was insulting? The man didn't do *anything* in a normal way.

"Actually, I meant no offense," he said softly near her ear. "There are women of vast experience who are still terrified of me when I . . . but an innocent girl would be even more so. You have that, at least, in your favor."

And nothing else? But he didn't say that. He wasn't *trying* to insult her, after all.

"*Some* innocents would react *just* like I do," she retorted. "But I don't suppose I will have to worry about it anymore, will I?"

He sighed. "I've made you angry again."

All Tanya noted was that he hadn't answered the question. "You can let go of me now, Stefan. The rain has stopped in case you haven't noticed."

She heard him chuckle, and he tipped her face up so she could see that he was smiling, his way of telling her that he at least was willing to forget the harsh words that had passed between them and start over—again. But he didn't know that she hated it when he smiled. He didn't know that her heartbeat sped up each time he did. She looked at those lips, felt the length of him pressed so close to her, and experienced that fluttering in her innards again. Hell and high water, how could he still do that to her after his recent nastiness?

She felt him tense just before he released her, giving her an idea that he had sensed what she was feeling and didn't like it. She turned away from him before she could see it in his expression too.

"What have you decided for our direction?" she asked in a neutral tone.

"South."

They *would* choose the opposite of the way that she wanted to go.

Chapter 21

Three hours must have passed since they started walking south, yet none of Tanya's companions had mentioned food. The change in her appearance was mentioned again and again, however, and each time she looked up, she caught at least one of them staring at her, even Stefan, as if they still couldn't believe she'd actually turned out to be pretty. Serge and Lazar seemed delighted that it was so. Vasili she couldn't read, except that he hadn't made any derogatory remarks so far this morning. And she already knew what Stefan thought, which made no sense when you figured that he could get more for a pretty exotic dancer than he could for an ugly one.

She tried not to think about being more valuable to them now, because that would make them even more vigilant of her. She thought about her hunger instead, easy enough to do with all the noise her stomach was making. And it finally occurred to her that as finely dressed and mannered as her abductors were, they might not know how to survive in the wilderness. That would be a laugh. No, it wouldn't, not when she was stuck with them.

Tanya was about ready to reveal that she knew how to hunt for food when Serge, scouting up ahead, called back that he'd found something. The something turned out to be a rather large plantation house, with all the accompanying outbuildings that made places of this size self-sufficient. This one turned out to have everything her abductors could have asked for—a hot meal already prepared, supplies to take with them, and four sturdy horses, all of which they could apparently afford to buy. There were more horses available, and the men had more money with them, but obviously she wasn't going to get a mount of her own.

She supposed that would have been too much to hope for. Nor was she left alone for a single moment, even to use the convenience, *especially* to use the convenience. Stefan escorted her to the outhouse himself. He even inspected the interior to make sure there were no other exits before allowing her those few minutes of privacy. She'd like to know how they were going to manage this when there wasn't an outhouse around. Did he think he was going to stand there and watch her? Like hell.

They didn't stay at the plantation any longer than necessary, possibly because they didn't trust Tanya around other people. She'd been warned beforehand not to cause a disturbance there, though the consequences weren't spelled out. Regardless, she wouldn't have heeded that warning if she had thought someone on the premises might have been able to help her. But the owner was an old man. His wife was an invalid Tanya didn't even get to meet. And everyone else was the couple's slave; they couldn't help her any more than they could help themselves.

When it was time to leave, Tanya didn't have to ask whom she would be riding with. With a hand on her elbow, which had been there during the entire visit, Stefan walked her right to the horse he'd chosen, a large sorrel mare, lifted her into the saddle, and mounted behind her. The position, which more or less placed her across his lap, she didn't like at all. With one of his arms supporting her back, she was comfortable enough, but she could see Stefan with no difficulty at all. It was bad enough that she was so close to him, touching him in too many places, feeling his heat—the man always felt hot to her— but looking at him as well was too disturbing by half. She could close her eyes, she supposed, or get a stiff neck looking forward. But trying both options left her with the clear impression that he was watching her, and that was just as bad.

It didn't take her long to inform him, "I want to change position, Stefan, and sit facing forward."

"Astride?"

"Yes."

"No."

She met those sherry-gold eyes and demanded, "And why not?"

He held her gaze only for a moment, and then he was looking over her head, his jaw clenched, his lips tight, for all intents and purposes ignoring her, yet he answered, "Your skirt won't allow it."

Her skirt was kind of narrow in comparison to one designed to accommodate innumerable petticoats, but it wasn't *that* narrow. "It would only show a little skin or none at all, since I'm wearing boots that already cover a third of my calves."

She thought that had sounded quite reasonable, but his eyes were a degree lighter in color when they dropped down to her again. "A little is too much. Kindly remember who you are, Princess, and begin acting with some decorum as befits your station, rather than as a tavern—wench."

The pause told her plain enough that "whore" had been his first choice in descriptions. For some reason that she couldn't imagine, she was annoying him enough to call forth the insults again. And if she was going to get them, she might as well deserve them.

"What was it? The word skin? Calves? I *am* a tavern wench, Stefan, and there aren't too many words that don't fit in my vocabulary. Would you like to hear a few more you might find objectionable, you son of a bitch?"

Their eyes did battle for nearly a full minute of silence, his definitely glowing now, hers shooting some green sparks of her own. And then he surprised her, conceding all.

"Sit as you like. Show as much skin as you like. You may also say whatever you like, little Tanya."

She made a face of disgust that he was giving in that easily after prodding her temper for a fight. But she still quickly rearranged her limbs before he changed his mind. And not being able to see those devil's eyes was much better for her peace of mind.

Now maybe she could start concentrating on her escape again . . .

Even as she was leaning forward to tug her skirt down as far as it would go, Stefan's arm slipped around her waist to draw her hips more firmly between his legs. Tanya wasn't alarmed, however, thinking he was merely assuring that she didn't fall off the horse. But he didn't let go when she straightened, and a moment later his forearm moved up until his hand flattened over her right breast with enough pressure to bring her entire back into tight contact with his chest.

The gasp no sooner left her lips than she heard his voice at her ear, continuing as if there had been no pause after his concessions. "But you will discover, if you haven't by now, wench, that the way a woman behaves is the way she will likely be treated."

Tanya's eyes flared wide with the realization that he was merely giving her a lesson, albeit an outrageous one, and not taking liberties because he had any desire to touch her. That was so humiliating, her eyes closed against the thought, but flew open again because the lesson wasn't over. His fingers curved around her breast, squeezing gently as his hand undulated, and although he probably didn't expect or want her to feel anything but shamed by this lesson, that particular caress aroused her anyway.

She pried his fingers off her, thankful that he let her, and pushed his hand aside. "I got your point," she said bitterly.

"I don't think so."

And his hand came back, traveled up to caress her

throat, then down, over both breasts, across her stomach, down one leg. Her skirt was stretched so tautly over her thighs, she shouldn't have felt more than the slightest touch of his hand there, but his fingers managed to curve around her leg anyway, making her feel as if the skirt weren't even there—and started back up slowly.

She caught his hand and pulled it off her again, but back it came to her breast. And this time she couldn't pry it loose.

"I'll scream," she promised.

"That will merely gain you an avid audience."

She had completely forgotten they weren't alone out here. As it was, they had probably already gained notice from one or more of the others. And his hand squeezed again.

"All right, damn you, I'll sit the way you want me to!"

"A wise decision, Princess."

But he didn't remove his hand from her breast until she had completely turned around and was settled back in his lap once more. She glared up at him then, frustrated beyond endurance that there was no way she could have won that little battle.

"Have I called you a devil's spawn, Stefan?"

"Yes."

"What about bastard?"

"That too."

"You know I despise you."

"That was inevitable."

She said no more and stared off to the side of the road they were now traveling on, refusing to look at him again. But his last remark lingered in her mind, bothering her repeatedly throughout the long afternoon. Was it inevitable? She wasn't so sure. But why did he think so?

Chapter 22

It was almost dark before Stefan directed them off the plantation road to find a suitable spot to make camp that night. Not so far back they had passed another plantation at which they could probably have spent the night, but since no one suggested they even try, Tanya could only conclude she was the reason they were going to rough it instead. They simply didn't trust her when other people were around. Actually, they didn't trust her, period, as she found when she asked if she could have a few moments alone in the bushes.

One of the things they had purchased along with the provisions was a long rope, likely Stefan's idea, since he was the one who tied it to her wrist and kept hold of the other end before he was willing to let her out of his sight. But she had to talk, sing, or hum continuously, he didn't care which, as long as he could hear her. That was taking precautions a bit far as far as she was concerned, but she did as he had instructed, well aware that he would come charging into the shrubs after her if she didn't.

She chose merely to count numbers aloud, and was back before she had reached fifty. She didn't even consider cutting the rope from her wrist while she had the chance, not when they were all up and alert. But she *was* going to escape tonight, somehow, and preferably with one of the horses if she could manage it. She just hadn't yet figured out how, and was shying away from the obvious conclusion that she would have to seriously hurt whoever had the watch when she was ready to go. Serge and Lazar? She couldn't hurt them, for they seemed to be merely following the orders of the two cousins. Vasili? Without a qualm. Stefan? She just wasn't sure.

Blankets had been spread out on the ground when she returned from the bushes and presented her wrist to Stefan so he could untie the rope. Serge was just lighting a fire, and Lazar was taking out the extra cooked meal they had brought along—a ham, sweet potatoes, and several loaves of sweet-smelling bread. They had bought enough provisions to last a week, along with a few cooking utensils and several rifles to supply fresh game. But from what she had heard in the general conversation that went on around her during the day, none of them knew how to cook. She wondered how much fuss she ought to put up before she agreed to do the task for them. None. She wasn't going to be there for another meal if she could help it.

They were settling down on their blankets around the fire, hers too damn close to Stefan's, in her opinion, when he asked her to dance for them. Tanya was so surprised by the request, she didn't answer for a moment. The man had been rotten to her all day, from his nasty insinuations that morning to his diabolical lessons in the afternoon. And whatever had attracted him to her before was gone now, so she couldn't figure out why he would want to watch her dance. Unless this was another attempt to humiliate her somehow. If she agreed, would he suggest she remove her clothes first?

It made her angry that that might be his motive, angry enough to reply, "For all of you, no. For your king—if he insists."

She said it merely to get back at Stefan, and because she was positive Vasili wouldn't ask it of her, not even to relieve boredom. That would, after all, be admitting that he had liked her dance, and Vasili wouldn't do that when he despised everything about her.

But she wasn't sure her answer had had the desired effect on Stefan. His expression didn't change. And his voice was no more than moderately dry when he spoke.

"Our king is too exhausted to appreciate it, is that not so, your Majesty?"

Vasili took one look at Stefan and said, "If I wasn't, I am now," and turned over to sleep.

Tanya heard a chuckle from Lazar on the other side of the fire, but he, too, turned his back on them. Serge, on her left, did likewise. That they were all three already going to sleep told her that Stefan had the first watch. And when she glanced back at him, it was to find him still reclined on his blanket, resting on one elbow and watching her.

"Will you reconsider?" he asked as their eyes met and held, and a tension suddenly built.

Oddly enough, Tanya became flustered, thinking about dancing just for him. Could she make him want her again if she did? Did she *want* him to want her again?

The drift of her thoughts was annoying under the circumstances. But she couldn't deny it. He might not find her desirable any longer, but she couldn't say the same. Unfortunately, she still found him *very* attractive, and right now even more so, lying there with his jacket and waistcoat removed, his cravat long since discarded, a wave of black hair falling over one brow, and his sherry-gold eyes becoming more and more intense with her silence.

But recalling his question, and that she wasn't likely to ever see him again after tonight, she finally shook her head in answer. And she refused to regret it. He might be the only man who had ever stirred up her innards, but the very fact that he could do that made him more dangerous to her than any other man. Because a man didn't fit into her future plans, no man did, and this one in particular, with his lies, his arrogance—his utter contempt for her. She had to be a little bit crazy even to consider enticing him.

All he did was shrug in response to her second refusal, but a moment later he sat up and said, "Then come here."

Her eyes narrowed on him suspiciously. She was already closer to him than she wanted to be, her blanket placed right alongside his.

"Why?"

"I will prepare you for sleep." He was drawing the rope across his lap as he said this, adding, "I regret the necessity, Tanya, but there is no reason for any of us to lose sleep now that we have this."

"This" was the rope. When she realized that he meant to tie her up with it, she almost laughed. Thank God she hadn't offered to hunt for food that morning, for she would have had to reveal her hidden knife to do so. That knife was now going to get her out of this mess with no trouble at all, because they would *all* be sound asleep, thinking her secure for the night.

She crawled closer to him, slowly, so as to appear reluctant about it. "Is this really necessary?"

"Absolutely," he assured her. "Unless you would like to sleep under me?"

That he could say something like that now was infuriating, especially since he didn't mean it, and was no doubt being sarcastic, but hearing it still set her pulses racing.

She just managed to keep from screeching at him to go to hell, and instead purred, "Oh, I don't know. I'm used to being weighted down, but you might not find it a very comfortable sleeping arrangement."

That apparently struck a sore nerve, for his lips tightened, his jaw clenched, and his eyes were definitely starting to glow. Interesting. Why would references to her familiarity with men still bother him? Damn, his attitude made no sense. It never did. Even when he had wanted her, he hadn't liked thinking she was a whore—except for that first night. It hadn't bothered him when he was willing to pay for her services, had it? In fact, that night he'd seemed glad enough that she was supposedly a whore.

She ought to prove the matter to his satisfaction before she left them. That would set him back on his ear, wouldn't it, in showing him how wrong they were about her. It would give her something to gloat about— *Where* did these thoughts keep coming from? The last thing she needed was to come away from this experience with knowledge of fornicating. It was bad enough that she'd found out how nice kissing could be.

She thrust out one hand to him, but he didn't take it, merely waited, so she reluctantly gave him the other. He made quick work of wrapping the rope around her wrists several times before he began tying knots that even he wouldn't be able to untie in the morning. That done, he proceeded to wrap the other end of the rope around his waist half a dozen times.

Tanya hadn't expected that, but all was not lost. There was about a foot of rope left between her hands and his chest, more than enough to enable her to raise her knees and reach her boot without touching him. But being tied to Stefan's waist left her facing him, and he her, and if he should happen to turn over once he was asleep, he'd pull her hands with him. Well, she'd just have to pull him back in that case—or be gone before it happened.

She lay down now since Stefan did, and instantly discovered the disadvantages to this arrangement. It wasn't very comfortable lying on her side without the support of at least one arm for her head. And if she had actually wanted to go to sleep, she would have found it next to impossible with Stefan so close, watching her. And he was watching her. His eyes were no longer glowing. They were shadowed now that the firelight wasn't shining directly on him. She could still make out his features clearly, but, unfortunately, nothing of his thoughts or his mood. Yet she had the feeling he wanted to say something, or was waiting for her to say something. Theirs was an intimate arrangement, after all, cozy even, almost private, and obviously neither of them was the least bit sleepy yet.

She tested her conclusion, asking, ''When are you going to own up to the real reason I'm here?''

''When are you going to accept that you are a royal princess?''

Stalemate. ''Good night, Stefan.''

''Would you like to know some of your family's history?'' he inquired softly.

She closed her eyes against the temptation to believe that he might really know something of her true family. But of course he didn't. Anything he told her would be a creation for his own benefit.

''Don't bother,'' she said with just a tinge of bitterness, adding, ''Iris used to make up stories for me when she put me to bed, but Dobbs made her stop when he found out about it. He didn't want me growing up soft and fanciful.''

''So you grew up hard and . . . ?''

''Pragmatic.''

''I would have said skeptical.''

''That too.''

''And distrustful?''

"I never thought about it, but I guess so," she said. "What about you?"

"Arrogant," he said without the slightest hesitancy.

She looked at him now and smiled. "You admit it?"

"I am well aware of my faults, little Tanya."

"Do you have so many, then?"

"Wouldn't you say so?"

"Oh, I don't know. I suppose . . . but I think I'm getting used to some of them. Your temper, for instance."

Now, why had she said that? Mentioning his temper could only make them both think of making love. And his hands weren't tied. She was within his reach. God, what a stimulating thought.

"Good night, Tanya."

The curtness in his voice told her plain enough he didn't like the reminder. Tanya closed her eyes again and sighed inwardly.

Good-bye, Stefan.

Chapter 23

Tanya couldn't ride straight for Natchez, as much as she wanted to. Her horse-riding skills weren't good enough to ensure that she could stay well ahead of any pursuit on a direct route. As it was, she'd been unseated nearly a half-dozen times in the first two days she'd spent getting acquainted with the horse she had appropriated for her use. So her roundabout journey home took five days in all. And if she weren't so worried about The Seraglio and how Dobbs was managing without her, she still wouldn't venture into town. But she'd been gone a total of seven days, and she couldn't begin to imagine what kind of shambles the tavern would be in. She had to get back.

Nonetheless, she was plainly and simply afraid Stefan would be there waiting for her. Of course, logic told her they wouldn't come all the way back to Natchez for her. And even if they did, would they wait when they didn't find her there? All she could do was hope not, and take as many precautions as she could.

Waiting on the outskirts of town until the wee hours of the morning was the worst, but she couldn't risk entering The Seraglio while it was open for business—if it was still open. If Stefan had followed her, then that would be where he would await her. But even if he wasn't there, she was without her disguise, so she had to wait anyway.

She had bartered the horse to get across the river, instead of Stefan's waistcoat. The ferryman had just loved that trade, but she had no further use for the animal anyway and was delighted to get rid of it. Dobbs would probably have a fit when he heard about it. Horses weren't cheap.

When Tanya deemed the hour was late enough, she made her way stealthily into town, keeping off the main streets as much as possible. The tavern was quiet when she reached it, the doors closed, no lights burning, but she had no way of knowing if it had opened today or not. Next door, the brothel was still entertaining customers. So was the gambling house across the road. But neither establishment was making enough noise to allow her to break into the tavern if the doors were locked. And both were.

Tired and hungry at this late hour, Tanya didn't relish her options. She could either climb to the porch roof and hope one of the upstairs windows was open, or wait until tomorrow for the tavern to be opened— if it would be—and risk what she had tried to avoid tonight.

She climbed the porch roof. It took all of ten minutes and one near fall, but she made it. And to her utter relief, Dobbs' window was open and easy to enter. Inside the room, however, it was pitch-black, the moonless night that had aided her through town now hindering her.

She found the bed by bumping into it. "Dobbs, wake up. Dobbs!" she whispered urgently, shaking the mattress. He didn't make a sound, not a snore, not a grumble at being disturbed. "Dobbs?"

"You won't find him there, Princess."

"No," she groaned as a match flared to life and she swung around to see Stefan sitting in a chair by the door. All she could think to ask at the moment was, "Why are you still here?"

"Still? Ah, of course. We *have* been waiting nearly three days for you. Did you think we wouldn't?"

"I had hoped!" she exploded and dashed for the window.

She didn't waste time climbing through it, she dived. Her knee hit the sill, her shoulder hit the roof, and her boot snagged on something. She was still cringing with the pain from her landing when the "snag" began to pull her backward. She immediately flipped over to kick at Stefan's hand, but got her other foot caught for the effort.

With dread, she heard him say, "Give me your hand or I'll pull you in by your legs, and at the moment I don't care how badly you get scraped in the process."

She didn't doubt that he meant it, but she tried kicking loose from his hold once more. That effort started him pulling.

"Wait! Here." She pushed herself to a sitting position to offer her hand. For a moment she didn't think he was going to take it. But he did, and she was hauled in so quickly, she had no chance to try anything else, even if she thought to.

The room was dark again, Stefan's light having been extinguished when he bolted after her. He let go of her now to light another. She wished he hadn't. He looked angry enough to wring her neck.

But his voice was merely mild when he informed her, "You are caught, Tanya. Accept it."

"I can't," she cried feelingly.

"You will."

Those two words seemed to hold more than a warning, as if he knew something she didn't. And he sounded so confident, triumphant even.

She turned away from the glow in his eyes. He moved to light the lamp by the bed. She stared at Dobbs' bed—without Dobbs in it.

"My God," she gasped suddenly. "Has Dobbs died?"

"Not that I know of."

She turned back to him, infuriated by his offhand tone. "Then where is he? What have you done with him?"

"I haven't done anything to him."

"Stefan!"

"First I'll have your knife, Tanya, the one that cuts so easily through thick rope." When all she did was stare at him, he started toward her. "You can hand it over, or I can strip you down to find it for myself."

"You aren't undressing me, damn you!" she told him as she bent to retrieve her knife.

"Whatever is necessary, Princess, will be done. Don't deceive yourself by thinking otherwise, because you are *not* going to slip through our fingers again."

She would. She had to. And that resolve made her stare at the knife in her hand.

"You might want to recall the last time you tried it," he said, guessing her thoughts. "You won't have any better luck this time." She met his eyes without answering, so he added, "You're determined to provoke my temper, aren't you?"

"Does that mean I'm in danger of being tossed on the bed?" she goaded sarcastically.

"It means you're in danger of ending up over my knee again."

"Like hell!" She slapped the knife down in his open palm.

"Is that the last of them?"

"Yes." But he was staring so hard at her, she shouted it again. "Yes!"

When he continued to stare, she knew he was debating whether he ought to search her anyway. And she couldn't blame him for doubting her. That he finally nodded his acceptance clearly showed how he felt about her now. He didn't *want* to search her. Last week he would have jumped on an excuse to do so.

Well, to hell with him. She was glad he didn't want her anymore. She had enough to contend with without letting his or her lust get in the way. She turned and headed for the door.

He sighed, then said, "Don't make me chase you again, Tanya."

She stopped, infuriated that he sounded so damn patient. Was he never going to lose his temper with her again? she wondered.

"I'm just going across the hall to bathe and change my clothes. Then I'm going to get something to eat— or were you planning on leaving town tonight?"

"You may clean up at the hotel. We have rooms there—"

"I prefer my own room, thank you," she said crossly, then swung around to give him a frosty smile. "But there's no reason for you to wait for me. You can come by to fetch me in the morning."

"Enough!"

"Oh, my." She widened her eyes with feigned innocence. "I haven't made you angry, have I? No, of course not. I'm still standing."

He really didn't like being reminded of what had passed between them as a result of his temper. Her taunts had made his eyes glow again, but he was exhibiting remarkable control. He didn't even take a step toward her.

His voice, however, cut like steel through her rancor. "It was Sandor's death wish that you be found and brought home to assume your rightful place on the throne. All of these delays you have caused could mean that he will die before we return. If that is the case, Tanya, then you can be assured that you will experience my full wrath . . . and my pain."

She wished he hadn't put it quite that way. "Who is Sandor?"

"Our beloved king these last twenty years."

"But you said Vasili—"

"Because of Sandor's ill health, he abdicated in favor of his only son just before we set out to find you."

More fairy tales again. Did he continue them to provoke *her* temper?

"Why don't you save that for someone a little more gullible than I am? I'm going to take my bath *now,* Stefan. Wait if you must."

She turned again, only to be stopped again. "You cannot make free with this place any longer, Tanya."

"Like hell I can't. This is my home, and before long it will belong to me outright."

"I don't think so."

She was beginning to really hate that particular phrase of his. "Look, Stefan, I've been pretty even-tempered, considering what you've put me through. No screaming, very little crying, no fainting. I didn't even go berserk when I found you here again. And do you know I could have cut all of your throats the other night while you were sleeping? But I didn't, did I? Because I hoped—stupidly, I now realize—that you would have sense enough to give up on a lost cause. So you go ahead and take me wherever it is you're taking me. But once you're out of it, I'll come back here. There isn't *anything* that will keep me from coming back here."

"Madam Bertha—I believe that is your neighbor's name?—would probably welcome you with open arms, but I don't intend to give her the opportunity."

Tanya frowned. "What is that supposed to mean?"

"It means that you will not be allowed to return to this country again. It also means that I bought this tavern from Mr. Dobbs for enough money to keep him in the lap of luxury until his demise. And rather than burn it down, and possibly the town with it, which was my first inclination, I then sold it to the brothel next door—at a considerable loss."

"You're lying! You couldn't have had that kind of money with you! Nor would you go to such extremes!"

"*Any* extremes, Tanya. *Anything* deemed necessary to fulfill Sandor's last wish," he said in a hard tone, only to add matter-of-factly, "Our letter of credit was water-stained, but still legible and more than sufficient to meet Mr. Dobbs' exorbitant price. But if you still doubt me, then I will take you next door this minute so that you may ask Madam Bertha exactly who owns this property now."

Lord help her, she believed him. He was too blasé about it, too ready to offer proof. The effect on her was awful. Pain pressed at her chest. Her face drained of color. And if she hadn't gone berserk before, she did now.

She didn't know how she reached him, but her hands began to hurt, drawing her to an awareness that she was pounding on his chest with both fists, and he was letting her, making no move to stop her, letting her shriek at him and call him every foul name imaginable. And then his arms wrapped around her and he was holding her while she cried her heart out.

"It isn't as bad as all that, Tanya."

"You don't know what you've done!"

"I've made it possible for you to walk away from this life without any regrets."

She stiffened. His arms tightened. She pushed away from him anyway, and the look she gave him, awash with tears, was incredulous.

"You destroy the life I had planned for myself and I'm not supposed to regret it? For as long as I can remember, I have worked like a slave in this tavern, and not once, ever, was I paid for it other than with food, a bed, and a slap every time I turned around. Even my clothes were Iris' and Dobbs' cast-offs. But finally, and only because that old bastard couldn't care for himself anymore, I was going to be compensated. And you take that away from me on an arbitrary whim?"

"Not arbitrary. Your continuous attempts to return here left us with only two options. To eliminate your reasons for coming back here, or to see you married immediately to settle the matter."

"What happened? Wouldn't that jackassed peacock you call a king volunteer to marry me sooner than he had to?" she sneered, telling him how little she believed him. "Not that it would settle *any* matter, because I'd take a leaf from that tale you told the captain of *The Lorilie* and leave him in a minute."

"I see," he said tightly.

"No, you don't. You'll never comprehend what you've stolen from me, my dreams, the one thing I wanted more than anything—control of my own life. Only rich widows achieve the kind of independence I craved, but I'm not willing to marry first to become a widow. I could have had it without that—"

She broke off, overwhelmed again by her loss—and the need to strike out at the cause. She gave in to the need.

He caught her fists this time. "Enough!"

"Never!" she cried. "I can never hurt you enough for what you've done. And as soon as I get my hands on a gun, I'm going to shoot you, you son of a bitch!"

To her utter fury, he smiled at that. "You will have to remain with us, won't you, to await that opportunity?" And he picked her up and carried her out of The Seraglio for the last time.

She fought all the way.

Chapter 24

Tanya's second riverboat ride wasn't as pleasant as her first would have been. The cabin wasn't as large or as nice, nor was she allowed out of it. And whether she would have been forced to share that other cabin with Stefan on *The Lorilie,* she didn't know and didn't ask. But that she had to share this one with him was of little concern to her.

She slept in the bed. He slept on a pallet on the floor. She wouldn't talk to him, wouldn't answer him, wouldn't even look at him. She totally ignored him as if he were merely another object in the room. The amazing thing was that he let her.

For the most part she had the cabin to herself, and without participating in any conversation when it was offered, she had little else to do but think. Of course, it wasn't hard to conclude that she had once again been far off the mark in her estimation of what was happening to her. Too much money had been spent, in the purchase of horses, in the purchase of tickets on two riverboats—in the purchase of a tavern. God, she still couldn't believe they had done that, and not even to make a profit, because they had turned around and sold the tavern at a loss.

Their action defied reason. It said money was of no account to them. It said they did it just for her benefit, as Stefan had claimed, to eliminate what kept drawing her back to Natchez. And she couldn't even hold out the hope that he might have been lying about it, because she had made so much noise that night when he carried her out of the tavern that Bertha and one of her girls had come out on their porch to investigate. And Tanya couldn't resist asking the damning question.

Actually, she'd screamed it. "Did you buy The Seraglio from this devil?"

"Sure did, honey," Bertha had shouted back, not even recognizing Tanya without her camouflage, and no more than amused by her struggles. "I'm gonna fill it with bedrooms. Care to occupy one of them?"

The madam had laughed and gone back inside. Tanya had stopped struggling to get out of Stefan's arms. She hadn't spoken a word to him since.

But she knew now how wrong she'd been in trying to second-guess Stefan and his friends. More money had been spent than could ever be regained by selling her to a brothel, so she was forced to let go of that idea as their motive. Yet their story of kings and lost princesses was still too fantastical for her to accept. The trouble was, now she couldn't think of a single other plausible reason for her abduction, unless . . . Maybe her family *was* alive and had sent these men to find her. Maybe they had been warned not to tell her about it for some reason. Maybe . . . maybe she ought to stop driving herself crazy worrying about it.

After all, there were a number of other things to worry about, like what she was going to do with the rest of her life, now that her one chance at independence had been sold out from under her. She would have to find work. She would actually get paid for it, at long last, but she would be following orders again, forced to please, to do things the way someone else wanted them done, not the way she did. She'd been so close to never having to answer to anyone again . . . damn Stefan to hell.

Her rage over what they'd done wouldn't go away. And it centered solely on Stefan, even though buying the tavern might have been a collective decision for all she knew. Revenge crossed her mind, but getting even was a new concept to her. She was so used to taking everything dealt her, with no recourse, that she wouldn't even know how to go about retaliating in kind, hurt for hurt. She had promised to shoot Stefan, but of course she hadn't meant that.

She thought about delaying the men some more. Time did seem to be important to them, even though she doubted the reasons given her. She also considered causing dissension among them, though she wasn't sure how that would work when she had yet to see them angry with each other—only with her.

But she couldn't do anything as long as she was locked away with only Stefan. He wouldn't even rise to the bait of her indifference. Not that she wanted him to; fighting with him never gained her anything but frustration.

"If you will change into one of the dresses we acquired for you, you may join us in the saloon for dinner tonight."

Tanya had been pacing and hadn't heard Stefan enter. She stopped now, but she didn't turn toward him. She hadn't even looked at the two dresses he had given her that night in the hotel. She had told him once that she wouldn't accept clothes from them, and she had meant it. She had been washing her own clothes, one item a day so she wouldn't have to strip down completely.

"I will need an answer this time, Princess, or I will assume that you prefer to eat alone again."

She wouldn't prefer that at all. She hadn't even seen the others since they had left Natchez for the second time. And she couldn't very well cause any trouble among them, if that was even possible, when she was kept isolated.

"All right," she said tonelessly, still without looking at him.

"And you will change?"

She glanced at the small trunk that contained the two dresses as well as a number of new items that Stefan had bought for himself in Natchez.

"Why must I?" she asked.

"Because we do not care to be embarrassed again by your mannish attire."

Tanya stiffened. Was he actually back to insulting her? Or was that the kindest way he could express the fact that she looked ridiculous in his waistcoat and shirt? That shouldn't bother her, since she had never in her life dressed to look attractive, but it did coming from Stefan.

"Show me a man wearing a skirt before you call my clothes mannish," she said merely to be disagreeable. "Never mind. I'll wear one of your dresses, but I hope to hell it doesn't fit."

"That is a possibility, in which case you may use your discretion to choose whichever is the least inappropriate."

So this order wasn't set in steel? Then, remembering that Stefan didn't like her to look pretty, she hoped she ended up looking downright beautiful. But that wasn't very likely, considering she hadn't been fitted for either dress, and men weren't very knowledgeable about such things as sizing.

"How much time do I have?"

"Thirty minutes."

"I will need some hair bobs."

"You will have to do without."

"You expect miracles?"

"Just something halfway presentable."

She detected amusement in his answer, but wouldn't look at him to be sure. "Then leave me to it."

"Will you require help with buttons and such?"

"Not from you. But you can send Vasili to escort me. If I do need help, as my betrothed, he can provide it."

The slamming of the door was her answer to that. Tanya smiled for the first time in days. She had forgotten how easy it was to provoke Stefan. She wouldn't forget again.

Chapter 25

It was Vasili who showed up to escort her to dinner.
But Tanya had made sure she wouldn't need any help
with her dress, nearly straining her shoulder muscles
twisting about to do up the buttons herself. They
could have chosen dresses easier to get in and out
of, but she wasn't going to complain. She was too
amazed by her appearance to do other than smirk
when Vasili looked her over with some amazement
of his own.

The two dresses she had to choose from were the
same size, one a beige plaid, the other a bright lemon
satinet with bishop sleeves and matching shoes. The
shoes were a bit small, but both dresses fit her better
than she could have hoped, except for one small
area—right across her breasts. Obviously the dresses
had been bought already made, and for a woman of
smaller proportions than she.

The necklines of the dresses were in the favored
boat shape, which exposed shoulders, neck, and a
great deal of upper chest, sloping to a point just over

the breasts. In this case, the point was rather deep on both dresses. A chemisette could have added some becoming lace to the area, but Stefan had said he would forget to include underclothing when he bought her clothes, and whether he actually forgot or intentionally forgot, there was none included with the dresses.

Under normal circumstances, Tanya would have been so self-conscious, she wouldn't have worn either dress. She'd always hidden her breasts under high-necked shirts in thick materials, so they were nearly invisible. Here she was exposing all, so to speak, or at least the upper curves of her breasts, made worse since they were squeezed together because of the tightness of the material in that area. But these weren't normal circumstances. In fact, her first look at herself in the large mirror above the dressing table in the cabin made her think of only one thing. Stefan would see her like this and wouldn't like it at all. And that made her determined to wear the dresses exactly as they were.

She settled on the bright lemon yellow for tonight, simply because its color was so opposite her usual dull ones and went well with her dark hair. Even her dancing costume wasn't as flattering to her figure. And this without benefit of a corset. Tanya was pleased, more than pleased. She'd never known that she could look like this.

There wasn't much she could do with her hair, however, other than tie it back. But she did remove the wide, lace-trimmed ornamental bow at the back of the dress to tie it at her nape instead. She could, of course, have tucked that strip of yellow into her deep décolletage to make the dress a bit more demure. But with Stefan's reaction uppermost in her mind, she didn't even consider it.

She had a few second thoughts about it, however, when Vasili stared overlong at her chest. But the rest of her also underwent a thorough inspection, so she let it pass.

"You look lovely, Princess."

Her brows shot up. "A compliment from you? Are you feeling well, Vasili?"

He laughed and remarked, "You are amusing if nothing else. Now, don't stiffen up on me when I have gone to so much trouble on your behalf." He held out his hand, which contained about a dozen hairpins in several different styles, then confided, "Two women on board now assume I am interested in them, although I regret that I am not. You can't imagine the difficulty that might entail tonight."

"I wonder why I can't dredge up any sympathy for you," Tanya replied.

He grinned boyishly, and for a moment she saw why women found him so irresistible. "I believe I have missed your wit, Princess. It was too bad of Stefan to keep you to himself the whole of this voyage."

"Did he send you for these?" She took the pins from his hand.

"He suggested that if we didn't want you looking like a trollop, one of us should make the effort. Naturally, I was elected."

How casually he tossed out that secondhand insult.

She ignored it on the surface, but deep down she was stung. She wondered how many other disparaging remarks were made about her when she wasn't around to hear them. Since she heard too many when she was around, she could only imagine that these men never said anything nice about her. Well, she hardly had anything nice to say about them either.

She reached for the bow at her nape. "If you will wait a few—"

"Leave it," he broke in and, at her inquiring look, added, "It is quite fetching as is."

"But after all the trouble you went through to borrow these."

He shrugged. "You can use them tomorrow for our arrival in New Orleans."

Tomorrow? Was that why she was being allowed out of the cabin tonight? Stefan had no doubt decided it was safe enough to let her be around other people since she wasn't likely to see any of them a second time. How much trouble could she cause in so little time, after all? She hoped she could find an opportunity to show them the error of that assumption. Trollop? She might not look like one now, but how hard would it be to act like one?

"Then shall we go?"

This riverboat was smaller than *The Lorilie,* though it had two decks as well. The dining saloon was on the lower deck, next to a large room devoted strictly to gambling. Passing that room, Tanya realized this was one of the boats referred to as a floating gambling palace. Professional gamblers made their homes on such boats. So did women of ill repute. For a moment she wondered if that wasn't the reason she had been kept isolated, but she dismissed the notion as being too unlikely, particularly when her traveling companions, one and all, thought her reputation couldn't be any worse.

Lazar and Serge were waiting at a table for them. Both stood as she approached. Both bowed slightly as Vasili seated her. Their deference made her uncomfortable, until it occurred to her that it was no more than an act to reinforce the fairy tale. Why they still bothered . . .

"Is Stefan still at it?" Vasili questioned before he sat down.

"You need to ask, when he has rarely left that table since we boarded?" Lazar replied.

"Why don't you go and remind him that food is a necessity?" Serge suggested. "He won't listen to us."

"Then I suppose I had better."

Lazar turned to Tanya when Vasili left. "Stefan has been doing a little gambling," he explained.

She had already gathered as much and asked with little interest, "Is he winning?"

"Actually, he's lost quite a bit."

She wondered how much "quite a bit" was to them, not that she cared. She couldn't wish penury on a more deserving group of men.

"Usually you learn how to play the game before you try your hand at it," was all she remarked.

"Stefan knows how to play well enough. In fact, he is quite skillful at it."

The way Lazar was looking at her couldn't have

said more clearly that she was somehow at fault, and that incensed her. "Now that takes nerve, to blame me for his bad luck when I wasn't even there."

The rebuke didn't phase him. "Your despondency *has* bothered him. I don't understand it either. You grieve for a hovel when you will live in palaces."

Tanya sighed inwardly. Obviously, they must believe that perseverance was going to make her accept their story eventually. She was definitely tired of telling them that it just wouldn't work.

"I wasn't despondent, Lazar, I was furious," she pointed out. "You would be, too, if someone showed up and tried changing your life around."

"Not if it was a change for the better," he insisted. "You had to be made to see that your life there was over. And you will be happy in Cardinia, Tanya. You will have wealth, power—"

"A husband?"

"Every woman wants to marry."

"Imagine that! Every single one? And here I always thought I was a woman."

Her exaggerated sarcasm had him flinching. "You really don't want to marry?"

"No."

"Not even Vasili?"

"*Especially* not Vasili."

Two hands settled on her bare shoulders, and warm breath stirred the hair by her ear. "Careful, Tatiana, or I will begin to believe that and be so wounded, I will have to exert some charm to change your mind."

Vasili, not Stefan, the voice told her. Her heart slowed its beat.

Before she could think of a reply to that outlandish promise, however, Lazar asked Vasili, "You couldn't drag him away?"

"He said he would join us later—perhaps."

Tanya's shoulders slumped. Stefan wouldn't join them. She knew it as sure as she was sitting there. He had ordered her to look presentable, but he had had no intention of seeing for himself if she complied. How dared he take away even the pleasure she had felt in the way she looked tonight? She wouldn't let him do that, too, on top of everything else.

"If Stefan doesn't join us later," she said boldly now, "then we must join him."

The suggestion was met with total silence until Lazar finally blurted out, "That won't do at all, Princess."

"I insist."

"But Stefan won't like—"

"You heard her, Lazar," Vasili cut in. "She insists. And she does outrank you."

Tanya turned to Vasili incredulously. "I do?"

"Certainly you do. Lazar is, after all, only a count."

Lazar was grinding his teeth by now. "This isn't the best time to point that out, *your Majesty*."

"Relax, my friend, and let Stefan handle the matter if he objects to it. He needs something to draw him out of his present mood, anyway."

Tanya was interested in only one thing right now. "Does that mean I outrank Stefan, too?"

"How hopeful you look." Vasili grinned. "But I must disappoint you. No matter Stefan's rank, responsibility for you is his alone until we return to Cardinia, so you must defer to him in all things. If you choose to argue . . . but you have dealt well enough with him so far, have you not? He is the one who seems to be having trouble dealing with you.''

Tanya hid her disappointment well. She should have known they wouldn't go *that* far to enhance their tale.

''You think so?'' she said in a neutral tone. ''I hadn't noticed.'' But oh, how she wished it were true, because any difficulty whatsoever that she could cause Stefan would delight her no end.

Chapter 26

They came in behind Stefan and stood at his back, so he was unaware that they were there. That suited Tanya. She was in no hurry to confront him now that she was in the same room with him. And the anticipation was pleasant, all the more so because both Lazar and Serge were sure that Stefan was going to be quite annoyed at her being there.

They were so certain, they had refused to come along, so only Vasili stood beside her as her escort. Without his intervention, she would have been taken right back to her cabin after dinner. She grudgingly acknowledged she had him to thank, though she hated being grateful to him for anything, even a means for some sort of revenge.

Merely annoying Stefan wasn't enough, though she hadn't figured out yet what else she could do. But an idea came to her when she noticed that the gambler sitting directly across from Stefan was paying more attention to her than he was to the cards in his hand.

He was a big man, very wide across the chest, and from what she could tell, none of his bulk was fat. He wasn't bad-looking either, probably a few years older than Stefan, with dark brown hair and darker brown eyes. Like one other gentleman at the table, he had removed his coat and rolled up his shirt-sleeves—possibly so no one could accuse him of cheating. At any rate, he had appeared to be taking the game in progress very seriously—until now.

There was a lot of money on the table, a very great amount, most of it before the brown-haired gambler. The other two players had modest piles in front of them. Stefan was throwing in his last two bills to call the present hand. The play went around, cards were drawn. The big gambler actually had to be reminded that it was his turn to bet, because his eyes were again on Tanya instead of his cards.

"Are you in or out, Mr. Barany?"

Tanya started when she realized the question was asked of Stefan by the man on his right. She had never heard his last name before, never even thought to ask what it was. Come to think of it, Lazar was the only one among them who had introduced himself fully to her. Perhaps there was a Thomas or a Johnson among them who would shoot down their story of being foreign nobles. Stefan reached inside his coat to draw out more money. More? The man didn't know when to quit, but she'd already learned that about him the hard way. Only this had to do with money—and losing it. Didn't he care? A glance at Vasili told her he wasn't the least bit worried. Of course, that man probably didn't know *how* to look worried, or anything else, other than bored or contemptuous.

She watched Stefan throw in more money to call the second bet. The man to his left dropped out. The big one turned his cards faceup on the table, revealing three fives. His eyes came back to Tanya yet again while he waited to hear if anyone could beat his hand.

It took a lot of nerve, but Tanya finally smiled at him, not timidly or coyly either. After all, she'd watched the tavern girls for years, knew their subtle signals and the way they moved their bodies when they were interested in a man and wanted him to know it. She wasn't sure if she was doing it right, however, but guessed she was when the man smiled back at her, a big, beautiful smile that made him look downright boyish and definitely interested.

But not to overdo it, she lowered her eyes—and just happened to see Stefan's three kings before he laid them facedown on the table, which declared without saying so that he couldn't beat the three fives. It didn't make sense. She didn't know all the intricacies of the game, but she did know three kings beat three fives. Didn't Stefan know he had the winning hand? She felt compelled to tell him. She held her tongue. Helping him wasn't in her plan.

Her eyes were drawn back to the big gambler as he stood up to rake in the winning pot. He was grinning, and looking straight at Tanya as he said, "You'll have to excuse me, gentlemen, but I feel compelled to sit out a few hands."

"It ain't wise to tamper with a winning streak, Corbell," the man to his right complained.

"Don't I know it." Corbell laughed. "But I'm merely going to direct that streak into other channels for a while."

The complainer followed the direction of his gaze and laughed, too. Stefan finally seemed to notice this interplay. Tanya tensed, expecting him to turn now. He didn't. He stood up and stepped into the path of Corbell, who was bigger than Tanya had guessed, a half foot taller than Stefan and much, much broader.

"I'm afraid you have made a mistake, Mr. Corbell," Stefan stated calmly. "She isn't available."

Tanya gasped. Stefan hadn't even *looked* at her, yet he knew she stood behind him, and knew what Corbell had meant with his subtle play on words.

But the mountain wasn't discouraged, though why should he be? A man would have to be crazy to tangle with someone his size.

"I'd say she feels differently," Corbell replied. "So why don't you step aside?"

Stefan didn't budge. "What she feels or wants is entirely irrelevant." Then, without turning around he said, "Vasili, return her to my cabin while I endeavor to convince Mr. Corbell of his error."

"Now hold on—"

That was all Corbell got out before there was the distinct sound of knuckles meeting flesh. Tanya only heard it happen. Vasili was dragging her out of there so fast she didn't even have a chance to look behind her. And then she was shoved into the arms of Serge, who had been waiting outside the gambling room with Lazar. Words weren't even exchanged. Vasili and Lazar went back inside, while Serge gave Tanya no choice but to return to her cabin.

"How much damage have you caused this time, your Highness?"

This time? Tanya tried to stop to address that, but Serge just kept walking and pulling her along behind him.

"Just *what* makes you think I am at fault here?" she demanded of his back.

"It was obvious even to me that you wanted to go in there expressly to make trouble."

That might be so, but how did *he* know it? And if he knew it, so did the others. Nor would it take Stefan long to figure it out. Well, so what? But she no longer objected to being returned to her cabin.

She thought about going straight to bed and pretending sleep. Of course, if Stefan was angry enough, sleep wouldn't prevent him from telling her about it immediately. She paced instead, and tried to think of a way to refute the allegations he was going to throw at her. And what if he was hurt? Was she crazy? Of course he was going to be hurt. That Corbell was a veritable giant of a man. But that wasn't what she had wanted. She had merely wanted to cause Stefan some difficulty, to get a little bit even.

The door opened much sooner than she had expected. Tanya whipped around with bated breath. Stefan was merely closing and locking the door as he did each night before retiring. Even when he glanced at her, he didn't seem to be annoyed with her or anything else. But in trying to assess his reaction to the way she looked, to judge his mood and if he was hurt, she was finally seeing him again, really seeing him without the red heat of her anger clouding her vision.

Lord help her, the attraction was still there, more powerful than ever. Her pulses picked up. The tenseness she had felt now turned to something else. How unfair could you get? After everything he had done to her, he shouldn't have any effect on her now at all, certainly not this giddy swirling in her innards that she knew to be desire. She couldn't still desire him. She refused to!

"Did you enjoy yourself?"

Considering what she was experiencing, it took her a moment to realize he was referring to what had happened in the gambling room. She tensed now, suspicious of his casual tone.

"Are you hurt?"

He shrugged as he dropped his coat on the clothes trunk. "A few bruises. Nothing to be concerned about."

"I wasn't concerned. I was merely wondering why you didn't just tell him I was your wife, like you've told everyone else. That might have made a difference."

"I didn't feel like it."

That was *too* casual for her mounting unease. "Didn't feel like it? Didn't *feel* like it!" she exploded. "You felt like getting beat up instead?"

"I'm not the one who had to be carried back to his room."

She tried to keep the surprise out of her voice. "You mean you won?"

"Certainly."

"Oh, certainly. How could I have doubted it? He was only a walking mountain."

"Sarcasm doesn't become you, Tanya. And he might have been big, but he was clumsy. The big ones usually are."

"You're big," she couldn't resist pointing out.

"Not that big, but then there are exceptions to the rule."

"And what rules were you playing by tonight when you threw in the winning hand?" At his frown, she clarified her question. "I saw your three kings, Stefan."

He actually smiled, though he flicked a dismissive hand. "That is merely an idiosyncrasy of mine. I feel a certain unfairness in letting kings win for me."

Which made no sense. The fact that he wasn't angry with her made no sense either. The fact that she was angry because he wasn't made the least sense of all.

"Well, I'm delighted you enjoyed yourself," she said crossly. "But of course you would. Gambling, fighting, those *are* diversions you men love the most, aren't they?"

She hadn't even noticed that he had been slowly moving toward her. He was now close enough to catch her arm, which he did, drawing her up against his body. She stiffened. He didn't acknowledge it. Both arms circled her now, keeping her firmly in place.

He only waited for her to look up at him before he said, "You forgot to mention the one diversion you are familiar with yourself, little houri." He grinned. "That means beautiful maiden, not what you are thinking."

"Sure it does," she scoffed, despite her confusion over whether he might be desiring her again. But that confusion wouldn't be quiet. "Stefan—"

"If you wanted a man, you should have asked," he admonished gently, "not tried to solicit a stranger."

"I didn't!"

Her denial didn't annoy him, he simply ignored it. "I knew the exact moment you encouraged him, Tanya. It was there in his face. But I excuse your actions because you haven't had . . . because it has been a long while since you . . ." The second explanation must not have suited him either. He actually looked flustered, and finally settled on skipping it altogether. "The alternative is that you deliberately caused trouble tonight. I prefer to think you need a man badly enough that you will accept even me."

Even? Didn't he know he was the only man she *would* accept? No, of course he didn't. He thought she'd done what she'd done because she was desperate for a man, any man, because they had kept her so long from the occupation they assumed was hers.

Tanya didn't know whether to explode with righteous indignation or laugh. Actually, she couldn't do either. Right now he was sure her motive hadn't been to cause trouble. If he started to think otherwise, he'd be angry. Yet he had enjoyed that damned fight, so he wouldn't be *that* angry—probably just enough to put her over his knee again. But she wasn't going to make love with him just to get out of that. And she wasn't going to make love to him while he thought he would be doing her a favor. If and when she ever did, it had to be because he was desperate to have her. She wanted nothing less than the exquisite passion he had offered her that night by the river, not this hesitancy that wasn't like him at all. Actually, she wanted a whole lot more from him, she realized, but she was realistic if nothing else.

"I have surprised you?" he asked carefully.

"Do I look surprised? I guess I am, which is understandable, after your reaction to my freshly scrubbed face. What happened? Did I pick up some dirt smudges tonight? Is that why I'm suddenly acceptable again?"

Her tone was just sneering enough to gain her release. "You are, as you well know, exceptionally beautiful tonight."

But not once had he really looked her over. Even Vasili had looked her over. And every man she had seen tonight had spared at least one glance at her cleavage. But Stefan wouldn't look below her face. And his compliment had been so toneless, he might as well have been speaking of the weather. And that was supposed to convince her that he wanted her?

She stated as much, plainly. "You don't want me, Stefan."

He didn't try to correct her. He said merely, strangely, "One night I give to beauties like you. One night . . . no emotion . . . just pleasure."

It was that "no emotion" that got to her, that cut through the hurt those words had caused her and left only a simmering anger. "What if one night won't do it? Do I then go visit Lazar tomorrow, and Serge after him?"

Those taunts finally got to him, too. He no longer looked emotionless. "You forgot to mention Vasili," he said tightly.

"No, I didn't. I still wouldn't have that condescending peacock, no matter how desperate I was. But you'll notice I'm no longer in need. Being pitied has a way of curing that."

"Pitied?"

"Don't pretend you don't know what I'm talking about!" she snapped. "But don't worry. If I find I need a man again, I'll know where to look."

She deliberately left him to wonder about that, turning her back on him and crawling into bed, fully dressed as usual. Stefan slammed out of the cabin. Good. *Now* he was angry—but not angry enough.

Chapter 27

Pitied? Try as he might, Stefan couldn't figure out why the woman had come up with that word. Who in his right mind would pity her? She was beautiful and of royal birth; she was going to have more money than she would know what to do with, a fortune left to her by her mother, estates scattered all over Cardinia that were hers alone, and more in Austria, not to mention the royal palaces, the royal jewels. She was going to be emulated at court, sought after. She was going to wield incredible power. And the only one who could tell her yea or nay was her future husband, whom she could have wrapped around her little finger if she had but tried. But she didn't know that. And she didn't believe the rest of it. Still— *pitied?*

The obvious answer was no answer. She had merely used that as an excuse to reject him. He should have expected it. He shouldn't have made the offer. Lazar had tried to tell him she had been looking for trouble, not a quick toss in the sheets. But like the fool he had been acting ever since he met the woman, he saw only what he wanted to see.

"Why don't you just bed the wench and get it out of your system?"

"Shut your mouth, Vasili," Stefan growled.

They stood at the bar in the gambling hall, three on one side of it, Serge behind it. Only one table in the room was still occupied. Two others had been broken in the earlier fight. But most of the passengers had found their beds. So had the bartender, after locking up his stock. It had taken a few more large bills, on top of those doled out for damages, to get the purser to reopen the bar.

"For once Vasili is right, Stefan," Lazar said. "It's better than drinking yourself into a stupor every night just so you can sleep in the same room with her, and then snapping at everyone the next day—everyone but her."

"Shut your mouth, Lazar."

"Why don't you two leave him alone for a while?" Serge suggested. "Drink is about all a man can resort to when a woman plays hard to get."

"Shut your—"

"He was on your side, Stefan."

Stefan merely scowled at his empty glass and grabbed the bottle of whiskey from Serge's hand. They had finished off the last of the vodka two nights ago, but had been lucky to find any at all on the boat. Beer and whiskey were all this country seemed to stock. But what could you expect of a country that produced bastards like Dobbs, who could raise a baby in a tavern? It galled the hell out of Stefan that that man was going to live out his remaining days having his every whim catered to—thanks to him.

Lazar tried again. "If you won't bed her, Stefan, then why don't you tell her the truth? It just might change her attitude."

Vasili nodded in agreement, adding, "And it will allow us to show her our credentials, so she can stop doubting every damn thing we say to her."

Stefan wasn't listening to them. He was still remembering Tanya's expression when he told her that he preferred to think she needed a man so badly that she would accept even him. She had looked so amazed by his words at first, confused even; then slowly her expression had changed, telling him she hadn't cared for the way he had put it, not at all. It had been all he could do not to kiss her, and she had gone all stiff and indignant on him. He should have kissed her anyway. She yielded to his mouth more often than not, a fact that delighted him as much as it enraged him.

He had to admit he had handled the whole thing rather poorly, but he wasn't surprised by that. Where beautiful women were concerned, he had no tact at all. Money usually spoke for him, was all that was necessary. But not with Tanya. She might have accepted much, much less from other men in her lifetime, but she was too set against him for money to make the least bit of difference in the way she felt.

Why did she have to turn out to be so lovely? It had been much easier dealing with her before her true beauty had been revealed. He hadn't been so self-conscious then—so vulnerable. And if that wasn't enough for him to work through, there was his bitterness over the fact that she hadn't been raised as she should have been.

Sometimes her lack of innocence wasn't an issue, like tonight. He had wanted her so badly, he had been afraid to overwhelm her with what he was really feeling. Other times, the way she had turned out was all he could think about. And still other times, both emotions would come at him at once, disgust for her vast experience and desire in spite of it. He was going to have to reconcile one or the other, to accept her as she was or not. He knew that. But that was still the least of his problems. What *she* felt concerned him the most now, and trying to figure her out was next to impossible.

"Stefan, you aren't listening."

He looked up at Serge, then turned toward Lazar, who had spoken. They were both getting blurry. Good; maybe tonight he could get some sleep. He certainly couldn't manage it sober, not with Tanya in the same cabin. But each time he had thought of sleeping elsewhere, he had rejected the idea almost immediately, and he couldn't even say why. *She* certainly had no trouble sleeping with him nearby, but until tonight, she had treated him as if he weren't there.

"Have you said something worth listening to?" Stefan asked.

"He's not drunk enough yet," Serge remarked and filled all four glasses again.

"Just because he doesn't slur his words—"

"Never mind that," Lazar interrupted. "Stefan,

Vasili thinks what you need is a woman, any woman.''

Lazar was definitely coming in blurred. ''Vasili thinks too much.''

''But in this case we all agree. And that pretty blond wench he has been spending his nights with ever since we came aboard is now awaiting him in his cabin. She's yours if you want her.''

Stefan swung his head around and experienced a moment of dizziness for the effort. ''Are you giving your women away again, cousin?''

Vasili shrugged. ''For a good cause.''

''Ever the generous one, eh? And I do appreciate it, Vasili. But if memory serves, and I'm not so sure it does right now, that little blonde is too pretty for me.''

''God, I hate it when you—''

''Dammit, Stefan—''

''Oh, enough,'' Stefan grumbled. ''You're becoming nags, the lot of you. Since when haven't I handled my own difficulties, in my own way? So go to bed. There is no reason for us all to wake up with headaches.''

''I fear it's too late for that.'' Serge grinned, swirling the amber liquid in his glass. ''Or weren't you counting how many bottles we've gone through this evening?''

''And we would just as soon keep you company,'' Lazar added.

Stefan drained the last of his glass and shoved it aside. ''Then I will take myself off to bed. But if you hear our little Tanya scream, just ignore her. I will merely be taking your advice.''

They all three gaped at him. ''Are you serious?''
Lazar asked.

''Why not? After all, I have your unanimous con-
sent. Do I really need hers?''

''Stefan, perhaps you should wait until—''

''Stefan, I don't think—''

''What is this now? Doubts? Perhaps you are suddenly remembering that she is a royal princess? But
don't worry about it. By the time I reach my cabin,
I will likely change my mind—or not.''

Stefan chuckled to himself as soon as he was outside the gambling room. But his humor over teasing
his friends didn't last more than a few seconds. He
was tired, exhausted really, yet wide awake. He was
pleasantly inebriated, yet his mind refused to acknowledge it. And he had his friends to thank for
putting tempting ideas into his head.

How much *would* a whore protest if he simply took
her? Not much, he realized, because she was probably used to men wanting more from her than she
was willing to give. In her profession, she would
meet all kinds and be forced to take the good with
the bad. But he couldn't do it. As much as he wanted
her, he wanted her willingness more.

And where did that leave him? Knowing what hell
was like. And he could see no end to it. If this trip
down the Mississippi River was bad, he still had an
ocean voyage to look forward to, and no gaming
room to distract him. A lot of good gambling had
done him, however, since just about every hand had
found him thinking about Tanya instead of his cards.

Standing outside his cabin with key in hand, he was almost afraid to enter. She would be asleep, but the difference that made could be measured on a pen point. So why did he put himself through this? He didn't *have* to sleep in there. But he knew why. There was the slim hope that the very thing he despised about her would bring her to him, in the dark, where she could forget that she knew what he looked like. Of course, he was deluding himself. She was too strong-willed to let a little thing like sexual need control her. He even admired that about her. Despite what the others thought, she was going to make a fine queen. He wondered if he would survive to see it.

Jesus, he must be more intoxicated than he'd thought. He was getting pukingly melancholiac, and that wasn't like him. She was only a woman, and they were easy enough to come by even for him, with the right amount of coin. And he had expected nothing from her before he'd found her. Actually, he had expected precisely what he was getting.

He opened the door carefully so as not to wake her. But that gesture suddenly struck him as being entirely too generous on his part, so he slammed the door closed. She sat up in bed immediately and looked straight at him without surprise. He'd noticed that about her before, how quickly she came awake, and without the least bit of grogginess or disorientation.

She had left one lamp burning low, but then she did that every night, probably out of a dislike for the total blackness that prevailed without it, rather than

any consideration for him. And each night he put the
light out, but she never complained about waking to
darkness in the morning. Of course, she hadn't been
talking to him before tonight.

She was still wearing the yellow gown, but that
was another thing she did consistently, sleeping fully
clothed. However, she had loosened some buttons
due to the constriction in the bodice of the dress, and
now one shoulder of it was halfway down her arm,
the actual bodice slipped low on that side but hanging
in place because of the fullness of her breasts.

Stefan wished he hadn't noticed. His eyes were
suddenly glowing so fiercely, the floor pallet he
turned toward should have burst into flames.

"What time is it?" Her voice came at him, not
annoyed, just flat.

"How the devil should I know?" he shot back,
definitely annoyed.

"It was a damned simple question. You don't have
to snap my head off."

He whirled around—too fast. Dizziness took over,
making the room sway for a moment until both hands
pressing against his temples brought it under control.
He fixed his gaze on her then and saw that she had
corrected the droop of the dress and was staring at
him wide-eyed.

"Lord help us, you're drunk, aren't you?" she
asked in genuine surprise. "No, don't bother to deny
it. My experience in this area happens to be life-
long."

"Vast indeed," he snorted.

"Scoff all you like, Stefan, but I was learning how

to handle drunks before you . . . well, before you could have had your first taste of whiskey.''

"Whiskey?'' he sneered. ''I'll have you know I was weaned on vodka straight from our Russian neighbors, so I believe I shall claim superiority in all areas of drink.''

"I stand corrected.''

His eyes narrowed on her. ''You wouldn't be so foolish as to try humoring me, would you, little Tanya?''

"Absolutely not.''

"Wise of you, because I wouldn't like that.''

"I knew that.''

His eyes narrowed even more, but her expression, wavering before him between a total blur and crystal clarity, was damned inscrutable. So he kept his suspicions to himself. Besides, he didn't particularly want to begin a fight with her now, when his exhaustion was catching up with him. Proof of that was the difficulty he was having just removing his coat. He ended up turning a full circle while trying to get the damned thing off.

"Do you need some help, Stefan?''

It took him a moment to find her on the bed again. Help? From her? He must have misunderstood.

"It's that damn whiskey,'' he explained to her, just in case he *had* heard her correctly. ''I believe it sneaks up on you.''

"That's a fact,'' she agreed.

"You—ah—weren't actually offering to help me undress, were you, Tanya?''

"No, but I thought you might need a little assistance in finding your bed tonight.''

His disappointment in that answer was acute—and enough to prick his temper. ''I will have you know there is not a single thing wrong with my eyes.''

''That's a matter of opinion,'' she mumbled.

''What's that?''

''I *said,* that was my opinion.''

He wasn't mollified. Arrogantly he continued, ''Besides which, a blind man couldn't miss that bed.'' He marched to it and sat down to prove his point. ''You see?''

''But, Stefan—''

''You are determined to annoy me, aren't you?''

''Absolutely not,'' she assured him. ''But are you aware that you don't sleep here?''

''Don't try to confuse me,'' he said as he leaned over to remove his shoes and nearly tumbled off the bed. But with one hand braced on the floor while he tugged on shoes that didn't want to come off, he added, ''I know damn well I have been sharing this cabin with you. It is driving me crazy, so I ought to know it.''

''Why is it driving you crazy?''

He scowled at his foot. ''Don't change the subject, Tanya. We were discussing this cabin.''

''You're right, of course. The cabin and sharing it. I sleep in the bed and you sleep on the floor. Have I got that right?''

She just had to rub it in, didn't she? Wasn't it enough that he had given up the bed for her and hadn't once tried to join her in it?

''You don't have that right at all, Princess.'' One

shoe finally came off and flew out of his hands to hit the far wall. "I might lie on the floor, but if I have managed to sleep there, I don't remember it."

"Is that why you're taking the bed tonight?"

Stefan straightened up so fast, he nearly blacked out. He dropped back on the bed the rest of the way as pain streaked through his head. And he was unaware that he was holding his other shoe when he brought his hands up to press them against his temples once more. However, the shoe was swiftly extracted from his fingers.

"Lord help me, what next?" she exclaimed. "You shouldn't have moved so quickly, Stefan."

He would have laughed if it wouldn't have hurt. And he refrained from saying, "No kidding," because it was finally occurring to him what all this nonsense was about. The damned woman *had* been humoring him. She should have told him to get the hell out of her bed when he'd mistaken it for his own. But no, that wasn't the way to *handle* a drunk. Just what had she thought he would do if she hadn't agreed with him? But he knew the answer to that, too. The same thing he had done before when his anger got out of control.

For a moment he wondered how far she would go to keep him a happy drunk. Wasn't she fortunate that he was too tired *and* too drunk to explore that thought fully? But he wasn't asleep yet.

He opened his eyes to see her staring down at him. She stiffened then, making him realize that her thigh was the soft pillow cushioning his head, and that he had surprised her by not being passed out, as she had likely assumed from his prolonged silence.

"As long as you're already here, Stefan, there is no reason for you to stir yourself. I can sleep on the floor for one night."

"That's generous of you, but speaking of no reasons, I can't think of a single one to prevent us from sharing the bed instead—only for one night."

"I can think of several—"

"Don't."

"I'll just—"

"Be *still*, Tanya! My head has just stopped aching, so don't make any sudden movements to start it up again."

He wasn't sure, but she seemed to be grinding her teeth together before she suggested, "Don't you think you would be more comfortable if you put your feet up on the bed and stretched out properly?"

If she thought he would release her thigh when he moved, he would have to disappoint her. "Thank you for mentioning it," he said and rolled sideways, curving his legs to fit at the bottom of the bed and throwing an arm over her legs. His head remained on her thigh, and if it wasn't the most comfortable position, he would suffer it just to thwart her.

"Stefan," she choked out.

"Shh," he grumbled. "Don't start nagging now, when you have been so pleasantly agreeable—and I am almost asleep."

Her sigh was loud and clear as she dropped back onto her pillow. It would be a grand stroke of poetic justice if she didn't get any more sleep tonight herself, about as unjust as his finally having her in this position, but being in no condition to enjoy it. At the moment, he didn't even care.

Chapter 28

Tanya awoke to the feel of lips moving with tantalizing softness over hers. She didn't have to wonder who was kissing her. What she did wonder was if Stefan was awake and knew what he was doing, or if he was merely reacting in his sleep to the warm body he found next to him. And if he wasn't awake, or completely aware, did she want to risk changing that by abruptly stopping him?

Reasonable questions, surely, but they didn't take into account that she found being awakened like this very pleasant, so pleasant that she didn't want to be the one to end it. In fact, she began participating, carefully at first—to avoid waking him if he was still half-asleep—parting her lips, inviting the thrust of his tongue, which came instantly to duel in slow, sensual motion with hers.

But how quickly she forgot about being careful when the more she yielded, the more Stefan demanded. In no time at all, passion raged between them, hers fed by his. Her heartbeat had become violent. She had to gasp for each breath when she could get one. And the sensations that manifested and pulsed through her innards were more exciting than ever before.

She held him close, marveling that each time she ever had, the man had been so very hot to the touch. Now was no different, and she found herself wanting more than anything to know the feel of that heated skin against her own. But she still wore her dress. He still wore his shirt and trousers. Even the blanket was still half covering only her, though she had kicked one leg free of it when she had turned toward Stefan.

Then suddenly he was pushing the shoulders of her dress down and tugging on the bodice until her breasts spilled out. His hand caressed her while his kiss deepened even more, as if he were afraid this new intimacy might inspire a protest. The only thing inspired was a new sensation that amazed and delighted her as he palmed the hard kernel her nipple had become.

When his lips finally left hers, she tried to draw him back, but he was determined to explore a new path. He found it and she gasped, the moist heat of his mouth searing one breast, then the other, as if he couldn't make up his mind which one he found more tasty. But then he latched onto one nipple and began to suckle, and Tanya discovered the heretofore unknown connection between her breasts and her loins, how heat could shoot from one part of her body to another, firing an achy feeling of need for his touch in both places. She arched into him, demanding what she needed with her body. His hand slid up her bare calf, her thigh, finally answering her silent call with the most sensuous of caresses.

There was no doubt now that he was awake, and no doubt either that nothing was going to stop them this time. And Tanya responded to that, giving herself over completely to what he was making her feel, wanting so much now to know it all, feel it all, though she couldn't quite believe anything could be better than what she was experiencing right now. His nakedness, though, that might be better, all that heat hers to touch . . . hers? No, she wouldn't let doubts or negative thoughts intrude to spoil this. She wanted this man to make love to her. She wanted . . .

The insistent pounding on the door registered and provoked a groan of frustration from her. Stefan was more vocal, snarling, "I'll kill them," as he raised his head.

The pounding continued a moment more, then: "Stefan, if you don't answer, I'll think she's murdered you and break this damn door down!"

Tanya's eyes flew open, but it was difficult to see anything with only a thin crack of light coming in from under the door. But the door wasn't locked. Stefan had no more than slammed it closed last night.

He must have realized that at the same moment she did, for he got up with a curse, then groaned as the headache from his expected hangover caught up with him in a big way. But he still managed to reach the door, opened it partially just long enough for whoever was on the other side to see him, then closed it again, softly, in deference to his head.

Tanya slowly pulled and pushed her dress back into place, not knowing what to expect now, especially when the door-pounder called out the parting tidbit that the boat had docked an hour ago. She could barely make out Stefan's shadow as he moved to light a lamp. She wished he wouldn't. She wished he'd come back to bed, but she knew that was impossible now with everyone obviously waiting for them to emerge from the cabin.

But when light surrounded her, Tanya had one more wish, that it would extinguish itself. It didn't. Stefan was standing next to the bed, staring down at her with the most inscrutable expression he'd ever worn, and all her doubts came rushing to the surface.

Had he meant to start what had happened, or had he in fact been sleeping to begin with and just got as caught up in their mounting passion as she had been? Did he wonder the same thing about her? And after last night and his magnanimous, arrogant offer to make love to her because *she* needed it . . . oh, God, this morning wasn't an extension of that offer, was it? And why didn't he say something? Why did he simply keep staring, as if similar or worse questions were running through his mind? Worse, she guessed, for his expression suddenly hardened, whatever conclusion he'd drawn not to his liking.

Tanya braced herself, but she still wasn't prepared to hear him say, "You really *don't* care who you bed with, do you?"

She would have hit him if he was close enough. She had to settle for rolling over to give him her back, because the rejoinder he deserved—"I guess not''—wouldn't get past the lump in her throat.

Her silent withdrawal must have surprised him, however, for he added, ''I'm sorry—that was un-called-for. But I know you hate me, so what else am I to think?''

What else indeed, but he didn't have to put it quite that way, did he? But it seemed that the more intimate they were, the more insulting became his remarks afterward, so she should have expected something like that. But she hadn't.

And what could she tell him? She *had* been so furious with him about his taking the tavern from her that she really would have shot him if she could have got hold of a gun. But the anger had petered out into despondency over what she was going to do with her future. Still, just last night her anger had returned and she had been hell-bent on getting a little even. So it was understandable that he would assume she hated him. Only she didn't hate him. She ought to, but she didn't, and she didn't understand that at all.

So again, what was she supposed to tell him to account for her passionate behavior? That she was so attracted to him nothing else mattered? He wouldn't believe that any more than she did. She didn't trust him, didn't accept half of what he told her. And she didn't like the uncertainty he caused her, or his attitude, which swung on such a wide pendulum that she was constantly kept off balance. And she really did hate his insults. All of these negative reactions were pretty hard to hide from him when she didn't have lovemaking on her mind. Then what *was* the reason she was drawn to him despite all that?

Lord help her, maybe she was as bad as he thought she was. Maybe she just liked those things he made her feel so much, she could overlook the rest. And maybe that was all she should tell him, or tell him nothing whatsoever, which was the same thing, since he already thought it.

This was her own fault. She had known full well she shouldn't have stayed in this bed with him last night. And she had tried to leave it a number of times, but each time his arm had tightened over her legs, he'd mumbled something incoherent and moved even closer to her, so she'd finally given up and tried falling back to sleep, a tall order under the circumstances.

And she'd been so sure she had handled that situation well last night, despite her frustration at having to give in on practically everything just to keep Stefan a happy drunk. But if she knew anything, it was that you didn't argue with intoxicated men. Too easily they could be moved to violence, serious violence that half the time they didn't even remember the next morning.

She'd long ago learned how to avoid that. If you agreed with them no matter what, you could steer them down the path you wanted them to go. That hadn't quite been the result with Stefan, but at least she had kept him peaceable. Only look what it had led to. Now his opinion of her was so low, it was a wonder he could even look at her.

But that was just as well, wasn't it? As usual, when

she wasn't aroused, she was wishing herself anywhere else but here with Stefan and his cohorts.

"Tanya?"

She shrugged the hand away that came to her shoulder, but said nothing. She heard a sigh and then movement as he left the side of the bed.

"I will leave you to change and pack your things," he told her. "But do hurry. We've kept the others waiting long enough." She didn't hear the door open and close, however, because Stefan had one more thing to say, though it took him several long moments to do so. "It bothers me more than it should, your experience with men."

Her eyes flared wide and darkened with rancor, but he didn't see that with her back still toward him. Was he actually trying to offer an excuse for his blistering insults? As if any excuse could make a difference. It *bothered* him? Well, she could fix that, couldn't she?

Without turning around, she said, "You should have said something sooner, Stefan, because I could have so easily relieved your mind. You see, I don't actually have any experience with men other than you, and that's not much, is it? But I don't expect you to believe that, which is why I haven't mentioned it before. After all, I worked *and* lived in a tavern, and all tavern girls are whores, aren't they? On second thought, I guess you'll just have to keep on being bothered by it."

She had spoken with enough sarcasm that he couldn't possibly believe her. But then she didn't want him to. She only wanted to give him something else to be bothered about. And by his new habit of slamming the door shut on his way out, this time despite his aching head, she guessed she'd succeeded very well.

Chapter 29

Sasha was there waiting for them on the dock with a large coach. Either he'd had remarkable luck in finding them himself, or one of the others had gone off to locate him while Stefan and Tanya kept them waiting. In either case, the little man didn't seem too upset at having been left to reach New Orleans on his own, though he might just be saving his complaints for a more private moment. He did have a number of things to say to Stefan, however, who merely nodded agreement without much comment of his own.

Watching them from the deck, Tanya wondered if Stefan was still angry with her. He probably was since Lazar and Serge escorted her down to the coach, and only they got into it with her. Stefan didn't even look her way, which was just as well, since she had worn her own shabby clothes again to annoy him further. But now she was regretting it. Of Vasili there was no sign at all, again just as well, since she hadn't bothered to use the hairpins he had troubled himself to obtain for her, which was carrying her own disgruntlement a step too far.

Expecting to be taken to a hotel, as she had been that last night in Natchez, Tanya decided she would rectify the mess she had made of her appearance before she saw her worst antagonists again and had to endure their disparaging comments about it. So she was annoyed to find herself transported only a short way down the dock to another boat, or ship rather, because this one was definitely an ocean-sailing vessel.

She didn't even have time to hope that they were merely stopping briefly for some reason, that this wasn't her actual destination, because the missing Vasili was on the ship, waiting for her at the top of the gangplank. When she reached him, he picked up a lock of her hair and merely clicked his tongue. A mild rebuke, surely, for that razor-tongued cad.

"Welcome aboard the *Carpathia*, Princess."

"When does she sail?"

"As soon as the rest of the crew can be found. They could not anticipate our exact time of arrival, after all."

Though he made that excuse, he still said it with a degree of annoyance, as if the crew should have had second sight—or else remained aboard the ship. But Tanya couldn't have cared less that he was letting his arrogance show. She was too busy trying to hide her surprise. So much for the wardrobe she had been promised.

"My first time in New Orleans, and I'm not even going to get to see it?"

Vasili quirked his brows in mild interest. "Was Stefan aware that you wanted to?"

As if that would make a difference, she wanted to snort, but all she said was, "No."

"Perhaps if you made your wishes known to him in the future . . . but in this case, time is of the essence, particularly since so much was wasted merely in locating you."

She was amazed he didn't mention her attempted escapes, which had delayed them more recently. That Stefan might grant her wishes, she didn't bother to address.

"Will I at least have a cabin to myself this time?" she asked.

He ignored that question to ask one of his own. "You haven't taken my advice yet, have you?"

"What advice?"

"To court Stefan's affection?"

"Affection? Ah, I remember—and it was his interest you recommended I cultivate, rather than his fury."

"You have his interest, Princess. You would do *better* with his affection."

"You'll forgive me if I consider that an impossible endeavor."

"Forgive you?" he shot back. "No, because I can see you won't even try."

"Why should I?" she demanded, becoming as annoyed as he suddenly was.

"For your own sake. For all our sakes. For your own happiness."

Her green eyes flared with feigned surprise, just

before she ruined the effect by scoffing, "I'm supposed to believe you wish me happy?"

"I want Stefan to be happy. You can go to the devil for all I care."

"I thought I already had," she retorted, but then she sighed, finding no satisfaction in sparring with him as she did with Stefan. "I'm being forced to travel with you, Vasili, but I don't have to converse with you, so kindly stay the hell away from me."

"Shield your claws, Tanya," Stefan said from behind her. "He doesn't deserve them."

She stiffened, first wondering how long he'd been there, then not caring. "But you do, don't you?" she said as she turned around.

"Today, perhaps," was all he allowed before dismissing the subject. "Do you wish to meet the captain first, or inspect your accommodations?"

"What I wish is to be let go so I can make my way back to Natchez."

"For what purpose?"

She honestly couldn't resist the chance to taunt him. "Why, I've been assured a job at Madam Bertha's. Don't you remember?"

His lips tightened. His eyes brightened a shade. Tanya didn't need any more evidence than that to tell her that she was right on target. Then he took her arm and propelled her forward, down a barely slanted stairway, and into the first cabin they came to, all without a single word.

Understandably, she was a bit wary by that point. She didn't expect to be tossed on the nearest bed, because his devil's eyes weren't glowing *that* much.

And she didn't think he could be so hypocritical as to punish her for taunting him when his own barbs were much more lethal. Maybe he just meant to lock her away so she couldn't aggravate him anymore.

However, he hadn't even closed the door before she was in his arms and his mouth was covering hers. But Tanya knew the difference now in his kisses, and this wasn't his in-a-rage kind. He was in perfect control and bent on—what? Seducing her into becoming a more agreeable captive?

Tanya pushed away from him before those feelings he was so capable of stirring could surface and take over. "*Why* do you keep doing that?"

"I am damned if I know!"

He must not have meant to admit that, for he scowled now. Tanya could have wished for a better answer, something a little more revealing, because trying to understand the way this man's mind worked was a lesson in futility and frustration. Unless . . .

"You know something, Stefan? You've changed my life around to suit you, not me. You've ruined what few goals I had for myself. It's time I had some truth from you. You owe me tha' much at least."

"You have been told the truth—mostly the truth."

"I'm not talking about your damn fairy tale and you know it. I want to know your feelings, Stefan. Do you still want me?"

"Yes!"

He sounded so furious about it, she cringed. "I gather you wish that weren't so?"

"Exactly."

"Why? Because you think I'm a whore?"

"No."

She wasn't sure she believed that, though he *had* admitted to wanting her before—before she was uncloaked, so to speak. "Then it's just as I supposed, isn't it? You can't stand the sight of me now."

"The sight of you is too beautiful for words, as you well know."

She frowned. "I don't know any such thing. But I do know that you aren't making much sense. Of course that shouldn't surprise me, since you never do."

"I did not invite you into my mind, Tanya; you forced your way in. If you don't like what you find—"

"Thanks a lot," she cut in impatiently. "All I asked for was a little clarification of motives, to know why you kiss me one moment but despise me the next."

"I don't despise you."

"But you despise the way I look," she pointed out. "I dare you to deny it!"

"Yes, because I desire beautiful things just like any man. Only I am a realist," he added almost tiredly. "You and I are not compatible."

Because she was a lowly tavern wench, and he a condescending bastard. No, they weren't compatible at all. But he'd give her one night. He'd said as much last night. Only she didn't want "only once."

"Why don't you do us both a favor and stay away from me?"

"I wish I could, but even now I want you. Name your price, Tanya."

She stiffened. If she didn't hate him now, offers like that would soon change her mind. How dared he try to buy her again, and after admitting he wanted her?

"All right," she said bitterly. "The price is my freedom—before this ship sails."

Hot golden color was back in his eyes. "So I must forsake my duty to have you? I think not, little houri. And I think it's time you had the whole truth. Vasili is not the King of Cardinia."

"Tell me something I didn't know," she snorted.

"I am king."

"My oh my, will wonders never cease," she said with exaggerated amazement. "From one whopper to another, eh? But it's kind of late to try that one, isn't it? At least Vasili looks and acts like a king."

"You think a king can't be scarred?" he demanded, his eyes really starting to glow now.

That caught her off guard. "Scarred?" She frowned, but only for a moment. "You mean yours?" Suddenly she laughed. "Oh, come on, Stefan. Who even notices a few little scars with eyes like yours? And how many times do I have to tell you I'm not stupid? You're telling me you're king just so you can have me. Did you honestly think I wouldn't know that?"

Something in her reply must have caught *him* off guard for a moment. The heat went out of his eyes, and he actually looked confused. Lord help her, the man must have really been working under the impression she was a half-wit, just because of where she came from. And here she'd thought *he* had more intelligence than that.

"I think we should have ended this conversation before it began," he said.

"It was rather pointless, wasn't it?"

"I really am the new King of Cardinia, Tanya."

She sighed. "Have it your way. I'm still not going to be your whore for a day, Stefan."

"No, you're quite right. That was too much to ask. And I will endeavor to stay away from you during this voyage as you requested."

He was being stiffly formal now. She found she liked that even less than his anger, which was at least a true indication of feeling.

"Does that mean I will have a cabin to myself?" she ventured.

"This one."

"But I suppose I will be locked in again?"

"That won't be necessary once we are at sea. Until then . . ." He left that thought unfinished, though its meaning was clear, but he abruptly went on to another. "Your new wardrobe will arrive shortly. Sasha took the initiative of ordering it for you, promising a ridiculous bonus to the seamstress to have it completed in so little time. He does love to spend my money, but in this case he has managed to gain us back the time we lost in returning to Natchez."

"Then that lets me off the hook, I suppose, if that Sandor fellow dies before we—"

"Sandor is *my* father, Tanya. Doubt me all you like, but use a respectful tone when you mention him."

Well, pardon her for breathing. Damn him, he was managing to annoy her again.

"I'm delighted everything has at least worked out to *your* satisfaction," she ground out tersely. "Now, if you don't mind—"

"Actually, *I* wanted to choose your clothes."

Tanya could only stare at him, fighting to keep her expression blank. Why did he have to say something like that, something so—possessive? It made her innards start to churn, when she'd been keeping her damned attraction for him so well under control during this whole encounter. Even when he'd said again that he wanted her, she'd been too angry to let it affect her.

He frowned now—because of her silence or his own words, she couldn't tell. The smile that came next, however, was unmistakably self-mocking. But his voice when he continued to. speak was clipped with impatience. Obviously, he couldn't wait to get out of there.

"Go through the trunks as soon as they arrive, because if you require anything else, it will have to be seen to immediately or not at all. And you shouldn't be disappointed in Sasha's taste *or* his thoroughness. He has a flair for fashion and, unlike myself, an eye for proper sizing. He assures me everything will fit you perfectly."

With a curt nod, he left her. And true to his word, it was the last Tanya saw of him for a long while.

As for her new clothes, they were the stuff of dreams, fit for a princess. And though she couldn't summon much enthusiasm for them, she couldn't find fault with them either—well, maybe one. Because Stefan had had no say in what was bought for her, she now had every conceivable undergarment known to women. She could have done without half of them.

Chapter 30

About halfway to Europe, Tanya began to believe the fairy tale. And it was Sasha who began to convince her by not even trying. While the others were annoyed with her again for putting Stefan in such a lousy mood—though she never saw this mood, she only heard about it—Sasha befriended her. Without fail, he was always respectful. He would grouchingly criticize Vasili, sometimes Lazar, and once even the usually quiet Serge, and in their presence no less, but he never had a condemning word for Tanya.

One day she finally asked him why he was being so kind to her.

"Because you deserve it more than most, your Highness. Your life has been hard, harder than mine, I think, before Stefan took me into his service."

"How would you know what my life has been like?"

Sasha explained. "Stefan has told me what you tell him. He doesn't believe all of it. Then he believes what he shouldn't. I think you throw him the truth, daring him to accept it, then toss him the lies to punish him for his doubts. He also told me what he saw for himself. That man who raised you, he should have been shot.''

Tanya grinned at that opinion. ''I've often thought so myself.''

''But you stayed with him, when you could have left.''

''He finally needed me, really needed me. I had to . . .''

Tanya didn't like the way that sounded, as if she had some daughterly feelings for Dobbs, which she didn't. She couldn't. The man was too mean-spirited to inspire affection. She discounted those years when she had thought he was her father and loved him despite his cruelties.

She continued almost belligerently. ''I was going to be paid for staying, with the tavern. I wanted to own that tavern more than anything. It would have been my support, my freedom from being under someone else's control.''

''Yes, Stefan realizes his mistake in buying it. He could have more easily, and cheaply, just burned it down without your knowing and placing the blame on him. But then your Mr. Dobbs wouldn't have had the settlement that will keep him happy for the rest of his days. And Stefan didn't want you worrying about the man—in case you might.''

''You know Stefan very well, don't you, Sasha?''

''As well as any man can.''

''Is he always so . . . at odds with his own feelings?'' she asked hesitantly.

The little man laughed. "You put that very well, your Highness. And no, he is not always so. Usually his feelings are in complete accord, whether they are good or bad. He doesn't like doubts, or conflicting emotions, and usually has none. Anything that will tip the scales, he stays away from."

"Like me," she concluded aloud. "Is that why he's been avoiding me?"

"He stays away from you because you asked him to—and because you two cannot come together without fighting. Why is that, do you suppose?"

"You're asking me, when he's the one with the short temper?" she snorted.

"He has a temper, yes, but of necessity he has learned how to control it."

"Sasha, do you know *how* he controls it? What he does, or wants to do, when he's so passionately furious?"

He was amused by her rising indignation. "Yes, and it began at his father's suggestion, because when Stefan was younger and became angry enough to fight with someone, he inevitably hurt them. They would not fight back, you see, because he was their prince, and not just any prince, but the Crown Prince. So he had to find another outlet for his anger, an outlet that would hurt no one. He would go to whomever he was currently . . . well, I think you get the drift."

"I'd already realized that, but *I'm* not his current mistress."

"No, but you are closer to him than a mistress could ever be. You are his betrothed by royal decree, which is as binding as any marriage. In his eyes,

Princess, you are already his wife. It only lacks a ceremony to make *you* believe it.''

It was not the first time Sasha had made mention of Stefan being the royal one, rather than Vasili. In fact, since Stefan had made his confession before they sailed, all of them, the crew and captain included, now spoke of Stefan as their king. Vasili had even made the remark that it had been tedious on his part, trying to be something he was not. Tanya had choked back her laughter, for the man was as arrogant and patronizing as ever. If he had pretended to kingly qualities, she couldn't imagine what they were.

The Cardinians had shown her some very officious-looking documents, shoved them in her face, actually, the day after they sailed, when she had made some caustic comment that betrayed her skepticism over Stefan's confession. The papers were clear testimony that Stefan Barany was the new reigning King of Cardinia. Any government would have rolled out the red carpet were it presented with such credentials. Tanya had suggested the documents could have been stolen, or merely faked, and three men had stared at her in offended outrage, which they continued to display to a lesser degree for a good week.

But after she thought about it, really thought about it, she realized how much easier it was to believe that Stefan, rather than Vasili, could be a king. After all, they had all, always, deferred to Stefan, followed his lead, even looked to him occasionally for silent permission before doing something. And it was Stefan who gave the orders, not Vasili. They had tried to tell her the reason was because he was the older cousin, but that had never rung true, and that, combined with the rest, was why she couldn't believe Vasili was their king, and so couldn't believe the rest of their tale either.

But then she recalled the time Lazar had asked her if she would prefer that Stefan were king. And even Stefan had asked her once how she would feel if she had another choice besides Vasili. Why, unless it was so? And it was Stefan who had taken charge of her from the beginning, as if it were his right—or as Sasha said, he already thought of her as his wife.

And how would she feel about it if she finally accepted everything they'd told her? It was actually much harder to consider marrying Stefan than Vasili. With Vasili there was no question. She simply refused. But with Stefan—she was probably as divided in her feelings as he was. There was the powerful attraction she felt for him while hoping it was all true, that he was going to be her husband. Then there were all her doubts while she hoped that even if it was true, she wouldn't be forced to marry him in the end.

The doubts, of course, took precedence. They were just too numerous. Incompatibility, hostility, the fact that the only thing they had in common was some distant relations she knew nothing about. Then there was marriage itself, the very thought of which she despised. To be under the control of a normal man would be bad enough, but Stefan wasn't a normal man, he was an all-powerful king, for crying out loud. And she'd already had a thorough taste of just how controlling he could be, with her own wishes being consistently ignored.

And she mustn't forget Stefan's baffling attitude toward her. He wanted her but wished he didn't; thought she was beautiful but wished she weren't. And his wanting her was only for one time. He'd admitted as much and was probably of the same opinion as Vasili, that royal marriages were political, not personal, and didn't require much intercourse of any kind between the couple. But where would that leave her? Still wanting Stefan with no hope of ever having him? Would she willingly put herself through that kind of hell? She'd have to be as stupid as they seemed to think she was.

As she would have done with Vasili, she'd have to refuse to marry Stefan—if it were all true. And unfortunately, she was nearly convinced that it was. And then she learned how naive she was about what she could or couldn't do. Stefan had said it once himself—that as a subject of Cardinia, she would have to obey the king just like everyone else. She had assumed that meant obey or get thrown in a dungeon or some such distasteful alternative. Again it was Sasha who enlightened her when they were having another of their daily talks.

It began when she asked how Stefan had received his scars. For once the little man didn't want to answer her and said as much.

"Stefan should be the one to tell you about it, if he chooses."

"It's been a peaceful voyage, Sasha." Her tone was as dry as parchment. "Do you really think I should change that by requesting an audience?"

He chuckled. "It is nearly five weeks since you have seen each other. Perhaps you could now manage a few minutes alone, only a few, mind you, without cutting each other to shreds. You haven't missed him?"

"Not even a little," she said with absolute certainty, but only for Sasha's benefit.

Actually, she did miss Stefan a little, or more exactly, the stimulation of being in his presence. What she didn't miss was the insults, and even Vasili was being on his best behavior now that they suspected she was starting to believe everything, even that she was a genuine princess.

"Has he said anything," she continued, "that would lead you to think he—ah—misses me?"

Sasha smiled at her hesitancy, but shook his head, saying, "The truth, your Highness, is that since he has been away from you, he has reverted to his normal habit of keeping his feelings strictly to himself."

"He's brooding?" she asked with interest.

"No. He simply speaks of nothing of a personal nature."

"You mean he hasn't even asked after me?" she demanded, not caring how indignant she sounded.

"For what reason? Everything he could possibly want to know is told him before he need ask."

Her eyes flared wide. "By you?"

"Certainly."

"You mean you tell him what we talk about?" she fairly shouted.

"There is no reason for this display of anger, Princess," Sasha said soothingly. "I haven't told him anything that might displease you."

"How would I know? And don't you dare tell him I asked if he misses me!"

"The subject is already forgotten," he assured her, only to venture to add, "But perhaps if he thought you wouldn't mind a chance meeting with him—"

"I would mind," she insisted stubbornly. "I would have to be a glutton for punishment if I *wanted* to talk to him again. Why, the very last time we spoke, he asked my price. My price, Sasha! Do you know how insulting that was? No, I like it just fine that he's arranged things so that we don't run into each other by accident or otherwise."

Sasha's cheeks flushed as he tried to explain. "If you were a whore, then you would surely be delighted at the mention of price. They all think you a whore, so half of what you take as insult is not meant as insult. Why do you not tell them it isn't so?"

She wasn't offended by such plain speaking, not from Sasha, and she didn't prevaricate either. "Why should I bother? Would it change their plans for me?"

"No. You are going to marry King Stefan of Cardinia. It is the old king's wish. It was the wish of the king before him, your own father. So there is nothing you can do to prevent it from happening."

"I can say no."

"It can be accomplished without your permission. You were raised in a country where many voices make the law, but you were born in a country where only one voice is the law. Stefan has merely to order it so, and this he will do because it is his father's wish."

"But not his."

It was not a question, but Sasha treated it as one, admitting, "It was not his wish when he came to find you. Now I am not so sure."

Tanya was sure. Duty before preference, as Vasili had put it. Stefan would marry her whether he wanted to or not. And now she knew that she would have no choice either. She wouldn't even be allowed the satisfaction of putting them to the trouble of forcing her.

Sasha became disturbed by her silence. "Perhaps I should tell you how Stefan came by his scars, after all, to help you understand him better."

"Don't bother," she said glumly. "I'm no longer interested."

Chapter 31

Tanya might have lost her interest in learning about Stefan's scars the day before, but it was the first thing she asked Lazar the next morning when he and Serge joined her for breakfast in her cabin.

"Stefan's scars? That is a touchy subject, Princess," Lazar began.

"One Stefan wouldn't like us to discuss," Serge added with a warning look at his friend.

"Well, heaven forbid you do something he wouldn't like," Tanya said with just enough scorn to goad them.

But Lazar merely grinned at her, aware of what she was doing. "That tactic won't work. If you knew how unpleasant it is to have Stefan annoyed at you—"

Serge wasn't amused, and he broke in, grumbling, "She knows. But like most females, she doesn't care how she goes about getting what she wants."

"That isn't so," Tanya retorted. She tried to look offended, couldn't manage it, so settled on a shrug.

275

"Never mind. I suppose I can just ask Stefan, even though it's *such* a touchy subject."

Both men were now scowling at her. "From one tactic to another—"

"Women *always* fight dirty—"

"Oh, for crying out loud." Tanya cut them both off in disgust. "You'd think it was a secret that could topple your whole country." And then she tossed out a challenge. "Or is it something Stefan is ashamed of?"

"Ashamed?" Lazar stood up to lean across the table so she couldn't mistake how angry she'd made him. "Stefan risked his life to save another's. There was no shame in that, your Highness."

"So why couldn't you just say so?" Tanya retorted, annoyed with herself now for pushing them. "It sounds like he was a hero."

"Tell her, Serge," Lazar said as he sat back down. "Maybe she'll be wise enough not to mention it again—at least not to him."

Serge began grudgingly, but soon he was merely relating the incident. "He was heroic, or foolhardy— depending on how you look at it. But he was only twenty-one that year, with no important duties weighing on him yet, no worries other than his studies, which, unlike for some of us, were incredibly easy for him, and his every wish granted—"

"Stick to the story," Lazar complained. "She doesn't have to know how wonderful his life was up to that point, when her own life has been so deprived."

Tanya blinked in surprise. Serge flushed with embarrassment. But she suddenly remembered Stefan's impassioned speech about what she'd suffered through fate when she was supposed to have been reared gently, with a fortune at her disposal. He'd been angry *for* her, not at her, though she hadn't seen it that way at the time. Did these two think she was resentful, perhaps, for not having had the privileged life that her birth should have guaranteed?

She hadn't even thought about it, but it was hard to feel resentment for lacking something she'd never expected to have in the first place. If she resented anything, it was how easily they all assumed she was tarnished goods just because of where she'd been raised, when one of the major concerns of her life, every day for the past eight years, had been how to stay *out* of men's beds.

"I'm sorry, your Highness," Serge told her with touching sincerity.

The man was apologizing for the wrong thing as far as she was concerned. But she would just get angry if she tried pointing that out to him.

"Don't be absurd," she said instead. "Stefan doesn't strike me as a man who feels very privileged right now, so what do I have to be envious about? The fact that he isn't allowed to choose his own wife?"

"There is no one else he wants to marry," Serge assured her, then added, "Not anymore."

"Serge!" Lazar admonished incredulously.

Tanya was amused by his objection. "What, am I supposed to be shocked that he wanted to marry someone else? He's thirty years old or thereabouts, isn't he? I'd be amazed if he hadn't wanted to get married at least once by now."

"I'm no older than he is, and I've never wanted to get married," Lazar said.

"Nor have I," Serge put in.

"But he did, and my oh my, that must have really set a fire under the royal temper when he was reminded he already had a betrothed. Is that about the way it went?"

Lazar nodded reluctantly. "But he found out he was better off without her. She was nothing but a . . ."

The fact that his face suffused with color told Tanya she didn't have to ask what the woman was. "I see. Another whore," she said evenly as she stood up, then with more heat, "Get out, both of you."

"Now, Princess, I wasn't comparing—"

"Like hell you weren't, or you wouldn't have stopped and turned ten shades of red! And to think I thought you two, at least, could contain your contempt."

"If the word is so objectionable to you, Princess Tatiana," Vasili said from the open doorway, his voice expressly dispassionate, "then you should have found some means of preserving your virtue."

She stared at him furiously for a moment until she realized he was actually scolding her for becoming upset over what they all considered a fact set in gold and minted. And he was right, of course. Until she denied the charges, she had no business getting angry over their allusions to them. Sasha had told her the same thing. And if she looked at it from their point of view, her offended sensibilities must seem very hypocritical.

The trouble was, it was hard to make her feelings be logical or tolerant. She supposed she was hoping the men would judge her by her behavior since they'd known her, not by their assumptions, but she was forgetting Vasili's first encounter with her, when he'd found her sitting on Stefan's lap. And she doubted Stefan had ever bothered to tell him that he had put her there. She was also forgetting the things she had said in her anger, lies to get back at them, but which they took as the literal truth.

But even knowing all that, accepting it, being ashamed for her part in it, she still couldn't exonerate them, not all of them. Lazar had blundered into offending her. Vasili did it deliberately every time.

So she sat back down and said curtly, "You're not welcome in here. They are, but you aren't."

Typically, he completely ignored her statement and sauntered further into the room. "We have been ordered to keep you company, occupied, and amused. I see we are doing splendidly well in the matter of amusement, but I doubt Stefan will appreciate the topic under discussion."

"She asked about Stefan's scars," Lazar explained, his voice uneasy. "Were we supposed to let her broach the subject with him?"

"Morbid curiosity doesn't deserve to be appeased," Vasili replied, and for once, *he* got angry. His amber eyes were glowing nearly as bright as Stefan's could when they came back to light on Tanya. "Was it too much to hope you might overlook a few minor flaws? You women are all alike, concerned only with appearance. You never look beneath the surface to what is inside a man, do you?''

She stared at him incredulously, unable to believe she was actually being accused of this, too. ''Now there you happen to be very wrong. With you, Vasili, *all* I see is what's beneath the surface.'' She didn't elaborate. She just gave him a look so full of disgust, he couldn't help but understand her meaning perfectly.

His smile was so brittle, it should have cracked. ''So you want to cross swords with me, Princess? I'd have you in tears in a matter of minutes.''

''I don't doubt it. That is your specialty, isn't it, belittling anything you deem unworthy? And, of course, I am beneath your contempt, a whore who must be constantly reminded that she is a whore, because I'm so dense I somehow keep forgetting it. But tell me something, Vasili, just out of *morbid* curiosity. What would you do if you found out you had misjudged me, that I'd learned at a young age how despicable men could be, and so I wanted no part of them, not even to better my life with a few extra coins?''

''Is this merely a supposition, Princess, or are you saying you had no choice in the matter, that you were forced to lead such a life?''

She wasn't sure what had prompted that question from Lazar, curiosity or indignation on her behalf, but she wished he could have contained it a little longer, until she'd had her answer from Vasili. The peacock was merely looking scornfully dubious. And how the devil had they drawn this new conclusion from what she'd said?

"Forced? I didn't wear that knife on my hip for decoration, Lazar," she reminded him. "Any man who tried to force himself on me ended up losing a lot of blood for his trouble." Except for Stefan, but since he'd never managed to finish what he started, he didn't count. "Now how about an answer, Vasili? Just use your imagination and picture me as chaste as the day I was born. What would you do?"

Vasili refused to cooperate. "I'm afraid my imagination is not that—"

"Never mind," she interrupted, losing her patience and temper. "I know what you would do. Nothing—except maybe find something else to condemn me for."

"Your opinion of me has sunk rather low, Princess," he said with some surprise.

"I assure you it didn't have far to sink."

He looked mildly annoyed. "Very well, we will play your silly game. If you are found to be virginal, Stefan will be furious because you never once proclaimed your innocence. I would have apologized profusely, probably on my knees, but Stefan will insist on a grander gesture to atone for us all, myself being the likely offering."

He wasn't being the least bit serious, so neither was she. "Your head?"

"My tongue, delivered personally."

"And of course you do everything he asks?"

"Certainly."

"Then start hoping he doesn't ask, Vasili. For that

alone I'd be willing to give up my virginity.''

"You better hope you don't have any to give up, Princess, because when I said Stefan will be furious, I meant with you. If you're going to turn into a virgin on your wedding night, miraculously, you damn well better make sure Stefan isn't surprised by it.''

That had come out so seriously, it sent a chill up Tanya's spine. But all she replied was, ''I see you have a splendid imagination after all, Vasili.''

Chapter 32

It wasn't until nearly the end of that long voyage that Tanya remembered to ask again about Stefan's scars. She was on the deck with Vasili and Serge this time, and the men were explaining that there was no easy way to reach Cardinia from the sea. It was situated at more or less an equal distance from the Adriatic Sea in the south, the Black Sea in the east, and the Baltic Sea in the north. The only reason they had sailed north was the possibility of being delayed by pirates in the Mediterranean or by the capricious Ottomans, who controlled the entrance to the Black Sea.

It made no difference to Tanya, who didn't know enough about Europe, anyway, to care which route they took. She had already been told that once they docked in Danzig harbor on the Prussian coast, it would still take another two or three weeks, depending on the weather, to reach Cardinia by land. The only thing she might have preferred was the warmer climate of the southern seas, for the end of October in the North Sea, particularly when they rounded

Denmark, was colder than anything she was used to.

Seeing the coasts of France and the Netherlands had been interesting, though, especially when the ship stopped to take on supplies and she got a much closer look at the foreign ports. The smooth, sandy beaches along the Prussian coastline were almost boring in comparison. But the conversation wasn't. Of course, it never was with these companions of hers. She was either learning something about where she was going, being taught, clumsily at best, court etiquette by two counts and a baron who didn't give a damn about court etiquette themselves, or putting up with Vasili's diabolical wit—or steering the topic to Stefan, which she did more often than she realized.

When she broached the subject of Stefan's scars now, Vasili didn't object. He merely watched Tanya carefully, which should have warned her she wouldn't like what she was going to hear. And Serge didn't elaborate this time either.

Briefly, he recounted, ''The royal family was traveling to their hunting lodge in the north woods, where they spent several weeks every year—Sandor, Stefan, his younger brother, Peter, and only about fifteen attendants. It was spring, the winter had been especially harsh that year, and there were reports of villagers being attacked by wolves in the area they were passing. Peter was warned not to venture from the camp alone, but at ten years of age, he rarely did as he was told. Stefan heard his screams and reached him first.''

''That's enough,'' Tanya whispered, but with the wind on the deck, Serge didn't hear her.

"I was there. So were Vasili and several of the guards. But we were all too far behind Stefan to stop him from charging into that pack of wolves to save his brother. He kicked, he slashed, he threw them off Peter, but they kept coming back. By the time we were close enough to shoot, Stefan had already killed four of the beasts. One had gone for his face. There was another still clamped to his leg that he was stabbing, and stabbing . . . and stabbing."

"For God's sake, Serge!" Vasili snapped, startling Tanya. "You're not entertaining a roomful of drunken louts who would appreciate all that blood and gore. A few simple words would have sufficed."

Serge glanced at Tanya's white face and his own pinkened. "I'm sorry, Princess. I am afraid I was seeing it all happen again . . ."

"You have nothing to apologize for," she assured him, while she tried to remind herself that it had happened so long ago, she had no business feeling sick to her stomach. "I asked to hear it, didn't I?"

"But can you now see beyond the scars?" Vasili wanted to know.

Tanya sighed. "If anyone has a problem with Stefan's scars, it's you. When I first saw him, those glowing eyes of his had me so fanciful, I thought I was meeting the very devil. It took me a while to even notice the devil was scarred, and when I did, I felt—"

"Revulsion?"

That he was back in form assuming the worst from her made her realize that a moment ago he'd actually got huffy with Serge on her behalf. And that so sur-

prised her, she couldn't manage to get angry with
Vasili right now.

"I was going to say I felt empathy for the pain he
must have suffered, because I understand pain."

He looked at her skeptically. "Princess, we *all*
saw you reject his touch."

"The devil you did. When?"

"In the common room of your tavern, when he
was questioning you about the mark Sandor gave you.
He was merely reaching for your face to regain your
attention, but you jerked away from him. What was
that if not revulsion?"

"That was protection, you idiot!" So much for
not getting angry at him. "He would have smeared
the powder on my face if he'd touched it. No one
was ever allowed to touch my face. And just for the
record, the only time Stefan disgusts me is when he
acts like you."

Something she'd said had surprised Vasili too
much for him to even react to her insult. Serge,
however, latched onto the last thing she had said,
and thought to defend his king to her.

"Stefan's emotions were more scarred than his
face by that incident with the wolves. He is still bitter
that it was all for nothing. His brother died anyway.
And that bitterness sometimes guides his thoughts
and actions."

That profound statement coming from Serge had
both Tanya and Vasili staring at him in amazement.
Tanya forgot her anger for the moment. Vasili shook
his head, made a face, then pinned his gaze on Tanya.

It was only half as menacing as Stefan's, but discerning.

"Protection?" he demanded. "You were protecting that hideous disguise of yours? You really *didn't* want to be bothered by men, did you?"

Lazar chuckled at Tanya's back, having come up behind them. "Careful, Vasili, or you may have to apologize before you even see the wedding sheets."

She turned to raise her brow at Lazar, but was caught by the sight of Stefan appearing on the quarterdeck at the other end of the ship. Her eyes followed him as he approached the captain and they began talking. She avidly took in everything, the way he bent his head to hear the other man because he was taller, the movement of his hand as he pointed toward the coast, then whipped back a lock of black hair the wind tossed in his face. His hair was longer, though not as long as that of some of the sailors, so he must have had it cut at some point during the voyage. And he was wearing the strange-looking coat edged with fur and wrapped and belted, rather than buttoned. She was just getting used to seeing that style of coat on the others, but on Stefan it no longer looked strange, it looked right.

Behind her, Vasili was demanding of Lazar, "Did you hear what she said?"

"Certainly. She was implying she managed to keep her virtue because of that 'hideous' disguise even we couldn't see through."

"They said she could be had for a few coins, Lazar," Vasili reminded him.

That gave Tanya back the breath she had been

holding, and brought her whipping around to face
Vasili again. *"Who* said that?"

"The patrons in your common room. Two of them,
as a matter of fact."

He had to be making that up. "They said Tanya
Dobbs could be had?"

"Yes—no, they said the dancer could be had, and
Stefan assured us you were the dancer."

Lord help her, all this contempt dumped on her
because April had broken her foot. She ought to
laugh. It was actually funny. No, it wasn't.

"Imagine that," she said, meeting Vasili's eyes
and holding them with the ire in hers that contradicted
her sudden smile. "And they were right. The dancer
could be had for a few coins. Everyone knew it,
except Dobbs, of course, because he didn't allow
fornication under his roof and would have given her
the boot if he found out, despite the fact that her
performance was the only thing making money for
The Seraglio."

"So you don't deny it?"

"How can I? I'd even caught her once myself out
back with her skirts up."

"Her?"

"April!" she snapped, her anger in full bloom
now. "The regular dancer. The girl who carelessly
broke her foot that day, leaving me high and dry with
an empty common room if I didn't perform in her
place that night. I hadn't been on that stage myself
since I was thirteen—fourteen . . . how the hell old
am I, anyway?"

"Oh, God," Vasili groaned.

"Twenty this past June, your Highness," Serge supplied. "June first was the day of your birth."

"The first day of June," she whispered, but refused to be sidetracked even by something she'd waited a lifetime to hear. "So I was fourteen the last time I'd danced. I had to stop when some of the regulars started figuring out that it was me up there on the stage instead of our original dancer, who'd run off, because Dobbs didn't want them getting ideas that I might be talented at other things, and neither did I. So he found me girls to teach the dance to, only he was too cheap to ever have more than one on hand at a time. But that's all I've done for the last six years—train the girls who come and go, and take care of every other job that needed to be done." And then she couldn't help herself from adding, "But don't take my word for it. Whores are notorious liars, aren't they?"

The goad didn't work that time. Vasili looked like hell warmed over. "Tanya—"

"Don't!" she hissed.

"Tanya, please—"

"Don't you *dare!* I wouldn't accept a saving hand from you if I was sliding into oblivion."

"I love him!" Vasili said passionately. "I couldn't stand that he was being forced to wed a woman who would play him false by her very nature!"

"All right. I'll accept that. I'll probably even understand that kind of motive after I give it some thought. But don't ask another thing of me, not now."

"Stefan will have to be told," Lazar said very quietly behind her.

She turned back toward him, but it was toward the quarterdeck she looked. Only Stefan wasn't there any longer, nor anywhere else on deck that she could see. He'd gone back to his cabin, or wherever it was he went when she was on deck. Had he even noticed her? Dammit, that glimpse of him had been too brief. But the voyage was almost over. He couldn't hide from her much longer. Could he?

She was suddenly tired. All that expended emotion, she supposed, that had nearly choked her. God, pride was a horrible thing. And it was still sitting in her pocket, though a bit worn out, too.

She glanced at Lazar and said calmly, "If you tell him what I've said, I'll deny it."

He didn't appear to believe her and said as much. "You can't be serious."

"I am."

"But why?"

"Because he has to want me despite what he thinks."

"He already does," Lazar said softly.

She shook her head. "Then he wouldn't have stayed away from me for so long."

"Don't do this to him, Tanya," Vasili beseeched her. "Stefan doesn't deal well with guilt."

She glanced over her shoulder and for the first time gave Vasili a genuine smile. "He won't be guilty, he'll be angry. You said so yourself. But I don't happen to mind his anger. Now, am I going to be your queen?"

"Yes," all three of them replied.

"Then respect my wishes."

"But he is already our king, and our friend besides," Lazar pointed out.

"So? I told you I'll deny it. Then he'll just be furious with you for misleading him."

And she walked away before she let them convince her that she was being unreasonable, prideful, and very likely foolish.

Chapter 33

Tanya hadn't expected Stefan to come for her when the ship docked in Danzig the next day. She had hoped he would and had dressed accordingly, but she hadn't expected it.

She had so many beautiful clothes to choose from now, it was actually a dilemma to decide what to wear that might impress him. She'd settled on a dark emerald skirt with a matching short-waisted jacket that buttoned primly to the throat, revealing only the delicate white lace on the high collar of the blouse beneath. Sasha had even supplied her with two choices for outer wraps. One was a long, thick cloak in pearl gray with a darker gray fur trim and a hood lined in the fur inside and out. The other was a coat very similar to the men's, black velvet with brown sable along every edge and in a wide, capelike collar. Hers fell to the ankles, while theirs cut off at the knees. What Sasha must have found amusing was having it made in the same material and colors as the one Stefan was wearing right now. Fortunately, she'd chosen the gray cloak to wear today.

He appeared stiff. The bow he offered, slight as it was, was formal. And she could read nothing in his expression as he looked her over, though his eyes were more amber than brown. But she had done nothing that could have made him angry, so that softly glowing color had to come from some other emotion, though she couldn't imagine which one.

"It is our hope the voyage was not too tedious for you."

Definitely stiff, and she didn't know what to make of it, if he was merely reluctant to have to deal with her again, or . . . Lord help her, had the others gone against her wishes and told him what she'd said yesterday? No, she wouldn't assume that. He'd have come straight to her to demand to hear it from her, wouldn't he? And be furious besides. Right now he was only—dammit, she couldn't tell what he was. But if she'd got anything out of his friends' revelations about him, it was that Stefan was even more complicated than she had thought.

She decided to behave just as she'd planned, casual, a little bit goading, a little bit friendly, maybe even a little provocative, whatever it took to keep him off balance until she could figure out where she stood. After all, his total indifference to her on this voyage was telling. If he could stay away from her on the confines of a ship, would she ever see him after they were married and he had a whole country to disappear in? If they were married. Maybe *he'd* find some way to get out of the betrothal. He was king, after all.

The smile she had planned to give him wasn't quite so dazzling now, but she still managed to speak in a friendly tone. "The voyage was quite pleasant, but of course it would be, with such charming companions to keep me entertained."

He obviously couldn't tell if she was being sarcastic or not, for he hesitated before saying, "My men are a lot of things, Tanya. But charming?"

"When they try to be, yes. I even found—to my amazement, of course—that I could like Lazar and Serge. And I have grown quite found of Sasha."

"You don't mention Vasili."

"Let's just say I've learned to tolerate your cousin, even when he's at his obnoxious best. No, I can't even say that. I have discovered, only recently, that I actually have a horrid temper. So I guess I haven't been very understanding of the close bond between you and Vasili that has more or less influenced his behavior toward me."

She smiled again, this time with satisfaction, for his new expression was a priceless combination of bafflement, irritation, and wariness. He really didn't know what to make of her now, and that was just what she wanted for the time being.

"It surprises you that I figured that out?" she continued. "Well, don't be. Vasili made the confession himself only yesterday. So I guess the most I can say is that I will *try* to tolerate him in future—your Majesty."

He raised a brow at the title, something he could at last deal with directly. "Was it the credentials?"

"Not at all. I thought they were faked."

"Then what convinced you?"

"Sasha, actually. He has an amazing way of getting his point across without even trying. He just kept going on and on about you, me, Cardinia—and the wedding." And then she pinned him with a direct gaze that had just enough angry sparks in it to indicate what was coming. "Why the hell did you tell me Vasili was king?"

He turned toward the door on the pretext of holding it open for her, but the question obviously disconcerted him so much that he couldn't hold her gaze. "You were being troublesome at the time. I thought you would be less so with him named as the prospective bridegroom."

She wasn't letting him off the hook that easily. "Why?"

"Because women become utter fools around him, and that is before he even sets out to seduce them. If he had made an effort to win you over, you would have succumbed."

Tanya snorted. "If you believe that, you are deluded."

He finally glanced at her and his look said she was deluding herself. "You say you know that Vasili's loyalty to me influenced his behavior toward you, so haven't you realized yet that some of his behavior was a deliberate effort to make you despise him? I merely wanted you to come along with us willingly, but Vasili saw the consequence of the lie. He didn't want you falling in love with him when you would have to marry me in the end."

"How thoughtful of him," she sneered. "But you

and he both put too much stock in his looks, for some reason thinking that's all that matters to a woman. And maybe that is all that matters to a woman with no sense. But most women aren't foolish enough to fall in love with a man without knowing what he's made of. Vasili is incredibly handsome, yes. There's no denying that. But he's also the most arrogant, condescending man God ever put breath into, and you aren't going to tell me that his obnoxious attitude was a pretense just for my benefit.''

He didn't like what he was hearing, probably because he knew he was arrogant and condescending, too, in no way as bad as Vasili, but Tanya was counting on his not making that distinction. The object here was not to let Stefan know that she was one of those foolish women she had just ranted about. Not that she had fallen in love. Lord help her, she hoped she wasn't *that* foolish. But she knew very well that she had succumbed to a purely physical attraction, one so powerful that she could want this man even when she was so furious with him that she could shoot him. And time hadn't made that feeling go away. She wanted him, enough to marry him, enough to ignore all his faults. But he had to want her just as much . . . he had to love her, whether she loved him or not. That was the only way she could willingly give herself over to the control of one man for life. And she didn't have much time to find out if it was even possible.

Before he could dwell too deeply on what she'd said, she asked, ''When you saw that the pretense wasn't working, why didn't you tell me the truth, that you were Cardinia's new king?''

"You already doubted everything. It was not the time to admit to a falsehood that you could hold up as a reason to justify your continued skepticism.''

"I see your point,'' she said, her brows knitted thoughtfully for his benefit. "Of course, you never saw mine, did you? It didn't matter who was being offered as my husband, I didn't want one.''

He didn't notice the past tense, he merely replied adamantly, "You have no more choice than I do.''

"Ah, that's right. How did you put it before, when Vasili admitted he didn't want to marry me? That the king will marry me whether he wishes to or not, because his duty demands it? But you know, Stefan, I've been giving that some thought, especially after being assured how all-powerful you are, so powerful, I'm told, that you can have us married no matter what I say about it. It strikes me that if you're that powerful, how can anyone make you do something you don't want to do? You could just break the betroth—''

"I happen to honor my father,'' he cut in stiffly, his eyes suddenly glowing with serious anger. *"Sandor* wants you sitting on the throne, so you will damn well sit on the throne! And if you ever try coaxing me out of my duty again.... I *will* marry you, Tanya. Nothing will prevent that, do you understand? Nothing!''

It was amazing how wonderful that promise made her feel, shouted or not. And she had her answer. *He* wasn't going to do anything to get out of the betrothal. Neither was she, but he didn't know that.

Nor was it part of her plan to let him know that. She'd keep him guessing, which would keep her constantly on his mind. But long before they reached Cardinia she'd have him in her bed, too. There was no help for that. *She* just couldn't wait anymore.

Chapter 34

"Why so stiff, Stefan?" Tanya asked as soon as they settled into the waiting coach.

He'd grabbed her arm, whisked her out of her cabin and off the ship, all without saying a word to her, but she was determined to open him up today, to get inside his thoughts, even if she had to get him angry again to do it. Fortunately, the others weren't there to try to stop her. Lazar and Serge were seeing to the baggage and would follow in another carriage. Vasili was disposing of the ship. It seemed it had been bought only to fetch her home from America. Cardinia having no navy, situated so far inland as it was, they now had no further use for the ship.

"Is it the clothes?" she persisted when Stefan didn't even glance her way. "Do they make you feel more kingly, less like a—commoner?" No answer. "Well, you were right. Definitely too conspicuous for Mississippi."

"What *are* you talking about, Tanya?"

He still wasn't looking at her. Trying to get his goat was getting her own.

"Oh, nothing important. I understand now why you didn't open up that second trunk of clothes for use while you were in America. You would have stood out like a sore thumb in such strange garb, wouldn't you?"

Actually, he looked grand dressed all in black, in an outfit that seemed military in design. The gleaming knee-high boots, with trousers tucked into them, were tight enough to define his leg muscles. The velvet jacket was more like a tunic, crossed with silver-gray braid and frogs from neck to waist, then with an open seam, also braided, from waist to mid-thigh, where the tunic ended. Around his waist was a thick belt worked in silver with a splendid leather scabbard also set with silver, and containing a sword that was so fancy, it had to be mere decoration. He wore a sable-edged velvet coat draped over his shoulders like a cape, held in place by a silver link chain with jeweled clasps. To top this off was a hat of the same brown sable fur that merely circled his head, what Lazar called a *kucsma*.

Although her question was supposed to rile him, all Stefan said in reply to her observation was, "Look out your window before you call my clothing strange."

He was right as usual. There was no denying she was in a foreign land where people dressed and looked like nothing she was accustomed to.

Tanya had been told the country they were in might be Prussia now, but it had once been the kingdom of Poland, and was still populated mostly by Poles, especially here in the old harbor city of Danzig. And these Poles, men and women both, seemed to favor extremely long coats with the most unusual sleeves, wide from shoulder to elbow, then slashed down the front from elbow to cuff. They were long sleeves, much longer than the length of the arm, and hardly any were cuffed. People just let the sleeves dangle down at their sides or threw them back over their shoulders. One man who looked like a soldier had his tied at the back of his neck. The hats or bonnets were different, too, mostly flat, some tall and oddly shaped; and the men's hair was either shoulder-length or cut extremely short in a round crop on the very top of their heads.

"I see what you mean," Tanya allowed and gave up attacking his clothes, which were actually very moderate in comparison. She tried the congenial approach again. "You know, Stefan, I've learned so much about you on this voyage, I feel like we're old friends now."

His expression hardened considerably. He didn't know what she was referring to, and she could see that annoyed the hell out of him. Good. She smiled to herself and abruptly switched subjects again.

"Lazar couldn't tell me much about my father, other than how greatly he was admired for continuing the tradition of his ancestors in keeping the Ottoman Empire from taking over Cardinia as it has so many of her neighbors. Your father has also kept those people at bay, hasn't he?"

"We have excellent treaties with the Turks, but

even more importantly, good relations. The Janaceks have always believed in offering a genuine hand of friendship—after they defeat the enemy. The Baranys are of the same philosophy.''

''Yes, well, Lazar said I should ask your Prime Minister, Maximilian Daneff, about the more personal side of my father, since he knew him well. But he said that you could tell me about the blood feud that killed him and the rest of my family in a matter of months.''

That finally made him look at her in surprise. ''You still don't know why you were sent away? Vasili could have told you—''

''I didn't care to ask him,'' she interrupted. ''But you, on the other hand, I can ask anything, since you're going to be my husband.''

That startled him even more, enough to ask, ''You have accepted it?''

Tanya shrugged with a degree of indifference. ''That depends.''

''On what?''

''You.''

''How?'' he demanded, his gaze suddenly so intense, she had trouble holding it.

''Oh, I don't know. You could try convincing me that you want to marry me, that you have found you can't live without me, that you love me madly.''

He was frowning so furiously now, she dropped her gaze. Well, she supposed she *could* have sounded serious instead of facetious, and ended with the words ''want to marry me'' instead of getting ridiculous

with the rest. Now he thought she'd been making fun
of him.

*Great going, missy. You had a golden opportunity
there that you just wasted. No damn guts.*

She wondered if she ought to apologize. She stole
a quick glance at him and nearly gasped. His eyes
were as hot as live coals. She'd made him so angry,
it was a wonder she wasn't already stretched out on
her back and being devoured with kisses . . . Desire
slammed through her system at the mere possibility,
one she hadn't realized until that moment. She'd only
been nipping at his temper to get him to reveal something of his feelings to her. She hadn't even considered the consequence of making him lose his temper
completely, but the consequence was there, and she
wouldn't mind if it happened right now. And how
much easier to have it taken out of her hands so she
wouldn't have to entice him and risk rejection.

"Do you require a reply, Princess?"

His voice was so low and menacing, she shivered.
He was controlling his temper by a thin thread. The
wrong answer to his question could snap it. Did she
want to be made love to in a moving coach, in broad
daylight? She didn't really care at the moment.

Her chin rose stubbornly. "Yes."

"Marrying me will make you a queen," he reminded her. "That is sufficient reason for you to
accept it graciously—if not willingly."

That was *not* the answer she had hoped to hear.
And it looked as if he was going to keep his temper
under control, no matter what.

She made an effort to readjust her expectations to

reality. Finally she sighed and turned to stare out the window again.

"I wouldn't know," she said to finish the subject. "I'm still adjusting to being a princess, and all I can say for that is the title comes with nice clothes." Then, more stiffly she said, "You were going to tell me about the blood feud."

"Was I?"

She glanced at him with a tight little smile. "Yes, you were, if for no other reason than because *you* feel I ought to know."

She waited, silently, while he just stared at her with those devil's eyes. When some of the heat went out of them, she knew he had decided that she would at least treat this subject with the seriousness it deserved.

Chapter 35

"It began with the execution of Yuri Stamboloff. He was the oldest son of a very powerful baron, which was perhaps why he felt he was above the law. He killed his mistress only because he suspected her of being unfaithful. It was an act committed not in rage or passion, but calmly, cold-bloodedly, and stupidly, before five witnesses. Because he was a baron's son, he was brought before your father, King Leos, for judgment and was executed. There was nothing else to be done. But Yuri's father, Janos Stamboloff, didn't believe his son was guilty of this murder. You see, the dead woman had first been the mistress of your brother."

"I had a brother old enough to have a mistress?" Tanya asked in surprise. "Wasn't I supposed to have been a baby at this time?"

"You were not even born yet when the murder took place," Stefan explained, adding, "Though you were expected. And you had three brothers. The oldest, the Crown Prince, was sixteen that year."

She was no longer surprised, but horrified. "Sixteen and he's discarding mistresses!"

"There are some women who would seduce a baby to advance their circumstances. At court, it doesn't matter who you use, as long as you use them to your advantage, and a sixteen-year-old boy would be a prime target for manipulation."

"I suppose you've discovered all these conscienceless women for yourself?" she asked tersely.

He smiled for the first time that day. "Of course."

Tanya couldn't believe how angry she suddenly felt, imagining hordes of women fawning over Stefan, seducing him, just to see what they could get out of him. And that damn smile of his said he had enjoyed every bit of it, whether the women's ploys had worked or not.

It was all she could do to keep from glowering at him, so she didn't dare pursue that subject any further. "So the dead woman was first my brother's mistress. Why would that lead Janos to believe his own son was innocent?"

"Because he couldn't believe Yuri was capable of such a crime. In his mind, someone else had to have committed it, and your brother was the most likely candidate. Janos claimed the boy killed the woman in a fit of jealous passion when she wouldn't return to him, then bought witnesses to blame Yuri for the crime. He also claimed that Leos had Yuri executed instead of banished because Yuri could prove he was innocent, and Leos was protecting his own son."

"Is it possible that Yuri *was* innocent?"

"No. One of the witnesses was a bishop of the

church. Another was Yuri's own servant. Only an enraged father would doubt them. Besides, your brother was well accounted for the entire day of the murder.''

''So then what happened?''

''Janos had your brother killed.''

''How?''

''How he did it doesn't matter, Tanya. Suffice it to say—''

''How?''

He stared at her for a long moment, his scars quivering as he ground his teeth together in protest at her persistence. She almost took back the question. But she already knew the end of this tale, so the details couldn't make it any worse. Her whole family had been killed. This was a known fact and she considered it tragic. But she had yet to actually feel anything personal about them. They simply weren't real to her because she had no memory of them. If she was going to grieve, it would be for that lack of memory.

She tried to explain that to Stefan. ''If you're hesitating because you think I'm going to get upset over any of this, don't. These people might be related to me by blood, but for twenty years I didn't know anything about them, and I still don't know anything other than what you tell me. And from what you've told me so far, I have as much sympathy for the Stamboloffs as I do for the Janaceks—with the exception of Yuri.''

''Then let me see if I can correct that, Princess. Your brother, innocent in all of this, was taken from his own bed one night, dragged before the entire

Stamboloff family for a mock trial, and found guilty. Janos then had him tied to a wall in his courtyard, and each member of that damn family put a bullet into him, even Janos' eight-year-old grandson. His body was left on the road outside the palace. The blood-soaked note attached to him said, 'A son for a son.' However, this wasn't enough proof against Janos—not until one of his daughters-in-law had too much to drink at a party and happened to brag about it to the wrong people.''

''I hope Janos was shot on the spot!''

Stefan raised a brow at her. Color came back to cheeks that had gone quite pale.

''You have no sympathy left for that fanatic?''

''None,'' she said more quietly.

''Well, he wasn't shot on the spot. He was tried and sentenced to hang. The day after the execution, Leos' only brother, sister-in-law, and their two children were found in their home with their throats cut. The note left behind this time was explicit. 'Every Janacek dies now.' ''

''But that was a wanton act of vengeance. How could they justify it?''

''They didn't have to. Two of their own had been killed. Those remaining now saw this as a personal war with the king, a blood feud, and there were a goodly number of them remaining—Janos' second son, five grandsons, two younger brothers, and three nephews. Janos had also called for revenge, his very last words on the scaffold before he was hung. But it was now treasonous, this revenge, with Leos himself being threatened. The five older men were killed resisting arrest. The grandsons and one remaining nephew, all under eighteen years of age at that time, were merely banished.''

''You didn't mention the women. What about that daughter-in-law?''

''There were two Stamboloff wives, and Janos had one daughter. They were eventually banished from Cardinia, along with the men, when it was suspected that one of them drowned your sister in her bath.''

''I had a sister, too?'' Tanya asked in a small voice.

''She was fourteen, the second oldest child. But getting every Stamboloff out of the country still didn't stop the killings. Ion Stamboloff, Janos' oldest grandson, was caught attempting to kill Leos' cousin, the only living son of your great-uncle, who was already deceased.''

''Why him?''

''He bore the name Janacek,'' Stefan said simply.

''But he survived?''

''No. A month later they went for him again and succeeded. It was Janos' daughter this time, found before she could leave the city. Then your two younger brothers were shot a few weeks before you were due to be born. This caused your mother to start her labor early. You were born small, but healthy. Your mother, however, never completely recovered. She had lost all of her children but you, and you were betrothed the very day of your birth. They say that Leos' insistence that the betrothal be finalized immediately was an indication he didn't expect to live much longer himself, and that contributed to your mother's decline. When you were three months old, she died of natural causes that a healthy woman could have easily withstood.''

''And my father?''

''Leos was stabbed in the back at his own table while he was eating dinner. The assassin had slowly worked his way up through the kitchen and had finally been allowed to serve at the table. He had no hope of escaping. He knew that. A confession revealed that he was dying of some disease, that the money he had taken to kill the king was for his family, the only way he could leave them cared for.''

''But did he reveal that a Stamboloff had hired him?''

''Not _a_ Stamboloff, Princess. That family was so arrogant by then in their hate for the Janaceks that there had been no secrecy in hiring this man. He named each one of them, the two remaining women right down to Ivan, Janos' youngest grandson, and since they each had contributed something of value for the assassin's payment, they all shared in this victory. And for them it was a victory. A Barany was put on the throne because the last Janacek wasn't expected to live out the year if she remained in Cardinia.''

''So I was sent away?''

''Not immediately, not until the first attempt was made on your life. Your nurse died instead. My father then devised the plan to send you away in secrecy, with only Baroness Tomilova to know of your whereabouts. He also put a high price on the head of each Stamboloff.''

''Even the children?''

"They didn't quibble about killing children," he replied harshly. "Your youngest brother was six years old. *You* were five months old when your nurse took the bullet meant for you. This was a blood feud, Tanya. It would not be over until one family or the other was completely destroyed. They wouldn't stop until you were dead. We couldn't bring you home until the last one of them was found and eliminated. But they were no longer children. It took years to find just one of those remaining, for they scattered and went into hiding when you disappeared. And only one of them was captured without a fight and brought back to be executed for treason, the rest all fighting to the end. And the last, Ivan, wasn't found until this year. Even then, he nearly escaped in a ship. But he left port so quickly, he didn't have enough crew to handle the storm they met. His ship went down in the Black Sea. Sandor's men were close enough behind to pick up any survivors, but Ivan wasn't one of them."

"Are you sure he was the last?"

"The Stamboloffs weren't just enemies of your family. Their assassination of the King of Cardinia made them enemies of the crown. A unit of twenty men was formed for the specific task of hunting them down. These men didn't make mistakes. It may have taken twenty years, but they were thorough."

"But a child, grown to manhood and not seen for ten or fifteen years. Who could possibly recognize him and say for certain this is a Stamboloff?"

Stefan grinned at her. "An excellent point, little Tanya." He went on without noticing the blush that his near endearment caused her. "But the Stambol-offs were one of those unique families whose members looked alike—at least the men did. The remaining grandsons were each dark of skin, blond, and blue-eyed, and all bore a striking resemblance to Janos and his sons when they were full-grown. And not one but five of Sandor's men knew the Stamboloffs personally. When they found one, there was never any doubt that they had found the right man."

Tanya shook her head slowly, denying the emotion churning inside her. "All those deaths, because one old man couldn't accept that his son was a murderer. Yuri must have hidden his true character well from his loved ones."

"It is human nature to do so."

"Is it?" she asked in a whisper. "I wouldn't know. I've never had any loved ones."

He couldn't mistake the mist forming in her eyes. His hand reached toward her, but drew back as the coach stopped. She didn't notice, turning her head aside to dab briskly at her eyes.

"Where are we?"

"At a house I have on the outskirts of town. We will spend the night here while everything is readied for the last leg of our journey."

His hand was offered again, but this time to help her from the coach.

"You own a house here, so far from home?"

"I merely leased it when we came through Danzig in the spring."

Tanya turned a look of amazement on him. "And you kept it all these months just so you would have somewhere to spend one night on your return? Lord help us, Stefan, someone ought to have a serious talk with you about the way you squander money.''

He laughed because *she* was serious. ''The house cost very little, Tanya.''

She looked up at the two-story edifice and exclaimed, ''Sure it did!''

''And it was needed for the attendants who were left behind.''

''Oh, well, that makes sense,'' she replied dryly. ''Especially since it only takes a few weeks to reach Cardinia from here—but you've been gone, what, seven or eight months?''

He frowned at her now and took her elbow to lead her up to the front door. ''The cost was negligible,'' he said with curt dismissal, ''and my attendants chose to wait for me here. I fail to see—''

The door flew open, and a lusciously curved redhead threw her arms around Stefan's neck and plastered her lips to his mouth. Stefan could ''fail to see'' till his eyes fell out, but Tanya could see perfectly well why this *attendant* had chosen to wait for him here.

Chapter 36

There was a positive benefit in being forced to stand there and watch her betrothed kissing another woman. It took Tanya's mind completely off that depressing tale she had just heard about her family. It also made her see red, and not just in the color of that strumpet's hair.

To give Stefan credit, however, he didn't seem to be returning the woman's enthusiastic kiss. He seemed to be trying to end it. But it was taking too damn long for him to do so, as far as Tanya was concerned. And she didn't doubt for a minute that if she weren't there to witness this reunion, he'd be participating in the kiss instead. But she was there, and he knew it, so what could he do but make this halfhearted effort to pry the redhead's arms loose from his neck?

When he finally accomplished that miraculous feat—the woman really was clinging to him—he was treated to a gushing explanation for her behavior. ''It was too bad of you, Stefan, to be gone so long that

I would miss you unbelievably. And we have been so worried. Your father even sent a man who will no doubt leave within the hour to take him news of you. The anxious fellow has been a pure nuisance hanging around here, but I suppose Sandor has been as concerned about your tardiness as the rest of us, and didn't want to wait even an extra few days to hear that you have returned safely.''

''My father still lives, then?''

''I have heard nothing to say otherwise,'' she assured him with a bright smile.

Tanya stiffened as the woman reached for Stefan again, obviously with the intent of showing him her delight in having him returned to her. Tanya felt a very strong urge to reach for the knife now strapped to her thigh, though she wasn't sure what she meant to do with it. It was merely a small eating knife that she had confiscated on the ship, and she had had to find a new place to conceal it after Sasha got rid of her boots, but old habits were hard to break. She might have one or more of four strapping, capable men always there to protect her, but she preferred to depend on herself.

Right now that knife would look very nice placed against the redhead's throat with a warning to back off. Of course, she would then have Stefan to deal with, and she couldn't imagine him being pleased by such an unexpected display of jealousy. And it was jealousy. She couldn't very well call it anything else when the sight of that woman kissing Stefan made Tanya mad enough to scratch her eyes out.

But how could she explain that to Stefan? He

would believe that as much as he had believed her taunt that she might be a virgin—not at all. Why should he? She had rejected him completely the very last time they were together, before the *Carpathia* had sailed. The best she could do was offer the truth, that since she had accepted their upcoming marriage, she now had it set in her mind that he belonged to her, and if she was going to have him, she wanted him exclusively.

But she couldn't even tell him that without making a complete fool of herself, because *he* didn't feel the same way. He had admitted to wanting her, but also to hating that he did. And his wanting her was so temporary, it wasn't worth mentioning. One time was all he was interested in, she supposed for the novelty or the challenge, because she *had* rejected him. Big deal.

What was more telling was his resentment that he had to marry her, and that resentment had always been crystal clear. If it wasn't a matter of duty, he'd never do it. And standing before her was still another reason that he wouldn't.

She had been told by Vasili that Stefan had a mistress. She just never dreamed she would have to meet her. Nor had it occurred to her that Stefan probably had no intention of giving up his mistress. Why should he, after all? He was being forced to marry Tanya, but standing right here was a woman he gave his affections to by choice.

It was fortunate that Stefan prevented the woman from plastering herself to him again, because Tanya honestly couldn't say what she would have done if she had to watch them kissing again. He put his arm around her waist instead and turned her toward Tanya, and in that moment of green eyes meeting blue, Tanya knew this little demonstration of devotion had been staged for her benefit. Stefan's mistress must feel threatened by her. What a joke.

Any satisfaction she might have felt from that realization was ruined by Stefan's expression. He was so delighted to be reunited with his mistress again, he didn't even try to hide it. Tanya didn't consider that his obvious pleasure had come from hearing that his father still lived.

"Princess Tatiana, may I present to you Lady Alicia Huszar? Alicia wanted to meet you before the rest of the court, because she desires to be one of your personal attendants when you are queen."

Over our dead body, missy. No, over hers, Tanya corrected herself. But she'd rather die than be as obvious as they were about their feelings right now. Stefan was *not* going to know she was pea-green with jealousy. So she didn't dare say a word. She merely nodded to acknowledge the introduction.

Alicia was forced to offer a perfunctory bow now that Tanya's identity had been established. Tanya was a royal princess, after all. To do even that must have galled her, but Tanya couldn't find any satisfaction in thinking that either.

"I'm sorry, your Highness," Alicia said, pretending surprise she couldn't possibly feel. "I didn't even notice you standing there."

Liar. She had seen them arrive from one of the windows, or Tanya would eat her new shoes. But she didn't say so, not directly anyway, since she still didn't trust herself to say anything to the redhead. She glanced at Stefan instead and raised a slim brow to accompany an expression as skeptical as she could make it.

He at least got the message, or she assumed he did, for he took his arm away from Alicia and frowned at her, perhaps finally realizing that she hadn't kissed him just in greeting, something he was no doubt accustomed to, but she'd done it in front of his betrothed.

Stefan, to give him his due, would want to be discreet, at least until the marriage was an accomplished fact. He probably hadn't counted on Tanya suspecting anything about his sweet Alicia. But did he really think she would accept his mistress as one of her attendants? His *mistress*, for crying out loud! If that was the way things were done in Cardinia, Tanya wasn't leaving Danzig.

For his part, Stefan was as embarrassed as Tanya was furious. He had left Alicia here with the promise that she wouldn't be supplanted. He had had no intention of giving her up for a woman he was being forced to marry, and although he would marry her, he had intended it to be in name only.

But he hadn't counted on his reaction to a plain-faced Tatiana, his delight that she wasn't what they'd expected, his anger that she was a whore. All he should have felt was satisfaction that she was what he could bring back to his father with the taunt, "Here is the princess you would bind me to, but neither of

us will ever know if her issue is royal or bastard.''
Instead he had been fiercely glad that she would be
his, had desired her from the first moment he saw
her, and by the time her beauty was revealed, it was
too late. His emotions were already thoroughly involved with her.

Now he knew exactly what he wanted, and it was
more painful than he could have imagined, knowing
that he'd never get it. She even teased him about it,
perhaps not cruelly, since she didn't know how he
felt, but it had hurt just the same that she could deal
with the subject so frivolously. Tell her that he
couldn't live without her, that he loved her madly?
He'd actually found the only peace he'd known since
meeting her by staying away from her on the ship,
because every time he was near her, his passions
were roused to either anger or desire. And he had no
control over what she made him feel. Anger, lust,
jealousy, love, it all went hand in hand where Tanya
was concerned.

Love her? ''Madly'' was an apt word. God, what
an utter fool he was!

Chapter 37

Dinner that night was an excruciating affair of tempers tested to their limit, at least for Stefan. He had been unable to have a private word with Alicia, and when he did, he still wasn't sure what he was going to say to her. On the one hand, she was the most amiable mistress he had ever had, and he would hate to lose that. On the other hand, he had absolutely no desire for her at present.

That would change, undoubtedly, when he stopped torturing himself over Tanya. But Alicia wasn't the type of woman who would just sit back and wait while he agonized over another. It wasn't even fair of him to ask. It wasn't fair of him, either, to put her aside when he had assured her that wouldn't happen. That he was undecided on what to do not only was aggravating, it wasn't like him.

Then he had found himself actually walking the floor in a state of nervous unease when Alicia had taken Tanya upstairs to show her to her room. The two of them alone together, one woman in the habit

320

of wielding knives, though thank God she no longer wore them, the other in the habit of protecting what was hers, and Alicia still considered him hers. It didn't bear thinking of, what could happen. But nothing did, at least nothing that either of them cared to let him know about. And that, incredibly, annoyed him more than the fact that he'd worried about it.

Even Sandor's man not showing up to speak with him, after Alicia had assured him the fellow would put in an appearance, had infuriated Stefan, especially since he had prepared a missive for the man to take to his father. But the man must have merely noted his arrival and left to return to Cardinia immediately, without even asking after the princess, whom Sandor would also be anxious to hear about.

And what was he going to tell Sandor in the end about Tanya? The truth? Only half the truth?

Sandor was going to blame himself for Tanya's deplorable upbringing. Stefan half blamed him himself. To have sent only one person with the child, and not to have taken into consideration that something might happen to that single guardian . . . no, he couldn't tell his father the entire truth. He was going to be upset enough that Tanya hadn't been raised properly. He didn't have to know just how improperly she had turned out. But Stefan had never lied to him before. That he would start doing so, and for a woman, was intolerable.

Obviously, he was in a mood to be irritated by the slightest little thing today, but he supposed, after all those weeks at sea, he was due to let off a little steam. No, it seemed more that Tanya was going to ensure that he did. First her strange behavior in her cabin, then again in the coach. He had expected her to be a little different after he'd been told that she no longer doubted her identity or theirs, but all that inane chatter? And such drastic mood swings? If she had set out to exasperate him, she couldn't have succeeded more thoroughly, for trying to figure out what she was up to—and he didn't doubt she was up to something—was unbelievably frustrating.

And what the devil did Vasili think he was doing, making over Alicia tonight as if she were his mistress instead of Stefan's? For Tanya's benefit? Since when did Vasili want to protect Tanya's feelings? And Alicia was only halfheartedly playing along with it. But Tanya wasn't stupid. And she had witnessed that kiss. And she didn't care. That was the most annoying thing yet today. She didn't give a damn that she was sitting at the same table with his mistress. Any other woman would, if only for the sake of form, but not his future bride.

He watched her now, sitting between Lazar and Serge, talking with them, laughing occasionally. He had never seen her like this before, at ease, apparently enjoying herself—not angry. Had he stayed away from her longer than necessary? No, he still couldn't be near her without wanting her. It was no more than she had said—she now liked Lazar and Serge both. That in no way meant she felt any differently about *him*. And for all her chatter that morning, she hadn't spoken one word to him all evening. In fact, she spoke to everyone but him. But every so often she would glance his way and smile, and he'd grit his teeth, wondering why.

Stefan didn't know it, but his eyes were lit to the scorching point. Tanya knew it, and that was the only reason she was able to act as if she didn't have a care in the world, when in fact she felt like breaking every dish on the table over Stefan's head. And she found she was rather good at pretense, much better than Alicia, who had offered friendship with malice in her eyes.

She still couldn't believe that woman's gall this afternoon. No sooner had they entered the bedroom where Tanya was to sleep that night than the redhead had asked, "Has Stefan told you yet that your marriage will be in name only?"

"No, I suppose he forgot to mention that."

"Oh, you poor girl." Alicia had oozed sympathy. "You must have been dreading . . . well, I'm glad I can at least relieve your mind on that score. And you needn't thank me. I know how disappointed you must have been when he showed up to claim you. Those scars do take getting used to."

"What scars?" Tanya asked, and was immensely pleased to see Alicia lose her whole train of thought, as well as her false smile.

"That isn't funny, Princess."

"It wasn't meant to be."

"Are you saying you don't *mind* his scars?"

Tanya turned and walked to the window to stare outside, saying nothing at all. Behind her, she heard Alicia snort.

"That's what I thought," the redhead sneered,

then switched back to her let's-be-friends tone. "But I was trying to tell you that you won't have to worry about him playing the husband with you, not while I'm around. And don't worry about being lonely either. Stefan won't mind how many lovers you take, as long as you don't make a scandal out of it. And I'll be able to help you in that respect."

"You know all about being discreet, do you?"

"Certainly."

It occurred to Tanya that if she had been dreading her coming marriage, she might have been naively grateful to Alicia for her assurances. However, she knew damn well those assurances hadn't been given to be helpful, but for the opposite reason. If she had fallen in love with Stefan, her expectations were now supposed to have burst. If she were merely undecided, she'd just been warned to forget it, that he was already taken. And she had the feeling, knowing how angry her imagined lovers from the past made Stefan, he *would* mind if she took new ones, so Alicia was also setting the groundwork to cause one hell of a lot of trouble.

Tanya turned around to face Alicia, though with the window at her back, the fury brimming in her green eyes went unnoticed. Her tone, however, was unmistakably frigid. "I know a little about discretion myself, so I'm going to be discreet right now and not tell you what I think of your kind of help."

Alicia's eyes narrowed, showing that she gave up the pretense. "You would do well to get along with me, Princess. With a word to Stefan, I'll have you begging my pardon."

"Is that so? You think you have that much influence with the king?"

"I know I do," she said with total confidence.

"Well, the king doesn't happen to have *any* influence with me—yet—so don't count on my begging your pardon for anything. Nor do I need him to fight my battles for me, as you do. *You* would do well to remember that."

Alicia merely stuck her nose up in the air and huffed out of there. Tanya turned back to the window and counted to fifty, then a hundred, then way beyond that. When she was finally calm enough to unclench her fists and think rationally, she decided she wouldn't kill that woman. She'd give Stefan the benefit of the doubt. Maybe Alicia had been told to wait for him here because he had doubted he would even find Tanya. Or maybe he had originally intended to keep his mistress close at hand, because what Tanya didn't know wouldn't hurt her. Well, she did know, and he was smart enough to know she did after that kiss that was bestowed on him at the door. So she decided to give him the rest of the afternoon to get rid of the woman.

Only he hadn't done that. She'd walked into the dining room tonight to find Alicia sitting there, and not at a prudent distance from Stefan, but right next to him.

The redhead was decked out in some very splendid finery that made her look almost pretty, and she'd been laughing at some comment from Vasili, who was sitting on her other side at the table. But when she noticed Tanya, her lips curved in a smug little smile that was almost the last straw. Tanya had given Stefan his chance and he'd tossed it away, proving that he didn't care what she thought or how she would react. So she wasn't going to react. That was, after all, her only pride-saving option under the circumstances. And, Lord help her, it was the hardest thing she'd ever done, containing that much seething anger without revealing one little bit of it. But her performance became easier when she finally noticed that her lack of reaction was, for some reason, annoying Stefan so much that his eyes were glowing like golden fire.

Chapter 38

Stefan had calmed down some by the end of dinner, thanks to the enormous amount of wine he had put away with very little food joining it. It had occurred to him that perhaps Americans were different in the way they handled certain situations, and that possibility was what actually took a big chunk out of his anger. After all, Tanya might lose her temper frequently with him, even with his friends, but he couldn't recall her ever letting it loose in front of strangers, and she would consider Alicia a stranger.

Then again, women adhered to certain rules of conduct when they were together. Two of them could be sworn enemies who would go for each other's throat in private, yet they could behave like perfect friends in public.

Once he'd begun, he came up with even more excuses for Tanya's seeming indifference to the situation. She could be intimidated by Alicia's sophistication and elegance. Tanya's upbringing made her ignorant of social protocol. She hadn't even changed for dinner, was still wearing the clothes she'd worn on arrival, while Alicia had turned herself out in grand style, her white silk gown new, her jewels abundant. And Alicia was cattily showing off.

He'd seen her do this before and it had never bothered him, the way she fingered her jewels in front of other women, drawing attention to them as if they were trophies. These trophies were three long ropes of pearls around her neck, diamonds at her ears, and not one but four rings on her fingers, each one worth a small fortune. And she took every opportunity to flaunt them in front of Tanya.

Tonight this habit of hers annoyed him, not so much Alicia's typical competitiveness, but that his mistress had jewels he had given her, while his future bride had not a bauble to her name. How much more was Tanya annoyed by it, though carefully keeping her envy from showing?

That was at least one thing he could rectify, and before he left the city—tonight, in fact, since they were leaving first thing in the morning. He didn't care if he had to drag a jeweler out of bed, he was not going to have his bride arrive in Cardinia looking less grand than even the lowliest member at court.

It didn't occur to Stefan as he set off to do just that, with Serge and several bottles of vodka to keep them warm, that he was procrastinating, clearly avoiding making a decision about Alicia, *and* avoiding being alone with her. When it did occur to him, he was naturally disgusted with himself. Yet by the time he returned to the house, a small, jewel-encrusted chest on the coach seat beside him, he had come up with still another reason to put off a confrontation with Alicia, and this one was more logical than all the rest. He was now too intoxicated to make a decision tonight, one way or the other.

Besides, he had reasoned that he really ought to wait until the morning and speak to Tanya first, alone. If she gave him hell about Alicia, then he would quite cheerfully send his mistress away. But if she said nothing at all about it, then he'd know that the excuses he had come up with were only that, and it really didn't make any difference to her what he did.

That was his final intention, but he hadn't counted on a mistress determined to reestablish her claim on him. When he stumbled into the bedroom Sasha had prepared for him, instead of the one he had shared with Alicia before he went to America, it was to find her in this new room anyway, curled up in bed and waiting for him.

"It wasn't necessary for you to change rooms, Stefan, just for appearances," she gently chided him. "Your little princess doesn't care where you sleep."

That was not the wisest thing she could have said to him just then. She realized it when he set down the jeweled chest he was carrying and turned glowing eyes on her. She also realized he wasn't exactly sober. That, at least, she could count in her favor. However, she doubted even that when his voice came out sounding so chilling.

"I don't recall inviting you here, Alicia."

She tried laughing that off. "You didn't have to, darling. I have shared your rooms for the last two years. Since when have I needed an invitation?"

She was right, of course. She was also forcing him to face his decision about her head-on, right now, when he no longer was clearheaded enough to do so. But there really was no decision to make, was there? He didn't just want Tanya. There was a lot more to it than that, a lot more that she had managed to make him feel for her. With Alicia, all he felt was a desire not to hurt her, bred from two years of familiarity and a certain fondness that their time together had produced.

"Alicia—"

"Come, Stefan, let me put you to bed," she cut in quickly, before he could actually tell her to leave. "I can see you have had a little too much to drink tonight, so you probably don't need me, but let me at least make you comfortable."

He came over to the bed and she immediately moved the covers aside for him, at the same time revealing that she was naked beneath them. The one thing he had always liked especially well about Alicia was her body, and she knew it. She also knew that, like most men, he became amorous when he was drunk, wanting to make love whether his body was agreeable or not. She had never liked accommodating him at such times, but tonight was definitely an exception: her future was at stake.

She wasn't stupid. She *knew* things had changed with him. One look at that damn princess was all she needed to tell her that Stefan wouldn't mind at all marrying the bitch, or bedding her. But such a beautiful creature would never want him in return. Didn't he know that?

If he didn't, Alicia had to make sure he did. She was finally the mistress of a king. She had put up with Stefan for two years, patiently waiting for Sandor to die or step down in favor of his son, and she didn't care which. Now that one of the alternatives had finally happened, she wasn't about to lose her position just because Stefan had to get married.

When he just stood there looking at her, but making no move to sit beside her, she began to panic, wondering if anything she could say or do would make a difference at this point. If he had actually fallen in love with that woman . . .

That horrid thought brought her swiftly to her knees in front of him. "Silly man," she pouted as she reached to remove his coat for him. "You could not have picked a more inappropriate time to drink too much. You may not want me tonight, but after such a long absence from you, I cannot say the same. But I suppose I can wait if I must. And I can't really blame you after I saw the way that woman behaves toward you. She could drive anyone to drink."

Stefan didn't bother correcting her about the state of his condition. He wasn't anywhere near so drunk that he couldn't cover her on that bed and make love to her all night. And after his own ridiculously long abstinence, it would undoubtedly take all night before he was finally satisfied. But since it was the wrong bed and the wrong woman, he said nothing. Her remark about Tanya, however, he couldn't let pass.

"What behavior are you referring to?"

"Why, the way she completely ignored you at dinner. And she didn't even care that you saw how friendly she has become with Lazar."

The insinuation cut with razor sharpness. The only reason he didn't bleed was that he knew where Lazar's loyalties lay. But the pain of Tanya's "friendships" with other men was still there, and he could not thank Alicia for reminding him of it.

Tightly, he said, "It has occurred to me that her behavior tonight can be attributed to her having witnessed that thoughtless display of affection you greeted me with on our arrival. She is my betrothed, Alicia. You knew better than to be so obvious in who *you* were!"

Anger was making him sober up, but it was the word "were" that increased her panic. "But I didn't even notice her with you," she insisted, hoping to placate him and exonerate herself at the same time. "And I was so happy to see you, I couldn't help myself. I know I was careless, and it won't happen again, but she didn't care about that, Stefan. I know she didn't."

"How do you know?"

Alicia lowered her eyes, pretending a reluctance to say any more. She even managed to get his shirt off while he waited for her to answer, his concentration so great he wasn't aware of what she was doing.

Finally he repeated the question, and none too softly. *"How* do you know?"

She still wouldn't look at him, was swiftly opening the front of his trousers. "I'm sorry, Stefan, but I spoke with her at length this afternoon."

She said no more, forcing him to drag this confession out of her. "And?"

"She said she was relieved to know you had a mistress to keep you from bothering her in that way."

He moved away from her as his anger increased tenfold. "Damn her, she actually said that to you?"

"And more," Alicia said as she sat back on her heels, wishing she could have at least removed his trousers before he started pacing. She might not love Stefan, but he *was* a magnificent lover, and she had missed that in his absence—if nothing else.

He whirled on her now. "What else?"

"Stefan, you really don't want to hear this." When all he did was scowl at her, she figured she'd evaded enough. "Well, she admitted she can't bear your . . . that is to say, she doesn't like . . ."

She didn't go any further, but she stared pointedly at his left cheek. The scars there twitched, then disappeared, his face had darkened so with heat. Alicia stared at him in amazement. God, he was a handsome man when you didn't notice his scars. It was too bad she had such an aversion to them herself. Of course, without them, she knew she would never have won this man, so it was an aversion she kept strictly to herself.

Now that the damage was done, Alicia felt safe in criticizing the princess. "She's just a vain girl, Stefan, so what can you expect? She knows how beautiful she is, and knows that she could have any man she wanted—"

"Enough!"

Stefan couldn't believe how much those words

hurt. It was exactly what he had feared, that Tanya wouldn't be able to ignore his disfigurement. He should have known she was lying when she'd claimed she barely noticed his scars because of his eyes. Her constant rejection of him proved it. And that she yielded to his kisses occasionally was just as he had first supposed—she was a whore at heart as well as in fact. But vain? No, about that Alicia was merely guessing. He'd never known anyone less vain or conceited than Tanya. But that was all he could see in her favor right now.

He hadn't noticed Alicia approaching, but he felt her cool breasts first as she pressed them into his bare chest, just before wrapping her arms around him. "Let me help you forget about her for a while, Stefan," she purred up at him. "You know I can."

He did know it. He also needed a woman, needed one so badly it was painful. And this one knew how to pleasure a man with the skills of a harlot.

Chapter 39

Tanya wasn't sleeping well at all that night. She missed the roll of a ship beneath her after being at sea so long, but that wasn't the only reason, not by a far cry. She simply had too much anger simmering inside that she hadn't released even a little bit. So it was no wonder the tiniest noise kept waking her, and no wonder she was alerted and wide awake again when someone turned the handle on her door.

Unfortunately, she didn't recognize what this sound was. And the fire in the hearth, which had blazed earlier to warm the whole room, had burned down to mere ashes now, giving off no light at all. So she couldn't see the door slowly opening when she tried peering into the darkness around her, nor was there a creak from the well-oiled hinges.

After a few moments during which she didn't hear anything else, she lay down and tried getting back to sleep for the umpteenth time. But then there was a creak, a very definite creak, in one of the floor-boards too damn near her bed.

Her eyes flew open again, and unlike the other times she'd been awakened by sounds that didn't alarm her, this time she was frightened, and was reaching for the knife she kept under her pillow, a habit from her days in the tavern that she could be glad she hadn't given up, even on the ship. But no sooner did her fingers touch the blade than the pillow was yanked out from under her head to land square on her face.

For a horrible moment Tanya thought she was being deliberately smothered. It didn't take her long to realize that her first guess was accurate. Someone didn't want her to breathe, was smashing the pillow down on her face so hard she really *couldn't* breathe.

It was the shock that someone was actually trying to kill her, that had her paralyzed with fear for nearly a minute, even though she was gripping a knife in her hand. And it was the pain starting in her chest that finally set her to motion. She could barely move though because her body was trapped under thick blankets, her hand with the knife in it trapped beneath the pillow where it was being pressed down on both sides of her face.

Her free hand found only an arm that wouldn't budge when she pulled at it, because whoever it belonged to was leaning his full weight into the pillow. She pulled at the pillow next, but it wasn't moving either. Her last option was to get to the knife with her free hand, and, thank God, she found the blade of it extended beyond the pillow's edge. But her other hand was still gripping it, and she couldn't open those fingers to release it, because that hand was right under the one holding the pillow down. She tugged at the blade, turned it around, wiggled it, but the grip she had on the handle with her trapped hand was just too tight. And she was running out of time, a streak of weakness racing along her limbs as the pain in her chest became excruciating.

All she could do then was what she wouldn't do under any other circumstances. Somehow she pushed that blade up and back toward the arm above it, probably breaking her fingers to do it, but she didn't feel that, because she was feeling too much pain everywhere else, and was losing consciousness when the pillow was released on that side of her face. Enough air rushed into her lungs to keep her conscious, and with her other hand released now and the knife still somehow in it, she made a faint swipe at her attacker. She struck nothing, but she was able to steal another breath before he tried smashing the pillow down again. Only he didn't. He knew she had something sharp that she'd stuck him with, and he'd moved back from it.

When she realized the pillow had been released altogether, Tanya didn't even try pushing it off her face; she just rolled out of bed before she could be stabbed or shot, now that the non-messy attempt had failed. Still gasping painful breaths, she landed on the floor tangled in her blankets, in no condition to fight if she had to.

She'd never screamed in her life, except maybe recently in a rage, but she decided this might be a good time to start, simply because she didn't know what her attacker was doing now, couldn't see him, and was still terrified. Nor did she want that son of a bitch getting away, and she wasn't quite up to chasing him herself yet. But trying to scream after she'd almost been suffocated was no easy task. She tried it three times before the sound finally came out loud enough for it to do her any good.

In less than a minute, her door was thrown open, but it was help arriving, not her attacker leaving. Stefan was first through the door, with Serge right behind him carrying a lamp. They stopped short when they saw only her head poking up from the other side of the bed. But Tanya ignored them for the moment, taking advantage of the light to scan the room. She even looked under the bed, but there was no one there.

"Do you always scream when you fall out of bed?"

The voice sounded so disgusted, Tanya stiffened. Was that really what Stefan thought, that she'd merely tumbled out of bed? "No, I save my screams for murder attempts," she said sarcastically and then dismissed him and looked toward Serge, who had set the lamp down and was lighting another. "If you hurry, you might find whoever it was who just tried to kill me, before they leave the house."

With Tanya calmly sitting there on the floor, only her head visible above the bed, and with that bit of sarcasm she'd tossed out, it was no wonder even that Serge asked doubtfully, "Are you serious, Princess?"

She still wasn't breathing normally yet, so her "Very" came out as a very loud sigh, but both men moved the moment she said it.

In seconds she was alone again, but she'd just happened to catch the glow that leaped into Stefan's eyes before he ran out of the room. She cringed, imagining that he was angry only at being put to the bother of searching for her would-be attacker, which he still probably doubted was real. And if they found no sign of him, that anger would likely be turned on her. As if she cared just now.

She let out another sigh, this one intentional, and dug her way out of her blankets, leaving them where they lay as she pulled herself up to sit on the side of the bed. That accomplished, she set her knife on the table beside the bed and began massaging her fingers. Amazingly, none were broken, but they were definitely sore from being pressed and bent by the knife handle, particularly her little finger and wrist. Her nose hurt, too, from being smashed, and her chest still felt as if it had burst and was merely patched back together. It would probably ache for days. But that was the least of her problems. Figuring out who hated her enough to kill her was the priority of the moment.

Naturally enough, the Stamboloffs came to mind first, but she had been assured they were all dead, so she let that possibility go as quickly as it had come. Her traveling companions she discounted, too. If one of them wanted to get rid of her, he wouldn't have waited this long. It would have been too easy to take her unconscious from her cabin and simply toss her into the sea, then suggest she had fallen overboard or even jumped.

But she knew of no one else here, and the only other people who knew of her existence were all in Cardinia. Of course, that didn't mean that someone from Cardinia couldn't have been waiting here for her arrival. After all, Sandor's man had been waiting here to bring him word of Stefan. Someone else could also have been waiting.

That supposition was logical enough, but she needed a motive. It came to her instantly. Someone didn't want her to marry Stefan. An enemy of his? But why should they care if he married or not? And it seemed as if *everyone* knew he hadn't wanted to marry her, so killing her would be doing him a favor . . . No, she wasn't going to suspect Stefan. Even if she thought him capable of murder, which she didn't, her instincts discounted him immediately. Besides, it was his *duty* to marry her, and his duty meant too much to him.

So if not an enemy of his, and she had none herself that she could think of . . . maybe some other woman who wanted to marry Stefan, but couldn't because of his betrothal to Tanya?

As soon as the idea of a woman entered her mind, she knew exactly who her attacker was. She had an enemy after all, but one so new, it was no wonder she hadn't thought of her first. Alicia. Hadn't the woman proved, by deliberately kissing Stefan in front of her, that she felt threatened by Tanya? And hadn't she taken the first opportunity she had to tell Tanya she was Stefan's mistress, just in case that kiss hadn't been obvious enough? Alicia was so worried that Stefan's affections would turn from her to Tanya, she felt she had to get rid of the competition. And she'd almost done just that.

It all fit, even why the attacker had given up as soon as Tanya had started fighting back. A man wouldn't have. A man would merely have grabbed Tanya back when she rolled away from him, or forced the knife away from her with his superior strength, or used some other means to kill her. But a woman only had the element of surprise as her advantage, and Alicia had lost that. Once Tanya had rolled off the bed, Alicia obviously hadn't thought she was capable of continuing the fight, and so prudently had got out of there—and slipped right back into her own room, which Tanya knew to be directly across the hallway from hers. And no one would suspect her, certainly not the men, because she was probably in her bed right now, pretending to be fast asleep.

Tanya was suddenly so furious, all her aches and pains were forgotten. That stupid woman! How dared she try to take Tanya's life, her *life*, just to hold onto a lover for a while more? Or would Stefan marry Alicia if he were free to do so? That would at least make this attempt understandable—but not forgivable. And Alicia wasn't getting away with it.

Tanya swept up the knife and headed for her open doorway, her eyes trained on Alicia's closed door across the hall. She was almost there, too, when Stefan appeared to block the way, bracing his hands high on the doorframe and giving her a look that said he didn't appreciate wasting his time.

"There was no one in the house, Princess, and all the doors were locked."

He didn't mention the windows and she didn't ask. Of course they had found no one. But did he have to sound as if that had been a foregone conclusion? The man didn't believe—nor had he believed moments ago—that she had had a harrowing experience. Did he think she had deliberately lied?

Before she could say anything in her defense, whether she would bother to or not, he snapped, "Where do you think you're going with that?"

His eyes had dropped to her knife. Her grip tightened on it, but her voice was perfectly calm when she replied, "I'm going to take care of this little matter myself, since you obviously won't."

He tried for a calm tone himself, but it came out more a growl. "Put that down and admit you merely had a nightmare."

"I don't have nightmares."

He was getting exasperated. "Fine, we'll assume an intruder bothered you. We'll even assume he might still be around, even though we've searched through every . . . damn . . . room . . . in the house."

"Not all, you didn't."

"Your room is next to the stairs, so if anyone was here he would have gone that way, since all the other rooms up here are presently occupied."

"Exactly."

His eyes narrowed at what he assumed she was implying, but he didn't address it. "It's over," he said with finality. "So either you can lose more sleep while I have a lock put on your door so you'll feel safe, or I can sleep in here the remainder of the night."

"Suit yourself. There's ample room on the floor. But I'm going to carve your mistress into little pieces first, so you'll have to excuse me for a few minutes."

She took one step, only to hear him command, "Stop right there! Did I hear you correctly? You think Alicia tried to do you harm?"

Did he realize he had just admitted Alicia was his mistress? She doubted it. And why should she care at this point? She'd already been told. *Yes, but you were hoping that vengeful witch had been lying, missy, or at the very least that she was going to be his ex-mistress.*

With the anger churning inside her came pain. It was a wicked combination that she could barely control.

"I don't think it, Stefan Barany, I know it. She was in this room when I screamed, or she sneaked out a moment before, but in either case—"

"Either case is an impossibility, you little liar," he cut in sharply, his eyes starting to glow again. "Because she was with me when you screamed!"

In the middle of the night? And he was only half dressed, she realized now, with no shirt, his trousers not even done up completely, as if he had put them on in a hurry. And Alicia had been with him?

It didn't occur to Tanya that Alicia had just been exonerated, which meant someone else had tried to kill her. She wasn't thinking about that now, wasn't thinking about anything except Stefan making love to another woman. Little wonder that she lifted her arm and threw her knife at him.

Chapter 40

Tanya was as amazed as Stefan that she'd thrown the knife at him, and she regretted it immediately. Not that she even came close to hitting him. The knife struck the wall to his left, then clattered to the floor. And she'd needed to throw something, to hurt him as she was hurting. It just shouldn't have been a damn knife.

Her regret, however, came more from the fact that his amazement didn't last, but changed almost immediately to furious rage. His devil's eyes weren't just glowing, they were now as bright as she'd ever seen them.

She was in deep trouble and knew it, so she offered, albeit lamely, "You weren't in any danger. I never did learn how to do that properly."

No answer. No change in expression either. And her nervousness was making her own anger return.

"But I wish I had," she added. "What the hell did you expect me to do when you tell me you're off making love while I'm being murdered? Nothing?"

Again no answer. But he closed the door and started to walk toward her. Tanya didn't hesitate. She whirled and ran. A hand in her hair jerked her to a stop. Another on her shoulder whirled her back around.

"You weren't being murdered," he said in a voice that was more ominous for being so low. "And I wasn't off making love."

"Liar!"

"I was refusing the offer that was made," he continued as if she hadn't got that "liar" in and wasn't pounding on his chest. "Because I decided that if I was going to have a harlot, I might as well have the one I really want."

The mouth crushing down on hers told her she was the harlot he was referring to, and for the moment, that was all she registered out of what he'd said. But she also registered that he'd been drinking, and anger and liquor were a frightening combination. So although she might have yearned to be in this position again, she continued to fight furiously to get out of it now. But she couldn't get out of his hold, and she suddenly knew why.

Lord help her, she had forgotten that this was how he dealt with his extreme anger. She had even contemplated doing something really foolish just to get him angry enough so she could have this again, so how could she have forgotten? But that was before they had joined up with Alicia. Stefan was accustomed to going to his mistress to relieve his anger. Vasili had said so. And with Alicia here, just down the hall . . .

That was when it clicked, the rest of what he'd said, that he'd turned Alicia away because Tanya was the one he really wanted. And he hadn't gone to Alicia, even though she was just down the hall, in his own room even. He was taking his anger out on the one who'd caused it instead.

Tanya didn't know what to make of that, though she stopped fighting for the moment. But her confusion kept her from yielding completely to Stefan's mouth.

Did she really want him to take her in this mindless fashion, merely as an outlet for his anger? If that was the only way she could have him, then yes. But was it the only way now, when he'd said that he'd decided to come to her, not in anger, but in need, because he wanted her? He'd made that decision before he got angry with her tonight, so angry that this was the result. And if she stopped him, he might not come to her as he'd planned to, because of his new anger with her.

He was furious that she had tried to kill him—as he saw it. Furious that she was lying about someone trying to kill her—as he saw it. So if she tried to calm him down now so they could make love for no other motive than mutual desire, his calm might take him right out of here and right back to Alicia, because his fury with Tanya would still be there, just under control again.

The decision was almost out of her hands, her senses already heightened, her innards already whirling with excitement. So she asked herself the simple question, did she love Stefan Barany?

She was afraid she just might, but she wasn't positive yet. But she was positive that she wanted him, and did not want him to go to another woman to satisfy his needs, even his present need to slake his anger with mindless fornication. So she had her answer. She'd take him this way, even if it was savage and over quickly . . . but it wouldn't be that way, would it? She'd been thinking only of the anger, and comparing Stefan with other men under similar circumstances, forgetting that even in anger, Stefan took his time at this, and wasn't rough with her, merely ruthlessly determined.

She was forgetting one other thing, too, Tanya thought with a shiver of pleasurable anticipation. There was very little that could stop Stefan from having his way. She had never been able to. But he *had* been stopped those other times, by a noise, by an imminent intrusion. Suddenly a measure of urgency entered her own responses. She let everything he'd already aroused in her loose, and began kissing him back with every bit of it.

He had been moving her slowly, unknowingly, toward the bed. The backs of Tanya's legs came up against it now and gave her a start of surprise. She wasn't surprised when she was lowered to the mattress, however, and that, too, was done slowly, carefully, without releasing her mouth. She couldn't seem to impart her urgency to him, but that shouldn't surprise her either. He was oblivious of everything but the anger, the compelling need to release it, but in his own way, not as she'd like, and his way was without haste, instinctively similar to how it would be if he weren't angry. She should be grateful for that, and she would be—if there were no interruptions this time.

The back of her sleeping gown had been raised before she was lowered to the bed. The front lacings had been untied without her notice. The kiss broke now as the white linen was whisked over her head, but his lips came back almost immediately. And now she had his heat, what she associated with his anger but was always there, his skin so hot to her touch. And his weight, glorious sensation, pressing against her breasts, her belly, settling between the legs she opened for him quite willingly.

While his tongue swirled with delicious languor inside her mouth, his hands slipped between their bodies, one to fully cover each breast, kneading, gently plucking at her nipples, then not so gently squeezing once they were quivering buds. It all had the same effect, however, making her wild to have more, the heat in her loins igniting, fast becoming an ache.

He was caressing her arms now, her face, kissing her fiercely one moment, gently the next. And she thought she would go mad because he still wasn't reacting to her own passion, which had already surpassed anything she'd ever felt before. Nor would he stop kissing her long enough for her to tell him. But she was hoping she wouldn't have to, for the fear was there that if he did stop, if he heard her voice now, he'd come to his senses and stop altogether, leaving her in this agonizing state of need.

She tried to calm herself, to relax, reasoning that

she must not be going about this right, that she should just follow Stefan's lead, because although she might know what went where, she was basically ignorant about lovemaking, at least the subtleties of it. But she couldn't do it. She writhed, she arched, she pulled at his hips, his hair, his skin. He was in no tearing rush, but she was going to be a cinder before long.

Finally, she found the thick bulge pressed to her loins and undulated against it in a simulation of what she wanted. That brought his hand to that area, but he didn't actually touch her there. When she realized he was removing his trousers instead, she almost melted with relief. And then he was entering her and she held on tight.

Somewhere deep in Stefan's mind, he knew Tanya wasn't fighting him anymore, was instead wantonly responding to him, and he knew there was something that should bother him about that. But what it was never quite surfaced in the quagmire of his thoughts, blessedly blank for the most part, rife with rage and passion the rest. He was functioning purely on instinct, primitive in nature, and thanks to too much alcohol, on the drunken assurance that he wasn't taking anything that didn't belong to him.

The anger was still there, but lust was now overriding it, and that was suddenly so strong at finding her so wet and tight, he didn't even notice his difficulty in entering her. The slight tug and give of her maidenhead was nothing next to all that moist heat squeezing him. And when he reached her depths, he stayed there, the pleasure so great he couldn't bear to move.

It was that pleasure that brought him to his senses, wiping out his anger completely. And with the anger gone, he knew exactly what he had done, and that damn near sobered him completely. He was inside her, deep inside her at last, and he couldn't recall with any clarity the details of having got there.

Guilt washed over him in waves and would have unmanned him, but he was still encased in the tightest, warmest sheath he had ever entered, and that exquisite sensation was separate from everything else he was suddenly feeling.

After the last time this had almost happened, he had sworn to himself that he would never take Tanya in anger. That was one of the reasons he had stayed away from her on the ship, where forced confinement could so easily make tempers flare. But he hadn't been back with her one complete day before he took her anyway. Only she had responded to him—hadn't she? Or was that wishfulness on his part, her wanton wildness actually resistance?

Even as he thought it, her arms suddenly tightened around his neck, and in his stillness he felt it; unbelievably, without his having moved at all for the past few moments, she was climaxing, the pulse of it surrounding him, squeezing him with each glorious throb, and firing him with a savage exultation that whipped his desire for her to a frenzied peak. He thrust, and thrust again, and went over the edge so explosively, he wasn't sure he would survive it.

Tanya held on tight and smiled very smugly to

herself when Stefan finally went wild in his release. She'd caused that, and if it was anywhere near what she'd just experienced, then the man ought to get down on his knees and kiss the ground she walked on. She was certainly ready to make that concession. Having someone tell you, "It's wonderful. Try it," just doesn't prepare you for that maelstrom of sensation. Nothing could.

He dropped his head on her shoulder now, his heartbeat slamming against her breast, his breath stirring the hair tangled about her neck. Her fingers smoothed his black mane, her other hand caressed his back. She felt so close to him just then, and that was a wonderful feeling in itself. She didn't want him to move, didn't want him to remove that part of him that was inside her, because it still felt so delicious, having him there.

He did stir at last, not to actually raise his head, but with a sudden tensing of his body. "Did I hurt you?"

The pain of her maidenhead breaking had been so minimal, it wasn't worth mentioning. "No, but why is that always your first concern when you calm down?"

"Tanya, I am anything but calm. Did . . . I . . . hurt . . . you?"

"Well, of course it hurt a little bit, but only for a second."

Stefan's guilt escalated. Only for a second? Dear God, had he hit her? He reared up to look at her face, but he could see no bruises. That didn't mean she wouldn't have them elsewhere, if not now, then tomorrow. Alicia had always claimed bruises galore, though he'd never actually seen any. If he had bruised Tanya . . .

Tanya groaned inwardly when he rolled away from her and swiftly fastened his trousers. Then he left the bed and started heading toward the door. Was that it? she wondered. Not even a reaction for discovering she wasn't the whore he thought her to be? Vasili had said he would be furious if he discovered her a virgin, but he wasn't. He was in the strangest mood, as if he felt guilty for taking her innocence, which was ridiculous, since it would have been his on their wedding night anyway, in the not-too-distant future.

"I really am fine, Stefan," she told him, stressing each word. "Better than fine, actually. You should know by now that I'm not some fragile flower you have to worry about touching."

He turned at the door. There was a glow in his eyes. She didn't know it was self-directed, or that he was referring to taking her in anger when he said, "You may be accustomed to variation in lovemaking, but that doesn't excuse . . . This won't happen again, Princess. You have my word on that."

Tanya stared at the door after it had closed, her eyes incredulously wide. Had he just promised what she thought he had? Never to make love to her again? And then the rest of what he'd said hit her. My God, he still thought she was a whore! He'd been so caught up in his rage, he hadn't even noticed her virginity!

Tanya almost laughed. It was too fantastic! Her only proof of innocence was gone now. He'd taken it and didn't even know it. God, what a joke—on her. Well, she'd wanted him to want her despite what he thought, and it looked as if that was the only way it could be now—except he'd had his "one night," and obviously, that was really all he wanted from her.

Chapter 41

"What does that look like to you?"

"Blood."

"Not *that*," Tanya said in exasperation tinged with embarrassment. "The tear in the sheet."

Serge moved up to the side of the bed for a closer examination. Tanya waited impatiently. She wished she hadn't had to do this, to drag him out of bed a second time that night to show him the proof of her attempted murder. If he and Stefan had had the decency to believe her before, she wouldn't have had to. And the only reason she had discovered the proof for herself was because that damned virgin's blood was right next to it on the sheet, and that had drawn her eyes to the spot. But when she did notice it, she had stopped fretting about Stefan and had gone straight to Serge's room. Someone had to believe her about what had happened tonight, and she wasn't about to try to convince Stefan again.

Besides, after she'd thought about it, and got angry about it, she decided she didn't want Stefan seeing that blood on the sheet, so she hadn't even considered going to him with what she'd found. If his anger was so blinding that he could miss something so monumental, the fact that she had willingly given him her virginity, then he could rot before she'd tell him— or show him.

That she hadn't heard Alicia return to her own room possibly had a little to do with her decision. And she had listened for her, too. But obviously Stefan had gone back to spend the rest of the night with his mistress, was curled up in bed with her now, sleeping or . . . He could definitely rot.

She watched Serge as he stuck his finger through the hole, right into a similar hole in the mattress beneath. "It's the cut of a knife, your Highness," he said, drawing the same conclusion she had.

"Exactly."

"I'll get Stefan."

"Don't bother. He'll just think I put it there. But I want at least one of you to believe me and take precautions, because I wasn't dreaming tonight. A sound woke me, I reached for my knife, but I was too slow. My pillow was used to try and suffocate me. I finally must have pricked one of the attacker's arms with my knife—"

"Then that is his blood on the sheet?"

"No," she gritted out. "As I was saying, he released the pillow and I immediately rolled off the bed. But it was so dark in here, he might not have realized I wasn't in the bed anymore. It looks like he tried to stab me then, and I guess he might have tried again if I hadn't started screaming."

"Then *you* were cut?"

She wished he would stop worrying over that red stain. "No, I wasn't."

"Then whose blood is that?"

"Mine," she said, hoping he'd conclude that it was her time of the month and let it go at that.

"I don't—" He didn't get any further, his face suffusing with heat. But he didn't draw the conclusion she had hoped he would. "Stefan returned here after we searched the house."

It wasn't really a question. And since Stefan might mention it to him, there was no point in denying it. "Yes."

"Was he very angry on finding you a virgin?"

Did he have to be so damn discerning? "He didn't notice. He was too angry to begin with."

Serge's cheeks got even hotter. "I will get him now. He has to see—"

"Like hell," she fairly snarled. "I'm not dealing with his anger again tonight, thank you. And I don't care what he thinks, so forget about that damn stain, will you? Just tell me you believe someone tried to kill me."

"I do."

She sighed in relief before asking, "Do I have enemies that no one has told me about?"

"None that I can think of now. Those you had are all dead."

"Would someone want me dead to keep me from marrying Stefan?"

"That is a possibility, yet there are not many who know of your betrothal, or remember it, and even less who know that you are still alive. You disappeared when you were only a baby. Most people think you are dead.''

"How nice."

He smiled at her tone. ''It was better to let them think so while there were still Stamboloffs lurking about. But even though Stefan was sent to bring you home, it is doubtful Sandor would announce your existence until you were there to prove it.''

"All right. Obviously we're not going to figure out who or even why. Tell me this, then. Why would this would-be murderer try to smother me—which was taking a good deal of time, I don't mind telling you—when he had that knife on him? He could have just stabbed me to begin with.''

"Perhaps he didn't want to take the credit for it.''

"What do you mean?''

"He could have wanted it to look like you merely died in your sleep—''

"I'm in perfect health!'' she interrupted indignantly.

"—for some inexplicable reason,'' he continued. "That way, no one would hunt him down.''

"And he would get away with it, no one the wiser,'' she grouched. ''I have to tell you, I really don't like this bastard, whoever he is.''

"But killing you, your Highness, was more important to him than not being hunted down, or he wouldn't have resorted to the knife when his first plan failed.''

"Then I guess it's fortunate I had enough breath left to scream.''

"Very fortunate," he agreed, then insisted, "Stefan will have to be told."

"About the attacker." She shrugged. "Fine. You can try to convince him, because I won't." And then her eyes narrowed threateningly as a blush suffused her cheeks. "But don't even think about telling him about that bloodstain, Serge. He made love to me and left here still thinking I'm a whore. And if he couldn't even feel my maidenhead, he'll never believe that blood is what it is. He'll think I cut myself to put it there, and I'm not going to be accused of deception on top of everything else."

Her plain speaking had his cheeks glowing again. "When he is in that kind of rage—"

"You aren't going to make excuses for him, are you?" she asked coldly.

"He had also been drinking quite heavily tonight, your Highness."

"I see you are," she said in disgust and turned her back on him. "I'm not going to get any sleep tonight until there is a lock on that door. Stefan was going to take care of it, but he got distracted. Would you mind seeing to it before you go back to bed?"

"Certainly, your Highness. I will attend to it myself, as well as sleep outside your door."

"You needn't go that far," she protested.

"On the contrary. Stefan would have it no other—"

"Hang Stefan!"

Chapter 42

The first thing Tanya noticed when she came out of the house was not all the servants scurrying about, getting the last of the baggage loaded into the coaches lined up there, nor the twenty guards already mounted, nor even Stefan standing by the first coach, waiting for her with his three personal guards around him. What she noticed was that Alicia wasn't there.

Well, she wasn't going to ask why not. If Stefan had decided it would be prudent to be discreet now and not travel with his mistress in tow, it was just too late, as far as Tanya was concerned.

"You're late," Stefan said tersely as she reached him.

"Fat lot I care," she shot back. "I'd just as soon not go at all."

He dismissed the others with his hand probably because he hadn't expected her to be as testy as he was. Serge, she noted, didn't look guilty, so at least he hadn't told Stefan what she didn't want him to tell.

"What is that supposed to mean?" Stefan demanded as soon as they were alone.

"You figure it out, your Majesty. You're rather good at drawing conclusions, after all."

She started to climb in the coach without aid. Stefan jerked her back around. "Why didn't you tell *me* what you told Serge?"

So that's what had him growling? "You weren't in a mood to believe me."

"You managed to convince him. You didn't even try to convince me."

"As I said, you weren't in a mood—"

"Tanya, you are *my* responsibility. Mine! If I doubt what you tell me, you damn well tell me again, and again, until I believe it. Something as important as this—"

"Shouldn't have been doubted in the first place," she retorted.

"I agree." When her eyes widened, he added, "If I had been completely sober last night, I likely would have believed you at the start. I apologize for being less than clearheaded in your time of need."

Was that a double entendre? No, he had taken her last night. He hadn't bothered to ask if she wanted him to. And he hadn't noticed any need in her response, just the opposite—he hadn't noticed anything.

"I don't think I can accept your apology, Stefan. Your drinking did a lot more damage than your merely doubting me. It helped you, along with your anger, to take something from me that I was prepared to give you, but you don't even know what it is. And you don't even know what I'm talking about, do you? Well, I could have forgiven you if you did, but since you don't, forget it.''

She turned toward the coach again. This time he caught her shoulders and drew her back against him. She stiffened, but all he did was issue a warning. ''If you think you are going to get away with that cryptic little riddle, think again. I will have an explanation from you, Tanya, and I'll have it now.''

''Or else?''

''I might just turn you over my knee again.''

Hot color rushed into her cheeks to accompany the ire his warning provoked. ''Then I might just throw another knife at you.''

He sighed and let her go. ''All right, Tanya, get in the coach. You have delayed us long enough this morning.''

''Because I didn't get much sleep last night, thanks to you and my would-be killer,'' she retorted.

That got her a boost up into the coach that almost sent her into the opposite door. He followed her in, taking the seat across from her. And there was the glow in his eyes that she'd been looking for, sparking fire.

''I promised it wouldn't happen again, Tanya. What more do you want from me?''

Damn him, he was sober and saying it now, telling her as plain as day that he was never going to touch her again. ''Not . . . a . . . damn . . . thing!''

She turned toward the window before she started crying. He didn't say another word. For nearly an hour that simmering silence continued between them.

And then Tanya felt a weight dropped in her lap.

"Those are for you."

It was a small, jewel-encrusted chest. *Those?* She opened it and stared at diamonds, pearls, emeralds, dozens and dozens, set in necklaces, rings, bracelets. She could buy a hundred taverns with what she was holding, but all she saw was what it represented. In a kingly fashion, Stefan was paying her for last night—because whores had to be paid, didn't they?

The gesture made her so furious she could have thrown that chest out the window—or at his head. But her fury didn't come through in her tone, merely in her words. "This ought to pay for my passage home." He snatched the chest back so fast, she blinked, then shrugged. "So I'll find another way. Don't think for a minute that I don't know how to earn money."

She was delighted to see him go red in the face. She had meant working in taverns, but she knew that wasn't what he thought.

"They told me you were at least resigned to the marriage," he gritted out.

"That was before I was reminded what a devil-spawned bastard you are."

His eyes flashed molten gold. "I will be eternally sorry for last night, but you are going to marry me, *and* live with me, whether you like it or not!"

"I am?"

She didn't mean it as a taunt, but he must have taken it as such. Before she even knew what he was doing, he reached over and yanked her onto his lap, slipped a hand into her hair to utterly destroy her coiffure, and took her mouth with an exquisite sort of hunger. Waves of giddy relief shot out to her extremities and came back in tides of sweet pleasure. He was touching her again, kissing her again, making her forgive him everything in her relief that he couldn't keep his promise, that what she could make him feel transcended even his given word.

She didn't notice that this kiss was skillfully calculated, designed to melt her resistance and leave her clinging to him. Clinging she was, and she hadn't even thought to resist. She would probably think later how unfair it was that he could do this to her when she was so spitting mad at him, but right now all she did was kiss him back.

And then he was only nibbling, at her lips, her earlobes, her neck, and she knew instinctively that what he was doing now wasn't going to lead to anything more. She felt a disappointment that helped her tamp down her rioting senses. She could protest at any time now; he was allowing that. But since she didn't want to anyway, she decided to wait to see what else he would do. Besides, the way he was leisurely toying with her was sinfully delicious, just stirring enough to keep her senses alert and hoping, but inducing a languor that had her melting into his body.

Finally he looked at her, tipping her chin up so she couldn't avoid his gaze. His eyes were merely sherry-gold, about as mellow as she'd ever seen them. And he didn't say a word. That alone brought her back to full reality. But she didn't stir from her position, half reclined in his arms, her right hand curled around his neck.

With a degree of smugness, she asked, "What happened to your promise?"

"I was only a little angry."

"The hell you were," she snorted.

He smiled down at her. "Then let me rephrase that. I was in perfect control."

"You *wanted* to kiss me?"

There went his smile. "Why the devil do you sound surprised?"

"Your promise—"

"Had nothing to do with it."

It didn't? Confusion reigned, until she thought to ask, "Stefan, what exactly *did* you promise me?"

The subject wasn't pleasing him, if his new expression was any indication. "I thought I was quite specific."

"Then refresh my memory."

"I gave you my word I would never take my anger out on you again."

Her relief was there, jumping up and down inside her, but there was another thought that had her brows drawing together in a scowl. "Then who will you take it out on?"

"I suppose I will have to find another outlet."

"Alicia?"

She could have bit her tongue for asking that, especially when he grinned. His mood might have suddenly improved, but hers didn't.

"You weren't jealous of Alicia, were you?"

"Not the least little bit," she lied. "Where is she,

by the way?'' *You weren't going to ask that, missy.*
Oh . . . shut . . . up.

''On her way to Cardinia, I would imagine. She
left quite early.''

''I thought she was going to travel with us.''

He stared at her for a long, pensive moment and
then he frowned. His hold on her tightened. His scars
twitched.

She was confused again, increasingly so when he
demanded, ''Did you want her along? Perhaps to
keep me from kissing you when I damn well feel like
kissing you?''

Now, what brought *that* on? she wondered in vex-
ation. Her innocent remark? Not likely.

''Whatever gave you that idea?''

''It's what you told her, isn't it?''

Tanya gasped in outrage. ''I told her no such thing!
In fact, that sounds pretty much like what *she* told
me—that I ought to be grateful for her existence
because I couldn't possibly want you bothering me
in that way, and she would make sure you didn't.
She had the unmitigated gall to assume, *assume,* to
know what I want. What other lies did that bitch say
about me?''

Stefan didn't answer. He didn't know whom to
believe at that point—Tanya, who said such outlandish things sometimes that he never knew what
was true or not, or Alicia, who had never lied to him
as far as he knew. And Alicia hadn't told him anything he hadn't already agonized over himself.

That was what had driven him back to the bottle
last night after he had unwrapped Alicia from his

body and sent her packing. He hadn't been gentle about it, either which he regretted now that he was sober. And now that he was sober, he realized that telling Tanya that Alicia had been with him when she screamed—when Alicia actually had returned to her room some thirty minutes earlier—had merely been his pain trying to inflict a like pain on Tanya. Obviously it hadn't worked, since her reaction had been fury that he might have been enjoying himself while she was in danger.

The accusation Tanya had made against Alicia, however, he still couldn't give credence to. Alicia might be petty and spiteful, but she wasn't capable of murder.

The hardest thing he had ever done was to finally ask Tanya outright, ''If you don't want her around, are you prepared to accept me as I am, scars and all?''

Tanya didn't know how important her answer was to him, or how much frustration she could avoid if she would just answer yes. She was too annoyed to answer yes.

''Your scars again? You and Alicia are two of a kind, aren't you? You're both obsessed with those damn scars.''

All he heard was that she had evaded his question, which was all the answer he needed.

He abruptly set her from him, waiting only until she had settled back in her seat to say stiffly, ''You may not like my touch, Tanya mine, but you had best get used to it. But then we both know that once you're being kissed, you don't care who is doing the kissing, or the touching. Do you?''

"I honestly wouldn't know," she shot back, only to realize that that particular taunt was the truth.

Chapter 43

"Would you mind kissing me?"

Vasili stiffened to his full six feet, impressive in his indignation. "I beg your pardon?"

Tanya flushed, but she wasn't giving up yet. They were close to Cardinia. Another three or four days, she had been told. But ever since leaving Danzig, Stefan had been deliberately avoiding her again, not as completely as on the *Carpathia*, but nearly as much.

Almost immediately he had stopped riding with her in the coach, sending Serge or Lazar, or both, to keep her company in his stead, while he rode with Vasili and the guards outside. Now she was lucky if she even caught sight of him through her window. Nor did he come to speak to her when they stopped at villages or great estates for food or to pass the night. Once they had camped in the open. She didn't know where he had slept.

When they had left Danzig, it was like leaving civilization behind. The countryside had been pretty bleak and barren, with winter upon it. Houses or farms became a rare sight, towns even rarer. The occasional castle held Tanya's interest the most, but not for long. Clouds or fog sometimes surrounded them so completely, it was difficult to see the road even a few yards ahead. She had yet to see a sunny day. It had rained often, and yesterday there had been a few snowflakes, though a frigid wind had whisked them away. The weather alone would have put her in a gloomy mood if the situation with Stefan hadn't.

She was definitely beginning to regret her childish behavior during their last conversation. She had let her temper get the better of her, as usual, this time because of her jealousy, and that in turn had alienated Stefan again. And just when she had discovered that he wasn't indifferent to her. Well, he was now. But that last taunt of his, that she didn't care who was kissing or touching her once it was happening, had really bothered her after she thought about it. He'd implied she might protest first, but she was easy to conquer once she got heated up.

It was an insult, not as bad as his similar one about her not caring whom she bedded with, but an insult just the same. Only how did she know if it wasn't true? She'd never given any other man the chance to prove it one way or the other, stopping them all from kissing her the way Stefan did. So what if he was right? She didn't *want* any other man kissing her. There were dozens of them now in their party, but she didn't want any of them. She wanted only Stefan. But if one of them kissed her, really kissed her . . .

She had decided at last to find out for herself. If

she was as wanton and fickle as Stefan claimed she was, then she damn well wanted to know it. And Vasili was a very logical choice to find out with. At that moment, he would probably like to vindicate himself, because he had actually been showing some guilt ever since he had accepted her innocence as fact. So he ought to delight in proving that if she wasn't an actual whore, she was at least one by nature.

He was also the most handsome man she'd ever known, and if she was going to prove this experiment beyond a doubt, she might as well use the big guns, so to speak, and make it as tough on herself as she could. And once she did prove it in her favor—and she was confident of that outcome—then she would have some ammunition to confront Stefan with. But she was going to have that confrontation one way or another, before they entered Cardinia.

Stefan said she *had* to live with him, but she wasn't going to go on living with him like this. If she wasn't positive that there was at least some hope of Stefan ever coming to love her, then she would just as soon leave before they reached Cardinia and the whole country knew about her existence.

Now she looked Vasili straight in the eye and repeated her question in a tone he couldn't doubt was serious. "I asked if you wouldn't mind kissing me."

"Actually, I would mind," he replied, still indignant, then glanced about the camp they had set up about an hour ago, looking for Stefan.

Tanya guessed as much. "He went with Serge to the village that is supposed to be a couple of miles from here. At least that's what Lazar said.''

Vasili's eyes came back to her, narrowed. "So if he isn't around, what was the point of that ridiculous request? It *was* to make him jealous, wasn't it?''

"As if he would be," she snorted. "No, I asked for my own benefit, because Stefan says that no matter who kisses me, they'll get the same response from me. I want to know if that's so.''

"You must be joking!" he exclaimed.

"Do I look like I'm joking?''

"But I seriously doubt that Stefan meant it. He hasn't exactly been in a good mood lately, in case you hadn't noticed. And when he gets like this—''

"He made the observation before we left Danzig.''

Losing on that point, Vasili tried another, his voice actually scolding. "You don't just go around asking men to kiss you, Princess.''

That had her blushing again. "If this weren't important, I wouldn't. But that *is* why I asked you instead of someone else, to keep it in the family, so to speak. Now, will you just do it and get it over with?''

"No, I will not," he said flatly, with finality.

"Why not?''

"Because Stefan would kill me if he found out.''

"He wouldn't do any such thing," she scoffed.

"I would just as soon not put it to the test, thank you.''

She was surprised. She really thought he would help. "Very well, I'll just have to ask someone else.''

She turned to leave. He reached out and grabbed her arm. He looked totally flustered now.

"You must have some past experience to go by for this comparison. At least one man who has kissed you before Stefan. Rack your memory, for God's sake."

"I did. The few other kisses I've had were stolen, and necessarily brief, because I tended to draw my knife very quickly."

Vasili gave in then, but with complete ill grace. "Oh, very well." He leaned forward to place his lips on hers for all of five seconds.

When he leaned back, Tanya was shaking her head at him in disgust. "You know what kind of kiss I meant, Vasili. That wasn't it."

He flushed furiously now and grabbed her hand, pulling her along behind him across the camp. "Where are we going?" Tanya demanded.

"If I am going to do this properly, it isn't going to be for public consumption that Stefan will be bound to find out about." And then he looked back at her suspiciously. "*You* aren't intending to tell him, are you?"

"If I do, I won't mention names."

That must have satisfied him, for he said no more. His destination was the other side of her coach, which she slept in when they camped out in the open like this. No one was near it now, but when she retired, there would be at least four attendants sleeping in front of either door, including the two women who were acting as her maids, as well as a number of guards set to watch the coach all night long. She might not have felt like a princess before they reached Europe, but she was being treated like one on this trip, with servants galore keeping her from lifting a hand to her own care.

Vasili stopped as soon as he was certain no one could see them, and immediately drew Tanya into a lover's embrace. The kiss began hesitantly on his part, but he soon got into the spirit of it. And Tanya was determined to participate as well, to relax, to open her senses to feel the experience. That was easy enough, since she was getting good at this sort of thing. Vasili, on the other hand, was an expert at it, quite as good as Stefan. But that's what she had hoped for, to really put it to the test.

The experiment ended about five minutes later, when she tapped Vasili on his shoulder. He released her and stepped back, running an agitated hand through his golden locks.

There was a soft glow in his eyes that was quickly extinguished as he gave her an inquiring look. "Do you have your answer?"

She grinned. "Yes."

"Well?"

"You don't *really* want to know, do you, Vasili?"

Her beaming expression told him plain enough that he'd failed to stir her. He burst out laughing.

"You never have been good for my self-esteem, Princess, so spare my feelings in this case."

Chapter 44

Tanya had waited impatiently for Stefan to return to camp last night. He and Serge had supposedly only gone to the village up ahead to get news of the area they were nearing, and to arrange to have breakfast prepared and waiting for their large group when they passed through the village in the morning, as well as more food they could take with them for a noon meal.

Lazar had told her this part of the country was known for its hill bandits and other types of lawless individuals. Because it was so remote and almost primitive in nature, it was ignored by the countries surrounding it: Austria; the kingdom of Poland, or what was left of it, since Poland was now under Russia's control; and Russia herself.

Unfortunately, the northern route leading to Cardinia cut right through this area. But it could be traversed in only half a day. And Tanya was assured that heavily guarded travelers, such as they, were never bothered. Not that she was worried about it. She had also been told, almost from the beginning

374

of the overland trek, that the land's natural inhabitants were a danger, too, for bears, wildcats, and wolves roamed the forests and sometimes beyond. It had been stressed again and again that she was never to venture off alone for any reason whatsoever. But she hadn't given that much thought, either, with so much else on her mind.

When Stefan had finally returned to camp last night, she had tried to speak to him, but he had put her off, saying he was too tired. When she tried again in the morning before they broke camp, he said he was too busy, it would have to wait until that evening—when she would probably hear that he was too tired again? Like hell.

It was then that she remembered all the warnings about how dangerous it would be to leave the group. She also remembered how thoroughly upset Stefan had been that time she'd jumped into the Mississippi River, just because she had put herself at risk. She decided that if she couldn't get his attention by asking for it, she'd get it another way—by turning up missing.

Of course, she had no intention of putting herself in danger. She wouldn't have to go far from the coaches to be "missing," certainly not beyond shouting distance. She just didn't have to answer when she was called. And she didn't have to show herself until Stefan was good and upset. Then that devil would damn well talk to her.

She also realized that what she intended might actually put Stefan's promise to the test, that he was likely to be livid with rage, just as before. But that only added some exciting possibilities to the plan, which made her even more determined to do it. And she didn't wait until that evening. She'd just as soon not go off in the dark, anyway. She chose that very afternoon, when they stopped to partake of the cold fare from the village.

Tanya waited until everyone had almost finished eating, since there was no point in going off into the woods for longer than she had to. She even finished the meat wrapped in thick bread and butter that had been brought to her. But as soon as her maids started cleaning up in preparation to leave again, she slipped behind the coach, waited another minute to make sure no one had seen her, then dashed into the woods.

She wasn't sure what she was going to say in her defense when she let herself be "found." She ought to just put the blame where it was due and tell Stefan the truth. No, that wasn't, after all, a good enough excuse to ignore all the warnings she had been given. Just because he was ignoring her? She could tell him that she'd wanted to be alone, to think, to decide if she was going to marry him or not, and then had fallen asleep. After all, she needed a reason to explain why she wasn't going to answer when she heard them calling for her. Being asleep solved that.

At any rate, she had a while to think about it, ten minutes probably, before they would be ready to continue on their way. Then she had a moment's unease when it occurred to her that they just might leave, thinking she was inside her coach already. But she laughed it off. They wouldn't be *that* careless. And someone usually rode with her.

But at that point, she decided she'd gone into the woods far enough. She looked about for some type of cover other than a fat tree trunk, though a trunk would do just as well for her purposes. Then she spotted what looked like a building just a little farther on and headed toward it. On closer inspection, she saw that at one time it had been a house or a farm, but was now in ruins, long abandoned. As shelter, it fell short of the mark, with most of the roof and one wall caved in, but as a place to "fall asleep," it was perfect. Only Tanya hadn't counted on anyone else being there.

When she came around the building to get out of the wind, she saw the three ponies first, once wild by the look of them, then the three men leaning up against the wall of the ruins. She no sooner let out a gasp of surprise than the man closest to her was hauling her forward and out of sight of the way she had come.

"Now just a—"

A hand over her mouth cut off Tanya's protest. An arm around her waist lifted her off the ground and didn't let go. Her wrists were swiftly being tied together by another man, who also had a gag ready for her mouth. It had all happened too quickly, before she could think, before she could get at the knife strapped to her thigh.

"What if she isn't the one?"

"She is," said one of the men with confidence. "You sent me close to watch them and I watched. She is the only lady in that party."

"Then she wouldn't be out here alone. She

wouldn't be this far from the road at all.''

"Who cares what she's doing here when what she did is make it easy to earn the payment.''

"Then if you're sure, I say kill her here and be done with it.''

"You would say that, Pavel,'' he was told with unmistakable disgust.

"Why bother taking—''

"Take a good look at her. I would keep her before I'd kill her. Besides, it's Latzko's decision, not ours. We don't even know if the payment is good yet, and I'm not killing anyone for nothing.''

"We'll be hunted,'' Pavel pointed out.

"We'll be hunted either way.'' The other man laughed. ''But how does that make a difference when we're *always* hunted? And no one finds us unless we want them to.''

Tanya didn't know she'd been given a reprieve or that her life had even been in imminent danger, because they had been speaking some Slavic tongue that she couldn't begin to understand. But she did know that she would be going with them, because as soon as she was tightly bound—and it took less than a minute to accomplish that—she was tossed up onto one of the small ponies, with the shortest of the men getting on behind her—for the sake of the pony, she supposed.

She didn't know what to make of this abduction, except that she hoped these men weren't associated with whoever had tried to kill her in Danzig, and since they hadn't killed her outright, that hope was strong. But if they were hill bandits, why didn't they just rob her and go? Why take her with them?

They looked no different from the people she had been seeing for the past few days in this part of the country, dark of hair and eyes, swarthy-skinned, except there was a marked difference in their individual heights. One was no taller than Tanya, one was a few inches above her, and one was actually quite tall. Their clothes were not quite the same as those she had seen in the area, looking more appropriate for riding: thick trousers, soft-skinned boots laced up the calves, short sheepskin jackets with the fur on the inside, worn over woolen shirts wrapped with wide cloth belts. They each wore brightly colored scarves knotted close to the neck and shaggy fur hats. If they carried any weapons, she didn't see them, but undoubtedly they did.

Stefan had been traveling in a gradual, southeasterly direction. These men rode directly south, straight for the Carpathian Mountains. And they rode as if the devil were on their tails. The only stop they made that evening was at some isolated farm, where they gave up their worn-out ponies for fresh ones. They avoided roads altogether, seeming to know every out-of-the-way path through forests and hills. And they didn't even stop to eat, chewing on stale bread crusts that each man carried.

They reached their destination sometime around noon of the next day, having ridden straight through the night. It looked like a typical village, except it was high in the mountains, reached by a path that Tanya was sure only those small ponies could navigate.

She was utterly exhausted by then, having gotten no more sleep than her captors. She was almost too tired to care what happened next, but she was definitely grateful for the warmth inside the house she was dragged into.

It was more like a log cabin, though with only one large room. Tanya moved straight to the clay-mounded oven in the center of it the moment she was let go. The first thing she noticed was how cluttered the room was, with crude furniture and the debris of a lifetime. The second thing she noted was the man sitting at a table eating; he didn't even look up at their intrusion. He was big, middle-aged, with the hardened features of someone who had not had an easy life.

A pouch was dropped before him, and a lengthy explanation was given by her captors that she didn't bother to try deciphering. Instead she looked at the many cots scattered about and wondered if anyone would mind if she made use of one. But she didn't want to leave the fire just yet. She had been chilled to the bone, despite the long gray cloak she was wearing. But then she wasn't used to winters like this, and it had become much colder the higher they had climbed into the mountains.

She finally noticed the silence and glanced toward the table to find only the older man there, the other three gone. He'd been watching her while he finished his meal. He didn't seem disposed to say anything, however.

Tanya decided to try her luck just the same. "I don't suppose you speak English either?"

"English," he said in disgust. "I know four languages good, three not so good. My English is not so good."

"Good enough," Tanya said in relief. She knew a smattering of French and Spanish herself, but she doubted those two languages were included in his seven. "Will you tell me what I'm doing here?"

"You should not be."

"Not be what?"

"Here. If my men knew the difference between rubies and pretty glass, then you would not be." He picked up a necklace from the table and dangled it from a finger to show her.

"I don't understand."

"This was given to kill you. It is not real, so you do not die."

It was nice of him to clarify that before she had time to be horrified. "Do I understand you correctly? Someone paid your men to kill me, and that necklace was the payment?"

"That is what I said."

"And since it's made of glass instead of real rubies, you won't kill me?"

"That is what I said."

It was that cowardly assassin of hers, no doubt afraid to try again himself. But she asked anyway. "Can you tell me who?"

He shrugged. "We do not deal with names."

She sighed. "Very well, what now?"

"My men waste much time getting you, ruin good animals getting here. Pavel, he thinks we should kill you anyway, for the trouble they were put to." He chuckled. "He hates all aristocrats after one beat hell out of him. Will your people pay to have you back?"

She shrugged. "Probably, though I wouldn't stake my life on it. Why don't you just ask whatever price you want and see if you get it?"

He grinned. "I like the way you think, lady." He waved a hand to the pot sitting on top of the oven. "Eat, rest, it will not be long."

"It won't?"

"Your people were not far behind," he explained, "not far at all. Hope they carry a lot of gold, lady, or we may have to kill them all."

He'd managed to horrify her after all.

Chapter 45

Stefan rode slowly into Latzko's village, his men spread out behind him. He had come here once before, about seven years ago, when he had had a fight with his new mistress and she had run home to her father. Latzko was her father. Stefan had come to make up with the girl, having decided he'd been unfair in their argument, a dispute he couldn't even recall the subject of, it had been so minor. And Arina had been delighted that he'd come to fetch her back. An old suitor of hers hadn't been, however, and had insisted Stefan fight for her. It had been a bother. He hadn't wanted the girl back *that* much. But he had obliged the fellow and won. Ironically, the affair with Arina had only lasted another month.

Latzko came out of his house to greet him now and obviously remembered him, if his welcoming smile was any indication. And why not? The wily brigand hadn't been satisfied with getting his hot-tempered daughter off his hands again, seven years ago. He'd charged Stefan fifty rubles before he could leave with her, and that was after Stefan had already fought and won that privilege.

"What brings you here this time, Stefan?"

Two other men had come to join Latzko in front of his house. Stefan wasn't pleased to see that Pavel was one of them, and looking as belligerent as he had the last time. But the rest of the village also turned out, the men coming quietly forward to surround Stefan's, their weapons concealed, but Stefan knew how quickly that could change with these mountain people.

He stared at Latzko and said without preamble, "I believe you have something that is mine."

"Yours?" Latzko laughed heartily. "I'll be damned. They didn't bother to tell me that."

Stefan gritted his teeth, doubting that, but at the moment he didn't care. "How much?"

"Five hundred?"

"Done."

"And he has to fight me," Pavel inserted loud enough for all to hear.

"Done."

From Latzko's expression, it was clear he hadn't expected the challenge. He even tried to protest. "You are supposed to learn from experience, Pavel, not foolishly make the same mistakes. Didn't he nearly kill you last time with his bare hands?"

"My mistake was not calling for knives last time," Pavel replied with appalling confidence. "This time we use them."

The older man made a sound of disgust before he turned back to Stefan. "He bears a grudge, this one.

He blames you for Arina's indifference to him, even though she now lives with some Austrian duke. But I have the last say here, and I say you do not have to fight him.''

Latzko was obviously worried that he wouldn't get his money if something happened to Stefan. But this time Stefan wanted the fight, had been fiercely glad to hear the challenge issued.

''I have already accepted, Latzko, and it will happen now, this minute.''

''Stefan!'' Lazar objected behind him, but Stefan merely sent him a silencing glare as he dismounted.

Vasili wasn't as easily shut up. ''Let one of us fight in your stead, then. Your position is such that you cannot take these arbitrary risks anymore.''

''I will decide what is a risk and what it's worth. This risk is needed to keep the skin on Tanya's back.''

Vasili's brow shot up in understanding. Stefan needed *something* to expend his anger and fear on before he faced his betrothed. It was a wonder he'd contained those emotions these past twenty-four hours.

''Well, heaven forbid she should lose any skin,'' Vasili said dryly now, knowing full well the girl was in no such danger. ''Go ahead and get it out of your system this time. But you are going to have to think seriously about curtailing these little pleasures in the future, Stefan, you really are.''

Stefan only gave a curt nod while he removed his sword and coat. He wasn't wearing a knife. Latzko supplied him with his own, a long-bladed dagger with a good grip on it. And he no sooner had it in hand than Pavel brought his own knife in a downward swing to stab him, to end the fight right there. But Stefan hadn't been expecting a clean fight, not after his last experience with this man. Pavel's dirty tricks had made Stefan angry enough to beat him senseless. He wondered if he'd have to kill him this time, as he caught Pavel's wrist, threw it back, and slashed with his own knife, drawing first blood in a small nick on Pavel's upper arm.

They circled each other now, knives extended, looking for another opening. Neither man had slept in a day and a half, but they didn't feel it; felt nothing but the raw emotion goading them on.

Pavel was eaten up with hate and jealousy. Stefan had relived the horror of his brother's death when he couldn't find Tanya in the woods. But how quickly that had turned to a killing fury when they found the tracks of those three ponies. If he had caught up with the ones who had taken her before now, he would have shown no mercy. Pavel could count himself fortunate that Stefan didn't know yet that he was one of them.

Pavel finally leaped, a false move, since he then dived for Stefan's feet to knock them out from under him. Stefan did go down, face first, but rolled, just missing the knife that ended up buried in the ground where his back had been. He responded with a kick to Pavel's head, which gave Stefan time to get back on his feet, but didn't daze Pavel nearly enough.

Pavel came up charging in an attempt to knock Stefan over again, but Stefan held his ground and they connected, hands locked to each other's wrists. It was now a matter of strength, of who could hold back the other's blade while making use of his own. They were almost evenly matched in this, both tall and muscular. Stefan still had the advantage—he was angrier.

It ended with Stefan's blade sinking into Pavel's shoulder. The other man stumbled back. Stefan retained his dagger, but he didn't need it anymore. Pain allowed Pavel's exhaustion to catch up with him and he sank slowly to his knees.

"You win a second time," Latzko told Stefan, officially ending the fight. "If he ever thinks to challenge you again, I'll kill him myself."

Stefan couldn't care less. "Where is she?" was all he wanted to know.

Latzko flipped his thumb toward his house. "In here. Sleeping. And she wasn't touched, other than to tie her up. But a word of caution, my friend. My men didn't just stumble upon her. I sent them to Warsaw on business. There they were approached and bribed to kill the lady. Fortunately for her, my men don't usually act on such things without my approval. Even more fortunate, the payment turned out to be worthless, rubies made of glass."

"So you decided to sell her back to me instead?"

The older man shrugged. "What else could I do with her? I'm too old to keep her."

"You're too greedy to keep her."

"True." Latzko grinned. "But come, you're welcome to stay the night, rest—"

"We'll leave now, Latzko, but thank you just the same."

In the house, Stefan found that Tanya actually was sleeping, totally unaware that he had come for her and, in a small way, avenged the ordeal she had been put through. But she didn't look the worse for wear, she looked exquisitely beautiful, peaceful in sleep, without a care in the world. He wondered if she ever knew how much danger she had been in, that if the one who was trying to kill her could have afforded better than jewels made of glass, she might be dead now. He wondered if she knew how much agony he had gone through, first thinking wolves had got to her, then fearing it had been the assassin.

He didn't wake her. He picked her up carefully and carried her out of there, handing her to Serge only long enough for him to mount and take her up on his lap. She did stir then, briefly opening her eyes to see him.

"Oh, hello, Stefan." She closed her eyes again and smiled, snuggling closer against him. "Did you meet Latzko? Nice fellow, but I hope you didn't have to pay him too much money."

"A paltry sum," he grunted. "Had he known it he could have asked for the moon, and I would have gotten it for him."

"The moon?" She yawned, but once that was done, her smile was even wider.

He was chagrined. He hadn't meant to admit something like that. He said what he'd meant to tell her, "You can thank your friend Pavel that I didn't g looking for a switch the moment I got here. Now I'm too tired to beat you.''

That took care of her smug little smile. ''Why would you want to beat me?''

''We'll discuss it later.''

Her eyes opened wide. ''No, I want—''

''Later!''

''Your putting me off was what led to this, you stupid man,'' she grumbled.

''A demonstration of your willfulness? I think you'll continue to wear those bindings until I get you home.''

But she didn't. He cut her loose himself when they met up with the coaches that evening at the estate of some baron, a man who bubbled over with welcome, ecstatic that King Stefan should honor him with a visit. The man's entire house was put at Stefan's disposal, including his own luxurious bedroom, which Stefan merely accepted as his due.

Tanya found herself sharing the same room. She'd been bristling the rest of the afternoon, getting no more sleep. She was prepared, thinking they'd be having their fight, which was going to be a royal one, then and there, but she was wrong. Stefan, after locking the door and pocketing the key, promptly lay down on the huge and rather ancient bed the room contained and went to sleep.

Chapter 46

Tanya spent the night in a very comfortable armchair, but she still felt a crick in her neck when she was awakened by a nudge on her shoulder. She opened her eyes to see Stefan looming over her—and nearly gasped at his expression. How long had he been up and stewing over the events of the past two days, to put that kind of fury on his features? Or was it that?

"Dare I say good morning?" she asked warily, only to find herself yanked out of the chair and roughly shaken.

"You were told there are wolves in this part of the country!" he blasted at her.

"Yes, and bears and—"

"Do you know how quickly a wolf can tear you apart?" was his second blast, the one that made her understand.

God, she had forgotten about his brother! After such an experience, that might be the only thing Stefan had thought of when they couldn't find her.

"I'm sorry, Stefan," she said sincerely, not even

thinking about lying now. "You were ignoring me. I just wanted your attention, and to tell you that you were wrong. I've been kissed by another man, and I didn't feel anything. It *does* matter who's doing the kissing."

Hearing, even if in a roundabout way, that she desired him had a very swift effect on Stefan. His anger, merely induced by fear, crumbled beneath his instant arousal. He was already holding her shoulders, had been about to shake her again. He drew her to him now and took her mouth almost savagely.

Tanya didn't have to wonder what had brought this on. His anger, of course, or so she assumed. So much for rashly made promises. But the fight was over as far as she was concerned. So was her own anger, which she'd gone to sleep with last night. It was really amazing how kissing could calm them both down in one way but fire them both up in another, more pleasurable way.

She was caught up in that pleasure very swiftly. The thrust of his tongue was met by some thrusts of her own. She helped him shed the blouse he unbuttoned for her. Her skirt just dropped at her feet. He didn't seem surprised that she was naked now, since she'd removed her underclothing last night to sleep, leaving on only the outer wear for modesty's sake, as she'd done on the riverboat. But he probably wasn't paying attention, no more than he had the last time, and that was something she'd just have to accept for now, because she had no intention whatsoever of stopping him.

Quite the opposite, actually, was taking place,

since she was the one who moved them slowly toward the bed this time. And once there, she was the one who made sure their kiss wasn't broken as she gradually lowered herself and him to the mattress. She had to worry not only about their being interrupted, which tended to recall him to his senses, but also about that damn promise of his, which would end this quicker than anything else could if he remembered it.

So she was frantic to keep Stefan in his mindless, rage-induced state, and wouldn't even let go of his head when he began removing his clothes. Only when he was as naked as she was did she relax enough to simply enjoy what was happening. And then she found herself caught up in that wildness again, that pure, wanton desire clamoring for release.

This time, it was she who wasn't paying close attention to everything he was doing. She was so centered on the sensations his hands were provoking in her, as they explored with maddening slowness from neck to loins, that it took her a while to realize he wasn't kissing her anymore. In fact, he was watching her in fascination. When she finally opened her eyes, he stilled his hands, their gazes locked, and she saw that he wasn't the least bit angry.

Tanya was struck by such a keen sense of frustration at that point, she blurted out, ''Damn you, Stefan, don't calm down *now!*''

To her complete chagrin, he burst out laughing and was still grinning when he asked baldly ''Why?'' He bent and gently bit her lower lip, then laved it with his tongue. ''You think I'm not going to continue making love to you?'' His lips nibbled now between words. ''Think again, little houri. You have belonged to me, with your father's blessing, since the day you were born.'' His hand swept her breasts in an unmistakably possessive manner. ''You are the only woman who has ever been truly mine. I won't take you again mindlessly, Tanya. Didn't I promise you that?''

She wasn't really expected to answer that just then, was she? She was so overcome with ecstatic delight over those key words ''belonged'' and ''truly mine'' that she had to give back some of that joy or burst with it. Her arm curled around his neck to draw his mouth more firmly back to hers, her tongue slipping past his lips to thrust and tease, while her other hand boldly sought his manhood, satin on steel, and caressed with the gentlest touch.

Her innocent touch brought a groan rumbling from his depths that had her innards curling up and sighing with satisfaction. She was making love to him, and he was letting her. And when she thought she couldn't bear another minute of it, he took over, gathering her close and filling her with his heat. But unlike before, he moved slowly this time, sensuously, deliberately prolonging the wonder of it, then finally with deep, grinding thrusts where he reached for the core of her, and brought her to a shattering climax that racked her body with fierce pulsations that continued to his final thrust, only with slightly less force, then nearly exploding again when she felt his own hot spasms.

She didn't want reality to intrude. It hadn't been

pleasant the last time. But of course they couldn't lie there forever, clinging to each other, much as she wanted to. It was morning. Everyone else would be up and readying to depart. And Tanya still had to account for her foolish behavior that had sent her right into the arms of bandits.

So it was with some surprise that she felt his lips softly grazing her cheek and heard him ask with only mild curiosity, "Who kissed you and made you feel nothing?"

Without the slightest guilt for what kind of fury her answer might bring down on his golden head, she said, "Vasili," then promptly exonerated him by adding, "But he hated doing it, grouched the whole time, and only gave in when I said I'd ask someone else to kiss me if he wouldn't."

Stefan raised himself up on an elbow to give her an incredulous look. "You went asking for kisses?"

"Only to see if you were right or not."

"You couldn't just draw on past experience for an answer?"

She didn't let that bother her. She was too sated and mellow to be bothered by anything just then.

"I hate to disappoint you, as I did Vasili, since he asked the same thing, but my past experience isn't as great and varied as you both think."

He smiled then. "And here I was going to admit, to my own amazement, a gratitude for it."

Tanya almost choked, but she knew what he was referring to and blushed, retorting, "That wasn't experience, that was pure instinct."

"I wasn't trying to insult you, Tanya," he said gently.

She knew that. That it was so was what she found hard to believe. But if this was the kind of reaction she could expect from him when he *wasn't* troubled by guilt, which she now understood had been the problem last time, then she'd just have to see that they made love more often.

"Could we stay here today to—explore this 'gratitude' of yours more fully?"

He laughed and rolled back, his arms tight around her so she went with him. His hand moved to smooth her hair and keep her face pressed to his chest.

"I wish we did have more time, but my father is anxious for our arrival. He will know to the hour when we *should* be expected, and this delay—"

"Will worry him." She sighed. "I understand."

He whacked her bottom then, and told her to get dressed. But she received four more delaying kisses while trying to do as ordered. The man couldn't seem to keep his hands off her this morning. She felt the same way. It was so unusual, having him like this, and she couldn't have been happier.

When they were ready to leave, she took advantage of his pleasant mood to ask, "What was that remark you made about Pavel sparing me a switching all about?"

"Nothing important," he replied, but then he caught her chin in his hand to add sternly, "Don't ever ignore specific warnings again, Tanya."

She smiled, aware that that was going to be the extent of his scolding. "Then don't ignore *me* again, Stefan. I do foolish things when I get angry."

"God, don't we all."

Chapter 47

The capital city of Cardinia was merely that, a city, not unlike Warsaw, which they had passed through, or Danzig. Tanya didn't know why she'd had a fairy-tale setting in the back of her mind, complete with castle and rosy countryside. There was no castle, but it snowed for her arrival, which added a wonderland beauty to this place where she was going to live. The city proper was enclosed in an ancient wall that was no longer guarded and crumbling in places, but the city had stretched beyond this wall centuries ago.

As in any city, there were many large, elegant homes in certain sections, then there were many not so elegant in other sections, but they all looked only slightly different from the homes she'd seen else-where in Europe. Commerce was thriving. There were large stores and small shops, open markets, vendors, even warehouses, next to parks, cafes, churches. Carriages and sleighs clogged some streets where the snow had been swept to the sides but an icy crust remained behind, while other lanes were empty, the snow pristine white and undisturbed. Tall bronze statues were centered in squares, and winter-naked trees lined many streets.

The palace formed a square by itself. If not a towering castle, it was incredibly large nonetheless. Three stories high, it covered an entire block in the city proper, with the majority of official rooms at the front of the palace and many more rooms stretching down the side blocks, a barracks comprising the rear of the square, and open gardens and courtyards in the center of these four long, connecting buildings.

Tanya was delighted with the city, after having seen nothing but small villages and the occasional estate of a nobleman for days. But she was totally amazed by the palace, the grandeur of it, the opulence. The entrance was mammoth, the entire three stories high, where an official with armed guards at his sides, many more stationed about the hall, would have stopped them if Stefan hadn't been recognized. Wide corridors of marble were lined with large portraits in solid gold frames, separated by consoles on the walls set with silver lamps, or pedestals holding busts or small statues, or doors with footmen standing at attention on either side.

She was dazed by it all as she was ushered down one corridor, then another. Was she actually supposed to live in a place like this? And if she was being taken to the room she would be given, Lord help her, it must be at the end of the next block.

But she wasn't being shown to her rooms, which were going to be in the same wing as Stefan's. She should have known he would go immediately to his father. She just wished he hadn't thought to bring her with him.

Stefan might be king now, but she hadn't always thought so, and she still thought of him only as Stefan. But his father had been king for twenty years, the length of her life, a *real* king as she saw it, and she wasn't up to meeting him just yet, was forgetting all the protocol and correct forms of address Lazar and the others had drummed into her.

It was no wonder she curtsied to the Prime Minister, who was seated at the desk in the anteroom outside the royal chamber, when he looked up in surprise. Fortunately, his surprise was such that he didn't notice her blunder.

"Stefan! Why did you not send word that you had returned?"

Stefan embraced the older man with a laugh. "I would have, except Sandor's man was waiting in Danzig and left immediately to return here, so I didn't see any point in sending another with news you would already have."

"What man? Sandor didn't send anyone. We assumed you would."

"Then—" Stefan paused to glance at Tanya. "It would seem your would-be assassin was rather clever after all. And that means Alicia would know what he looks like."

"Assassin?" Max exclaimed.

But Tanya interjected first, with eyes narrowed. "If you're going to see your redhead to question her, Stefan, I'm going with you."

"I don't even know if she was returning to Cardinia, but in any case, someone else can question her.''

Tanya was only slightly mollified. Maximilian Daneff wasn't at all. *"Assassin?"* he repeated, and regained Stefan's attention.

''Someone has made two attempts on her life since we reached Europe,'' Stefan replied, then added in what was clearly an order, ''I don't want another, Max.''

''I will see to it personally. But I do not think Sandor should be told. His health has improved, but worry could cause another setback.''

"How improved?'' Stefan asked suspiciously.

''Now, my boy, none of that. You cannot really think your father would have staged—''

''Would he not?''

Max grinned. ''Well, possibly, but as it happens, he did not. Your crowning *was* official. And I said his health had improved, not that he has made a complete recovery. However, the physicians are hopeful that he might have a few more years left, *if* he stays out of the throne room. Now, if I may welcome your betrothed, who certainly needs no introduction.'' Max turned to Tanya and bowed formally, then said, ''You are the very image of your mother, Princess Tatiana, except for your hair, which is pure Janacek. Welcome home.''

She would never understand why tears suddenly sprang to her eyes, but they did. Perhaps it was because this man had known her parents well, had known her as a baby, could tell her things not even Stefan could. Or perhaps it was simply because home had been such an elusive thing to her all these years and now she was finally feeling as if she really had come home.

At the first sign of tears, Stefan drew her into his arms and grinned over her head at the Prime Minister. "It was nothing you said, I'm sure, Max, so don't look so stricken. The wench is just emotional and high-strung. You would not believe what I have had to put up with—" At that point he got a fist in his side and grunted. "You see?"

"You arrogant devil's spawn, you haven't had to put up with half of what I have. I'll have you know—"

"Behave, Tanya, or I'll have to think seriously about putting you over my knee again."

"Like hell you will."

"Now, children." Max chuckled, because it was obvious neither of them was truly angry at the other. "I think it will do Sandor good to see how well you are getting along." At Tanya's glance, he explained, "We were worried that Stefan would—"

"That's quite enough, Max," Stefan cut in, and there was no doubting that this time he was displeased.

Tanya looked up at him and smiled. "Secrets? As if I can't guess he was going to tell me how much you hated having to fetch me home, that if you'd had your way, I would have been left to rot in America. I keep telling you I'm not stupid, Stefan, but you keep forgetting."

"That is a matter of opinion, as far as I'm concerned."

"Ouch." She grimaced.

"*Now* will you behave long enough to meet my father?"

"If he's anything like you, I'm not at all sure I want to meet him."

"Don't pout, little houri. Princesses concede gracefully."

"But tavern wenches go for the jugular."

He flushed. She did, too, realizing that no one here yet knew of her upbringing. But Maximilian made nothing of the remark, assuming they were merely jesting with each other, a private joke perhaps. And he was so delighted with this change in Stefan, he was barely listening to them. Sandor would be delighted too. They had both been so afraid that nothing was going to make Stefan accept the girl, whether he brought her home or not. But it looked as if he had more than accepted her.

"I'm sorry," Maximilian heard the girl say.

"Don't be," Stefan replied. "They, at least, have to be told, and it might as well be now."

"Told what?" Maximilian asked, suddenly alarmed by their seriousness.

"We will tell you both together, Max, so warn him that we're here. I don't want to surprise him by just walking in."

Max did as he was told, though reluctantly, and the next hour proved uncomfortable for all of them, but especially for Tanya as she listened to him sum up her life as nothing but a bleak and depressing existence. To hear Stefan tell it, you'd think she had suffered the agonies of hell, so she finally broke in to paint a less severe picture, leaving out the hardship and remembering only the lighter moments, in particular the years shared with Iris.

But Sandor was visibly affected nonetheless, and she realized why when he said to her, "You must hate me, girl."

"Why? I don't even know you."

"I'm the one who sent you off with Tomilova. She was your mother's closest friend. She would have protected you with her life. But not once did I consider she might die, leaving you helpless and at the mercy of peasants."

Tanya doubted Dobbs would appreciate being called a peasant. White trash he was used to, but peasant? The thought made her smile. She turned it on Sandor to reassure him.

"You don't regret what you never knew about in the first place, just as it would be pointless to regret what is done and past, so don't think I regret my life up to now. I don't. It taught me a lot, qualities a pampered and spoiled princess would never have learned. And there is something to be said for total self-reliance. I believe my upbringing has made me strong, certainly strong enough to put up with your son and his royal temper."

Sandor hooted with laughter. "Spoken like a Janacek. That branch of the family always did have the better diplomats. We are grateful for your understanding, child. You are going to make a truly splendid queen."

"When?" she and Stefan asked almost at once.

"Will next week be too soon? After all, this is

something we have waited years to see, and the preparations have been in the making for months.''

A mere week before the wedding? Tanya didn't mind. Sandor might have been waiting for years to see it happen, but she felt as if she had been waiting forever for this ceremony that was going to give her the right to call Stefan her own.

Chapter 48

It was the day before the wedding when Tanya finally realized she hadn't seen Stefan but a few times all week, and those times only briefly. The making of her wedding gown was a major affair that had required hours and hours of fittings. Then there had been even more fittings for another wardrobe that was being made for her, for which gowns had appeared each day for her to wear to the special functions she had to attend, where she'd been introduced to the court and the more important nobles of the land, as well as to the foreign ambassadors and dignitaries who would be present at her wedding.

There also had been the hours of interrogation she had gone through, when Maximilian had shown up with his security men to learn every possible detail of the attempts on her life. She had had to almost reenact that first incident, right down to her rolling out of bed, before they were satisfied she could tell them no more. But their very seriousness had brought home the fact that she was still in danger, and it was a horrible feeling, knowing that someone was very intent on killing her.

Then there had been the tutors who had appeared each day and taken up most of her time. Lord help her, the lessons she had to learn, on the history of Cardinia, the history of her ancestors, on deportment, foreign policy, diplomacy, even language. She hadn't realized how fortunate she was, for communication's sake, that English had been one of the six official languages taught at court for the last forty years. There was even a woman whose task it was to gossip with her, or at least that's how Tanya saw it, for the lady was instructed to apprise Tanya of all current scandals so she wouldn't make the mistake of being friendly with anyone who was presently in disgrace.

The interviews had also begun that week, whereby she had to choose her Women of the Bedchamber, those ladies in waiting and maids of honor who would be her constant attendents once she was queen, one of the positions Lady Alicia had been so sure would be hers. In this Tanya had had the help of Stefan's aunt, a lady who wasn't at all like her arrogant son, Vasili, and for whom Tanya was already developing an affection. But at least she hadn't had to make any definite decisions there. Next week would be soon enough, she'd been told.

All in all, she'd been kept so occupied, there hadn't even been time to miss Stefan or wonder what he was doing. But on the eve before the wedding, a time quite natural for introspection and doubts, she realized that although she and Stefan had arrived in Cardinia on amicable terms, they hadn't actually resolved any of their past difficulties.

She knew she wanted him, knew he wasn't quite as adverse to her now either, but was she actually going to marry him without knowing how he really felt about her? Knowing that he had decided he liked making love to her just wasn't enough. What about his aversion to her looks, his remark that they just weren't compatible? What about all those insults he'd heaped on her every time he was reminded of her supposed past? Was she going to have to deal with those things again and again in the years to come?

The man didn't even know that she loved him. Of course, it was plainly obvious that she did. Hadn't she forgiven him for everything? But he'd never heard her say it.

Tanya was on her way down the corridor before she knew exactly what she was going to ask Stefan, or tell him. Her personal guards fell into step behind her. She had been assigned twelve of them until the assassin was apprehended; they worked in three shifts, standing outside her door and following her everywhere she went, so at any given time she had four men dogging her footsteps, or stopping anyone who wasn't expected from entering her quarters.

But she didn't reach Stefan's rooms. Maximilian Daneff was coming down the corridor with his secretary and paused for a word with her.

"You should be resting, your Highness."

"Yes, I know, but—"

"If you are looking for Stefan, he is spending the evening with his father. He has been so busy since his return, they haven't had much opportunity to talk.''

Did that ever sound familiar. And she wasn't about to interrupt them. But she looked so disappointed, Maximilian asked, ''Perhaps I can be of service?''

''No, I . . . well, actually, maybe you can.''

She looked pointedly at the secretary until Max dismissed the man. Her own guards had stepped back discreetly. There weren't too many people they would do that for. Their own Prime Minister happened to be one.

''Now, what can I do for you?''

Tanya simply came right out and asked it. ''Do you know why Stefan wouldn't like the look of me?''

''The look of you?''

''He liked me better when he thought I wasn't pretty. I never have understood that.''

Maximilian smiled. ''I would imagine it has to do with the same reason he was against bringing you home.''

''Just because he didn't want to marry me?''

''Because he was certain you would not want to marry him. He left here expecting you to be a beauty. If he saw you as other than that to begin with, he was likely greatly relieved to find it so.''

''I still don't understand.''

Maximilian frowned. ''Has no one told you how sensitive he is about his scars?''

''Those damn scars again?'' she scoffed. ''Yes, suppose they have been mentioned or implied. But what do they have to do with how I look?''

''Everything. Stefan stopped pursuing beautifu

women after he was scarred. He felt they could not see beyond his disfigurement. I have seen it happen myself in a crowded room, how some women turn away from him, hoping he won't give his personal attention to them. I am sure he has had worse experiences. But the truth is, he did not want to marry you because he was sure you would be as repulsed by his scars as those other vain women were.''

Tanya shook her head, bemused. All that difficulty she'd had, at least half of Stefan's hostility, all because he'd thought *she* wouldn't like the look of *him?* Alicia had insinuated the same thing. His men had asked her if she minded the scars. Even Stefan had finally asked her if she was prepared to accept him as he was, scars and all. God, what it must have taken for him to ask her that. And she hadn't even answered him. Why hadn't she seen that he considered himself less than attractive? Because she didn't see him that way; in fact, she saw him as too attractive for her own good. But she still should have realized what the problem was.

''And I keep telling Stefan I'm not stupid?'' she mumbled in disgust. ''He knew better all along.''

Maximilian merely chuckled. ''I could see from the day you arrived that you were different. Stefan must have been greatly relieved to discover this.''

''Stefan doesn't know it, but if you'll leave him a message to come to my rooms before he retires tonight, I'll make sure that he does.''

''You mean he still thinks—''

''I don't know what he thinks. That's what I intend to find out.''

* * *

It was a little after ten o'clock when Tanya heard the knock on her door, so light in sound that she knew Stefan thought she was likely asleep by now, and he wasn't going to disturb her if that was so. Throwing open her bedroom doors without knocking had been his way before, but her king was being much more considerate these days.

She smiled to herself as she called for him to enter. He closed the door behind him before he located her in the large room. When he did, he visibly tensed.

"Did you invite me here to seduce me?"

Tanya laughed, knowing exactly why he said it, and in such a suspicious tone. She sat curled up in a chair by the fire, her black hair loose and flowing about her shoulders; she was wearing the white negligee that had been made for her wedding night, having decided it could be put to better use tonight. It was cut very low, and so thin it was almost transparent. The long sleeves *were* transparent.

"Actually, that's not a half bad idea, but no, I felt we ought to talk."

"You still aren't sure, are you?" he demanded as he came forward and, instead of taking the chair next to hers, stood glowering in front of her.

"Sure?"

"About marrying me."

His belligerence was acting up, and she didn't quite know why. "I'm sure, but what I want to know is if it wasn't a duty, if you weren't bound by your father's wish to see it done, would you want to marry me?"

"Yes!"

The vehemence of his response startled her. "Then what are you angry about?"

"When the bride asks to see the groom before the wedding, it is usually to cry off."

A tender warmth entered her eyes. "Couldn't she just need a little reassurance?"

"You?"

"I did happen to have some doubts today. I mean, you've never made any pretense about not wanting to marry me. You said we weren't compatible—"

"Can a man not change his mind?"

"And you hate the fact that I'm, as you say, beautiful," she went on as if he hadn't interrupted and given her a measure of the reassurance she'd asked for. "Which I never understood—until today."

He stiffened. "What do you understand?"

Again she went right on without acknowledging the question. "Are we going to have a normal marriage, where we sleep together, make babies together—?"

He jerked her up out of the chair so fast, Tanya gasped, but his intention was only to kiss her, albeit very fiercely. The subject, she supposed, had got to him, where her negligee had not. Or maybe he was only trying to shut her up long enough to get a word in edgewise, since she hadn't been acknowledging his interruptions. But it was a long time before he ended that kiss, and then he said nothing, merely held her in his arms.

Tanya sighed into his chest and said very softly, "You don't have any idea how attractive I find you, do you, Stefan Barany? I don't even think it's just your looks, though I'm grateful you aren't ugly since I *have* to marry you, but more your personality—aside from your anger, that is, though even that I never really minded after I got accustomed to it. It's the way you—"

"Enough!"

She stopped him from setting her away from him by reaching up and clasping his cheeks. "You don't believe me, do you? I'm sorry, I shouldn't have tried adding a bit of levity to a subject you are so touchy about. But personally, I don't understand why it's a touchy subject to begin with. When I first noticed your scars, and it took me a while to notice them because I found your eyes so fascinating, I merely felt an empathy with you, thinking here was a man who had suffered pain just as I had." She smiled then, bravely, because he was looking so stern, and gently ran her fingers over each one of his scars. "These aren't even there when I look at you, because all I see is the darkly handsome devil who first introduced me to passion. No other man has ever made me feel what you do, Stefan." And then she asked him outright, "Do you think I could want you so much if your scars bothered me?"

He didn't answer her, and she knew instinctively it was because his answer would have been insulting, something to do with her sordid past, probably that she could want any man if the price were right, and he was going to give her a whole damn kingdom, wasn't he?

She stepped back and an unbidden spark entered

her eyes, but she just couldn't help it, he was being so pigheadedly stubborn. "All right, this is a night for confessions, so you might as well hear the big one. When I arrived in Danzig with you, I was still a virgin. And let's be clear about this, since you barely remember that night. You didn't take my virginity, I *gave* it to you. But if you think I'm going to repeat that again and again until you finally believe it, think again."

"Do you honestly believe I wouldn't know the difference?" he asked incredulously. "What you are suggesting is impossible, Tanya."

"Of course it is," she snapped back. "I've been a whore for years and years."

That got her a hard shake. "Enough sarcasm," he warned severely. "I don't care anymore about your past. Do you hear? I don't give a damn what you were. You're mine now and I . . . that's all that matters."

All Tanya could do was stare at him, too amazed for words, her instincts telling her that he had been about to say he loved her. What had stopped him? Those damn scars? Was he still unsure, even after everything she'd said? Of course he was, and he would be, as long as he still thought her desire for him came with a price on it. Now, there was a joke, and a no-win situation. Her pride had kept her from showing him those bed sheets, and her pride was going to keep her from asking Serge to tell him the truth. She'd just have to prove to him, over and over again, that she wanted him, just him. That shouldn't be too difficult a task, quite an enjoyable task, actually . . .

He didn't care about her past? My God, wasn't that exactly what she had wanted, for it not to matter to him, for him to want her despite what he thought about her? And he did. And if she wasn't mistaken, the man already loved her, too. Well, he must, if he could overlook the kind of wicked past he thought her to have.

She gave him a smile that was dazzling in its warmth, and threw herself against him to pull his head down so she could do the kissing for a change. She was so happy she could barely contain the emotion. She lost her breath for a moment, he had squeezed her so hard in response. And his mouth took over the kissing now, some really voracious kissing that went on and on. But then he stopped and just held her against him, pressed very tight. She could hear his heartbeat pounding in his chest, feel the sexual tension gripping his body. So it was quite a frustrating surprise for her to hear his next words.

"I'm not going to make love to you tonight, Tanya mine, because it would take all night before I would be satisfied this time, and I don't want you tired for the ceremony."

"Stefan!"

He lifted her chin to brush his lips very lightly on hers and then gave her an incredibly beautiful smile. "The day after the wedding it will be understandable if you sleep late."

With a promise like that, how could Tanya argue?

Chapter 49

Tanya's wedding dress was a grand concoction of white lace enhanced with silver thread over white satin, with tiny seed pearls dotted throughout. With the immensely long train, it was too elaborate for her to move easily in it without the aid of attendants to take up some of the weight. These she would have, even for her long walk down the aisle on the arm of Sandor, who had autocratically claimed the honor of giving her into his son's capable care.

She should be tired. It had taken her quite a while to fall asleep last night after Stefan had left her; glorious happiness, unfulfilled desire, and anticipation had all kept her mind from resting. But she was too excited now to be tired. And the women had arrived almost with the dawn to begin preparing her, dozens of them bustling in and out of her rooms all morning.

As soon as the last diamond-studded pin had been placed in her hair, a silence fell over the group behind her. It took Tanya a moment to realize that her women weren't merely awestruck by their handiwork.

She turned to find that Alicia Huszar had been allowed into her chamber. Tanya stiffened. She was definitely going to replace those damn guards at her door for this. By their very silence, all the women present obviously knew who Alicia was, so how could her guards not know? Or was this nothing out of the ordinary, the ex-mistress coming to congratulate the soon-to-be-wife, with no hard feelings? Like hell.

Tanya dismissed her women curtly. This conversation was *not* going to be food for the gossip mills. And once they were alone, she waited to see what face Alicia would show this time. If it was to be the friendly, helpful one again, Tanya would probably get nauseous.

But Alicia was more her true self this time, if her smug little smile and first volley were any indication. "Do you know where Stefan spent last night?"

Tanya had a moment's doubt, which she swiftly squashed. She decided to play the game Alicia's way and smiled back with some smugness of her own.

"Indeed I do."

That Alicia didn't call her a liar or come right out and state that Stefan had been with her told Tanya that her moment of doubt had been for nothing. Alicia had no idea where Stefan had spent the night, but it certainly hadn't been with her.

"If all you wanted was to cause trouble, Alicia, you can leave right now."

Angry now that her first tactic hadn't worked, the redhead tried another. "That isn't why—I had to come before it's too late. If you cry off, refuse to marry Stefan, you'll give him the excuse he needs to get out of this marriage without shirking his duty. He doesn't want to marry you. Don't you have any pride?''

''More than is good for me, I don't doubt. But I happen to know—''

Tanya broke off when she caught sight of Alicia's ruby necklace. It was almost like—no, it was *exactly* like the one Latzko had dangled from his finger to show her what had paid for her demise. And here was a copy of it, or more to the point, Latzko's necklace had been a copy of this one.

A furious rage rose up to nearly choke Tanya, because there wasn't the slightest doubt in her mind that the person who had tried to have her killed, not just once, but twice, was standing before her. Yet none of that rage showed. She merely reached slowly for her knife, then recalled that it wasn't on her thigh because she hadn't wanted to shock all those women who were dressing her from head to toe this morning. So she got up and walked casually to her bureau, opened the drawer, took out her knife, and palmed it.

She then turned toward Alicia, offered a tight little smile as she approached her, and continued where she'd left off. ''I happen to know you are utterly deluding yourself if you think any of what you said is true anymore. It might have been true before Stefan left for America, but his outlook has definitely changed. He happens to love me, Alicia, just as I love him. But I'll wager you've already guessed that.'' Close enough now, Tanya shoved the redhead up against the wall and set the knife at her throat. ''Isn't that why you tried to have me killed?''

Alicia blanched as white as Tanya's gown, her blue eyes circles of horror as she felt her skin break under the sharp blade. ''Don't . . . please!''

''Give me one good reason why I shouldn't,'' Tanya hissed ominously.

''I was out of my mind with anger because he told me we were finished, completely finished. I had given him two years, waiting for him to become king, but when it happens, he discards me. Yes, I had guessed he had fallen in love with you. It was *him* I wanted to hurt through you. But after I had calmed down and thought about it, I was horrified at what I had done. I swear to God, I'm not a murderess. I was just so angry—Tatiana, if I had truly, seriously wanted to assure your death, I would have used the real rubies.''

That explanation was likely true, but it didn't incline Tanya to be forgiving. ''Do you think that will matter to Stefan when he hears about it?''

Whatever color had been coming back into Alicia's cheeks because Tanya was at least listening to her, blanched right back out now. ''Oh, God, please don't tell him. Even though you still live, he'll have me executed. He'll have to. Any threat against the royal house is considered treasonous, and he'll see it in no other way.''

''I wouldn't worry about him just yet, when I haven't decided whether or not *I'm* going to cut your throat,'' Tanya said, pressing the knife in just enough to make her point.

Alicia's eyes flared wide again. "I swear, Tatiana, on my life, I'll never do anything so foolish again. I'll leave the country, I'll—"

"I get the idea, for crying out loud!" Tanya snapped impatiently. "I'll accept your word for now, though God knows why I should be that foolish. But I'm also going to leave a message with Maximilian Daneff—that if another attempt is made on my life, he won't have to look any further than you for the ultimate responsibility. Now get out, Alicia. And see that you *do* leave the country."

After the door closed behind Alicia, Tanya shook her head, wondering if that wasn't the most foolish thing she'd ever done, letting that woman go with no more than a thin scratch on her neck to pay for all the trouble, fear, and worry she'd caused. And what was she going to tell Maximilian's security people, who were even now out searching for her would-be assassin? Was she just going to let them go on wasting their—

"You are very good at dealing with your enemies, Janacek—except for the ones you don't know about. Perhaps I will let you write that little message for Daneff before I kill you. It will be amusing to see someone else pay for my deeds."

Tanya had whirled around at his first word, finding him standing in the doorway to her sitting room, where she had been having her lessons all week. And included in the lessons on her own ancestry had been miniature portraits of Janos Stamboloff and several members of his family. She knew she was looking at one of those people right now. Stefan had been so right. Swarthy-skinned, with blond hair and blue eyes, the man was a younger replica of Janos himself. And he held a gun pointing right at her chest.

"Ivan Stamboloff?" she guessed.

"Very clever, Princess." He gave her a mockery of a formal bow.

"How did you survive that shipwreck?"

He smiled beautifully. He was actually a handsome man. There certainly wasn't anything sinister-looking about him to warn that he was a cold-blooded killer. Perhaps that was why her heart hadn't jumped into her throat yet.

"I'm a good swimmer," was his cocky answer to her question.

"You swam across a whole sea?"

"I swam away from the wreck. Death awaited me there, not rescue. Leaving the area was my only chance."

"But that was suicide!"

He shrugged at her amazement. "It was my salvation, as it turned out. I was found the next day— a miracle, surely, that a Turkish ship should sail so close by to see me and take me aboard. A miracle, because it was God's will that I finish what my grandfather swore would be done."

Did he really believe that? And even with his having stated it clearly, that he was going to kill her, his expression didn't change. If he was harboring a deep, abiding hatred for her, it didn't show.

"If you shoot me," she pointed out reasonably,

"my guards will be in here instantly. You wouldn't have a chance of escaping. You'll die, too."

"I would prefer not to, but I am prepared to die if I must. Now come away from that door, Princess."

She moved slowly away from it, but only because he was walking slowly toward it. She realized too late that he was probably going to lock it, bettering his own chances for escape afterward.

She tried distracting him. "How did you get in here, anyway?"

"The window in there." He nodded toward the sitting room. "I thought dawn the perfect time, so imagine my dilemma when your damn women showed up that early. I barely had time to dash behind the drapes."

"You climbed up two stories?"

"I came down from the roof. It was much easier."

And he was dressed in the lightest gray, the same color as the stones of the palace. It would have been very hard for anyone to notice him outside dangling from the roof.

"So you've been hiding in there all morning?"

"I am nothing if not patient, Princess. Haven't I waited twenty years for you to show yourself again?"

She wished this seemed more real to her, that she felt even half the fear she'd felt the last time she was in danger, to keep her from saying things like, "That doesn't sound like patience, it sounds like fanaticism."

Her remark didn't annoy him, however. He actually chuckled as he reached for the door.

"Touch that lock and I'll scream," she snapped.

He hesitated, even lowering his hand. "That wouldn't be wise of you, Princess."

She shrugged. "You're going to kill me anyway. Why shouldn't I take you with me?"

"Perhaps you would like to try talking me out of killing you first, as your little friend just did with you. I wouldn't mind hearing you plead a little."

"I don't think you'll hear that. But you have a knife," she said, looking at the dagger stuck beneath his belt, and knowing full well that that was what he meant to kill her with if he could, to keep the noise down to a minimum. "And I have a knife. Dare you try this fairly?"

He laughed. "You want to fight with me? You think just because you surprised me with your knife once, you're any good at wielding it?"

Her eyes flared the slightest bit as she heard what he was admitting. "So it was *you* that night in Danzig?"

"Of course it was. I had been waiting there for months for Barany to return with you."

"But how did you even know to expect me?"

"Because they thought I was dead, which I knew would bring you out of hiding at last. I couldn't have planned that shipwreck better if I had thought of it myself."

"Well, you haven't asked me to put down my knife, not that I would. So are you willing to break with tradition and do this fairly?"

She had finally managed to prick his calm exterior. "Are you implying my family conducted itself in an unfair manner, when *your* family began this vendetta?''

"Your uncle Yuri started it, by turning out to be a murderer. My father merely dispensed justice as it was deserved. But then your whole family turned out to be just like Yuri, didn't they?''

He didn't answer. With narrowed eyes he pulled out his dagger and stuck the gun in his belt. And Tanya finally felt her heart lodge in her throat as he started toward her. He was going to fight her fairly, she'd goaded him into that, but he was a man; and she might know how to wield a knife when it was in her hand, but she'd never had to use it on a man equally armed. Suddenly she knew how Alicia had felt just moments ago, and the feeling wasn't pleasant. To hell with being fair about this when her life was at stake.

She opened her mouth to scream, but never got it out. The door flew open first, and Stefan stood there, again entering without knocking, obviously, and already in a rage before he even noticed Ivan. But he couldn't help but notice him and, when Ivan whirled about, see plainly the knife in his fist.

What happened then was incredibly fast. Stefan hit Ivan in the face with what he was carrying, a pair of trousers, a trick he likely had learned from Tanya herself. The guards at his back came in next, but Stefan wasn't waiting for them to take care of the problem. He also had recognized Ivan, and while the man was reaching up to unblock his vision, Stefan lifted the gun from Ivan's belt and, without even hesitating, shot him.

Tanya merely watched as the guards toted Ivan out of there, but then she began to tremble, not because she had just witnessed the death of a man she had been having a conversation with—there had been at least seven deaths in The Seraglio that she had witnessed—but because the worry was over, and she had been much more frightened than she had realized.

"Are you all right? Did he hurt you?"

She looked up at Stefan, surprised to find him holding her. "I'm fine—really." But a shudder passed through her, making him tighten his arms around her.

"How the devil did he get in here?" he wanted to know.

"The window."

"Tanya, it's over. You have no more enemies, and if you did have, I would kill them for you. I'll never let anything hurt you."

"I know that." She started to relax the tiniest bit, but she badly needed a distraction. "Why did you come in here?"

She felt him stiffen. She was going to get a distraction in a big way, she was afraid. And in fact, he let go of her to fetch the trousers he had hit Ivan with. She couldn't help but notice that his eyes were glowing when he came back with them.

"I go to dress for my wedding, and what does Sasha lay out for me to wear? These!"

"The wrong color, perhaps?" she asked, bemused.

"They are stained, Tanya."

"Oh, well, I can see why that might displease you, but—"

The trousers almost got shoved in her face as he growled, "With blood!"

She make a *tsk*ing sound with her tongue. "Sasha must be slipping. How could he have missed that?"

"He didn't miss it. He was making sure *I* didn't miss it." And then he said pointedly, and much more quietly, which should have given her clear warning, "You haven't asked whose blood it is, Tanya."

"Yours?"

"No."

"When you fought with Pavel—?"

"No. I haven't worn these trousers since we arrived in Danzig."

"Oh." And then her eyes rounded in perfect understanding, and she said, "Oh—well, what are you so upset about? You said it didn't matter anymore."

"It didn't matter that you were *not* a virgin when I met you, but it damn well does matter that you were!"

Since his voice was going up again, Tanya thought it prudent to take a step back. "Now, you'll really have to explain that one to me, Stefan. I was under the impression, back then, that you objected to my not being a virtuous woman."

"You know *exactly* what I thought! And you never once tried to correct that mistake!"

"I beg to differ. I believe I told you, the morning we arrived in New Orleans, that I hadn't had any experience of men other than with you."

"And you laced that statement with enough sarcasm that I couldn't possibly believe it!''

She frowned then. This was their wedding day. Were they going to march down the aisle snapping at each other?

''Stefan, what are you really angry about? That I was a virgin, or that you didn't know it?''

''Neither . . . both . . .'' He sighed, dragging a hand through his hair, and continued in a low grumble. ''I am furious with myself.''

She grinned. ''Will wonders never cease.''

''*And* you.''

''I'd already guessed that.''

''Every time you responded to me, Tanya, I thought it was because you were a whore and a long time without a man. And every single time it infuriated me, because I was so damn jealous of all those men you had known before me. But you let me, *let* me, slander you with the vilest of accusations, and you never said a word to defend yourself—that is, not one word that I could believe. Instead you admitted that what I thought was true. This you did at every opportunity—''

''No, only when you were particularly insulting.'' She shook her head at him. ''You recognized the sarcasm when I said I was innocent. Couldn't you recognize it when I said I was not?''

''I was always angry enough to believe you at those times. But when I think of how easily you could have put my mind at ease—''

''How is that? How was I supposed to prove my innocence, except by giving myself to you? And when I did, it didn't prove anything, did it?''

He flushed at the reminder. "I have to ask your forgiveness for that, and for doubting you even last night, when you were finally sincere."

"No, you don't," she said gently and felt it was safe now to approach him. This she did, laying a hand on his scarred cheek. "What you said last night made up for everything, Stefan. You said my past no longer mattered, and that told me that you love me. You do love me, don't you?"

"More than I thought it possible to love anyone," he said with feeling. But there was still the slightest uncertainty lurking in his sherry-gold eyes, and she knew why when he added, "My scars really don't bother you?"

"Of course they do," she said flippantly just before she leaned upward and kissed each one of them. "They are so grossly grotesque, after all."

He grinned and wrapped his arms around her. "I suppose I will get used to that sarcastic wit of yours."

"You'd better. It will probably be around as long as I am, and you're stuck with me."

"If you can bear my ugly face, do you think you could also love me, even with my horrid temper and—"

"I just happen to *like* your horrid temper. It lands me in the nicest places." He laughed, but she wasn't through. "Stefan, I swore I would never marry any man, that I would never put myself willingly in a position where a man could have so much control of my life. That I am very willing to marry you ought to tell you something."

"That you already love me?"

"Yes, you foolish man."

The joy in the smile that came to his lips made him so handsome just then, it nearly dazzled her. "I think we should get married, Tanya mine—if you are over your upset."

"What upset? You just try and keep me away from that church today, my Majesty."

"That's *your* Majesty," he corrected her.

Tanya just grinned. "I know. From now on, you're *all* mine."